D1041413

OLIVER HARRIS

A
SHADOW
INTELLIGENCE

AN ELLIOT KANE THRILLER

MARINER BOOKS | HOUGHTON MIFFLIN HARCOURT
BOSTON | NEW YORK

First Mariner Books edition 2021

Copyright © 2020 by Oliver Harris

For information about permission to reproduce selections
from this book, write to trade.permissions@hmhco.com or to
Permissions, Houghton Mifflin Harcourt Publishing Company,
3 Park Avenue, 19th Floor, New York, New York 10016.

hmhbooks.com

Library of Congress Cataloging-in-Publication Data
Names: Harris, Oliver, 1978– author.
Title: A shadow intelligence / Oliver Harris.
Description: Boston : Houghton Mifflin Harcourt, 2020.
Identifiers: LCCN 2019041570 (print) | LCCN 2019041571 (ebook) |
ISBN 9780358206651 (hardcover) | ISBN 9780358308959 |
ISBN 9780358311805 | ISBN 9780358171898 (ebook) |
ISBN 9780358561941 (pbk.)
Subjects: GSAFD: Spy stories.
Classification: LCC PR6108.A7658 S53 2020 (print) |
LCC PR6108.A7658 (ebook) | DDC 823/.92—dc23
LC record available at https://lccn.loc.gov/2019041570
LC ebook record available at https://lccn.loc.gov/2019041571

Book design by Chrissy Kurpeski

Printed in the United States of America
DOC 10 9 8 7 6 5 4 3 2 1

A SHADOW INTELLIGENCE

1

THE SECRET INTELLIGENCE SERVICE PUTS TWO YEARS AND OVER £100K into the training of new field officers. You're shown how to steal cars, strip weapons, hack bank accounts. There are courses on the use of improvised explosives, two workshops dedicated to navigating by the stars. But nothing about what I had heard one old spy call *whiplash*. No one tells you how to go home.

You're marching through the bowels of Tripoli's Ain Zara Prison on Thursday; Saturday night you're at a dinner party in Holland Park. Cutlery tinkles. There is something you've forgotten. You lock yourself in the bathroom and call a restaurant on Martyrs' Square to hear a particular woman's voice and when the phone's answered there is automatic gunfire in the distance. The world cannot all be real at the same time. You apologize to your hosts as you leave, blaming jet lag, then sit on the Central line hearing mourners wail. After the first few times, officers switch to a desk-based role or they find ways of managing the transition. I can't do desks, so I had to learn.

I accumulated rituals, which veered in status between superstition and procedure. A lot of these involved returning to particular places — ones that I could touch as if they were charms and say: Everything's under control, you're here again. The Premier Bar in Jordan's Queen Alia Airport was a favorite. Travel between the lucky and unlucky parts of the world regularly enough and you'll find yourself killing time in Queen Alia. It was one of the twenty-first century's great crossroads. The Premier Bar tucked itself away in a corner of the main terminal, a fridge and three aluminum tables, with a clear view across the departures hall. It had Arabic news on a flatscreen TV and bottles of Heineken in a fridge. I thought of it as my local pub.

On this occasion, I was on my way from Saudi Arabia to London, with strict instructions not to stop until I was on English soil. This in itself was ominous—most of my debriefs were held in third countries. My operation had been pulled suddenly. I had one bag and the clothes I wore, which I was starting to realize stank of smoke and petrol. The pale jacket and chinos of a certain type of Englishman abroad are not made for arson.

I sipped a beer and tried to unwind, letting the adrenaline seep out, enjoying globalization at its transient best. A Congolese family in green and purple robes filtered through a charcoal-gray swarm of Chinese businessmen. Two dazzling white sheikhs led faceless wives in gold-trimmed burkas. Eastern European sex workers pulled Samsonite cases, heading to the Gulf, Southeast Asian ones in denim cutoffs on their way to Europe. The skinny, bright-eyed Bangladeshi and Sri Lankan laborers clutched mobile phones and scanned the departure boards. Staff of NGOs and media organizations sipped water, restless or exhausted depending on the direction of travel. I watched to see who responded as flights were called: Erbil, Jeddah, Khartoum. There were other solitary individuals like myself, traveling between identities, meeting each other's eyes but not for long. You found a lot of snapped SIM cards in the bins. Private security contractors favored duffel bags. They looked well-fed, and walked with the stiff swagger of men who'd been heavily armed until recently.

I could have done with some of them earlier today, I thought. Six hours ago I'd been in an abandoned mansion on the edge of Asir in Saudi Arabia, close to the border with Yemen. The mansion had been trashed. The previous night a local group of unknown affiliation stormed the place, looting what they could on the pretext of combatting decadence. The occupant—a notorious playboy, discreet funder of terrorism, and precious agent of mine—had fled. I now knew he'd been arrested by the time I got there. At that moment, all I'd been told was that I had ten minutes to clear the place of anything sensitive before a more purposeful crew arrived.

I walked through with an empty rucksack, my footsteps echoing as I searched. I'd been inside once at a party, two years ago, amid crowds of prostitutes and coked-up Saudi royalty. I hadn't been memorizing the layout. It was a fifteen-bedroom, thirty-million-dollar palace: fun to trash, difficult to search. Crystal teardrops from the chandeliers littered the floor among balls from an antique snooker table. There were scattered books, broken glass, trails of blood where the intruders had cut themselves climbing through windows. They'd shot his pets, ransacked his wardrobe, slashed some dubious abstract art and one haunting Fantin-Latour still life. A single word of spray-painted Arabic livened the wallpaper: *Irhal.* Leave.

Which was good advice.

"Are you seeing this?" a voice in my earpiece asked.

The satellite image on my phone showed a convoy of five Toyota pickups heading straight toward me. Unclear who they were, but there were no good options. The barrels of the rifles sticking out the windows were clear enough.

"I see it."

"Probably get a move on."

I climbed the stairs. The first floor gave a view across the grounds. Most of the buildings I used in the Gulf were built with anti-ram walls, barriers, ballistics window film. This wasn't one of them. It had a defiant lawn, some cacti, date palms, and an elaborate sprinkler system. A Ferrari belonging to the man who used to live here remained beside those gates, a white shell of carbonized metal. Silver puddles gleamed in the burnt dust beneath it, which perplexed me until I realized it was the metal of the brake pads, melted and resolidified. That was surreal and beautiful. My own driver leaned against the gatepost, binoculars raised. A plume of dust from the convoy reached up from the suburbs of Abha, the nearest city. That was 3.4 kilometers away.

"Eajal!" Quick, he shouted, turning.

I estimated ten minutes before the men arrived, two more to breach the gates. The local Saudi police had vanished, the SAS unit attached to the intelligence services for scenarios such as these was caught by checkpoints on the highway. I was left with three temporarily loyal members of a carjacking gang high on anti-epileptic medication that they consumed by the handful, claiming it gave them courage. Maybe it hadn't kicked in yet.

One of my current allies, Samir, appeared in the corridor behind me, fat, eyes bulging, a pistol gripped in his hand.

"We go now." He was agitated. Beside him stood a cousin or nephew, no older than sixteen, in an FC Barça top, barely able to lift his Kalashnikov.

"Five minutes."

"Two minutes."

"Here, swap." I reached into my jacket, gave the boy my handgun, and told him to forget the rifle. "I'll be back down before they get here."

I took a breath, mixed some oxygen in with the fresh adrenaline. Nice and alert; let's get this done. I opened doors, looking for electronics and paperwork, for the secure room he had somewhere, finding abandoned Kevlar, fine china, leather-bound encyclopedias.

I had one minute left.

At the end of a second-floor corridor I found the door I needed, punched a code into its electronic lock, saw inside, and my heart sank.

Seven or eight crates of material filled the small, windowless space: bank statements, shipping documents, loose cash. I counted four laptops, seven concertina files, stacks of invoices for the weaponry he was funding. No doubt, somewhere within the mess was evidence of UK ties.

Samir appeared behind me, saw the haul, swore.

"We must leave it," he said.

It would take an hour to remove it all. If we had a van. A call came from downstairs: They could see the convoy approaching. I threw the rucksack into the pile.

"Get a can of petrol from the fuel house."

"We don't have time."

"We've got time. Go."

I began to sort through, taking the cash, ensuring the hard drives were exposed. A sheet of the *South China Morning Post* caught my eye. It had been folded small, tucked into a box of necklaces. I unwrapped it and saw what looked like two uncut diamonds. Even in the murky room they sparkled: yellow-tinted and unmistakable against the newsprint.

I pocketed one diamond, wrapped the other back in the paper with half the money. When Samir returned with four jerry cans, I gave him the wrap of newspaper and told him it was a present for later; I needed him poor and wary for a few more minutes. We both splashed petrol over the hoard, and then he ran down to start the car. I took a final breath before lighting the place. Sometimes it's left to you to perform the ceremony alone, to lower the flag. To admit defeat.

An hour to the airbase, a flight to Medina, then a private jet into Jordan. No one had offered me a change of clothes. And petrol smoke sticks to you. Messages kept coming in on the phone belonging to Christopher Bohren, my cover identity: fellow art dealers, drug dealers, a company that specialized in installing infinity pools. All wondering why I'd disappeared.

I had no idea.

So the opportunity to catch my breath in the Premier Bar was more than an indulgence. I washed the taste of blood out of my mouth. The situation was a mess, I didn't doubt that. My agent had vanished, Saudi Arabia looked like it might kick off, and someone somewhere in Vauxhall Cross was worried about my own potential capture. But I had also been expecting this: The intelligence service liked to keep you moving, to stop you from building empires and attachments. The longer you were in the field the more vulnerable you became, so the thinking went. As well as the dangers of overexposure, the theory involved some old-school notion of going native. Operations got pulled overnight and you rarely, if ever, got an adequate explanation. I sometimes wondered about HQ's envy of field officers, whether they created their own secrecy just to keep you in your place. Sometimes it was as simple as a budget cut.

For now I wanted to enjoy a last moment of freedom, of being Christopher Bohren. For all the professional setback and geopolitical consequences of my departure, I was pleased to be here. The magic of returning to places never diminished — of finding them still there: the tables, the weary face behind the counter. It felt like keeping a rendezvous.

On the TV screen: *Saudi funder of terrorism arrested.*

There he was: my agent, at a party beside Lake Como. I must have been a few meters off camera. The caption beneath his face: *Is Saudi pact with extremism over?*

That was the question posed by RT Arabic, the Kremlin's new Arabic-language station. They had good footage: a reporter standing beside smoldering ruins, with the carbonized Ferrari visible over his shoulder. I finished my beer and got another.

"You used to show Al Jazeera here," I said. The manager shrugged. "You prefer Russian TV?"

"My staff prefer it."

I took the drink to my table, wondering at the way the world changes in small details. The journey from the counter gave me an opportunity to scan my immediate environment. There had been one man sitting at the Starbucks across from me for fifteen minutes now. He'd taken a seat facing in my direction, although he hadn't looked directly at me once. He had an Arabic paper spread in front of him but his eyes didn't track the text. Not airport security, but I thought I glimpsed a holster.

I finished my beer, watched a group of businesspeople speaking Russian hurry toward the flight to Damascus. After another few minutes my

Starbucks friend departed, slinging a laptop bag over his shoulder. I put my phone on encrypted mode and dialed a Syrian number.

"I've had to pause things. There's a few bits and pieces arriving which may be traceable to me. I'd like you to dispose of it all."

"Yes."

"And then I think you should also go quiet for a while."

"You are abandoning us."

"The situation's become precarious."

"We are ready."

"I appreciate that. I have to follow instructions."

"It is very bad here," the man said. "Very bad."

"I know." I rested my eyes on a video screen above the concourse, a woman in a field of lavender pressing a perfume bottle to her throat. "I will be doing everything I can to ensure you have no problems," I said. "If you speak to Leyla, will you tell her I'll be in touch as soon as possible?"

He hung up. I closed my eyes. The fabled license to kill is nothing beside the very real license to die; to walk out of a life and its responsibilities. No farewells, no last confession. I picked up my phone again and called CIA's station in Islamabad.

"Tell Reza, Courtesan's been arrested," I said. "Everything on ice for now."

"What happened?"

"I don't know. I'll message when I do."

I moved a British passport from my bag to my jacket pocket, booked a night at the Mandarin Oriental in Kensington. Then I went and bought a suit and a clean phone.

I knew from experience that in five or six hours I'd be facing men and women in ironed clothes who would determine, from how I presented myself, the level of mishap they could pin on me. Luckily, routes to and from war zones make for good shopping: Rolex, Ralph Lauren, and Prada do their own sleek profiteering. The woman in the Prada concession — elegant, flirtatious — didn't blink at a man who stank of petrol smoke digging out his money belt and buying a three-grand suit.

"You have been staying in Jordan?" she asked.

"Just passing through."

"English?"

"Canadian. What about those boxes? What's in those?"

"Watches."

I chose a watch.

"Can you wrap this?"

"Of course." She wrapped it, tied a ribbon and offered me a choice of message tags. "Just a blank one, thanks."

Doors of carved dark wood led between potted palms into the Royal Jordanian Crown Lounge. No familiar faces inside. At the back was a disabled toilet that had served me well over the years. I changed, tore and flushed my receipts and tags, checked that my paperwork was in order. Then I took a condom wrapper from my wallet, removed a pouch of duct tape, and pried it apart. Inside was a small key, the key to my own life. I rinsed off the glue and transferred it to my pocket.

I shaved, used the corner of my boarding pass to get the dirt from beneath my fingernails. Finally, I tried looking into my own eyes. I was thirty-six, five-eleven, 160 pounds, ash-brown hair faded by the Middle Eastern sun. I started operations looking well: groomed, trim but not so worked-out that I could be mistaken for military. I ended them haggard and bloodshot and with a wired edginess that triggered attention.

I eased the tape off the new wrapping paper and removed the gift box, took out the watch, then tucked the diamond into the velvet lining and rewrapped it. I found the tag and wrote: *Let's quit.*

At the boarding gate, the usual sunburnt crew gripped their Western passports as if they might try to wriggle away. The flight took off at ten thirty a.m. I stayed awake over Lebanon, trying to see how much power was on, caught a glimpse of western Turkey, slept through Europe.

Heathrow was unusually quiet. No issues at the border. I walked into the UK, part of me hoping there was no one there to meet me, but I was out of luck.

2

MY DRIVER HELD A SIGN WITH MY COVER NAME. YOU COULD ALMOST believe he was a standard chauffeur if it weren't for the eyes that scanned the people around me as he took my bag. Square-jawed, broad-shouldered — an army physique at odds with the gray suit.

"How was the journey?"

"Very smooth, thank you."

The car was convincing too: black Audi, authentic private hire license in the window. Its bulletproof glass and run-flat tires weren't easily identifiable for untrained eyes. The sky above it was gray, the bite of English winter refreshing.

"Alastair Undercroft apologizes for not being here in person to welcome you home," my driver said, when we were inside. "We're to proceed directly to the meeting."

"That's fine."

He kept his eyes on the mirrors as we drove, watching security and police. After several years living the life of Christopher Bohren, the most likely source of trouble was New Scotland Yard. I let him get going before leaning forward.

"I'd like to go via Marylebone High Street."

"Sir?"

"I have something to pick up."

"I've been asked to take you straight there."

"We have time."

"Okay."

He looked uncertain, put a call in to someone announcing our change of plan. Everyone had their orders. But his was the last deference I'd get for a while, and I wanted to use it.

London looked solid, fortressed in a thick, impregnable peace. A dream that had congealed. How long was I going to be here? I directed him to a Caffè Nero across the road from a Balthorne Safe Deposit Centre and he pulled up.

"How do you take your coffee?" I asked.

"I'm fine, thank you."

"Go on. Flat white?"

"No sugar."

I crossed the road to Balthorne. A row of classical columns obscured the front window. Reception was wood-paneled. They minimized human interaction. Four cameras and a smartly suited elderly guard watched you approach the entry gate and place your palm on a glass panel that read your veins. If your veins lined up, you got to enter a six-digit PIN code and walk in.

It became more functional inside: another desk, a brightly lit corridor, and finally stairs down to the vault. By this stage, the key seemed quaint.

In my box there were a few photographs, some handwritten poems, souvenirs of past operations, and a manila envelope containing a SIM card. I unlocked my briefcase and removed a couple of grand in various currencies, depositing it along with a fragment of pottery that might have come from the Temple of Artemis in what was now northeastern Libya. I kept the diamond. Then I took the SIM and placed it in my new phone.

I crossed the road to the coffee shop. As far as I was concerned, since the operation had been pulled six months early, I had half an hour for a coffee. And I needed strength for what was to come, whether or not it included re-entering my own life. I took the driver his flat white, with a pain au chocolat, which I felt should buy me ten minutes. Then I returned to the café and sat down.

Peace throbs. You're alert to threats that aren't there anymore, and the senses overload. Three young women came in, talking in Cantonese. A man in a corner of the café muttered Turkish into a Bluetooth headset. The coffee shop window was bare, no defensive blocks between it and the road. But there would be no attacks. I tried to re-enter the complacency. A copy of the *Times* had been folded on a rack beside the tills so that you saw a strip of flames in a front-page photo, but they were somewhere far away.

My hands looked tanned in the English light. My lips were cracked. I stared at the screen of my new phone. When you charge up a phone, you entertain the fantasy that a life will return. I'd always brace myself for the personal business I'd have to deal with but forget to brace myself for its dwindling pressure. When you expend your energy maintaining another person's identity, your own becomes neglected. In the last seven weeks I'd missed two birthday parties, one wedding, several job offers. There was an invitation to lunch from an investor friend who owed me for some timely information, but no message from the woman I wanted to hear from. At least, that's what I thought at first.

Emails likewise: irrelevant things or those I was too late for. I checked the junk folder in case that was where my life had been diverted, saw something strange.

It was an email from a Tutanota address with a string of letters and numbers for a name. Tutanota was an encrypted webmail service based in Germany. This was a procedure I used for agents. Subject line: *Lottery Win.*

The message had been sent twenty-two hours ago. I scanned the email for malware, then opened it. The content of the email was two lines:

HAPPY BIRTHDAY.
CLAIM YOUR PRIZE.

"Happy birthday" meant danger: I was in danger, or the agent in question was in danger, and I needed to initiate exfiltration procedures; i.e., time to get out of town. "Claim your prize" meant that a file had been uploaded to a message board hidden deep within the dark side of the internet.

When you've refined systems that work in the field, it's good to stick with them. But you make sure each agent has a unique signature, procedural details that identify them so you know who's contacting you in the absence of formal identification. I'd used this system with an agent in Turkey code-named Mescaline — Khasan Idrisov, a young man I had been fond of, with his pale eyes and thin beard; the frayed handkerchiefs with which he'd mop his brow. His decapitation was still up on YouTube last time I checked.

So the message was a surprise.

I looked around Caffè Nero, sipped my coffee, read the message again.

There was no way anyone should have had the code, let alone my personal email address as well. Now I looked through my missed calls more closely. Around the time of the email there were three attempts from a foreign landline. At 8:12 p.m. last night, 8:14 p.m., then 8:21 p.m. The prefix was 87 172. A check online confirmed it was a landline in Astana, Kazakhstan.

I'd been in the country twice, briefly—both times near the start of my career, more than fifteen years ago. There was little MI6, activity there; the service ran a minimal station out of the embassy. It provided some shallow cover for intelligence operatives and electronic surveillance, and had enjoyed a moment of inflated importance after 9/11—Kazakhstan was a supply route to Afghanistan—but in the resource-strapped world of MI6, nowhere retained staff without good reason. The world is big, and intelligence operations are expensive and politically complicated. Nothing came up online for the number: no individual or business. I set up GPS scrambling so my location was concealed, dialed the number back. It rang but no one answered.

My driver stood watching me beside his Audi, cigarette cupped in his palm. I needed a clean device with which to access the darknet. That wasn't going to be easy today. As I got up, I wrestled with a thought I didn't have the capacity to process at the moment. One other person alive knew the contact system, the person I wanted to hear from more than any other—but not like this.

3

I CONSIDERED ASKING FOR ANOTHER DIVERSION, PURCHASING A LAPTOP, retrieving whatever had been sent. But we were running late, and I was starting to feel any further action needed to be as inconspicuous as possible.

We followed the river east, sank into the Blackwall Tunnel, through the shabby tranquility of southeast London into Kent; bare branches, a splash of rain, suburban oblivion before the M25 reduced the world to litter-strewn verges.

I didn't get invited into Vauxhall Cross anymore. They'd have to disinfect the place afterward. The ideal of HQ was to remain a sterile domain in which transgressions by men and women like me echoed only faintly. It was a truism in the intelligence service that the better you were in the field, the less London wanted to know you. On a shaded lane outside Sevenoaks, the driver stopped, checked his mirrors. When no other vehicles appeared he turned left down a rough track between stone pillars to a gate. Two men in Barbour jackets approached the car, an Alsatian straining at its leash. They let the dog sniff around, checked the driver's papers, peered into the back, and gave me a nod. They pulled puncture chains off the track and we continued.

After another minute we arrived at a sprawling redbrick manor house with stables at the side, marshy paddocks at front and back. A Mercedes had been parked in one of the stables. Two armed men in gray suits sat in the main building's flagstone hallway, breath steaming.

"Home again," one said, recognizing me. "Phone, please."

That was new. I handed over my phone. He winked, nodded toward the stairs. "They're waiting for you."

Not quite Miss Moneypenny. Still, the environment offered a shred of comfort. I had been here years ago, crafting the Bohren cover in the first, optimistic flush of the Arab Spring.

You have experience with revolutions.

How's your Arabic?

Up to speed with the Muslim Brotherhood?

Rolling coverage on, courtesy of Al Jazeera; me, fresh from Ukraine, still filled with ideas of extending the color revolutions to Russia itself. Why not? But the Middle East was where the story was happening: freedom blossoming, a chance to remake the world. That seemed a very long time ago, with a lot of optimism and ideals crushed along the way. I allowed myself a flicker of nostalgia as I climbed the rickety stairs, breathing the same country air. I remembered the view of low hills and forest. A landscape for deer hunting, I had thought at the time. Tudor country: Thomas Wyatt, Kit Marlowe — men entranced by the power they served, who thought they could borrow some of its glory.

My debrief took place in a large room, a mesh of gray conducting material over the walls, rendering it a secure communications facility but giving an air of dust sheets and decline. Three people got to their feet when I entered: Alastair Undercroft, Director of Operations, Martina Lansdown, Section Chief: Libya, Syria and Yemen; finally Damien Mitchell, an advisor to the Foreign Office, though not one you'd come across very often. Undercroft was first to shake my hand.

"Good to see you, Elliot." The pink ridges of his bald head looked raw under the lights.

"Welcome back," Lansdown said. Her suit was the olive green of military fatigues. Mitchell offered his hand but didn't smile. He sported a five-o'clock shadow and his black hair gleamed with whatever kept it scrupulously parted. The walnut desk in the center of the room bore two laptops sitting on their secure cases of nickel- and silver-plated nylon, plus a Panasonic Toughbook showing satellite imagery. Beside this was a tray of sandwiches, untouched.

Six years ago the FO had identified an urgent need to bolster our connections with rebels in Libya and Syria. They wanted to know about activists, but also more battle-ready opposition. I was already tuned in to some of the movements from my time in Tunis and Cairo. The plan was to monitor and control the flow of arms, men, and communications equipment as much as possible. Prevent massacres, fight dictators, empower the right kind of rebels — ones who would owe us favors when the dust settled — all without the kind of military intervention that made news bulletins. Overseeing this was a small, ex-directory unit of MI6 set up in the 1990s after the fall of the Soviet Union, incorporating those familiar with the movement of Islamic fighters, as well as the intricacies of the diplomatic relationships that concerned them: Pakistan, Turkey, the Gulf states. CIA were on board, keen to make it a liaison operation with Six, because liaison operations didn't need to be reported to Congress. MI6 and those cabinet members in the know wanted it kept out of HQ to avoid the need for formal ministerial sanction. I was needed because you can't do everything with drones.

The taciturn overseer of this plan, Alastair Undercroft, had wanted me to enter that world, as someone who could befriend funding sources for rebels of all stripes, to map out the web of shifting alliances between Riyadh, Ankara, and Tripoli. I thought it sounded like an opportunity to immerse myself rather than run around another desert, sticking targets on backs. I would have to win trust, which took time, which was what I'd trained for. I convinced him that art dealing involved as much mysterious movement of funds as any other pursuit, that it incorporated a genuine passion of mine, and that our chief target—the terrorist sponsor Rashid bin Talal—was already in discussions about setting up a museum of modern art in Riyadh. So we created Bohren. I engineered an encounter with bin Talal six months later at Basel art fair, established that he was serious about collecting, that he nursed a crippling hard-on for young white men, and that he was shipping over five hundred grand a week to militant Islam. Those were the kinds of contradictions that appealed to me. I recruited him five months later, which was quick, but still felt luxuriously gradual by the standards of the modern intelligence service. I code-named him Courtesan and insisted that no more than six individuals knew his real identity. We kept him in play for the sake of his knowledge, his cash, the cover he gave our own schemes, and diplomatic relations with the Saudis. It was win-win all the way round.

"We've had confirmation," Undercroft began. "Courtesan was arrested, six a.m. our time, Saudi side of the border. Believed to have been taken to Ulaysha Prison. Obviously we're monitoring the situation. I know you'll want him out. Intervening now risks drawing attention."

"So will him talking."

"It may be too late."

"Where was E Squadron?"

"Wrong side of town, it seems. Total cock-up; no one's pretending otherwise. There's going to be a full review. We think perhaps the Turks stuck an oar in. Washington's got its new tunes, as you know, and that's causing pressure. Things were going to come to a head sooner or later."

"It's too many people to abandon. Too late in the day."

"The office feels the whole thing's gone too far, Elliot. They're saying you took it too far."

"They didn't want it to succeed."

"They don't see this as our cause. Not anymore."

I bit my tongue. Fieldwork sometimes felt like being told to build elaborate and very fragile constructions next to the sea; one day the tide of diplomacy turns, swamping it all, and you wonder why you bothered.

"We appreciate the work you've put in," Mitchell said.

"We're all frustrated," Undercroft elaborated. "But those theaters aren't the priority they once were. And there's an additional problem."

The problem was five million dollars' worth of Chinese assault rifles which had vanished off the face of the earth.

"Are we correct in thinking these were purchased via Courtesan — they came via his channels?" Mitchell said.

"That's right. You requested them, to arm our allies. Or those you considered allies until twenty-four hours ago."

"They're nowhere to be found."

The situation could have been written off as another "cock-up" if it wasn't for the troubling source for the information — a contact in Switzerland's Federal Office of Police, which had apparently made some tentative inquiries about Bohren. The Foreign Office had got jumpy and instructed us to cut all ties before MI6-sponsored weaponry turned up on jihadi YouTube. They were very concerned about what "bore our fingerprints."

So that was that.

Christopher Bohren had two homes I had decorated, as well as friends, prospects, magazine subscriptions. Obviously, some of this would linger. His work would be reabsorbed by the legitimate art dealership housing him; his personal contacts had been primed for an unannounced departure. Soon Bohren would be a curious memory, an individual who had passed in and out of lives, barely there in the first place. Operations Security would fade him out of existence over six or seven months. But he would not be me anymore.

When we'd exhausted our thoughts about the events of the last forty-eight hours, they brought out lists of names. Mitchell had the air of a man who was about to deal with individuals even less patient than himself. He wanted me to treat former contacts "unsentimentally" in order to "clarify the situation." It was a phrase the Russians used to mean "kill someone."

Every deal I'd made had been cleared. Yet they had a way of asking about it as if I'd sat alone in the desert wondering how to equip the Free Syrian Army. I existed because of the things the government wasn't allowed to do, and that brought vulnerability. I began to think through the individuals who might have been here but weren't, and what their absence signified. It felt like sobering up at a party to find yourself alone.

I cooperated with Mitchell's questioning, but you learned to give London what it needed and not much more. The Foreign Office cannot bear too much reality. When you travel between a world of reports and the one that people die in, intelligence product becomes a dubious thing. You impose order on chaos, give other people a false sense of understanding and authority. It involves the transformation of friends and brothers into agents or targets. That was the border crossing that eventually exhausted you. I wasn't prepared to endanger someone who'd recently had my back just because of a policy change in Whitehall.

As we worked through the details of deliveries and payment chains, I kept wondering about the email contact and the missed calls. What was waiting for me on the dark web? The more my welcome home began to feel inadequate, the more this contact seemed the real business. Eventually I let the thought that I'd been fighting surface. The one other living person who knew those protocols was the officer from whom I'd inherited the agent concerned: Joanna Lake. I hadn't seen her in six months, but the thought of a reunion had sustained me.

On a break I went outside, asked for the temporary use of my phone, then took it as far from the house as I could go without attracting suspicion. I found the last number I had for Lake and rang it, but the line was dead.

Three calls from a landline in Astana last night. Online, Kazakh news sites focused mostly on snowfall. There had been a storm for three days, beginning on the night of the calls. Roads were closed, whole villages had been buried. Other than that, the president had made a speech about diversifying the economy. Some industrial strikes continued. Nothing that brought the missed calls into focus.

After lunch I was interviewed by a man of around sixty with the patient, lethal air of Security Branch. He gave his name as Howard. He was curious about why I'd chosen to burn the contents of the secure room rather than bring them home as instructed. Curious about a lot of things, including my visit to the safe-deposit box this morning.

But most of all he asked about contact: who I'd had contact with, who I was in contact with, relationships I was in or had, or had left behind.

"Your lifestyle under cover has been somewhat hedonistic, am I right?"

"That would be one way of describing it."

"Funded independently? We know you have to have a loose rein. But we need to be sensitive to financial vulnerabilities. And expense, of course."

"I'm not financially vulnerable. But I didn't keep all the receipts. Is that a problem?"

I kept my flickering anger behind a cooler mask—humored him, answering questions accurately. There's always security concern, and minor panics of one sort or another. I caught him staring at my new watch. I didn't know if he was going through the motions, reminding me of my place, or if they harbored genuine suspicions. Perhaps I should have taken it more seriously, but it seemed petty and domestic. Part of me remained in less comfortable rooms, alongside men and women who'd risked their lives for British schemes and had been left holding empty rifles.

At three p.m., Howard departed. Undercroft and Lansdown returned with fresh satellite imagery. I talked them through the towns and alliances of Syrian Kurdistan, while making my own tour of what survived, distracted by new rubble.

"They've destroyed the old mosque," I said.

I reached over and enlarged the image. A nineteenth-century mosque I'd been fond of during a brief stay in Al-Hasakah had gone, replaced by a mound of beige stone. It had been bulldozed; militiamen, enraged no doubt by the tiled calligraphy. I tried to imagine that rage. Their iconoclasm was more than just an aversion to beauty and I found it fascinating, even while the results were awful. To them, the sites themselves were blasphemous; not just art or ornament, but the very existence of the past.

As we were wrapping up for the day, exhausted, I said:

"There's an officer who works in I/OPs: Joanna Lake. Do you have any idea of her whereabouts?"

They said they didn't.

4

WE CONCLUDED THE SESSION AT SEVEN P.M. I WAS TO PROCEED TO THE Mandarin Oriental. Next meeting would be in thirty-six hours in the back room of a private bank in Mayfair.

"Get some rest," Undercroft said. "But don't leave the country." He smiled.

I was driven to the hotel beside Kensington Palace Gardens, Bohren's bolt-hole when staying in London. The place was a cliff face of redbrick Edwardian ornament facing the darkness of the park. Usual doorman, crinkly smile as I was ushered into luxury. The receptionist smiled too.

"Mr. Bohren, so nice to see you again. We've given you the Master Suite."

"That's very kind."

"Not at all. No luggage?"

"Not this time."

I could feel my physicality adjust as I accompanied a bellboy to the lifts. Bohren was gregarious and slick. Not a man I personally liked, but others seemed charmed. They took to him more easily than I remembered anyone taking to me. The bellboy bowed gratefully as he received his ten-pound tip. I closed the door and stood among the suite's art deco–inspired features and custom-designed furniture: a chandelier like a starfish stuck to the ceiling, small sculptures of stags sat on a mantelpiece above the digital fireplace. I turned the virtual fire off, put the diamond in the safe. My phone scanned for electronic surveillance devices. No detectable signals, but it was best to assume you were being watched. I drew the blinds against the view of Knightsbridge. I hated west London, which always made being here somehow comforting; it told me I wasn't in my own life.

I lay down for two minutes and felt the icy creep of depression. Hotel rooms were good for suicides and blackmail, not much more, in my experience. Whiplash, I thought. How does one just stop? Keep moving. Keep a pace ahead of the anxiety. I went back downstairs, walked to PC World just before it closed and bought a cheap Toshiba laptop, then sat at the back of Starbucks, out of range of the cameras, and used their Wi-Fi to download privacy software.

Beyond the daylight realms of the internet were the places where people gathered anonymously, and which you could only enter by becoming encrypted yourself. The right technology routed you through a maze of servers, losing your identity in the process. Websites weren't able to track the geolocation and IP of their users, and users couldn't get any of this information about the host. You could talk and meet and share in pitch darkness.

I went to the file-sharing site I had used with my agent, Idrisov, entered the password, scrolled down the board looking for a file named *Dalia,* the name we had agreed for uploads.

There it was.

November 27, an audiovisual file had been uploaded with the title *Dalia dances.* The thumbnail preview showed a girl in a leotard. It was only if you looked at the file size that you'd notice it was several megabytes larger than it should have been.

Steganography was the art of concealing a message within another message. The intelligence service's technical department had come across a lot of men hiding images of child abuse in apparently innocent jpegs. It was an obvious enough idea to use similar ploys for our own purposes.

I downloaded the file, ran it through decrypting software, and braced myself for whatever revelation demanded such concealment.

A new filename appeared: *Catalyst.avi.*

From the opening frame it looked like CCTV or a spy cam, black-and-white, wide-angle lens, high on a wall. The room was plush — white furniture, glass coffee table. I thought maybe a hotel room, but the décor wasn't coordinated enough. Not one I recognized. A suited man stood alone at the window, turned so that his face was obscured.

From the angle I'd guess the camera was concealed in a thermostat or vent. It looked down on the top of a chest of drawers by the far wall and a sofa directly below. There was a window through which you could see an area of roof then what may have been an adjacent wing of the same building.

I glanced around the café again, then clicked play.

No audio. There was a briefcase on the glass coffee table, a decanter, a heavy-looking square ashtray. There was a framed picture on the wall: a horse and rider traveling through a mountainous landscape.

He browsed a bookcase at the back, checked his watch. I still couldn't see his face.

Watching people who think they are alone had never lost its appeal for me. The first few times I expected some revelation, but now it was the very absence of secrets that I found fascinating, the quiet thrill of a shared mundanity.

At fifty seconds he turned and poured a drink, and his face was visible for the first time.

I hit pause. Then I checked the room again and enlarged the image to see the face more clearly.

It was me.

I was clean shaven, smart, in a suit similar to ones I owned but not exact. I stood in a room I'd never been in. It was my face, my build. I hit play, watched myself sit on the sofa, pick up cigarettes, change my mind and put them down. I sipped a generous measure of what looked like whisky or cognac. At one minute and forty-five seconds, another man entered.

He was Central Asian. Dark hair swept in a heavy fringe, holding an old-school Nokia 130.

I didn't recognize him. The man said something, locked the case but left it lying on the coffee table. I gestured toward the decanter, appeared to offer him a drink. He went to a room at the back and returned with a glass of water. His movements were stiffer than mine. We touched glasses. You could see my jaw muscles tense. Then I checked my watch again.

He left the room with me. A second later the clip ended. The footage lasted three minutes, twenty-five seconds in total.

I remember most rooms, let alone most individuals I've shared them with. I'd never been in that room or met that man. I looked more closely at the shadows cast by objects, the movement of faces and hands: light reflections, skin texture, blinking. It all appeared real. There was a mirror on a cupboard at the side with a crack across it. The reflection matched the room. I studied the architecture visible through the window: It looked like we were high up, in a modern skyscraper with a glimpse of an adjacent wing and the roof of a lower tier. The façade was ornamented.

Neo-baroque spires fenced the rooftop off from the sky. It didn't look Western, more like something you'd find in a former Communist country.

I clicked back, watched myself again as I left. A triangle of light fanned out across the floor. Two shadows disrupted it, and then both were gone.

5

"HAPPY BIRTHDAY."

I imagined the chain of events behind this. Someone had come across the video file, illicitly or otherwise, and felt I needed to see it. They wanted me to know I was passing through rooms I'd never been in. There were implications. They chose an ultra-discreet means of communicating: not via official channels, but via a dead man's code.

I took the box from the safe, unwrapped it, and held the diamond in my palm. I closed my hand around it, then tried Joanna's number again. The silence was becoming loud.

Memory erodes from the inside out: Beginnings and endings sharpen as the rest grows vague. My last glimpse of Joanna Lake was in a lorry driver's café on the M1, beside the Newport Pagnell motorway services' area. She was following new security protocols. This was one of them: I couldn't be seen within five miles of her workplace, which was a governmental facility with unique sensitivity.

We had spent a weekend together, shadowed by its own brevity and the dark unknown beyond it, ruined by a fight of unprecedentedly personal dimensions. I was heading back to Saudi Arabia, to live another life. She was heading back to a UK-based role she wouldn't tell me about.

We weren't good at farewells, which aren't easy when both of you are embarking into secrets. And it didn't help when we tried to rescue the situation with promises that demanded more faith than we retained. This time when we spoke about leaving the intelligence service, I think we both meant it. We ended with a show of reconciliation but I had emailed twice in the intervening six months without reply.

The first time I met Joanna was fifteen years earlier, in an anonymous central London building where two men and three women had been invited for second-round interviews. They kept us sitting in a draughty room at the back of the ground floor for more than half an hour. I had been working the room, introducing myself to the other candidates, believing it was part of the test and already enjoying the newfound liberty of a fraudster. She spoke to no one. After half an hour she opened a window, perched on the sill, then swung her legs over. Four of us watched Joanna Lake lean into the flame of her lighter before exhaling smoke at the London sky.

When she turned up again at the IONEC—the Intelligence Officers' New Entry Course—I was surprised by how glad I was. And friendships forged on the IONEC tended to stick. They're some of the last you form with people who are allowed to have a foot in both your first life and your life in the service. We got put in different streams. She was more technically attuned, grasped the psychological aspect of operations better: propaganda, information warfare. Part of me still saw intelligence work as a quest for knowledge: to be at the heart of things, the one who knew what was actually going on. She found that endearing and naive.

We worked together only twice, briefly, once in Kiev in 2005, once in Turkey, three years ago, when she handed over the agent, Mescaline.

I imagined her coming across the clip, somehow. Then sending it in the most secure way possible.

I uploaded it to an encrypted cloud account, deleted it from my emails, called an operational data analyst at Government Communications Headquarters. GCHQ was the technological surveillance wing of the intelligence services, gathering comms and data from around the world. I gave the Kazakh number, asked them to check the databases, see if it came up anywhere. They processed six hundred million call events a day—networks tied to several thousand individuals of interest. It was a big net, finely meshed. I told them I was also going to email a screen grab and wanted to know if the face of the man supposedly with me connected to anyone on the system. Authorization was on its way, I said, but I needed it now.

I watched the clip again. The room looked real. Was the other individual computer-generated too? It was hard to tell. I searched for other clues. No books visible, one newspaper on the table at the front. The headline appeared to be in Kazakh. I could make out a few words: ұлт—*nation*; ұлтқа шок—*nation in shock*. The plug sockets took two round pins. The other building, or continuation of the same building, visible from the window could have been anywhere. I enlarged the lighter in my hand. It looked like a dented Zippo given to me by a journalist in Kiev. It was in the safe-deposit box, along with my other mementos; I'd hardly ever used it. The amount of work that had gone into this forgery was incomprehensible. For good CGI you needed multiple angles, to know the person from all sides. As far as I was aware, there were very few images of me easily available.

Deepfakes, they were called. Human image synthesis. Computer-generated images were being used in propaganda all the time now—Russia's Internet Research Agency generated social media content using politicians' faces superimposed on actors' bodies. It had employed them in online influence operations, mostly domestic politics. You got some sophisticated stuff from Turkey on behalf of the Justice and Development Party: people making speeches they never made, etc. Otherwise it was used for faking celebrity porn. Maybe there were plenty of unknown figures being electronically manipulated as well; we just didn't pick them up. I watched some deepfake porn posted on Reddit, then some of the political videos, and wondered how many teams were currently producing it.

I used the hotel gym, trying to work the acid out of my muscles and force some clarity into my brain, ran through some Vinyasa flows, which a former Marine once told me was the only way he got through five months of captivity, then ordered a plain omelet and a carafe of Pinot Noir from room service. I drank two large glasses, sitting on the edge of my bed.

If the service had allowed me social media of my own, now would have been the time I took solace in it. Instead I logged in to the Facebook account I had set up for a nonexistent thirty-two-year-old woman in Afrin. Her friends were posting photos of a child's funeral, and a glossy meme of an attractive female soldier alongside a quote comparing their struggle to the Paris Commune. I logged out, logged in again as Yuri Cherchesov, a twenty-year-old second rank seaman in the Russian navy, changed my status to *horny and restless,* browsed the gossip among Russia's young navy and their admirers. Then I checked Bohren's accounts and read messages from people who didn't realize he no longer existed: *Christopher, I hope you don't mind me writing. I dreamed of you last night. I know you are not superstitious but it made me worried.*

There were a couple of social media accounts that always seemed to get news first, one curiously with Selena Gomez as an avatar but definitely run by the Electronic Syrian Army. Currently it declared: *China sending troops to prop up Assad.* There'd been another behind-closed-doors agreement between Moscow and Beijing over the future of the Middle East, details to come. European news sites were heartbreaking enough: *"You're on your own," US tells rebels.* I watched the news twice until I realized that the BBC presenter was saying *Syrian government* rather than *Syrian regime.* Sometimes a word is enough to tell you the game is over.

The lingering adrenaline of the operation had got me through the debrief, but now I was slowing up. I'd had very little sleep in the last three days. I opened the window, took a lungful of cold air, listened to London hum. The streets were still busy, men and women walking at a measured pace, knowing their homes would be there when they arrived. A Porsche accelerated away from traffic lights, its radio on news, the words *escalation of violence* fading with its engine.

My phone rang. The GCHQ analyst said she'd run the face on the video through every database she could and no name came up, which was conspicuous in itself these days. The Kazakh landline wasn't on any lists either.

I tried it again, and still no one answered.

I called a colleague in the Counterterrorism section, Linda French, who had worked with Joanna.

"Are you back?" she asked.

"Just in," I said. "Quick query: Have you heard from Joanna Lake recently?"

"No, I haven't seen her for a year or so. And I heard she wasn't with Six anymore."

"Really?"

"Yes."

"Since when?"

"Not sure. I heard this a few weeks ago."

"Where did she go?"

"I don't know. Why? What's happened?"

The situation had just got a lot stranger. I tried three other people. None had seen or spoken to her in the last five months.

Intelligence services are labyrinthine, and for obvious reasons, you can rarely see much further than the room you're in. There isn't an easily accessible directory of personnel. Not for operatives.

The "Happy birthday" code meant danger. Meant: *Get out.* Get out of where? The UK? Out of an imaginary room?

I sent a message to the Tutanota account confirming I'd received the file, asking for more information.

Meanwhile, the events in Saudi Arabia that had ruined several years' worth of my work seemed to have blown over. There'd been some further arrests: clerics, intellectuals, activists accused of acting on behalf of "deviant groups." Fifteen women had gathered in Jeddah, calling for the release of imprisoned relatives, surrounded by a circle of green-uniformed police holding hands so it looked like a country dance. My arrested agent had disappeared from news entirely, and I knew Six would be working to keep it that way.

Bohren's phone kept flashing. I couldn't bring myself to remove the battery, but it was almost dead anyway. I ignored calls from a CIA contact, answered calls from Christie's New York confirming the sale of one of my agent's Paul Klee ink drawings. There was a message from my loyal hacker and all-round cybertechnician, Stefan Janikowski, an employee of Evotec Digital Security: *Confirm situation.* He was still stationed in a hotel in Riyadh. I wondered what he'd make of the CGI.

"What's going on?" he answered.

"I've had to go back to London. Are you able to look at a file for me if I send it over?"

"I've been told no more jobs."

"Who says?"

"Head office. Apparently payments from your side have been canceled."

"When were they canceled?"

"A couple of days ago."

"Do you know who gave that instruction?"

"No."

"Stay in place for now."

"Get them some money or I'll be back in Bucharest."

That was a setback. Evotec were the legitimate, daylight front of a hacking team that had been known to authorities as Hotel California, a motley and lucrative crew combining cybercriminals and former NSA analysts for the most part, based in Romania. Before they had the office and the business cards, they made their money through ransoms: They'd hack defense contractors and major infrastructure and squeeze money for fixing the situation. I liked Eastern European cybercriminals; they tended to work in small teams — not eccentric loners but still under the radar. The criminal background was good cover, and Six wasn't the only state agency using them. Outsourcing kept things deniable, which was everyone's favorite word, and a lot of criminals jump at the chance to work for governments, with the protection it implied. They'd received enough work from me to reply fast to my encrypted communication.

I checked with the Evotec HQ in Bucharest and spoke to the boss there, Marius, a charmingly malnourished, unshaven, and business-savvy chain-smoker whom I had eventually identified as a former colonel in the Romanian Foreign Intelligence Service. The payments for my account with them had been stopped last week, he said. They couldn't process any requests. It looked like Six had canceled them even before my operation was pulled.

I looked at the message again: *Lottery Win.*

Only Joanna knew the protocols. Only living person aside from myself. Were they a clue in themselves?

I thought back to the handover of Mescaline, which had been as tricky as most handovers. I could see Joanna, and the venue she'd chosen, dark and sweaty and debased. Where there's a war there will be a border, and over the border places like the Lighthouse. It was one of several neon-signed nightclubs on a new strip in the middle of Hatay Province, near Turkey's border with Syria — young girls, refugees, forced into the sex trade, wearing sequined belly dancing costumes, paraded for local men and bride tourists: men from Kuwait and Qatar, and the richer of the Iraqi refugees.

All intelligence officers have superstitions. Joanna didn't like using hotels. She had a nose for the dark corners in which rival agencies rarely ventured. The Lighthouse worked. I could never figure out the logic of the name. Joanna kept a room above the club itself. Heat and music rose through the floorboards.

It all felt rushed. She had met me at the Trabzon airport a few hours earlier. I hadn't recognized her at first: she'd dyed her hair dark for the job. She wore a blouse and skirt, managing, as ever, to be imposing at five-four. Chameleon ways; clear, well-bred English features that transformed from glamorous to businesslike with the application of a hair clip. She was skilled at looking like a variety of Western women who made it to exotic places: intense, ambitious, outraged — well-meaning, even.

She looked genuinely pleased to see me. That was what I remembered. And even though I realized, in retrospect, how desperate she was to get out of there, I don't believe that was all of it.

"Of course I'm pleased to see you," she said. "Elliot, you trust your instincts with other people. Trust them with me." Then: "It's been hell the last few weeks."

She'd been blamed for a questionable bit of intelligence that shouldn't have mattered, should have been dismissed at analysis, but got rushed into the public domain and ended up stalling UN action. It shouldn't have been her thing at all. Joanna was I/Ops. Information Operations covered a lot, from briefing agents before missions abroad to more covert psychological operations: planting stories, attempts to influence events in another country or organization in a direction favorable to Britain. Hearts and minds, which wasn't always as fluffy as it sounds. On the wall of their HQ in Basra I'd seen a drawing of someone's brain exploding, with the unofficial slogan *Because physical wounds heal*.

In Turkey, she was in charge of what she called triage. Hundreds of people were fleeing over the border from Syria each day. Joanna had to identify those with military intelligence, those who might be turned and persuaded to engage in various missions, those with propaganda potential. The morning after the handover we drove to the border and she showed me the big white tents set up with rows of fold-out tables inside: a front line of UN staff, a back line of spooks dividing up the refugees. It looked like a careers fair. She'd spent four weeks collecting horror stories for her own propaganda operation. She photographed what she could, distributed secure phones and laptops to any rebels heading back east and willing to blog, hooked them up with reporters via WhatsApp. She ran workshops with the US State Department, tutoring cyberactivists on how to craft their message. Later, in the bar, she'd joke about it: "*There's three of them, bandaged to the eyes, and I'm trying to establish if they've used Wordpress . . .*"

Then Mescaline turned up. He was meant to be for propaganda value only—*life in ISIS not such a bed of roses*, that kind of thing. Then one day he said he could get footage relating to a chemical attack by Assad's troops. We knew a village held by opposition forces had been hit by sarin the previous week, that casualties numbered close to a hundred. He said he had evidence.

Joanna took the evidence—shaky footage of a military convoy, men with shoulder-launched assault weapons firing at night—and passed it to London. It made waves in Whitehall. Hawkish elements in the government were thrilled and bumped it straight to selected journalists. It hit the news. *How Assad Gassed His Own People.*

Within five hours Russia was running the clips, demonstrating that they showed the opposite story—nongovernmental groups launching the attack from rebel-held territory. The canisters had Turkish markings. Everyone knew the Turkish were desperate for US intervention. They controlled rebels on the ground. Were these individuals desperate enough for American assistance that they were willing to bomb innocent civilians to provoke it? It seemed insane, grotesque, implausible, but not without precedent. It was enough to stall everything.

Mass humiliation. No movement from Washington. The Russians were having a field day. You could almost hear the laughter in Moscow.

I don't know what was true. No one ever sees the whole picture, but on the brink of entering a war, momentum is truth, and we lost momentum. Plans for intervention stalled. The UN froze. Russia walked in.

I was sent over under the new Bohren cover to assess what had happened. Had Mescaline planted the disinformation intentionally? As part of a bigger, Russian-led psychological operation? If so, could he shine a light on their schemes?

Joanna briefed me as we drove from the airport. She was putting a brave face on, having been told to step away. Her agent was a nineteen-year-old, Khasan Idrisov. He'd led a turbulent life. Orphaned, adopted by Chechens, he'd headed to Syria a few years previously. Supposedly he wanted out. That was why he'd approached Joanna in the first place. There'd been no one else on hand to receive what he'd described as time-sensitive information.

"You're going to try to get to the bottom of it?" she said.

"I'm going to see who he is, first of all."

"What are they saying about me in the UK?"

"I don't know. But that's what the analysts are there for: to catch this kind of thing before it blows up."

"I was played."

"It's Russians. Russians fuck with your head."

Muddying water with false flags, steering Western intelligence into a collision with fake news—the whole thing had the hallmarks of a GRU disinformation campaign. The GRU was Russia's largest foreign intelligence agency, more active internationally than the FSB, which was technically civilian rather than military. The GRU's main declared function was military intelligence, but it also did special ops, and under its umbrella of special ops came some curious ones: mind games, crafted with a dark ingenuity that the West struggled to replicate.

Hence Idrisov might lead to more than just terrorists, I thought.

The handover was as awkward and dangerous as ever. Idrisov was evidently traumatized—he chain-smoked, avoided looking at me. We were all sweating. Joanna had her headscarf down around her shoulders. Idrisov had survived a drone strike twelve months earlier, and his badly treated wounds smelled acrid and gangrenous in the heat. We agreed the communication protocol was unchanged. He kept asking when he could move to the UK.

Joanna had been drinking. My bosses said she was being rotated. She said she was being fired, and if she wasn't fired she'd had enough anyway, which is what you say at the end of missions. After the meeting, Idrisov had returned to risking his life or betraying us, or both—a pawn in whatever games the Russians were playing; the two of us got shashlik at a place Joanna liked: no glass in the windows, good-natured men with Kalashnikovs guarding the door. She said she was burned out. The way she saw it, all our work had been undone. We'd been outplayed.

When she passed out in the hotel room, I sat up watching news until I wasn't watching anymore: images of the chemical attack, unblemished corpses, men and women fallen alongside pets and birds as if all nature had succumbed to some overarching fatigue. I tried to imagine the moral equation that could justify perpetrating that.

Over the next few months, Idrisov continued to send his steganography. Hidden within the jpegs was some superficial insight into ISIS leadership structures, supply chains, oil sales, recruitment drives. Once a fortnight he crossed over the border for a face-to-face debrief. I moved us out of the Lighthouse to a safe house in the suburbs of Iskenderun. Vauxhall was pressuring me to get whatever scraps I could. He remained poker-faced, claiming ignorance as to the ultimate source of the footage that had got Joanna into trouble.

I didn't trust him anymore, but, I suspected, neither did his own side. He gave me nothing valuable. Two months later, just as I thought he might start opening up, he missed a meeting. An execution video turned up the following week. His confession to camera was that he was spying on ISIS for the UK. According to a later assessment, it looked likely the Russians had used him enough and decided to blow him. I wanted to talk to Joanna about it, about this vindication of our theory, but at that time she'd gone off-radar as well, busy with a new role. I knew she was somewhere within the UK, within the most covert corners of the intelligence service.

Now no longer at Six?

My confusion was enhanced by jet lag. It was ten p.m. here, one a.m. in Saudi Arabia. I was awake—an exhausted wakefulness. I finished the wine, found some English money, and went out.

The cold November night caught me by surprise, but I couldn't be bothered to return for a coat. Walking felt good. The area suited me: international students, business travelers, tourists. The pubs were small enough to monitor entirely from your seat. I favored the Queen's Arms. It didn't play music, which meant you could hear conversations, sometimes even relax.

I ordered a pint of IPA and the ease of acquiring alcohol seemed briefly hilarious. It put me back in the land of the infidel, of personal space, cautious eye contact. Out of the realm of sweet teas, hookah pipes, and close, wiry bodies. Reacquainted with the blunt functionality of the pint, solid enough to grip and stop yourself from falling. A TV in the corner of the pub showed what passed for the news: rail fare increases, the departure of a football manager, dresses at an awards ceremony. I heard someone laugh, a chesty public school bellow. The man was one of a group of five beside the bar: white shirts, fresh haircuts. The laugher had a cashmere scarf loose around his neck, elbow on the bar, delivering an anecdote about turning up to someone's place in the country uninvited. He reminded me of Christopher Bohren, in the bar of the Belvedere Hotel; in Istanbul's Club 29. I had always been fascinated by people with acts, performers who know that so long as you make life more interesting, you can commit whatever evil you want. Close by him, but not part of the group, a young woman turned in circles. She held her phone in front of her face. I tried to see if she was Skyping or recording. She had strong makeup, a dark fringe, ankle boots with silver studs. A friend with hair scraped back in a ponytail watched her from a table in the corner. I angled my face away and tried to remember if they'd been here when I arrived. They were noticeable, yet I hadn't noticed them.

When I went up to get another drink the woman with the fringe appeared beside me, clutching a purse.

"Long day?" she said.

She sounded Eastern European, maybe Scandinavian. Neither of the drinks on their table was finished; the trip to the bar seemed premature.

"Long year." I smiled and extended a hand. "Christopher."

"Anna."

"Where are you girls off to tonight?" I asked. She named a club a mile or so away. I tried to imagine what route would bring them via the Queen's Arms. It was a down-at-heel start to the night.

"Can I get you a drink?" I asked.

I bought them drinks, joined them. The friend, Inga, was taller and quieter. They were art students, apparently. They had just started at Saint Martins. I spoke at length about art auctions, private galleries, offered to guide them around London. My persona of the last twelve months was a bon vivant, a racketeer at ease with his demons. It was a relief to resurrect him briefly.

"Do you both have student ID?" I asked.

"Yes," Anna said.

"You know the government's trying to persuade universities to put nationalities on a hologram. And then if your visa expires, you won't be able to get back in."

"What?"

"Take a look."

Anna took the purse from the bag and clicked it open. It was thick with cards. She removed a student ID from among them.

"Where?"

"Can I see?" I took it from her and memorized the name and the ID number. "Maybe they haven't yet. Should be the same technology on the bank card." I pointed at her open wallet. She slipped a bank card out. Same name: *Ms. A. Nailand.* Bank account at Rietuma Banka in Latvia.

"You know a lot," she said.

"I'm just paranoid about the government."

Maybe they were real. I took a mental step back; a pause for reflection. Loss of faith in reality was one of the first signs of psychosis. And of being in the game too long. The laugher and his crew moved off, the girls remained. If this *was* something, they knew where to find me. Tailed from the airport? Picked up at the hotel? That would be concerning. If it wasn't anything then I needed to wind down and shake off the tension of the last few months before I made a fool of myself.

After twenty minutes I'd probed as much as I could without appearing excessively suspicious. I checked my watch.

"I've got to run." I focused in on Anna. "I know a few gallery openings next week. I don't suppose you'd be interested in coming along, would you?"

"Sure," Anna said, too readily. I took her number.

"And can I take a photo of us all?" I said. "Something to make my friends jealous?"

I checked them out online when I got back to the suite. Anna Nailand, Latvian art student, appeared across a few social media sites. So did Inga. How much social media do you need to be real? It was a question I'd spent more time contemplating than was healthy.

I had a message from a contact in Switzerland: Bohren's gallery in Lausanne was under surveillance. The Swiss had received a tip-off, possibly from Moscow. So much for a discreet drawdown. Bohren might not have had my name or any other details, but he had my face. I needed him to disappear from existence on the right side of legality. When I tried to see if any of his contacts had been approached, I discovered that Bohren's email accounts had been closed down.

And no sign of Joanna.

I watched the road beneath the hotel window, then the park across the road, then drew the curtains again.

Whatever was going on, the clock was ticking.

I opened my laptop. I had a full suite of passwords for bin Talal, obtained over two years by my cybersecurity team. I disguised my IP and logged in to his Deutsche Bank account.

Balance: $1,792,021.

They hadn't frozen it yet. Payments were still coming in. I'd watched these figures a lot over the last year: debits and transfers signifying arms and alliances. I'd never stuck my hand in before, but it was simple enough. I clicked "Transfer money," went into payees, and found the details for Christopher Bohren's own sharia-compliant account with the Jersey branch of the Abu Dhabi Commercial Bank. I set up three transfers of nine and a half grand—just below the threshold for triggering fraud and anti-laundering alarm bells—clicked "Send now."

It cleared in minutes.

I transferred the money again, from Jersey to an account with Union Bancaire Privée in Geneva, sent 20K to Evotec's Cyprus account, and submitted two tasking requests: information on the Tutanota address that had emailed me the message — where it had been set up and what device the email was sent from. I also sent the video file and asked for a forensic analysis: what CGI software was used in its construction.

I did my own research as well. The technology involved used deep-level machine learning: you fed in images of someone's face and the program taught itself how that face worked, how to generate new versions. It split itself into creator and critic, creating examples and then seeing if it could convince itself that they were real, feeding back errors until it could.

You needed the bodies, though, onto which the faces were mapped. Who was my body double? More seriously: Who had the resources for all this? The process required a high-speed graphics-processing unit. Supplying it with adequate training data meant having access to hundreds of images of that person. For someone moving around, like I was in the clip, seen from all angles, you might need thousands to be convincing.

I tried to sleep, got up an hour later, and watched the clip again. I took a screengrab of my face and used it to set up a recognition alert on Tru-Vision, the only facial recognition software that tracked online appearances rather than just CCTV feeds. I did the same for my companion. My sleep-deprived brain turned over the file name: *Catalyst*. It was a code. A code for the man with whom I was meant to be meeting? For whatever clandestine operation threatened my life?

6

I WOKE, SWEATING HARD, AT FIVE THIRTY A.M. THERE HAD BEEN NO MORE messages for me, from known or anonymous sources. I checked world news, then found shorts and a T-shirt, and ran hard across Hyde Park, outpacing the shreds of last night's dreams. A mile and a half in eleven minutes. It would get me into infantry, but not paras anymore. I didn't pick up any surveillance. I drank a bitter coffee at a cabdriver's shelter, the only place open in the dawn, watching the mist on the ponds and feeling a strange mixture of anxiety, melancholy, and relief. I had been looking forward to the challenge of today, to a tentative attempt at being myself. It wasn't going to happen quite like that.

At nine thirty a.m. I walked to the Maghreb Bookshop on Sussex Gardens, behind the Edgware Road. It was a cornucopia of secondhand books from around the world, most languages represented, forgotten poets gathered in the dust, shelves that squeezed you as you burrowed in.

I looked for books to distract me with old passions — Arabic poetry, Russian fiction — found myself flicking through works on Kazakhstan. After half an hour, I took my haul to the counter and the owner studied them. Among others, I had chosen some poetry in Kalmyk — the Kalmyks in Russia were Buddhist descendants of the Mongols — plus a nineteenth-century account of traveling in Central Asia. The owner was a neat Algerian man who wore V-neck sweaters and glasses on a chain. He handled the Kalmyk collection thoughtfully.

"You understand this?"

"A little. I am interested in endangered languages."

He nodded, lifting his glasses to study the blurb, then checked the rest. "Do you teach?" he asked.

"Sadly not."

"You travel the world in books." He smiled.

"Some are for friends," I said.

I put the Kalmyk collection and the Kazakh travelogue into my jacket pocket, then took the rest to a house on Lisson Grove. It was identical to the elegant houses on either side but for a small brass plaque beside the door announcing the Healing Foundation for Victims of Torture. The door was open. I walked into a long hallway with clients' artwork on the walls, leading directly through to a well-tended garden, where a Sudanese couple were arranging bunting and tables for a party.

"Is Hany around?"

At the sound of my voice, Hany Aziz appeared, grinning, from among the foliage.

"Martin." He smiled, because Martin was the name he knew. He clasped my hand. I savored the sweet incongruity I felt every time I saw him in London, a man I had first set eyes on in Cairo's Tora Prison. That crippled figure had been banished. Aziz's tightly curled hair was now a London gray, but his eyes had grown more youthful. A fine access agent once I'd acquired his freedom and services, not so much valuable for himself as for who he knew, introducing me to the intellectuals and firebrands that passed through his basement. He had established the healing center five years ago, after arriving in the UK.

I gave him the bag of books as a donation for the center, and we asked after one another's lives. He told me how he was faring; I lied about mine.

"You must come to the party this afternoon, Martin. Old friends will be there. You remember Sania."

"Of course."

"They remember you fondly. And the children."

"Not today."

"Then next time."

"I promise."

I told him I had an appointment and left him to the garden. Walking back down the corridor I thought: I got him out. Even if Egypt went to shit. I don't abandon them.

Café Rakka was nearby. Early in my career I had sought out London cafés popular with various émigré groups, and used them to practice going gray, becoming unnoticed. At the time, I thought maybe I would pick up snippets of information, but people didn't often talk politics, and when they did it was usually to parrot the editorials of the popular Arabic newspapers. Still, the food in this one was good, as was the fresh mint tea. You found yourself searching faces. Who might have made it over? Café Rakka had yellowed tourist posters of Syria on the walls: the Al-Madina

Souq, the Great Mosque, Palmyra with the Temple of Bel, all bombed to memories now. Early in the uprising, they had installed a TV and kept it tuned to news, but at some point it had been switched off.

I ordered tea and kibbeh, balls of bread stuffed with ground meat and walnuts. The men in the café wore harsh eau de colognes and ragged mustaches, cracking sunflower seeds with their teeth. Stirring sugar into their mint tea, with the sound of small bells ringing. Sometimes, in Egypt, you would hear that sound as you spoke on the phone: security officers from the dreaded Amn al-Dawla stirring their tea as they listened in.

A group of four young Yemeni men entered, accompanied by an older man. I eavesdropped on them as they talked about their trips to the home office to claim asylum. I tried to ascertain which towns they'd come from but couldn't glean any details. One of them phoned his parents, who had made it to Malaysia by the sounds of it, but had experienced trouble of a kind that I failed to ascertain before his credit ran out.

My final stop of the morning was the Royal Mail delivery office on Harrow Road, which housed the post office box to which my own post got diverted, serviced fortnightly by the intelligence service's housekeeping team. I would have to wait until the next debrief to collect the bulk of it. Currently inside the box was post that had arrived since their last visit: pension information, alumni fundraising, a postcard from a university girlfriend, Laura, showing Marrakech at night: *On honeymoon. We visited Morocco and I thought of you. Did you get the wedding invitation? Don't worry—I know you've been out of the country.*

I took the letters to a bench across the road, sat down, and read the postcard again. It was a generous communication from someone I had been in infrequent contact with. The fact, increasingly obvious to me at least, was that we maintained the contact not so much with each other as with a part of ourselves and a moment in our lives. Which didn't make it any less precious. I checked her Facebook account. The wedding had taken place six weeks ago. It looked appropriately joyful. Neither the groom's name nor his face meant anything to me. For some reason, the image that came to mind was a Saudi facility for returnees from Guantanamo. I had been shown around as their chief of intelligence explained that marriage was central to the program of deradicalization: a wife and a job.

I called the number listed on her page.

"You're back," Laura said.

"Just got in." I smiled into the phone, wondered why I was faking a smile she couldn't see. "I got your invitation. Congratulations. I'm sorry I missed it, I wish I could have been there." I tried to remember the cover story I'd given. North Africa, a posting on behalf of the Department for International Development. "How are you?"

We spoke about what she'd been up to. She taught French literature at Kings, had a doctorate in symbolist poetry. She was poised, articulate, with a life lived locally, with work and interests and friends around her, and now a husband. I found, as I always did upon returning, that without a role to play I suffered from aphasia. I opened my mouth and had nothing to say. I felt a blankness behind my face. Perform, I thought. Imagine you're trying to recruit her.

"I thought of you," I said.

"Really?"

And then, because I had backed myself into a corner, because I wanted to share something, I said: "Yes. I visited the house where Rimbaud lived, in Aden."

It was true, though—I had thought of her then. I had persuaded my fixer to show me where Rimbaud lived when the poet's self-exile led him to this corner of the world. She would have been fascinated. And I thought of Rimbaud himself, and the line in his letter from Harar that I thought of frequently: *Je ne compte pas rester longtemps ici. Je n'ai pas trouvé ce que je présumais. I did not find what I had expected.* What had he expected in dusty Yemen? A twenty-six-year-old, picking up exotic languages and diseases and a lot of secondhand Remington rifles, waiting on the edge of the desert as he prepared to head to Abyssinia to sell guns to the king. Poet turned arms dealer. At university, when I first stumbled upon his trajectory, it seemed wondrous and inexplicable. And I had surpassed it without the slightest scrap of insight.

"His house is still there?" she asked.

"Just about. It used to be something of a tourist destination."

It had been closed down at the start of the war, but I found the old caretaker chewing khat; when I bribed him to unlock the door, he spasmed with a cough so violent, he sprayed blood over my wad of tissue-soft rials. Inside, there were empty glass cases, rotting wooden furniture, scattered papers that weren't, to my disappointment, anything to do with Rimbaud but recent governmental directives on agriculture.

"Why didn't you let me know?" she asked.

"I was so busy."

"Do you have pictures?" she asked.

"I didn't think to take any."

"And what development work were you doing in Yemen?" she asked.

"Water," I said. "Mostly. For the refugees. The war's caused a bit of a crisis. Also some education projects."

"The war," she said, uncertainly. "Of course."

We didn't arrange to meet. I got up, checked the parked cars in my vicinity for any watchers, continued back to my hotel.

If Joanna had left Six, I thought, where would she go? Former spies move into banking or private intelligence. Joanna Lake doing nine to five in a bank was unimaginable. I called around a few ex-colleagues now working for private intelligence companies. None had come across her on the scene.

As a final punt I called Olivia Gresham. Originally at Six, she'd moved swiftly on to more lucrative pursuits: Citigroup first, then her own investment fund. She didn't know Joanna but she liked me, and she wanted to treat me to lunch.

Flax and Kerrigan's had been open two days—a "soft opening," which meant members of the public couldn't get in but Olivia Gresham could. She had set up her own fund concentrating on energy commodities around the time I started working in the Middle East, finding her natural home among the flows of capital. But she hadn't jettisoned contacts, and neither had I. Like a lot of jobs, ninety-five percent of espionage came down to who you knew. Swapping thumb drives in underground car parks can be fun, but an astonishing amount of the work simply involved belonging to a group of people able to exchange information that others didn't have. Like a journalist, you cultivated a network of off-the-record sources, only for a paper with the smallest distribution possible.

Investors were good. The exposure of several million pounds seemed to sharpen their appetite for knowledge. They, at least, knew where the wars were.

"My favorite spy," Gresham said. "You look like you could do with a square meal. Go wild."

She passed a menu over. She looked immaculate in a charcoal Dolce and Gabbana suit, smiling at me. I'd put some cash into her fund, but that wasn't why she sought me out. The mutual professional interest was enough to keep the sexual tension productive. The restaurant she'd chosen was unromantically bright, with wood and chrome, high ceilings, and white-tiled walls like a butcher's; light glinted everywhere you looked, as if you were inside a bubble. The menu swam in front of my eyes. I kept reading the words *Experimental Cocktails*. In Saudi Arabia that meant a bag of raw alcohol and a Coke.

We ate duck egg and asparagus, and shellfish on ice. She insisted this was a thank-you, which meant regularly topping up my glass, the bottle dripping water across crab shell. I'd given her a heads-up on Turkstream — a proposed line pumping gas under the Black Sea — and a Goldman Sachs fuckup in Libya, which her fund had turned to profitable use if the crustacean still life in front of me was anything to go by. I hadn't done it for the sake of a seafood platter, but it was all part of the play. She asked about Syria, Yemen, and the Gulf, and then it was my turn.

"Who's big in Kazakhstan these days?" I asked.

"Why?"

"Curious."

"Right now, Chevron, Gazprom. PetroKazakhstan was bought by the Chinese last year. JP Morgan are trying to get hold of the financial sector. A lot's still bound up in state-owned companies."

"Got a contact there? Someone who knows the scene?"

"I can make a call. I know a guy building retail units, big box–style. Tesco's moving in."

"Is it politically stable?"

"It's a dictatorship. You don't get much more stable than that."

7

I PICKED UP A ZIPCAR AUDI FROM FINSBURY CIRCUS, BOUGHT A BLACK baseball cap from a sportswear store beside it, curved the brim and pulled it down toward my eyes. The last address I had for Joanna would take me into dangerous territory, though you wouldn't know it to look at it.

In a sleepy corner of southeast England, a few miles north of Luton and south of Bedford, you find the village of Shefford. There are flower baskets, a winding road past a Norman church, tea shops with white tablecloths. Drive out of the village, past fields of sand-colored barley, and you get to one of the most classified sites in the UK. Signs stuck into the ground behind the chain-link fence warn NO TRESPASSING, but they don't tell you it's government property.

Shefford Park housed the experimental wing of the Secret Intelligence Service. That included technology, but also psychological research. Since 2002 it housed the Psychological Operations Group, which drew on MI6, GCHQ, and the British army. There had always been a psychological unit in the military, but after the first Gulf War it started to get serious funding. Analysis revealed that a large number of Iraqi surrenders and desertions could be attributed to coalition psyops—leaflet campaigns, loudspeaker teams, even a radio station. This success led the UK to create a permanent capability. They took over Shefford Park.

The facility was situated off high-speed roads that didn't let you get much of a glimpse at what looked, anyway, like an anonymous research campus—modern blocks of beige brick and turquoise glass, arranged around the original seventeenth-century manor house acquired by the Foreign Office after the Second World War. That had been in order to establish what it described as a "listening post," a phrase that usually concealed more than it revealed. The radomes and radio masts had gone, replaced by less visible technology. While Bletchley, a few miles away, eventually gained the plaudits, Shefford was happy to stay in the shadows. Which was how you knew somewhere was still important.

It made sense combining technological research and psychological operations. The world moved on from leaflets and loudspeakers at breakneck speed. More recent work by the unit included jihadi DVDs that placed trackers on users' computers, and cyberattacks on Islamic State websites, replacing bomb-making instructions with cupcake recipes. Joanna was proud of that one. But those kinds of operations barely scratched the surface of what went on under the umbrella of psychological warfare. There was more to it—sides I didn't hear about—so I was never quite sure what Joanna was up to.

I walked past the church, past a low-ceilinged pub, to the edge of the village, the point at which I'd usually leave her, beyond which she said surveillance began. There were hidden cameras set up in the village. She said they monitored all visitors.

I didn't have a choice. I headed for her home.

Joanna didn't explicitly talk about Shefford when we were together. We both wanted to escape thoughts of work anyway. So we usually just walked, often in silence, amused by the brazen beauty of the countryside.

I never knew what she was doing, but on more than one occasion she talked about the notion that fieldwork—the basic craft of recruiting human agents in a hostile environment, my business—would become irrelevant in the future. That triggered an argument the last time I saw her. We'd been walking in the woods, stopping occasionally to pour wine into plastic cups. I was mentally preparing myself for a return to the Middle East. I wasn't in the mood for someone implying that I was wasting my time. She even presented her own removal from overseas operations as a conscious choice, which was clearly designed to get a rise out of me. And, I thought at the time, reflected personal bitterness. She had been a better field officer than me. A group of us had been selected to spend two weeks in Brunei learning advanced weapons skills, some abseiling and parachuting. She was in her element, to the extent that there had been talk of moving her to the Special Reconnaissance Service, which they were in the process of setting up, a dedicated subunit of the SAS designed for the new era of cyber-inflected warfare. Unlike the SAS and SBS, it took women. Like them it comprised an elite group with the mental and physical ability to work in small, independent teams under life-threatening pressure. She said she wasn't one for painting her face and lying in puddles.

One fragment of that last, needling, semi-drunken conversation had stayed with me more than the rest.

"They have software that can tell you how long a relationship will last," she'd said.

"Based on what data?"

"Everything: geographical movement, sleep patterns, conversational rhythms, vocabulary, choice of entertainment options."

"What does that allow you to do? Marriage guidance?"

"It means, theoretically, if you wanted a relationship to end, you could run the program backwards and see what steps would engineer that outcome."

That was a loaded anecdote to share, I thought. I wondered if the ruthlessness was meant to impress me. We were sitting beside a tree, on the third bottle. She looked strikingly beautiful, her eyes large and liquid, as they became when drunk, and which was sometimes a warning sign. Head held high on her long, pale neck, hair escaping its knot to hang around her face, a wildness in her echoing the woodland around us.

"Is that what you're doing? Breaking hearts? People seem able to ruin their own relationships."

"You'd be amazed how useful it can be."

What riled me with the trend for high-tech forecasting wasn't so much my own potential redundancy as the idea of fate: that lives were inevitable, and you were born with your destiny coiled inside you, awaiting its own birth. *We think we are living our lives, but they are living us,* she had once said. My life had been a war against that.

"People will always surprise you," I said. "One person who wakes up and has had enough. Lights the fuse. You're not going to eliminate that. And no software's going to get you the nightmare they were having before they woke. Not in the way I've had agents talk to me. When you have software that understands hate, revenge, and trauma, then I'll start job hunting."

"Is that what you deliver?"

"You know what I deliver."

"A horizon watcher, connoisseur of men's hearts and nations' souls; detached, paring your fingernails."

"Come on, Jo."

"Anthropology with guns."

"Anthropology started with guns."

"I don't think you know what you do."

"Don't I?"

"You fall in love with foreign places, then destroy them." She knocked her drink back, as if this might deflect my own anger. But I wasn't angry. I was in awe at where we had arrived. She said I started wars out of boredom. I said something had broken inside her, whatever mechanism distilled an ultimate value from our work. Five minutes later I was suggesting she get professional help for what she went through in Turkey.

"No, Elliot. You get help. Look at yourself."

There aren't many places an argument can go once you reach the imperatives to seek counseling. We were both burned out in our own ways. And how would therapy work? A spy goes to a psychologist. I cannot tell you what I do, or the precise events that haunt me. My unconscious is covered by the Official Secrets Act. Obviously, the services anticipated this and wheeled in some shrinks of their own, so petrified of the information they received that they'd close you down at the first whiff of anything classified. And, of course, they were equally concerned with assessing your risk to the service as to yourself. None of which helped the free and frank revelation of psychological turmoil you craved. If you were lucky you got some MOD psychiatrist on his way to retirement who gave good prescriptions—powerful enough to knock you out, some might say —but little by way of empathy.

And what would that free and frank revelation be, anyway? I can no longer feel the things I once felt. My dreams have become warehouses for the dead. I remember men and women whose fates I am entwined with, but cannot remember which war they are from, and this troubles me, but maybe not as much as it should do. Every night, when I close my eyes I see a piece of shrapnel melting the synthetic fibers of a hotel carpet. Every morning I wake up and check the pillow for blood. The problem with trauma is that it's a plug hole, and every bad thing got drawn toward it, toward a thought: *That was where I lost the life I was meant to have.*

We were burned out, and after we'd kissed and made up again we agreed to leave Six. To run away. We joked about hot countries that had no extradition treaties with Britain. I suggested Cameroon, Namibia, or Venezuela.

"Caracas has a thriving literary scene."

"And it would be easier to blend in," she said.

Neither of us had worked the South American beat. The Caribbean

would be our playground: Montserrat, Grenada, Saint Lucia. I would ignore the drug boats, the private jets, the officials behind high gates. I'd
stare out to sea.

We talked unimaginable things: a home, children, jobs we could admit to. Our lives would be quiet and apolitical. Love would demarcate
our cares.

"You couldn't do it," she said.

"Did your software tell you that?"

"Just think: You'd have to decide what you want, who you want. You
know what I mean, Elliot."

"I know who I want."

"Let's do it now, then." I could still feel the challenge of her stare. With
something more in it, a plea, which was so unlike her, I didn't recognize
it at the time.

"Are you serious?" My incredulity killed the moment. The plea vanished.

"We'd need money," she said.

Six months ago. I had assumed she was still here. I walked past the
house in which she'd been living, one of a cluster of semi-detached homes
close to the railway station. The front garden had recently been mowed,
then strewn with plastic toys: a tricycle, a slide for a toddler. A maroon
Citroën people carrier occupied the driveway. Through the windows, a
woman in an apron was washing up.

I went to the end of the street and bought a pair of gardening gloves
from the shop opposite the station, tore the tags off, wiped them in soil.
Then I knocked on the door of Joanna's old home.

The aproned woman answered, drying her hands.

"Sorry to bother you," I said. "I live around the corner. Borrowed these
off the woman who was living here but a while back."

"She's not here anymore."

"Oh. When did she move out?"

"We've been here five months."

"I don't suppose you have any forwarding details?"

"None at all. And nor does the former landlord, apparently." She
looked at the gloves. "Sorry."

Joanna's parents were in the phone book. They'd met me once. A
Christmas. I usually try to hole up in a lawless terror haven at the holiday, but my own mother had died the previous year and Joanna, be-

ing supportive, had invited me on her annual pilgrimage home. Her parents were mannered, English. Father ex-City, a wine trader, womanizer; mother discreetly Christian and frail. She liked me. "Joanna never brings anyone home," her mother said, and gazed at me with hope. Joanna's personality with them was hilarious; all smiles and self-deprecation: the dutiful daughter with her rising career in the civil service. I wished they'd seen her firing an Uzi.

She was protecting them from herself, I realized. Your closest family members don't have to be completely in the dark about an MI6 career, but you have to ask yourself why you'd give them that to think about. I felt they deserved to know of her coolly walking into a room of Eastern European fascists, enduring enhanced interrogation training, setting up radio stations in the Afghan desert.

"It's Elliot," I said, when her mother eventually answered the phone. "Joanna's colleague."

"Oh yes. Elliot. Hello."

"I've been having difficulty tracking Joanna down. Any idea where she is, or how I could get hold of her?"

"We've not heard from her for ages. I thought she was abroad. She never tells me much. Should we worry?"

"No need to worry. I'll tell her to give you a call. When did you last speak to her?"

"It must have been over a month ago."

"Any idea where she might have been?"

"Not in the UK. I know that much. We had another man calling up looking for her just yesterday. He couldn't get in touch with Jo either."

This didn't feel like good news. The individual was someone who shared my anxiety or it was a professional hunt. Neither great, but a lead.

"Did he give a name?" I asked. "Maybe we can pool resources."

"Hang on . . . Patrick Dolan. He left a mobile number. Do you know him?"

"Rings a bell. I'll give him a call."

I didn't know Patrick Dolan. I put the mobile number she gave me through Facebook and WhatsApp, then Truecaller—a search tool that found contact details globally. No sign of Patrick. I went to an out-of-town Sainsbury's, bought a pay-as-you-go Nokia, and messaged:

It's me. Can you meet?

Five minutes later he messaged back.

You ok?

Possibly not. Where can you meet?

New Pag caff? Can you make 5.30?

That was our café: the one where Joanna and I used to have a last breakfast before parting. It gave me a kick of jealousy alongside relief: Someone else she trusted? The incautious approach to arrangements told me he wasn't a trained field officer, at least. Unless I was being lured. He'd chosen five thirty, an after-work stop for someone who worked locally—a few minutes' drive from Shefford Park.

See you there, I messaged.

The caff was aging, in need of a lick of paint, attached to a ten-pump truck stop, with grumpy staff, filthy toilets, signs advertising beds and showers for thirty pounds a night. I got there early, bought a coffee, took a seat at the back, near a rear exit, just in case.

The man arrived cautiously, looking around—which only made him more conspicuous. As did the hi-vis yellow cycling jacket. He was tall, early thirties, clean shaven with a mop of brown hair. He held a bicycle helmet under his arm, phone in hand.

I recognized him from the birthday of a mutual friend last year. I had a memory of him flirting with Joanna outside a restaurant in Clapham, one of the technology wizards. Tom someone. Tom Marsh.

"Tom."

He glanced over, eyes narrowed. Then he looked around again, still searching for Joanna, slowly putting two and two together. He turned back to me and walked over.

"It was me who messaged you," I said. I waited for one final beat of comprehension. "We're both concerned about Joanna. Get a coffee, take the battery out of your phone."

He considered this, then put his helmet on the table and joined the queue. At the party, he'd struck me as hyperintelligent, if a little sheltered. He was working on the technology for mass holographic deception. He had shown us a photo on his phone: Tehran with a three-dimensional Allah several hundred feet high, rising over the Azadi Tower. I had bristled, ignoring the jaw-dropping aspects of this and pointing out that most Iranians were too secular and astute to care. "Well, this was what we were tasked with," he said. Talent leads you on strange journeys.

By the time he returned, splashing down a mug of Nescafé, his memory had done some work.

"You're Elliot."

"That's right. We met at Hugh Stevenson's fortieth."

"Do you know where Joanna is?"

"No. I'd like to find out. Why did you contact her parents?"

Marsh breathed deeply. I smelled fresh aftershave and wondered what kind of encounter he'd been hoping for.

"I was questioned about her, at work. On Monday afternoon. I was taken for what they said was a routine security check. They were very interested in Joanna, whether I'd had contact with her since she left, the nature of our relationship."

There it was, I thought: the creep of an intelligence agency turning against you. My suspicion was that they knew the answers to those questions. They were shaking him up to see what came out. I had no idea why.

"And have you had contact?"

"No."

"What's the nature of your relationship?"

"We're friends," he said, cautiously.

"When did she leave?"

"April."

"Know why?"

"No."

"Escorted out? Leaving party?"

"Definitely no party. I don't know if she was escorted. The next week her unit was shut down."

I felt another tremor as the ground gave way, exposing new depths of trouble. Marsh stared at me, as if my response might give him some insight. I was showing my concern.

"What unit?" I said.

"I really don't know much, and I can't say much. I didn't work with her. And . . . you know what it's like."

"Of course. Only, I'm worried, Tom."

"Me too."

"Was this unit shut down suddenly?"

"Overnight."

"Do you think it had been compromised?"

"That would be one explanation."

"Where did Joanna go after leaving?"

"I've no idea. That's what got me worried. That and the interrogation."

"You'd tried to contact her."

"Of course," he said. "What's your involvement? Why did they think you were connected?"

"What do you mean?"

"The security officer asked about you."

That gave me a lurch. Something ominous was coming into focus.

"What did he say?"

"He asked whether Joanna had mentioned you, if I thought the two of you were in contact. I said I had no idea. What's going on?"

"Someone you'd seen before?"

"Never. Big guy, maybe sixty. No name."

"Was this in-house security?"

"I don't think so. He didn't sound like he knew the place well. We spoke in an empty office."

"Did he have paperwork? A file?"

Marsh considered this. "I don't remember seeing any."

"Was the interview filmed?"

"Not to my knowledge."

"Anything else strange that you've noticed recently? Break-ins? Computer viruses?"

"Nothing."

We finished our coffees.

"Does the code name Catalyst mean anything to you?" I asked.

"No."

It had been a long shot. But people always know more than they think they do; they have seen or heard things that mean nothing to them but hold the keys to understanding a situation.

"I need you to tell me a bit more. What was Joanna doing at Shefford?"

"She was part of a research group, I think."

"Researching what?"

"I could never find out"

"Do you know when it was set up?"

He considered.

"Mid-2014."

After Ukraine, I thought. Russia in Crimea. It had been a febrile time in the intelligence service.

"Targeting anyone in particular?"

"I have no idea."

"Who else in it? What kind of staffing?

"I don't know." He looked around, lowered his voice. "They were isolated from all other units. They even had their own canteen."

"Where was this unit based?"

"The old house; Building D. It's at the back."

"How many in the building?"

"Hard to say. It had a separate entrance and parking."

So within the most classified of government sites they had created an enclave of enhanced secrecy. That usually meant the technology involved was sensitive, or the ethics. Often both.

"You must have some idea of what was going on in there," I said.

"She joked it was seeing into the future."

"Forecasting? Pattern analysis?"

"Maybe."

I thought back to that conversation: relationship breakdowns; dreams and nightmares. I still struggled to imagine Joanna cooped up with predictive software all day, no matter how advanced it was. Tom's questioning by unspecified officers worried me a lot. The security concerns could be real or they could be part of a discrediting campaign. Six and GCHQ collaborated on an "effects" unit. Its job was using dirty tricks to make life impossible for those it chose to destroy, and that ranged from the manipulation of bank accounts to dropping child abuse images onto someone's hard drive. You didn't want them turning against you.

"What's your hunch?" I said to Marsh.

"Maybe the program they were working on predicted something they didn't want getting out. Maybe she saw too much."

He said it deadpan, staring at me. I tried to disguise my skepticism. There was a difference between forecasting and seeing into the future. Still, if I could keep Marsh out of the hands of security, he was a potentially useful ally. I recommended he set up a new email account for contacting me, one that disguised IP addresses.

"Joanna told me you'd help," I lied. "If anything happened."

"Really?"

"You were one of the few people she trusted. See what you can find out."

I walked back to my car and checked a satellite view of Shefford, locating Building D according to Marsh's description. They had partitioned the building off from the rest of the grounds. New trees had been planted, alongside more robust fences. Upper windows and skylights had been blocked.

I felt a prickle of surveillance, glanced around. No one that I could see. But it was time to get out.

Shefford village looked cold and empty as I took a final drive through. It had been spring the first time I visited Joanna here. We walked from the farms into woodland with thick carpets of bluebells, everything so simple and bright that it seemed to mock us and the austere rooms in which we strategized the world. We picnicked in a clearing, lay back on the grass, an unthreatening English sun above us.

I had that moment and one other that served as the sun and moon of my recollection. Her face with the sun on it, and then her face in moonlight, on our last night together in Turkey, driving along the Iskenderun-Aleppo road. The pavement was slick with contraband oil dripping from supposed vegetable trucks. The route saw a lot of oil smuggled out and a lot of people trying to reach the refugee camp in Reyhanli. A complex of Byzantine architecture remained close to the border, ruins which had been largely destroyed and reused to enforce the border itself, but leaving the better portion of a triumphal arch as testament to Rome's northeastern frontier. Joanna had been amused by my interest in it. In moonlight the arch was ghostly. One wall of a tower remained, so it looked like a tool with a handle and blade.

We had stopped and got out of the car and she took my arm. Stars blanketed the sky. "Look," she said. And, after another moment, "When was the last time you kissed someone you weren't trying to recruit?"

We had kissed before, but not with necessity. Perhaps we had been waiting to become desperate. To prove something. It occurred to me then that maybe she thought I was going to die, that this was her last chance. Or perhaps she had decided that she was going to die. Instead, she returned to the UK, into Shefford.

You're taught to cultivate trusted insiders. What they don't say, but becomes obvious, is you need some inside Six as much as anywhere else.

The party where I'd seen Marsh flirting with Joanna was Hugh Steven-son's fortieth. Stevenson was someone I considered a friend. I called him from a public phone for his sake: I didn't want to show up on his records.

"Hugh, it's Elliot. I wondered if you'd heard from Joanna recently?"

"You're in town?"

"Yes."

"Can you meet? Now?"

Stevenson lived in Hampstead, close to the Heath. He shared his inher-ited townhouse with three dogs, his father's collection of Southeast Asian puppets, and a Nepalese man I had never met. It was a beautiful house on a beautiful street. He answered the door with his coat on and a leash in his hand.

"I fancied a walk. Do you fancy a walk? Let's walk."

He leashed his German shepherd and we progressed as a trio through the golden spotlights of the streetlamps toward the Heath.

"Good to see you, Elliot."

"You too."

"You've lost weight."

"It's possible."

Stevenson was climbing the ranks in Vauxhall. He had cultivated an ageless donnishness although he was only a couple of years older than me. There was a sense of succumbing to class, becoming the person fate had always had in store for him. But he was brilliant in his own self-dep-recating way. I first met him in the library at Vauxhall Cross. My favorite part of the building.

I used to get in early. In through the airlock doors. I enjoyed the place when it was quieter: the central courtyard, with its fountain; the central atrium with cool green light filtered through the triple-glazed windows. It always reminded me of the interior of a mosque. I could imagine peo-ple removing their shoes upon entering, prostrating themselves toward the Union Jack.

The library was a gem, and underused. In those less digital days, it kept newspapers from around the world, along with academic publica-tions and the less sensitive reports from rival agencies. It had lamps and leather seats that nodded toward private clubs or the archives of presti-gious legal chambers. Stevenson was always there first thing. We devel-oped a friendship based on this convergence. He was curious about my work in the field. I could already see that he was going to rise fast, and knew he would be useful. Also, we liked each other.

He allowed himself a careful glance at my face in the streetlight. I understood the precautionary ritual of small talk, that we would get to Joanna when he was ready.

"Heard you did pretty well out there," he said.

"I'm not sure about that."

"Not your fault it got pulled."

"Pulled suddenly. Left people exposed."

"Your man got into trouble, no?"

"He should have been protected. That was taken away. That's what caused the trouble."

"Ours is not to reason why."

"Fuck that."

We lapsed into silence.

"How's Sunil?" I asked, remembering his partner's name.

"Fine. Tired, overworked."

"And Legoland?" I asked, before he felt obliged to inquire into my private life. "What's news from Vauxhall?"

"The new regime's isolated pretty much everyone. Douglas Doyle's in the Secretariat now, still obsessed with the Arctic Circle. Ann Swan went to Citibank. Did you hear Etienne had a flap of sorts in China?"

"No."

"Triad-run billiard halls. The word is: Don't mess with them."

"I'm glad we've established that."

"Once and for all."

I momentarily missed HQ. The gossip, the etiquette of careful eyes. The locked doors and hushed corridors where you could nod at men and women who saw you every day, and if they didn't know exactly what you did or who you were, at least they had an idea, and that was permitted.

"I kept a review I thought would interest you." He extracted a folded clipping from his pocket: *An Islamic Utopian: The Life of Ali Shari'ati*. "Islam, Marxism, revolution. I thought it sounded like your kind of thing. Know it?"

"I skimmed a copy when it was in hardback."

"Any good?"

"Not bad. The usual line: CIA ruined the Middle East, et cetera. Everything's our fault. The publishing house is Kremlin-sponsored." His silence made me conscious of my irritability. "It's worth a read," I said. "I have nothing for you, I'm afraid."

"It's just good to see you alive and well."

We skirted the pond, turned onto a footpath that led into the Heath. Stevenson stopped to bag dog shit and I saw him glance at the road behind. We were alone. We continued into the trees. When the darkness had closed around us we sat down on a bench. He wrapped the leash around its arm. "Joanna's AWOL."

"What do you mean?"

"Definitely not working for us anymore, it seems. Stopped six months ago. I've been trying to ascertain where she's gone. It's not proving easy."

"I would have thought you could get some information."

"I would have thought so too. I'm still trying. Via staffing, I just about got confirmation she had parted company with us. It was a struggle finding that out. My request for contact details received silence. It's unclear if this is because they don't have them, or don't want me to have them, or I slipped down someone's inbox."

"What on earth's going on?"

"Seems she left under a bit of a cloud. Type of cloud unknown. Incommunicado since May."

"Security concerns?"

"Possibly. All I've got to go on is how little people are telling me."

"She was at Shefford."

"Yes."

"I met up with Tom Marsh. He's still based there."

"What did Tom know?"

"He was questioned about her. And about me. Something's happened that's turned Vauxhall against me. A loss of trust, or something worse."

Stevenson shook his head.

"Say Joanna's become toxic," he said. "Persona non grata. They'll be on you as well, as a matter of course."

"What do you know about Building D at Shefford?"

"Nothing. Shefford is as much of a mystery to me as anyone else."

"Anything code-named Catalyst that you've come across?" He shook his head. "New tech in development? New software?"

"I'm not the man to ask about that. I'm still waiting for my pen gun. I can have a sniff, Elliot. But you know what Shefford's like."

I got my phone out.

"I received an encrypted file three days ago. I believe it came from Jo-anna. It contained this; the footage is computer-generated."

Stevenson watched the video twice in silence.

"It's not real?"

"No. There's something odd about the way we physically interact. That's not my body. And the box at the back, there's no shadow. See how the vase casts a shadow but not the box?"

He looked again, nodded.

"You think Joanna sent it to you?"

"It was sent using a system only she knows about. No one else could have done it."

"Is there any more?"

"No. I've never been in that room. I've been in Kazakhstan twice, but not for many years."

"Has Joanna?"

"Not when I last saw her. That was a few months ago. I had three missed calls around the same time I received the video — from a landline in Kazakhstan."

Stevenson stared at the screen. I could see professional appraisal. He was looking for signs of provenance.

"Do you know the other man?" he asked.

"No."

"The location?"

"The plug sockets are type F, which doesn't narrow it down much. But it looks like there's a newspaper in Kazakh, which would fit. The newspaper's dated two weeks from now, thirteen December."

Stevenson wrinkled his brow.

"It seems convenient that the date's visible."

"Seems overdetermined. The message that accompanied this clip was a duress code. It means the sender needs to get out of the country, that I may be in danger too."

He sighed and shook his head.

"Why so enigmatic?"

"That's what I've been wondering. Maybe the sender was interrupted or in a hurry. It takes time to encrypt files. Perhaps if I'd got the accompanying phone call more would have been explained. Or perhaps the whole thing's deliberately mysterious because it's a trap, a lure. An attempt to play with our minds."

"By her?"

"More likely someone who's got information out of her." I regretted saying it immediately. This touched on the world he didn't operate in, and deepened the darkness around us.

"What's going on in Kazakhstan at the moment?" I asked.

"Desert, I imagine. Some oil. Benign dictatorship and shaky post-Soviet nationalism. Why?"

"Who's on it for Six?"

"There's no permanent station. I think the ambassador's called Suzanna Ford, but I've never had any contact."

The dog barked and we both fell silent. A figure passed up by the pond, male, walking fast, hands in the pockets of a short jacket. He continued toward Hampstead Lane.

"How was the debrief?" Stevenson asked.

"Hostile. Suspicious. I was questioned on contacts, lifestyle."

"They're covering their backs."

"Their backs are safe enough. I'm starting to feel somewhat isolated. What have you heard about Saudi?"

"Nothing. I mean, only— There's a sense of . . . Things got carried away."

"Carried away."

"What do we know, right?"

I didn't answer. He continued: "All I can say with regards to Vauxhall is there's changes: changes in priorities, in tactics, maybe. That's the atmosphere. The new C's in place, heads have rolled, morale is low. Russia's got the wind in their sails, seems to be the common belief. Syria's a test bed."

"For what?"

"I don't know."

"Maybe Joanna knows."

"Maybe."

I sighed.

"Someone could be manipulating HQ against us."

Stevenson shrugged—the kind of shrug that says: Of course, who can say, where does one start?

"Look, Elliot. Why would they turn on you? You're celebrated."

"As what? Their gun runner?"

"You achieved what you set out to do."

"That's the problem."

"What do you mean?"

What I meant: Success is never straightforward in intelligence work. It rests on a lot of things no one wants to think about. You sink deep into a role, become invaluable to both ends, because you have extra powers, but no one ever forgets that you're forbidden and to be jettisoned when the moment comes. You get an aura, a reputation for making things happen. Then you become a repository of other people's guilt.

"It was fun while it lasted, but you know how that goes. You do people's dirty work and it just means you're the last to be cleaned away."

Six years as Bohren, I thought. Libya to Syria and now Yemen as well, with a declining sense of moral justification. Yet this was meant to be the project that went well. That meant I could leave with my head held high, even if no one knew anything about what I'd done. The absurd image that wouldn't go away involved somewhere homely, where I was talking to a child. They held a yellowed clipping while I said something like: *I played a part in this. This is who I was, even if you won't read about me here or anywhere, except between the lines. In this old shoebox is the relevant medal in silver. No, I don't feel any need to display it. The Queen leaned in to my ear as I received it and said she understood I had contributed a huge amount "behind the scenes."*

"This is the end of the road for me," I said. "It's overdue—I'm moving on."

"To what?"

"I'll see. I have some notes for a book—the poetry of Islamic Spain. The invention of love. I want to retrace the steps of the troubadours, lose myself somewhere foreign that I don't have to spy on."

But as I said it I realized, with a chilling clarity, that I wasn't leaving anything without Joanna. Certainly not while she remained missing. Stevenson checked his watch, wrapped the leash around his hand.

"Listen, Elliot, I should go. Sunil will be wondering where I am. But will you keep in touch? And not do anything reckless, for anyone's sake?"

"Of course."

"You've been through a lot. I know it's all a day's work for you, but you deserve a break."

"Can you sniff around?" I said. "Keep an ear open?"

"They don't close anymore."

He placed a hand on my shoulder then returned toward the streetlights. I watched for other silhouettes but none came. I stayed on the bench, enjoying the darkness and the sensation of being alone.

AWOL. Where would she go? She was impulsive, a thrill seeker. Given how ill-advised our relationship was, it's a wonder she hadn't initiated it sooner. But I had always thought there was an unspoken agreement, an understanding that this final step would destroy us. We had always found alternative kicks. We would slip into improvisations while out, snap covers, games we'd developed during training; introduce one another by names made up on the spot, find ridiculous environments to penetrate: a meeting of Quakers, a protest against undercover police, a far-right march.

"It will be interesting," Joanna said, pulling me into the thin flow of marchers, adjusting her hair, her voice, ending up three hours later almost being glassed by a coked-up skinhead in East Ham. All of which was exhilarating and made you feel like you were both special, and deferred the awkward honesty of a relationship.

Two years after training, I was back from Chechnya. My mother had died and that was when Joanna invited me to Christmas with her family. She had always depicted her own life as a home counties nightmare of perfection: Cheltenham Ladies College, parents trying to marry her to stockbrokers, doctors, clergy. *I mean, fucking clergy . . .*

They didn't seem too nightmarish to me. After lunch she showed me how to pick the locked drawers in her father's study, which contained photographs of his lovers, some teenage, some sadomasochistic.

"So which locks do I pick for you?" she asked. "You don't talk about your background. Is that some stupid Six thing? I don't know how you got here. You were in Cambridge, you were playing soldiers on the side, get a tap on the shoulder . . ."

Boxing Day, we borrowed her father's Aston Martin and drove to where I grew up, a former local authority house on the edge of London. I had intended to sell it. This was something I never got around to, in the end. All it housed now were the conversations I hadn't managed to initiate and wasn't quite ready to give up on. Death had made me aware of how many people live suspended in the midst of half-completed gestures. I was embarrassed by Joanna seeing the place.

She wandered from room to room, picking up vodka bottles, blister packs. There were few traces of my mother's succession of boyfriends, who evaporated once it was time to put her out of her misery. Most of the bulbs had gone, and the winter light was hard.

"Your father?"

"Left when I was quite young. I don't really remember him."

"I should have guessed."

She lifted an unopened pack of oral syringes and gave me a quizzical look. I filled one from a Smirnoff bottle.

"Open your mouth."

I described my mother's late embrace of alcoholism, and the nine months spent feeding her vodka and orange juice as her body closed down, a scene that wasn't without its own raw beauty. It brought me a cool, enveloping nihilism that later became the foundation of what others perceived as courage and determination. I could survive anything after that.

I found a candle, lit it.

"What are you thinking?" Joanna asked.

"I'm enjoying this. I feel at home."

It took me a long while, taking out the memory of those two days and handling it, before I realized why she had invited me for Christmas. She wasn't using me to deflect attention. She liked me. She had picked through books in my room, found some old photographs.

"P Coy?"

"Pegasus Company. Training for the Parachute Regiment. Playing soldiers, as you said."

"You look like you've been boxing."

"They call it milling. It's part of the selection process."

"What does it involve?"

"Punching your opponent in the face as hard and as frequently as you can. One minute, no pausing, no trying to defend yourself."

"Why on earth do they make you do that?"

"I never thought to ask. To see if you're as dark and troubled as they are, perhaps. It made sense at the time. When they can, the officers pair friends, brothers, get them to knock each other unconscious."

"Lovely. Why did you want to get into the Paras?"

"More class-free, less hierarchical."

"And you ended up in Six."

"I know."

Joanna was the only person I had told any of this. I remember, at the time, thinking we were old. We were twenty-four. We survived several years' acquaintance before succumbing to the inevitable. Other partners helped. Joanna used to say: This one had better work or we will end up together. It was a joke and not a joke, brought to comic perfection when we were assigned cover as a married couple in Ukraine.

There was a drunken one-night stand in Kiev, but I think of us getting together in Turkey. And then she returned to the UK, to ignominy, and the distance allowed us to begin a relationship. That we could only see each other every few weeks made it easier. We should have notified our line managers. I didn't; I can't imagine Joanna having that conversation either.

It's a mixed feeling when someone's turn for the worse involves agreeing to a relationship with you. I had been worried about her, post-Turkey. Shame can drive people to all sorts of things, and it had driven her to me. There was a current of rage and humiliation sweeping her. I understood something of that. Her reputation was destroyed but she had survived, emerged intact on the other side of ruin, and that brings a disconcerting freedom.

Two recollections: sun and moon, night and day. Half an hour after that moonlit kiss by the Iskenderun-Aleppo road, we're half dressed on the dusty ground. Joanna's phone buzzes. It's one of her contacts saying Kurds had tapped into a pipeline beside the refugee camp. This had been going on for weeks, Turkish intelligence claiming the PKK were conducting sabotage operations. We both suspected it was the gangs running the camps. Under cover of night, they'd drill into the line, stretch a hose to a rusty tanker, then drive off when they'd finished, leaving the oil flowing into the ground until the place was swimming in it—and the villagers would come out and start scooping up fuel.

"Let's take a look," she said, already dressing.

We were approaching slowly when a flame danced through the darkness ahead. Someone was crossing toward the spillage with a kerosene lamp. Joanna swore. *That's a naked flame.* I was trying to decide whether to intervene or turn around when the place lit up, as sudden as a camera flash, only the illumination held and I could see all their faces, the people who'd been hiding. The fuel was flowing down into the stream, igniting through the trees, the night suddenly wild like a storm. Then there was a scream: A girl with her clothes on fire was running. I couldn't understand where she was running to. We were getting closer, Joanna unclipping her gun hopelessly, and I saw the girl running to the stream to dive in, only the stream was on fire.

That was the image I was left with. The scene from which she was calling me. It was the following day that Joanna received the cable from London recalling her, the news schedule still filled with lies she'd propagated. And hidden within my sympathy for her was a small sense of vindication: This is why I spy, and why I do so as a human spying on other humans.

Over the past six months I had thought of that night a lot, along with the days leading up to it. I had imagined the many schemes Joanna might be involved with, the many reasons it was best to maintain radio silence. No news was most certainly good news. I understood she would get in touch on her own terms.

Now she had.

8

When I woke the next morning there was a message from Evotec. They had accessed a recent Kaztelecom directory. The landline I'd been called from came up registered to Nurlan Pokatilov, Apartment 603, 9 Malakhov St., Astana 050059, Kazakhstan. It was listed on Airbnb as a holiday rental, entire flat included.

The Tutanota address used for the Catalyst link had been set up just before the message was sent, on a machine with an IP address that belonged to a PC in Kazakhstan. Evotec had gone one step better: The PC itself belonged to a café going by the initials KS, on Daraboz Street, Astana.

The resolution of the clip conformed to several models of concealed camera. The level of compression suggested it had been copied twice. There was no form of watermark on the video clip aside from a time and date stamp. Like the newspaper, it had been set to appear as if it originated two weeks from now. In terms of CGI, it wasn't like anything they'd seen before.

I brought up a satellite view, found the street address. The café was on a back street. Nurlan Pokatilov's address is one of many large apartment blocks in the north of the city. Kazakhstan was seven hours ahead of the UK, which enhanced its impression of dangling off the edge of the future. Which meant I'd been contacted around three a.m. their time. I tried calling again, but no one answered: on neither the number that had called me or the number listed as host. The place had poor reviews — for communication, above all — which might have been what attracted Joanna in the first place. It was dirt cheap.

I tried to log in to Bohren's Jersey bank account. The online portal didn't recognize my password. I tried twice more, with no luck.

Access denied.

Same with bin Talal's accounts. I received an automated instruction to contact the bank.

That gave me a guilty jolt. And a problem. I didn't want to touch UK current accounts in my own name. I could still access the eight grand in

Geneva. I converted it to cryptocurrency before that situation changed. The 20K I'd paid to Evotec left me with enough credit for one more request. I sent new tasking: Kazakh hospital records for the last week, plus recent arrests in Astana, then flight manifests in and out of the country for the days around the contact. My guess was that Kazakhstan's bloated bureaucracy used outdated technology that wouldn't prove too much of a challenge for the hackers.

I looked up routes to Astana.

Breakfast was brought to the suite, which let me spend half an hour browsing Kazakh websites and seeing how much of the language I remembered. Like in a lot of the former Soviet Union republics, Russian had remained the lingua franca, but Kazakh still held on strong, especially once you were out of the cities. My Russian was okay; Kazakh itself was a Turkic language, not quite as close to Turkish as some, but plenty of crossover.

When I visited all those years ago, most of my time had been spent around Aktau, in the far west of the country, on the coast of the Caspian. My job was to assess routes between Aktau and Baku in Azerbaijan, on the other side of that contested body of water. Aktau was pure ennui and I loved it: I had always sought out places that felt as remote as possible, which wasn't just a question of distance. Aktau had been built in 1962 as a camp for oil workers in one of the world's most lifeless deserts. There were no addresses, just three-digit numbers assigned to each home. The place was dependent on seawater desalinated with the help of a nuclear reactor, and the few trees that clung to existence had been planted using pneumatic drills. Camels wandered the concrete, coats matted. The town's main statue was of a Ukrainian poet exiled there by Russia in the nineteenth century, who wrote: *There is only sand and stones. You would gaze around and feel so dreary that you might as well hang yourself.* In the 1960s they briefly named the town after him. I spent most of my time watching oil service vessels heading for the platforms, wondering when the water froze. Kazakhstan had the biggest extremes of temperature in the world, and this seemed at least partly responsible for its stark beauty.

A lot of time had passed since then, with big changes in the country. I checked their local news, local bulletin boards, then went to an open-source search tool for videos and skimmed through all recently uploaded footage geotagged to the region. People were filming the snow. Eight inches had fallen in the capital over the previous night. Right now it was minus fifteen degrees Celsius. News-wise, workers at a metals factory had gone on strike. Presidential initiatives had been announced regarding the environment and social values. I noted what people were wearing, styles of coat and boots and hair.

Perhaps because I knew I was going to go, because I knew that absconding from the UK meant there would be no straightforward return, I decided to go to Croxley Green, to the place I still considered home.

My hotel arranged a chauffeur-driven BMW to Saint Pancras, where I walked into the station, loitered for a moment watching reflections in the windows of the Eurostar ticket office, then continued out to York Way and hailed a black cab. I kept watching the cab's mirrors, then I closed my eyes, opened them again in Hertfordshire.

In Kabul, children wandered between cars selling gum and phone cards, chanting "No mother, no father." They chanted in English, beelining to the white SUVs of Western organizations, and I had begun to wonder if they even knew what it meant. *No mother, no father.* I still heard their small voices, especially in Croxley Green. I felt an obscure shame each time I returned. The gilded origins of those I worked with were nothing to envy, I had learned that much, but one's own background always represents a personal lack. Croxley made me feel it acutely. I wasn't entirely sure why I kept the flat. There was some superstition around maintaining it, a sense that if I discarded this final connection with my own biography, the cover lives themselves wouldn't work. What would they be? The center would not hold. I think I had believed that my career would serve as a tourniquet, and that my roots, starved of blood, would wither away of their own accord.

Croxley was on the northwest edge of London, just inside the M25 but over the border of Hertfordshire. Its low suburban streets constricted around my heart. The historic windmill, the flat common, the interwar high street. Even before she'd seen the house, Joanna had looked around and said: *Do you think every life is a form of revenge?*

Shops and pubs had closed, a new beauty parlor arrived. The public toilets, with their scrawled lists of times for anonymous gay sex, appeared to be open for business. The modern redbrick church had a new noticeboard carrying photos of refugees.

I walked past my old secondary school where I had fallen in love with languages because they belonged to places utterly different from here.

How benign that had seemed, to foster a relationship with places that were not yours. A love of history too, which also seemed to happen elsewhere, and was somewhere you might escape to. I cleared some broken glass from the children's playground, as an opportunity to check the road behind me. No one except for a small boy on a bike, who yelled "Pedo!" and cycled off. I had been right at fourteen: This was the edge of the universe.

At my childhood home I went to the back, climbed into the garden, found the keys, and let myself in. The place still smelled of stale cigarette smoke and floor polish. My mother's art crowded the walls. I thought of Christopher Bohren's living room, up above Montreux, glass looking out over the Swiss town to Lake Geneva.

The bathroom was unchanged, the strip light harsh. I looked at my hands, the scar in the left palm where a woman extracted from the rubble of Baghdad's police station had dug her nails through my skin. I lifted the blind.

A van passed, stopped at the end of the road. It had a ladder on the roof. It reversed and parked. I dialed a number for the maintenance company advertised on its side and got a busy signal. Two minutes later, it drove off.

I let the blind fall, went out to the garden, took a trowel from the shed, left the property through a back gate.

Five minutes of walking took me past a postal depot and the first gray-brown fields to a municipal cemetery. I stopped at a clean, new headstone, bowed my head, then looked around. No one. I continued to the far end of the cemetery, over the fence, into the woods.

I brought up a compass on my phone and checked coordinates. I remembered the forms of specific trees as I traced the route: ash and beech trees planted twenty years ago, an abandoned cooker, a broken trough. A few meters north of the trough, I began to dig. Just as I was thinking I'd chosen the wrong spot I hit thick gray plastic. A couple of moments later I was able to retrieve the canister. The top was stiff but opened eventually. Inside: two passports, bank cards, driving licenses, cash in five currencies totaling three grand, plus a few basic items of kit: bump keys, a pay-as-you-go mobile. Most field agents organize their own emergency stash: contraband and leftovers. Few entirely trust their well-being to anyone else. I checked the dates on the passports, then returned to the house. I sat on the sofa and brought up a map of Kazakhstan on my phone. Vast and blank. The empty center of the world. I wasn't the first to feel it calling.

9

FIGURING OUT AN INCONSPICUOUS ROUTE TO KAZAKHSTAN WAS COMPLI-
cated by the fact that UK flights routed via Kiev. Flights from London to
Ukraine were closely monitored by more than one intelligence service, so
I flew Easyjet to Zagreb.

It was walking through Gatwick that the reality of it kicked in:
check-in, security, smiling at the air steward as he scanned my boarding
pass. Walking out of my life into renegade status.

I used my own card and passport for the Croatia trip, booking a holiday apartment in Zagreb for a week. No issues getting there: Zagreb's
Franjo Tuđman Airport was as busy as ever and no one could have
tailed me if they tried. I caught a bus into the city. The apartment was
up steep stairs, with a view down to a church with a red and white tiled
roof forming a Croatian flag. A street beside it filled with people over
the course of the afternoon, drinking at the bars that lined each side. I
let myself be briefly taunted by that imagined holiday. The paperwork
I used for the next leg dated back to a job in Tajikistan and had never
been used. The name was Toby Bell. It would get me into Kazakhstan,
at least, before any potential alert had been processed in London. I went
to a darkweb site that let you buy Mastercard details for twenty pounds
and used one to book my flight to Kiev, and another from Kiev to Astana.

That left me with twelve hours in Zagreb. I called Olivia Gresham and
set up a meeting with her property developer contact in Astana. I told
her the cover name I was using. "I see," she said crisply, and asked no
questions. Then I found a place to print while-you-wait business cards.
When I had cards in the name of Toby Bell, I printed out graphs and
spreadsheets concerning the Kazakh economy. My cover was going to be
a consultant for investors in Central Asia: something that put me between
business and government with plenty of room for unaccounted cash and
minimal infrastructure. As far as I could tell, that was what the word

"consultant" had been invented for. And businessmen were unthreatening: universally explicable, their politics transparent.

I set up Toby Bell's online presence, club membership, dating sites. Used a social media marketing company in Hyderabad to stock my new life with friends and contacts, likes and followers. I wove in a hint of concealed bankruptcy. The best cover for deceit is deceit; people always look for a secret, but they usually only look for one.

In a shopping mall on the edge of Zagreb's old town I bought thermals, boots, a couple more pre-paid phones. I loaded up the phones with apps—privacy vault, military-grade GPS navigation, police scanner, and an app that detected radio signals, including surveillance devices. I set them to erase all content if anyone entered the wrong password.

Hotels in Astana were one-star or five-star. I decided to head for the very economical Lion Hotel in the center of the capital, but didn't book in advance. December in Kazakhstan wasn't going to be overcrowded.

Evotec sent through passenger lists for all commercial flights in and out of Kazakhstan over the past week. I searched them for any females aged twenty-five to forty but there were none of the covers I'd known Joanna to use. Same with arrests and hospital records. I was going to have to take a look myself.

I marked up a satellite map of Astana with government buildings, police stations, and transport options out of the city. Then I added the address of the landline registered to Nurlan Pokatilov from which I'd been called.

At dawn I got up, switched on some lights, tuned the TV to BBC World News, dropped the keys in the lockbox, caught a train to the Zagreb airport, and flew to Kiev.

I had to stay a night in Ukraine, which felt okay. I thought it would sharpen me up. And I had spent time there with Joanna. Some superstition made me want to touch base. I brushed up my Russian and Kazakh on the flight. It wasn't so unusual in Six to have minimal time to immerse in a language before deployment, but this felt rushed. Like turning up naked.

The huge, blocky Hotel Ukrayina had a view of the Maidan. During the Orange Revolution, the hotel served as headquarters of the opposition. Ten years later I had seen footage of the same rooms being used as a makeshift hospital and morgue, the square around it divided between protesters and the paramilitary units cracking their skulls.

Quieter tonight, and repainted. The fallout from those events was seven hundred kilometers south in Donetsk and Crimea. I drank in the hotel bar, among the red and gold Soviet-era décor, and rehearsed Toby Bell: his enthusiasm for what he would describe as enabling policy environments, his knowledge of the EU's development cooperation strategy. Above all, his sense of opportunity. A man who had never been quite as successful as he wanted to be, perhaps. But he saw, in neglected places, the chance to cash in. He sought approval and had few memories that kept him awake at night.

Two or three days, I told myself. That was all I was going to spend in Kazakhstan. Long enough to determine whether there was anything I could do, short enough to remain under the radar. I'd follow the leads I had and ensure discretion while doing it; that was what I was trained to do. If Joanna was there and needed help getting out of the country for whatever reason, then a fresh presence could be invaluable. I was wary about crashing into someone else's field of operations, though, if that was what it was. Without knowing which direction the threat might come from, there's always the opportunity to make things worse.

Around eight p.m. the bar became a strip club. I tried out Toby. I flirted with escorts, flashed some cash, got in a conversation with an Israeli who owned an IT company, convincing him that Kazakhstan was the future. I left at ten p.m. and spent a couple of hours poring over Kazakh news clippings, identifying useful social media accounts and local journalists. Then I stopped and read some of Fredrick Burnaby's nineteenth-century account of traveling in the region, spying for the British empire when Tsarist troops were encroaching on its domain. And I felt the tingle again: entering a country as a spy, your own mystery momentarily equal to the world's.

I flew into Kazakhstan on Friday, December 2, a Ukraine Air flight. There'd been no issues in the Kiev airport. No one on my trail, as far as I could tell. The plane was half filled with businesspeople, some families, one or two backpackers. I boarded last so I could walk the length of it and see the faces of my fellow passengers, but nothing triggered any alarm.

I'd asked for a window seat. The desert began a few miles east of the Volga River, Caucasus mountains flattening, a flash of the Caspian. By the time we were beneath cloud again the world looked like Mars: rippled rock, pink then gray, running lifeless to the horizon. I experienced that ominous feeling I always got flying over deserts. You think you have diminished me, they seem to say, but it is you who are diminished.

Kazakhstan. Eighth-biggest country in the world, over a million square miles of land, and a population smaller than London. We flew over bare planet for three hours, then began to descend toward the capital. My neighbor pressed his face to the window to witness civilization bursting out of nowhere. Astana's glass towers burned with the low sun, office blocks of iridescent blue casting turquoise shadows across the business district. In front of the Presidential Palace, two perfectly conical towers of beaten gold stood side by side. The rest was snow.

Twenty years ago there was nothing here but a few crumbling Soviet blocks in a desert as flat as the sea. After his country gained independence, the president of Kazakhstan decided to move the capital here. He renamed it Astana, meaning "capital," and it appeared: ministerial buildings, business parks, futuristic shopping malls, arising from the dusty ground on his command. Or, more accurately, from the hundred-and-fifty-dollar barrels of oil beneath the dust. And it was only when you dropped below a thousand feet and saw the absence of people on the broad, straight streets, that you heard the echo of the old name — *Akmola,* "white grave." Hard to forget once you knew it.

Few of my fellow passengers looked up to observe the miracle of Astana when it appeared. The Ishim River had frozen — a winding white road through the city — and as we got lower you could see snowmobiles and sledges scarring the ice. Expensive new apartment blocks hugged the left bank, all glass and curves, older Soviet neighborhoods to the right: sullen, square-shouldered, like individuals who gambled on the wrong future.

Landing was bumpy. Outside it was snowglobe frenzied. Mid-afternoon but that didn't seem particularly meaningful. As we left the jet bridge into the terminal gate a woman in a pastel blue suit smiled and pointed a Sony mini DV camcorder at our faces.

Welcome to Kazakhstan.

At immigration control I chose a line with a young and tired-looking officer who barely glanced at my passport. I got a standard fifteen-day tourist visa on the spot, waited for the official stamp, admired a mural of horses running across the steppe.

The warmth of the arrivals hall thawed the atmosphere as far as the taxis, then the cold bit. Exhaust fumes billowed as thick as factory smoke in the freezing air. I changed some currency, then chose an alcohol-bloated driver in a dirty Nissan, who grinned at me as if amused to find me in the back of his car. I gave an address a block away from my chosen hotel. The driver grunted as he set off, and then the road vanished beneath snow.

"Where from?" he asked, speaking English.

"England."

"God Save the Queen."

"That's the one."

"First time in Astana?"

"In Astana, yes. It's exciting to be here."

He laughed. "Business."

"Hope so." We approached flashing lights that I thought were emergency vehicles but turned out to be a convoy of snow plows. "Quite some weather," I said, switching to Russian but keeping it tourist standard.

"This is nothing," he replied in Russian. "Last week, the snow was . . ." He gestured up to the tobacco-stained roof lining. "Now it will get colder. Less snow, much colder."

Astana's roads were broad and straight. We passed abstract sculptures, positioned without apparent logic, like someone trying to make an oversized flat look inhabited, then huge new residential developments. I couldn't see many lights on. Very occasionally a human could be seen moving between them, head down against the wind.

I tried to assess whether I felt alone here, or if I was sharing this city with Joanna. I thought of the calls, the fake video that had brought me to Kazakhstan. There was no way I could have stayed away. But Astana's scale and impenetrability were a reality check.

One face was repeatedly visible: the Kazakh president. He gazed enigmatically from billboards: Nazarbayev; wise, inscrutable, charismatic, seventy-eight years old, and, given that he'd been running the place as a Moscow-loyal Communist when it was still part of the Soviet Union, he'd ruled the country for longer than it had existed. Which was one of the reasons he maintained popularity. As father of the nation, he *was* Kazakhstan. Plus, he'd steered a careful path without relinquishing power, keeping Russia, China, and the West sweet. Keeping peace. His citizens couldn't start a magazine without governmental permission, let alone form a political party, but they voted largely in his favor in relatively clean, if meaningless, elections.

A few more of these citizens appeared after we'd been driving for ten minutes. My first impression of them was that they were suicidal. They wove through the cars, which were themselves skidding, appearing from between the gray mounds of slush at the side of the road. I had no idea if somewhere underneath the black ice there were lane markings, but no one would have been able to keep to them anyway.

Astana's landmarks came in and out of view as we drove: the gold-paneled governmental ministries; the soaring Bayterek Tower. A glass pyramid lit alternately pink and green. We passed three presidential billboards in a row. Across the last, in dripping red Cyrillic, someone had written: WATER FREEDOM WITH BLOOD.

Patrol cars sat in front of the billboard, lights flashing. As if sensing my interest, three men in dark uniforms turned their heads to watch me pass. I angled my face away, checked them in the wing mirror.

"How are things here?" I asked. "There's a lot of police about."

"Now, yes."

"Why's that?"

"Terrorism."

"Have there been terrorist attacks?"

"No."

Lion Hotel was in a concrete block that had been painted lemon yellow from the third floor up. The hotel actually occupied the top of the building only. The lift was broken so I walked up, which afforded me a glimpse of a brothel on the floor below, VIP Massage, with women in dressing gowns checking their phones and waiting for the VIPs.

The hotel reception desk was empty. It was brightly lit, with the city's eager artifice continuing inside: a lot of translucent plastic furniture, an incongruous chandelier spray-painted gold. Fish swam across a twenty-seven-inch screen on the wall. Everything seemed a little startled, as if called into play at the last moment.

After a couple of minutes, I went around the desk and leafed through the reservations book. There was no one else staying here. I returned the book, went and lay down on the reception sofa. Eventually a young woman turned up, sleepy-eyed, apologetic, in jeans and a T-shirt; she took my details, gave me a keycard, and rustled up a smile.

"You are here for work?"

"Some meetings."

"But you will visit Bayterek?"

"Of course."

"This city has many wonders," she said. Then: "Have you been to the old capital, Almaty?"

"No."

"It is very beautiful. There are mountains, trees. Perhaps you will have a chance to go."

My room was small, with a painting of a nomad asleep beside a camel on the wall and a view between tower blocks to the business district. I checked the window locks, then the devices currently connected to the hotel's Wi-Fi network. I logged on and sent an email, unsecured, to the property developer Olivia Gresham had put me in touch with, confirming arrival, saying I was looking forward to our meeting tomorrow. I logged out, connected to a private network, and checked for my own messages. Nothing from Joanna, one from Six asking me to confirm availability for a meeting tomorrow. I hesitated, then confirmed my availability. They'd become aware of my absence soon enough, no point preempting it. I went to the window and tried to understand where I was.

Across the business district, entire buildings masked themselves in LED displays, others flickering up their height in colored sequences. A block away, on the side of some offices, a pale-skinned woman twenty floors high repeatedly lifted a Samsung 7 to her ear and smiled. Any city can look utopian from a hotel window at night, but Astana was particularly dreamlike. Snowflakes cluttering the air added to the sense of unreality, of looking at an architectural model put together by a teenager with ADHD and a love of science fiction. Only the Central Mosque refused to blink, steadfast in its floodlights like an admonishment.

I remembered why I had loved the country the last time I was here: its sense of newness, of gazing out to a future as open and unencumbered as the steppe. But this city wasn't entirely without baggage. The President's excuse for creating a new capital was that the old one sat in an earthquake zone. One look at a map showed you the more pressing threat. Almaty was way down south, tucked into a corner near China. That left a huge tranche of northern Kazakhstan looking lonely and neglected next to Russia, and ripe for the taking. Shiny new Astana was a flag stuck firmly in the north. *Ours.*

I put my less sensitive paperwork in the room's small safe, then found a communal bathroom at the end of the corridor. There were cisterns, vent units, loose ceiling panels. I went for the ceiling, stashing two thousand dollars in cash and the more incriminating equipment up among the pipes. Back in my room, I searched online for car hire establishments and selected the one with the lowest Trip Advisor review, on the principle that it would show the least interest in me. Finally I mapped a route to the flat the phone calls had come from, then I headed out.

10

SNOW FILLED MY MOUTH WHEN I TRIED TO BREATHE. SKIN BURNED WITH the cold anywhere it was exposed. Ears were the worst. I pulled my hat down, used the act of turning away from the wind as I zipped up my jacket to check behind, in case anyone had followed me from the hotel. I could see about two feet. My nostrils stung as the mucus began to freeze. I covered my face with my scarf, moved on. I wanted to feel out Astana's energy.

The big, underpopulated streets meant it was a city without cover, which was both a good and bad thing. It made you conspicuous but also anyone trying to follow you. Anyone crazy enough to be out was wrapped up to the point of anonymity anyway. Locals called it the *buran*, the storm wind that came west from Xinjiang over bare planet, gathering ferocity as it advanced. Nature in Astana was limited to occasional thin stalks demarcating car parks. Vehicles were new for the most part, with little variation: Toyotas, Subarus, Hyundai, usually white or gray. They emerged from underground car parks, driving on compacted snow with the tick-tick noise of studded tires. They descended again beneath office blocks and shopping malls without anyone setting foot outside.

I got to sightsee alone. In the park that ran alongside the river there was a display of ice sculptures, miniature wonders of the world, the Taj Mahal, the Acropolis, lit by colored lights. All the older buildings across the water had been painted in pinks and blues. I walked three more blocks, which was as long as the exposed skin of my face could take, then hailed a car. In Kazakhstan, like a lot of former Soviet countries, pretty much any car doubled as a taxi for some extra income. Even in shiny Astana this held true. I got into the second car that stopped, waving off the first — I never took the first, as a rule, and I also tended to avoid ones that looked new, with central locking and powerfully built men at the wheel. I landed a battered Daewoo, driver maybe twenty years old. I mentioned a dive bar on a street near, but not too near, the car hire. Pronounced it badly so he asked me to repeat before nodding, unimpressed.

Just another entitled foreigner, stupid enough to be outside in these conditions. Easy money. He asked for five hundred tenge, which was comfortingly extortionate, and I got in. The car skidded onto Cosmonauts Street, wheels flailing on black ice, onto the main avenue heading away from the river into the governmental district. The windscreen wipers swept uselessly. A lone figure lost in snow dived out of the way as my driver turned.

A black Subaru Impreza cruised behind us for four or five blocks. I watched until it U-turned at a broad, empty intersection and disappeared back into the storm. We passed some frozen water fountains and began making better progress.

I thought of the graffiti I had seen. *Water freedom with blood.* The line was from a poem, but I couldn't think which. When we were close enough I told him to stop, then got out and walked. Someone barreled past, mummified in a parka, scarf over their face. I waited for them to disappear, then crossed the road, which gave me a chance to take a good, inconspicuous look in both directions. I was alone.

I found the car-hire place on a back street and picked up a white Hyundai Tucson. Half the vehicles on the road seemed to be Hyundai Tuscons. The owner was as indifferent as I'd hoped, hands stained with oil, writing down my details with a pen he had to smack on the desk to work. Things felt like they were coming under control. I collected the car and went for a drive.

Multiple state agencies patrolled the city. Police wore fur caps and long gray jackets that hid their weaponry. Closer to the Presidential Palace you got military in camo fatigues and sky-blue berets. The elite and more shadowy National Security Committee officers wore black tactical vests and carried Russian-made AN-94 rifles. Alertness was high. I saw two temporary checkpoints, with cars directed to the side of the road, drivers being made to open the trunks of their vehicles.

I cruised past the British embassy. It lay within a block of offices on the edge of the business district. No indications it had upped its game for any reason. No conspicuous security or aerials. The current ambassador, according to Stevenson, was Suzanna Ford, a career diplomat with previous postings in Stockholm, Nairobi, and Brussels. Nothing to suggest that this was MI6 cover, although one never knew. I memorized the vehicles parked in front of it. The place didn't feel like the sanctuary it would have once represented.

Now that I knew the local look I stopped at a department store and bought a balaclava, trapper hat, beanie, ski goggles, and a reversible down jacket with a hood—which was useful for quick changes of appearance. For the car, I picked up water, food, a first-aid kit, two spare phones, a shovel, and two liters of vodka.

Almost nine p.m. I drove while I could. Conditions were getting worse. It was time to put a plan into action.

I headed to the address of my missed calls.

The area was all half-constructed new builds. They looked desolate, the towers haggard. The block I was interested in had a roof, but if it weren't for lights in some of the upper windows I wouldn't have been sure it had been completed. Up close you saw ill-fitting window frames and protection tape. A courtyard remained half built. This was what happened when oil booms came to a crashing halt: Grand projects lurched into ruins before they were fully born.

I pushed the entrance door, and it opened onto a bare concrete entrance hall, walls covered with protective sheeting. Junk mail stuck out of post boxes, suggesting some habitation. Nothing in the box for apartment 603. I took the stairs to establish their viability as an escape route. They smelled of fresh paint, and I wondered if I was the first person to use them. Then, at the fifth floor, I passed an encampment: a man, woman, and two children beneath layers of tarpaulin. They were darker than most Kazakhs; refugees, with a propane gas heater. The man watched me pass, stiff with fear. I nodded, kept moving.

The sixth-floor hallway was freezing. No lights anywhere except for the light under the door of 603. I dialed the landline and heard it ring inside. So I was at the right place, at least. Still no one answered. I knocked on the door, listened for movement on the other side. No sound.

I didn't know who or what the apartment represented. I wasn't quite ready to draw the attention of a break-in. Not unarmed.

On my way back down, I spoke to the homeless family.

"Have you seen anything strange recently? A woman?" I tried various languages, got stares. "Know who lives in 603?"

"One night," the father eventually said, in faltering Russian. "We stay here just tonight. Tomorrow we go."

I told them not to worry and gave them some cash.

I needed to find a cathedral.

Black Mass was Joanna's system, and she'd chosen the name. Her idea was that even in an unfamiliar city, you could still communicate a location by code. So you had to think what landmarks every city might have: one code for general post office, one for town hall, one for cathedral.

The Assumption Cathedral in Astana was only five years old, though you wouldn't have guessed it. White towers with narrow, prisonlike windows supported blue and gold onion domes. A brass plaque announced that its construction had been funded by Gazprom. The towers looked a bit like distillation towers on a refinery.

The car park was empty, as was the security booth at its entrance. There were few surrounding windows, roofs, or ledges with a sight onto the cathedral square. I couldn't see much, but then neither would anyone watching. The cathedral remained open for evening prayers. I went in. A few pensioners sheltered from the cold, or appealed to God—it was hard to tell. The place didn't feel new. I was impressed by the sense of age they'd installed—the tallow candles and incense-darkened icons. I sat in a back pew, thawed out, breathed in.

It would do.

I sent the cathedral code to the Tutanota address, along with a number for my new mobile, then drove on, praying she got it, that she turned up. I should have settled in properly first, I thought, assessed security, familiarized myself with the terrain before trying to set up a meeting, but I didn't know how long I had.

11

I FILLED THE TANK, GOT SOME FOOD AT A CAFÉ WITH PLASTIC FURNITURE
and unshielded neon bulbs, waited for midnight. I checked the exit routes
I'd marked on my map; exits from the city, then from the country. The
scenario I was preparing for was one in which we had to get out fast. Kazakhstan had China to the east, across the Altai mountains; Russia to
the north, a long, porous border, the only downside being that on the
other side was Russia. Uzbekistan to the south was a strong contender
for exit of choice. I had connections there; it led deeper into the Stans,
into a complexity where you could hide. To the west was the Caspian Sea,
boats crossing to Azerbaijan. Shipping routes were always useful: chaotic,
bribeable, potentially off-radar. But it was all difficult terrain. All a lot of
steppe away.

The café served only one dish: *lagman,* noodle soup, with a few
pieces of mutton floating in oily broth, but it tasted better than the Hotel
Ukrainya's steak and potatoes, which was almost all I'd eaten in the last
twenty-four hours. As customers came in, I studied how people looked at
each other—eye contact among strangers, use of mobile phones, hands-
free mics. I hadn't seen anyone using a phone indoors yet. People were reserved. Men and women interacted coolly; glances were quick. You could
tell someone was unfamiliar to them but only just. I couldn't hear any
other foreigners about.

What none of it told me was how much of a mistake I was making by
being here. I sensed I was doing precisely what someone intended me to
do, which was never an entirely reassuring feeling.

At quarter to midnight, I returned to the cathedral. Floodlights around
its base caught the snow dancing furiously, seeming to race back up into
the sky. I parked beyond the edge of the light, with a view in all directions.
This was as clear an observation point as I was going to get. I turned off
the interior lights and watched the snow.

No one showed.

I waited, feeling conspicuous, checking my messages every few minutes. At one a.m. I drove back to the block on Malakhov Street. To apartment 603 and the landline that had called me.

I parked well away from it, covered my face, took a set of bump keys, which worked on ninety percent of locks. I used the lift this time, wary of witnesses. The sixth floor was unchanged. I knocked again, then went to work on the lock. It gave after a minute.

The flat contained no personal effects: no books or ornaments on the hallway shelves, no shoes or coats. Windows had been left open, dropping the temperature to below freezing. Snow had blown in. At the end of the corridor I could see a living room with snow over a sofa. I walked through. A black rucksack had been emptied across the floor: men's clothes, some money, painkillers, contact lenses. A bottle of vodka and two glasses stood on the coffee table. One glass had pink lipstick smears.

I turned toward the kitchen, saw blood up the wall.

A man lay on his back on the tiled floor. He'd been shot three times, twice in the face, once in the shoulder. The shots to the face had been done close up, bullets shattering upon impact, leaving a bloody gap where his right eye and the bridge of his nose should have been. They'd removed the lower jaw entirely. The back of his throat glistened icily, white knobs of spine among the flesh. Pieces of brain, tooth, and hair had frozen to surfaces in all directions.

A few distinguishing attributes remained. He was white; the condition of his skin and hair suggested someone under forty. He wore jeans, civilian walking boots, gray jumper, and a dark blue quilted jacket. The clothes were mostly global brands, neither cheap nor expensive. I felt a draught and saw a doorway in the corner of the kitchen leading into a bin area with chutes for rubbish disposal and a steel emergency door that had been left open a fraction. Beyond the steel door was an external fire escape.

I returned to the living room and checked the glasses on the table. In one, the liquid had frozen, but not the other. The man had been drinking vodka, but the lipstick-wearer had been drinking water. She had been controlling this situation, I thought. It was her safe house.

My mobile swept the place for devices, surveillance or otherwise. Nothing was currently transmitting. I checked the visible realm: the cupboards, the open window, and fire escape. No clues. No shell casings that

I could see, no prints. A crowd could have come and gone via the fire escape but their footprints would have been obliterated by the snow of the last forty-eight hours.

He'd been moving toward the fire escape, I felt sure. Trying to escape.

No ID on him: no phone, no wallet. I used my own phone to take pictures of what remained of his face, his fingers, then put it in his mouth and tried to take photos of the remaining teeth. Rinsing the phone, I allowed myself a sigh. *Thanks, Joanna.* I wondered what I was meant to do now. I wasn't in a position to seal the place. I wasn't in a position to stick around.

The lift was in use when I returned to the corridor. By the time it had stopped at the floor below I was already moving down the stairs. The sheltering family were all awake, eating out of tins.

"Excuse me," I said. "Apologies."

The four of them stared at me, new fear in their eyes. I kept my head down and kept walking.

When I looked at myself in the rearview mirror of the car, I saw why they'd been scared. I had someone else's blood smeared down the side of my face. I got out, used mineral water to wash, swore again. I sat in the car and briefly shut my eyes. I'd left prints all over the place. I'd be on cameras somewhere. The car certainly would. I had witnesses to my face and voice. The lock of the apartment was now broken, and it was only a matter of time before someone walked in.

I parked a couple blocks away from the Lion Hotel, and watched the street for two minutes before going up. The same girl sat behind reception, reading a magazine.

"How was your night?" she asked.

"Excellent."

"You saw the city? Bayterek?"

"Yes, Bayterek. Has there been anyone here looking for me?" I asked.

"No." She shook her head. Then, as I moved away: "Mr. Bell?"

"Yes?"

"I've put an extra blanket in your room. Let me know if you need more bedding."

"Thank you. I will."

The state of the dead man's face made facial recognition impossible. The frozen temperature made gauging time of death difficult. Nothing on local news about a man missing. I tried the owner of the apartment again. Still no reply. Online, a calendar showed it was booked for another four days.

Death's contagious. I made up an emergency go-bag in case I had to move quickly—phone, cash, some first aid—placed it under my pillow. But I wasn't just uneasy for myself. The thought of the body lying untended in the sixth-floor flat perturbed me; as if it had become my responsibility and I was failing obligations to care for the dead. I could call it in anonymously, find a phone box, use my Russian. An ID would surface once media reported it. But did I want to trigger an investigation?

Three days, I thought: in, out. How was that going? I stood at my window and watched the snow, the business district flashing, the river beyond it. The art of espionage involved remembering where you were. This wasn't London, Washington, or even Moscow. Mankind, as a whole, had never sunk any flag very deep in Kazakh soil. Frederick Burnaby, passing through one hundred and fifty years ago, heard talk of a Russian expedition against the Khans that set out in midwinter. A thousand men, nine thousand camels, three thousand horses, never seen again. Not even the bones.

You could build a hundred skyscrapers, but you were still in the desert. You had maps and plans, but they meant little here.

12

THE STORM HAD SUBSIDED WHEN I WOKE AT 5:45 A.M. THE WORLD outside lay entombed in moonlit snow.

The silence was jarring. My mind spooled through countries I might be in, arriving at Kazakhstan. Astana. And flicking immediately to the image of a man's destroyed face. I turned the TV on, checked online. No word of a body being found. By the time I was dressed, the sky had lightened a shade. I dressed as I had seen locals do — ski mask first, scarf, beanie, hood up over it, then trapper hat over the hood. Armored, I went out.

MI6 drummed into you the importance of "surveillance detection runs." They were best performed at times and in places when any possible tail was made conspicuous. Six a.m. in most places was ideal. It felt like starting the day clean. And confirming you were alone converted the loneliness into relief.

The first blast of subzero dawn took my breath. I walked as fast as I could over deep, pristine snow, through the last of the silence. I looked for vehicles without snow on the roof, individuals appearing from side streets. There was no one. It felt like the desert beneath the city had begun reclaiming it overnight. In other locations where I'd practiced this routine you felt the imminent life of the city around you, but not here. There was a thin tension to the dawn, an uncertainty as to whether Astana would summon the will to exist again.

Still, it was nice to be able to see it.

Ice had molded itself around the few branches in sight, around satellite dishes and street furniture as if it was concerned about preserving these things. On east-facing streets, cars had been buried entirely. I saw a man with a shovel carving out a Peugeot 308. Workers in luminescent orange marched behind snow plows, molding banks of snow on either side of the road. At the entrance to Nazarbayev Square, soldiers struggled with steel crowd barriers they were pulling from an open-backed truck;

the barriers had frozen together, and the voices of the men made an angry dawn chorus.

I cut through the park alongside the river and the central mosque appeared, its call to prayer opening up and startling me. Our song, Joanna used to joke. Plaintive as ever, at odds with the glossy, frozen city it appealed to. I slowed, made a rough headcount of those removing their shoes and boots to file in. It didn't seem more than a handful. Unbearded for the most part. Across the road, two stiff-backed men in an unmarked Toyota Land Cruiser also watched.

Terrorism, the cabdriver had said. I thought of the evident security tension and wondered what it indicated beneath the surface. Kazakhstan wasn't a hotbed of radicalism. Even if the Soviets hadn't spent fifty years trying to stifle religion, Islam was a relatively late addition, a sheet laid over older creeds involving tribe and land. The Islam that did take root was Sufi-inflected: mystical, superstitious. Still, Kazakhstan bordered the northwest of China, Xinjiang Province, where you found twelve million oppressed Muslims occasionally losing patience. Uzbekistan, to the south, had been having its little resurgence. In the other direction was Chechnya. Quite a neighborhood.

I stopped at the edge of the river, a spot where I could see the embankment and anyone on it for half a kilometer in both directions. A few defiant fishermen had carved holes in the ice, huddling under plastic windbreaks that encased them like body bags. No sledgers or skaters yet. No visible surveillance.

I returned to the hotel, collected my hire car, and drove back to the block of flats on Malakhov Street. I parked across the road and looked up at the windows. They were still open, light still on. No police vehicles around.

There was a kiosk at the end of the road. I bought a copy of *Kazakhskaya Pravda*, the national paper, then looked for cafés near police stations.

The one I eventually chose didn't have a name, as far as I could tell, but it was next to the central police station and had a view of the grandiose construction housing the deputy president's office and the Ministry of Oil and Gas. Cheap cafés near important buildings were a potential gold mine: You found cleaners, maintenance staff, security guards, employees having affairs—all sorts of lures to a spy. It had just gone eight a.m. Inside: ten men and women. Two tables of uniformed police, heads dipping to noodles and soups. A boy of nineteen or twenty continually mopped graying slush from the floor. A gruff man behind the counter took my order of coffee and a pastry. I sat for a moment watching the vast ministry building. It takes three or four minutes to become inconspicuous. I sipped my coffee, waited. Listened.

Eavesdropping brings language alive. You have a few hours on a new posting when your ears are still sensitized. There was that Turkic flavor, the harmonizing vowels that preserved the passage of nomads westward. I listened to the police, then two workers with the faintly Persian edges of Uzbek in their speech, then a woman with splashes of a dialect that sounded like Uyghur, from near the border with China. She had arrived just after me. From her various complaints about work, it sounded like she cleaned on most floors of the Ministry building. She lived with an elderly mother. Her daughter's upcoming wedding was a source of grievance. She sat close to a man who did maintenance in the same government offices — he had an identical pass to her, on a keychain. At his feet lay a toolbag containing wire strippers, electrical tape, a socket set.

The police barely spoke. I would have given a lot for a potential recruit. These were the wrong crew: young, professional, sober. I felt a cultural wall between us. The newspaper gave some carefully filtered insight into the country I was in. There was a lot about officials launching schemes in rural villages. A wind farm symbolized a possible future; Touch-KZ, a new dating site for Kazakhstan's youth, was taking off. Protests against Chinese companies renting agricultural land simmered in rural areas, but overall there was a lot less hate and a lot less sleaze than in a free press. Nothing about a missing or murdered Englishwoman. I checked what neighboring devices came up on my phone then logged in to the café's Wi-Fi.

New dating app popular among Kazakh singles. I found Touch-KZ on my phone, downloaded it, and joined with a fake profile.

A minute later I had a match. One girl, two miles away. Tia Zhang, twenty-eight years old, pretty. Catfish pretty. She looked like stock photos, sounded like a robot.

Hey. Great to meet you. What are you doing?

I messaged back: *Camel racing.*

Cool! You seem interesting. Check out this site — lots of fun there.

I ran a virus scan and clicked. It was a website advertising pop bands and TV shows. I declined the invitation to subscribe.

Twitter and SoundCloud were blocked, but a virtual private network was easy enough to download and allowed you to search the internet without going through government servers. I looked for prostitutes. Prostitutes were often a good first step to finding both the political elite and the underworld fixers. There was little information on prostitutes or red-light Astana generally. One gay traveler on a bulletin board asked where he might meet men. Someone mentioned a sauna, someone said Grindr worked. I logged in to Bohren's Grindr account. The only men within range currently looking for gay sex were two other Western travelers in a nearby hotel.

I ripped a photo of a young man from the internet—out of courtesy, I chose one safely domiciled in Toronto—and set up a profile on the Kazakh social network Zuz.kz. Adilbek Antropov was twenty-seven years old, an engineer, loved Italian cars, European football, Kazakhstan. I sent some friend requests, then linked to a piece in the *Washington Post* about kleptocracy in Central Asia. After five minutes it was still up, and I hadn't been arrested.

Dictatorship is sometimes hard to put your finger on. People don't go around visibly fearful or furious; you have to attune your senses. Something was brewing, I felt. *Water freedom with blood.* Now I remembered where it was from: a poem by Taras Shevchenko. *Bury me, be done with me, rise and break your chain; water your new freedom with blood like rain.* 1840s, maybe 1850s. He was Ukrainian, exiled to Kazakhstan when he started agitating for independence. It was a select few who knew Shevchenko's poetry these days, and not many of those painting graffiti. I wondered if any of this connected to Joanna.

The door chimed. A man walked into the café: clean shaven, in his forties, a pale, sullen face. European, maybe English. He ordered a black tea in passable Russian, took a seat at a table in the corner. Beneath his smart gray winter coat was a pale, slightly crumpled suit. In Europe he would have been a perfect gray man, utterly unnoticeable, but not here. I gave it another moment, then finished my coffee and left.

I crossed the Presidential Park, then doubled back over a low barrier and into the grounds of the Keruen shopping mall. Shopping malls are good for countersurveillance, and it seemed Astana had a fine selection of them. A lot of the world was inhospitable a lot of the time, but that wasn't going to stop consumerism.

I rode escalators up, then down again, with a nice clear view of faces.

No indication the pale man had followed. The mall was still quiet. A kiosk at the back sold cigarettes and bus tickets. I bought a packet of Chunghwas and two lighters.

"And a travel card, please; something that gets me on buses across the city."

She slid one across the counter.

"How long does this last?"

"One week."

"Any bus? Unlimited?"

She nodded, her palm waiting for coins.

I returned to the hotel. What I really needed was someone who had access to police files, an ear to the street, a local journalist or detective. Instead, thanks to the kindness and connections of Olivia Gresham, I had an appointment with a property developer. But that was better than nothing. He was local and would be sensitive to political currents, ones that could pull someone under.

I ironed a shirt, brushed my teeth, thought: *Toby Bell. Economic opportunity.*

We met in the lobby of one of the sapphire-blue towers in the business district. There were two huge photos on the walls, one of the governor of the Mangystau district opening the region's first supermarket, the other taken inside a Siemens factory close to the Chinese border, with smiling Kazakhs in white coats and hairnets. Dimash Toreali appeared a minute after I arrived, hand outstretched, black polo neck under a gray blazer, thinning hair gelled back.

"Mr. Bell." He walked me into the lift and up to the office. "You know Olivia Gresham?"

"Very well."

"A clever woman. If she recommends you, you are clever too. And lucky. She says your clients are looking to make significant investments here."

"Hopefully."

"Worked in Central Asia before?"

"Not as such. I've had some involvement in China."

"And you studied in England, of course?"

"That's right."

"Oxford or Cambridge?"

"Neither, I'm afraid."

"I spent a blissful year at Oxford."

His office was decorated with two portraits of the president, one with a gold shimmer like a novelty postcard. In between them was a poster declaring: THE CITY OF THE FUTURE IS DIGITAL. Toreali beamed at me. I was reminded of Moscow a decade or so ago, the excitement of money when it's flowing free and there's no end in sight. But I also got a sense that Toreali ran a tight ship.

He talked about entrepreneurship, a rising middle class, Kazakhstan as a link between China and Europe. As evidence of the country's appetite for modernity, he described his flagship development, Khan Shatyr — "Tent of the Khan" — Astana's biggest retail complex and, technically, the largest tent in the world.

"Its glass walls are suspended by cables from a central spire, you see? The whole center is modeled on a traditional Kazakh yurt."

I gazed across the promotional images and nodded. Gap, Zara, Occitane; an air-conditioned paradise where history came to die. The upper levels were encircled by a jogging track and monorail. On the top floor was a beach with rippling chlorinated water and sand imported from the Maldives.

"Did you know Astana had a beach?"

"I might have read about it."

"Open until midnight. You can relax on the sand while it's minus forty outside. Locals love it."

"I'm sure."

After another twenty minutes, the bottle and glasses came out. Ten thirty a.m. I'd had worse. And I respected the tradition. The vodka in the drawer was like a confession: *Of course, none of this is really bearable.* It made you conscious of its absence in Western offices, and wonder what psychopathy replaced it.

We raised a toast to the unbreakable friendship between Kazakhstan and the UK, then one to peace, understanding, and friendship.

I raised a toast to the president, and then he said, "Let's go for a drive."

Four armed guards accompanied us through the center of town, in a civilian-model Humvee, as Toreali pointed out the largest aquarium in Central Asia — "Possibly the only aquarium in Central Asia" — and a new ovoid national archive building under construction. I probed for insight into the political situation, but he was in sales mode and I didn't get anything useful.

"We call Astana city of the future, *gorod budushchego,* and the city of dreams, *gorod mechta.*"

"Not quite the same thing," I said.

"Where does the future come from but dreams?" He smiled. We approached the Bayterek Tower, its slender tower opening out to cradle a golden orb. "This is the centerpiece of the city," Toreali said. I realized what it reminded me of: the sculpture in Bahrain's Pearl Roundabout, flattened by Saudi tanks five years ago when it became a magnet for pro-democracy crowds.

"Does it do anything?"

"It embodies a Kazakh legend, about a mythical bird that lays a golden egg in a tall tree, beyond human reach. The egg contains the secrets of happiness."

"You can go inside?"

"Go in, go up, see the view."

"Do you discover the secrets of happiness?"

"You discover a cast of the president's hand. And when you put your own hand in it, a recording of a choir plays."

We lunched in the Palace of Peace and Harmony. The Palace was the pyramid I'd seen from various points across the city, sixty meters high, its apex formed of stained glass featuring giant doves. It had been constructed for a World Congress of Religious Leaders, Toreali explained proudly. "The palace expresses the spirit of Kazakhstan. Different cultures, traditions, and nationalities coexisting in peace and harmony." It also housed an opera house, a national museum of culture, and a projected "university of civilization," about which I tried to get information but failed.

We ate in a huge dining area right at the top with sloping glass walls— myself and Toreali and two Korean businessmen with Louis Vuitton bags to whom I was introduced as a successful British investor. The Koreans were in the process of building residential compounds in the style of English townhouses, and wanted to impress on me the potential scope for investment. They showed me a promotional clip on their iPad: Georgian buildings set among trees, bridges, duck ponds. They'd already built two identical villages in Moscow, one near Shanghai. I flicked through, past the images of golf courses, Western shops, and high-end restaurants, and thought of Egypt in 2011, which had had places like this opening every week and was soon in the throes of a revolution.

"It's going to have the country's first Burberry outlet," the Korean said.

"The Chinese must love this."

"They buy them off us five or six at a time."

We ate sliced meats and an Uzbek-style *plov* of mixed rice and meat. The developer, Toreali, made me study the bottle of Châteauneuf du Pape, reading the label out loud. He filled my glass to the brim but drank Coke himself. His guards stood by the door. I kept thinking about a guy lying in an empty flat with his face shot off.

"I hear the president's daughter likes to sing," I said.

"She is a beautiful singer," the developer said.

"I have some connections. If she'd like any bands to perform, to play with her."

"Oh, she'd love that. Her birthday is coming up. Do you know Coldplay?"

I said I might be able to help. When desserts were done, the Koreans left and Toreali led me to the sloping glass wall. He pointed past a library that looked like a giant contact lens.

"See that railway being built?"

I could see a dark line where earth had been turned, workers in hi-vis orange, small as ants.

"It connects down through the country to the East–West highway, all part of China's One Belt, One Road scheme. They are building it for us, connecting up the world. Last week I was having dinner with a couple who have just made the first overland delivery of laptops from Chongqing in southwest China to Duisburg in Germany. This is the return of the Silk Road."

I looked past the skyscrapers. Roughly the Silk Road, perhaps; the northern route: Khorgos, Alashankou. Six centuries ago the speed of British ships had drained this route of logic. Within a century or so, some of the greatest cities on earth had withered. Maybe someone then, on the Cape of Good Hope, had seen the galleons sailing past and got the same vertiginous sense of history turning.

"The beauty of the route is it bypasses Russia." He winked. "Now that Russia's put up trade restrictions on Western produce, people are bringing chickens over the Caspian. Yesterday I had reps from Jiangsu Province sealing a commitment to invest six hundred million dollars in related projects. So, as you can see, you have come to the right place at the right time. Think of Dubai."

I thought of Dubai. Toreali continued: "These are places created on the basis of logistics. Dubai was a small port where they made an economic zone. Now look at it. We are the next Dubai, and more."

I gazed across the landscape outside. Almost, I thought. Only, where Dubai carried a certain regal cruelty, Astana remained more earthbound. It wanted to be liked, which gave the pomp an air of Disneyland. But both were built out of oil. I said: "Someone once described the world to me as countries with long histories but no oil, and countries with lots of oil but little history."

I'd spent time trying to divine the lesson in this, but Toreali took umbrage. "Kazakhstan has as much history as anyone else. Just because there are not kings and castles."

"Of course."

"Not everywhere can be European."

"You're right. Can I ask, as one investor to another, how stable you think things are here? A country like this, with its oil, its location, it must be a magnet for unrest and interference."

"It is very stable."

"But this is Russia's backyard, right? How do you manage that?"

Toreali hesitated. "They know not to push it. The Russians can play a clever game when they want to."

"Cleverer than the West, perhaps."

"They have shown that."

I had the sense, as often when arriving in a country, of waiting for the key to decrypt it; the one that made sense of things and brought disparate pieces together. It was always a shared narrative—not the events that made it into the papers, but the prism through which they were viewed, the stories told at home. The meeting had gone well insofar as proving to myself that I could live my cover. I didn't feel any closer to understanding what I was doing here.

"And the police—are they cooperative? Trustworthy?"

"No more or less than the UK. We are not Nigeria."

I nodded, gazing across a country that wasn't Nigeria and considering the world's gradations of prejudice. Then one looming building caught my eye. More than a building, a sprawling residential fortress on the horizon. It stood away from the others, slightly monstrous, centered on a tower with a spire, additional wings of various heights appearing to have conglomerated around it, each with its own battlements. It would have been chilling at the best of times, but it had an extra layer of uncanniness here. I thought of the CGI clip.

"What's that?"

"That building? That is the Triumph of Astana."

"Know anyone who lives there?"

He laughed. "I have always wondered who lives there. People making money and people making trouble. It is not a place I have ever been."

13

WHEN I WAS BACK IN MY HOTEL ROOM, I WATCHED THE CLIP AGAIN, studying the view beyond the window, the glimpse of exterior visible, the shape of the room's own windows. Money and trouble. We were in the Triumph, I felt sure.

I paid it a visit. According to property sites, the Triumph of Astana had 480 apartments, plus shops, restaurants, and a cinema. The closer you got the more outlandish it seemed, a fusion of Stalinist and baroque, evidently modeled on the Seven Sisters apartment blocks in Moscow. Stalin had demanded those skyscrapers as a point of pride after the Second World War to compete with Western ones. They were heavier, though, and to achieve a scale commensurate with twenty million dead had to expand outward, mutating as they rose. Their silhouettes haunted the Moscow skyline, and even before I knew their origins I thought they had the cold gravity of war memorials. They made you realize that the scale of other buildings was born not of necessity, but a cultural sense of the humane.

Last night the Triumph had been lost in the storm. Twenty-two floors high in the center, rising to a pointed tower with wings either side, eighteen floors each. Four hundred and eighty apartments. Which one provided a stage for the video?

It felt strange crossing the threshold onto a polished checkered floor, smiled at by a guard. I felt an urge to ask if he'd seen me before. I headed toward the supermarket, bought a gift box of nuts and dried fruit, registered the various security cameras.

The apartments were accessed past a concierge controlling barriers to a set of lifts reserved for residents. Akhmetov being the most common Kazakh surname, I told the concierge I was here for Mr. Akhmetov, and could he let me through. He said he'd need to call up to the relevant apartment. I said I'd check I had the right number, took my phone out, and stepped back toward the doors. On the wall was a screen with time and date display. December sixth. The date on the faked video that placed me here was the thirteenth of December, a week away.

I found an internet café a few minutes back toward the center. I wanted to check for photographs of the Triumph's interiors. The café was small, no cameras. Good for anonymous searching. Or so I thought.

A young woman at the counter put down a medical textbook when I arrived. I asked to use a computer, and she asked for ID.

"What kind of ID?"

"Do you have a Kazakh ID card?"

"No. I'm from the UK. I'm here on business."

"Then your passport."

"Why?"

"It's the law."

"Since when?"

"Since last year. For security." She looked apologetic. Her face said: *Obviously this should not apply to wealthy white Westerners, but the law is the law.* "We are sorry."

"No need to be sorry. That's fine. That's good."

Joanna had sent the email from a place called KS. If they were as rigorous as the café I'd just tried, then I had a potential lead to whatever ID she was using. I found KS on Daraboz Street. It turned out the initials stood for Kiber Sports, or Cyber Sports. You had to knock to get in. It was small, with booths divided by plyboard screens. One security camera focused on the door rather than the PCs. The *sports* in its name presumably related to the old arcade machines at the back.

Two men in their early twenties sat behind the counter, working on a broken hard drive.

When they asked for ID, I gave them the Bell passport and watched them make a photocopy on an old beige Xerox. They scribbled down the details in a logbook, then assigned me a PC and wrote the number down too.

"Can I see which computer I used last time?"

They looked confused. I took the sign-in book before they could object, leafed back to the date Joanna was here. I ran a finger down the page until I got to the right time. Eleven people signed in that afternoon, one woman: Vanessa McDonald.

The handwriting was Joanna's. Joanna in a hurry. They even had which PC she used: number three.

Number three was farthest from the window. I requested it for myself and the staff acquiesced with a shrug.

The booth came with a sticky Dell PC and a torn leather office chair. When I clicked into the computer's control panel, the IP matched. She'd been sitting here. I checked files on the desktop, then searched the browser history for that date. It had been wiped.

More recent searches involved a lot of porn. The computer was running anti-block software. The country had a blanket ban on adult websites, so a lot of these cafés put on various forms of circumvention and made their money selling access to that part of the web. I sifted through the searches for various sexual practices, through Kazakh sports sites, social media, scrolled slower through news and local politics, but couldn't see any leads.

I went up and paid.

"One more favor. This woman, Vanessa McDonald . . ." I pointed at the name. "Presumably you took a photocopy of the ID."

They found it. The passport matched the name she'd given. In the passport photo she had shoulder-length brown hair. I wrote down the passport number.

"This mark beside it — the star. None of the others are marked."

"She didn't pay."

"Why not?"

"She just got up and left."

"Do you have CCTV footage?"

"No. The cameras don't work."

"Did the woman seem scared when she was here? In a hurry?"

"In a hurry."

"She was hurt," the other one said. He gripped his arm. "Maybe injured."

14

I BOUGHT A FRESH MACBOOK FROM AN ELECTRONICS STORE IN THE Keruen Mall, unboxed it two floors down in Big Ben Coffee, beneath a painting of the London skyline and the dictum LOVE COFFEE, LOVE PEOPLE. I got online, downloaded a virtual private network to mask my identity, and ran a search for Vanessa McDonald.

Plenty of women with that name on open source, but it was the sixth hit that caught my eye: a *Telegraph* piece from eight months before on blacklisted journalists trying to report from Russia, Ukraine, and Belarus. *The dangers journalists face in Russia have been well known since the early 1990s, but concern over a number of unsolved killings has soared in recent months. Now Western writers are reporting threats and obstruction. Those refused entry to the country this year include Martin Yates, Rachel Hodgkinson, and Vanessa McDonald.*

I searched "Vanessa McDonald journalist." Top hit, curiously, was a right-wing Russian discussion board devoted to media figures deemed unpatriotic. One member had uploaded a crowd photo from the Remembrance Day of Journalists Killed in the Line of Duty, observed in Moscow every December, if not unanimously. Joanna's face had been circled.

Anyone know this bitch? She caused trouble in Donetsk. Looking for address, phone number.

The individual who posted it gave a name that translated as Russian Truth. A "patriot." It was only their second post. Russian Truth suggested Vanessa McDonald worked for an organization called Reporters for Human Rights.

This all struck me as the kind of information you put out there if you're trying to build a cover identity: name and photo ID and backstory. Enough to make Vanessa McDonald real if someone was trying to establish her credentials.

The *Telegraph* journalist who'd included her name in the article wasn't one I knew as being a "friend of the department," in Six's parlance, but the

Telegraph was joined to the intelligence service at the hip. It could have been slipped in at any level, including source.

Which would mean, one way or another, she was in the field again. On an operation.

If she was playing a campaigning journalist, that was good reason not to be too visible. But people would run searches. Hits like this would be convincing. The organization she supposedly worked for, Reporters for Human Rights, had a website on which it described itself as a ground-breaking organization using documents and video footage obtained both openly and covertly to tell the stories of people suffering at the hands of various oppressive forces. *Our writers and filmmakers tap in to a network of organizations and workers in the countries concerned, some of them at enormous personal risk, to expose corporate abuse, modern slavery, and political violence.* No names came up on the site, for obvious reasons, just an email address and a guide to PGP encryption for those who wanted to get in touch with a story. It got good dirt, some military documents, governmental papers: Standing Rock, Occupied Territories, water disputes on the border of Uzbekistan.

I clicked tabs of the other regions where they worked: Belarus, Philippines, Sri Lanka, Kazakhstan. Under Kazakhstan there were images of prisons and oil pipelines, a quote from a UN report on ongoing detentions, a detailed report on the arrests of individuals associated with a charity called Testimony. That was the most recent story.

Reporters for Human Rights were working closely with Testimony, a local NGO. According to its own website, Testimony concentrated on human rights abuses in Central Asia. This included disappearances, unlawful imprisonment, and the use of torture. Established in 1993, it had Kazakh offices in both the old capital and Astana, which was unusual — most of civil society had stayed in the more attractive, bohemian Almaty. That had been part of the president's thinking, perhaps: No one wants do-gooders complicating utopia. I checked their address, decided to pay a visit.

The office was inside a crumbling building on the unfashionable right bank. It looked like someone had recently put a battering ram through the door. The wooden sheet that had been hammered over as temporary protection pried open easily enough.

Inside it was dark. The few windows were small and dirty. I left the lights off. The linoleum of the hallway floor was blackened where a fire had been started. Water damage had done the rest.

To the left was Testimony's small office. It had been trashed. Posters, leaflets, ledgers, old filing cabinets opened, one beige PC askew on a desk heaving with paper. There was a sulfurous stink of wet paper and ashes. All the drawers had been opened and rifled, so I took a seat and sifted handfuls of paperwork: it came from lawyers, doctors, journalists, and documented activists who'd been arrested; records of assaults; threats sent to families. The correspondence gave me staff names and contact numbers.

The director was a woman called Elena Yussopova. I knew the name. She was a long-term organizer in the fight against corruption and injustice in former-Soviet states, and a brilliant lawyer and writer. Her charity maintained additional offices in Moscow, Grozny, and Tashkent, staffed by individuals who'd made their peace, one way or another, with the price on their heads. If you spend your time fighting the violent, powerful, and corrupt, there are two approaches: Be discreet or be very visible. She'd gone for the latter. In truth, neither will keep you safe.

A few years ago, Yussopova's husband, also a lawyer, had been found bloodied and unconscious with a fractured skull in the lobby of their apartment building. He died in the hospital two days later. Police declared it the result of a hit-and-run, and nothing to do with the oligarch he'd been investigating. No one went to prison for it, of course. Since then she'd been outspoken, moved to Kazakhstan, pursued justice with even greater zeal. Was she acquainted with Joanna?

I found Yussopova's mobile number among the printed emails. She answered with a brisk "*Da?*"

"I'm a friend of Vanessa McDonald's. Is this a good line to talk?"

Yussopova sounded hesitant.

"Who is this?"

"My name's John Sands. I work with Reporters for Human Rights."

"No, it is not a good line."

"Can we meet? I have very serious concerns about Vanessa. Do you know where she is?"

"No. Have you heard anything?"

"Nothing. I am desperate to find out what's going on."

"Where are you?"

"In Astana. I have just arrived."

She gave the address of a café and said she could be there in an hour.

I swung by my hotel, set up email accounts in the names of Reporters for Human Rights and John Sands and Vanessa McDonald. I missed having access to Six's Changeling software, which enabled me to spoof any email address and send messages under that identity. But sleight of hand goes a long way. The Reporters for Human Rights email address was a .org. I set one up at .co.uk and emailed myself an urgent few lines about tracking down Vanessa. I sent one to myself from Vanessa, backdated to last week, saying if there were any issues I should speak to Elena Yussopova. I changed out of the suit into a shirt and jumper, practiced the speech and body language of a campaigner.

Unprofessional, I thought. Unprepared. But a step closer.

15

YUSSOPOVA'S CAFÉ OF CHOICE WAS IN SARYARKA DISTRICT, NORTH OF the railway line, where the industrial and poorer residential areas remained. Bare parks showed empty pedestals, snow piled up where the Communist heroes used to be. Yussopova's designated café sat opposite a war memorial. A statue of a grieving mother towered opposite the grate for an eternal flame, which had gone out. Mounds of chrysanthemums and gladioli lay frozen across a slab of pink marble. A bride and groom posed by the memorial having their photograph taken, a tradition in this part of the world that had always struck me as odd but also in some ways understandable. Love, death, the realm of serious things. Her dress was brighter than the snow; the groom wore a scarlet bow tie. After five minutes the newlyweds piled back into a VW people carrier, and it sped off toward the next photo opportunity. Elena Yussopova walked in.

She was alone. She was unmistakable, lined face accentuating a hard brightness in her eyes. Her hair was dyed dark red and she looked frail, eaten away by fury. She clutched a phone and a packet of cigarettes, studied the other clientele as she approached. Then she studied me.

"John?"

I stood and shook her hand.

"Thank you for meeting me so quickly," I said. "This is obviously terrifying for Vanessa's family. For all of us."

I glanced at the street outside. There was a better chance she was being tailed than that I was, but I couldn't see any new vehicles. Yussopova took a seat, ordered a coffee. I showed her the emails.

"You work with her?" Yussopova said.

"Yes. But more than that, I'm a friend."

"When did you arrive here?"

"Yesterday."

"Have you had any trouble?"

"I don't think so."

"No one following you?"

"No. Why? What's going on?"

"We don't know."

"When did you last hear from Vanessa?" I asked.

"Three days ago. You?"

"She called on Monday afternoon, around three p.m. UK time."

"And she hasn't gone back to London?"

"No."

"We thought perhaps she'd just left. It was only when your organization contacted us, saying you'd lost track of her, that I worried."

So someone else had called; someone else was missing her.

"Obviously it's sensitive stuff she was working on," I said.

"Yes."

"How did she explain the project to you?"

"She said she was making a documentary about Western oil companies in Kazakhstan. She wanted to highlight our work. That is right, no?"

"Yes. We've been amassing evidence of abuses by oil companies for a long time. Where was she staying?"

"I don't know."

"When you spoke to her three days ago, did she say she had any plans? Any concerns?"

"No. She was excited. She said the project was going well. I think . . . she had something."

"What do you mean?"

"I don't know. Andrei knows more about it — the communications director. He is flying back from Armenia at the moment. Did she not tell you about any of this?" Yussopova looked puzzled.

"I know she had something, some story. She told me too. I got the impression it was too sensitive for her to give us details at this stage. She thought our encryption might have been compromised. She was going to tell me in London. You've no idea what it was about?"

She shook her head. Her ignorance struck me as honest. But Yussopova would know the general objects of investigation. My cover was limiting how ill-informed I could appear. At the same time, I had none of the advantages of spying — the networks and know-how that would have been useful. It was excruciating.

"What happened at your office?" I asked.

"An attack. No one has been caught."

"When?"

"Two days ago."

"Do you think it connects to Vanessa?"

"Maybe. But there is no shortage of enemies. Have you told police about Vanessa?" she asked.

"No. I take it you haven't mentioned anything."

"As I say, until now I wasn't sure. And the police may not be on our side."

"That's why I'm here. I wanted to assess the situation first. You haven't had any contact with the British embassy?"

"No."

"Do you have any sympathetic contacts in police or government? Someone who might be able to help?"

She laughed. "Sadly not."

A man and woman came in, took a table one away from us, which seemed unnecessarily close in a near empty café. I checked the windows and saw a black Renault SUV outside. It hadn't been there before.

"Is there somewhere more private we can talk?" I asked. Yussopova looked around, understood.

"Follow me," she said.

We walked to one of the old apartment blocks nearby, a five-story Khrushchev-era slab with knots of ice spreading from its drainpipes like tree roots, making the approach treacherous.

Once inside, we climbed narrow stairs to a triple-locked security door, behind which was a surprisingly ornate apartment, with crowded bookshelves and a writing desk covered in leaflets and loose papers and copies of *Literaturnaya Gazeta* from Moscow.

I wondered if this was where Astana's intelligentsia gathered. Every city had some pocket of cultural pretension, and I was always drawn to them, not least for their inevitable political connections. Yussopova went to a small kitchen at the side and put a kettle on. I checked my phone, picked up the emissions of recording devices nearby.

There was a radio on the desk. I put it on to drown our voices. Rachmaninov. I turned it up. A framed photograph beside it showed a family of four, including a thirty-something Yussopova and her murdered husband. There was an unframed one of Yussopova being dragged away from a protesting group, megaphone in hand. There are good people, then people who will die for the good. It's a different breed, and one that always fascinated me. Joanna used to joke that I spied on them to find out what morality meant. I wanted to know what made them tick, but I didn't idolize them. It was a mistake, as a spy, to think you preserved good conscience through being detached, but at the same time, when your job was following the various strings being pulled in each direction, morality became a question of when someone chose to turn away. It simplified things, and could start to seem a form of self-defense, if only against the unknown. These were just some of the attempts at self-justification I'd used over the years.

Without getting too close to the windows I checked sight lines: nearby apartments with a view, somewhere you might stick a camera. The same black Renault SUV was on the street below, one man sitting in it. Yussopova came back with tea.

"Did you turn the radio on?"

"I usually do. We've had some serious issues with intelligence companies."

She nodded.

"Please, sit down."

I moved papers to sit on a sagging sofa, balancing my tea.

"Who exactly did Vanessa meet?" I asked.

"She met a lot of people." Yussopova assumed I knew most: fellow activists, lawyers, even some oil company staff.

"If she had run into trouble with authorities, where might she be held?"

Yussopova looked uncertain where to start. She listed police stations and prisons. She'd received no information that suggested Joanna was in any of them.

"But there is a precedent for individuals being held in secret," I prompted. "Without due procedure?"

"Yes, but usually word gets out after twenty-four hours or so."

"Did she have a car?"

"I don't think so."

"Can I see exactly what she was working on?"

We looked through recent campaign material. It covered disappearances, deaths in detention. There were names and organizations familiar to me from campaigns against labor conditions in the Persian Gulf. The biggest file was marked simply *Saracen*. Saracen Oil and Gas Exploration was a UK-registered energy company. The file contained FOI requests, diagrams of governmental connections, lists of UK figures on the board.

From what I could see, Saracen had been bought up by a British fund billionaire called Robert Carter. They'd drilled a few speculative holes in Kazakhstan and were now excited enough to be looking to expand their role: Extraction, transportation, and more exploration rights were being sought. I extracted a tattered *Herald Tribune* clipping from Yussopova's file:

> Carter, whose gambles on Central Asia have been increasingly stymied by geopolitics, has made what he describes as a last throw of the dice. Saracen have been in Kazakhstan for four years with little luck, accumulating an estimated 20 million in debt on wildcat drilling. Carter's hope is that new technology leads to fresh discoveries. But both rivals and shareholders claim he has paid well over the odds on a quixotic and personal mission.

Saracen weren't necessarily who you wanted moving in next door. Campaigning literature contained diagrams of corruption, evidence of lobbying in the UK, Brussels, and Astana, evidence of slush funds. Then there was their use of private security, a company called GL5 who protected rigs and personnel. The presence of GL5 necessitated the hiring of PR companies to cover up anything that seemed too heavy-handed. Finally there was the use of private intelligence firms to spy on the people accusing them of overstepping the mark.

"Do you know which private intelligence firms?" I asked.

"No. It is very secretive."

"Do you think Saracen could cause Vanessa trouble?"

"They are a British company." Yussopova gave another shrug. "You would think they have more . . . British values. But here, everyone becomes different. Now that Saracen has new owners, they are very aggressive."

I studied a protest flyer depicting a drilling rig gushing blood. Then I looked at the other work lying around: an article about the bribing of local officials, another focusing on censorship. Kazakh police had detained an activist trying to unfold a poster in front of the Presidential Palace. He was expressing solidarity with an independent magazine shut down last month. The editor had been arrested and was now on hunger strike. Testimony were battling official silence to get the story out.

"Things are starting to happen here," Yussopova said.

"What kinds of things?"

"A revolution. In expectations, at least."

"To an outsider, this seems quite a solid country."

"Countries seem solid until they begin to change. Nobody in any of the Arab Spring countries would have predicted those systems could collapse. When there are powerful police and security services and a leader who is feared and respected, a lot of people think nothing will change. But systems are more fragile than we think."

"The Arab Spring didn't go so well."

"This is different. There is optimism. More and more people are online—"

Yussopova's phone rang before she could tell me that the internet was ushering in democracy. She took the call in the kitchen. I made a physical search for the listening device: book shelves were good cover, a lot of visual information to lose a bug in; light fittings work, and mean you can mask the electronic emanations. Finally I knelt, felt under the table and found it. A disc the size of a ten-pence piece, attached magnetically. Inside was a voice-activated micro-transmitter. You wouldn't know what it was unless you'd planted a few yourself. I considered removing it, then heard Yussopova returning and straightened.

"Did Vanessa ever come here?" I asked.

"Vanessa? Yes, several times."

"Did she help you with equipment?"

"She gave us laptops, phones. All more secure than the ones we had. She recommended software, VPNs."

"Flash Free?"

"Yes."

Nice to see Joanna had kept her styles. Flash Free was known among intelligence operatives as inherently compromised software, which meant whichever crew she was spying for would have access to all the activists' computers.

"Vanessa has been so helpful for us," Yussopova said. "She is a brave woman."

"She certainly is." I took a final look through the anti-Saracen literature. "Have you had any direct contact with this company?"

"Only through petitions."

"Probably best to keep your distance for now."

"We will not back down. Not at this stage."

"Then be careful."

We confirmed the appropriate phone numbers to use, if anything happened.

"What are you going to do?" Yussopova asked.

"I'm going to find her. Please, please let me know if you hear the slightest thing."

"I will."

The black Renault followed me when I left.

16

THE DRIVER WAS EUROPEAN-LOOKING. TALL IN HIS SEAT, A TOUCH OF flab around the face, something very English about him in a former-military way. He kept close behind me; it was conspicuous: either a rushed job, a lack of training, or meant to intimidate.

I was driving into the center, trying to think how to play this, when I saw Toreali's vast tent of retail, Khan Shatyr. It was a plausible place for me to be going, and my follower would be forced out of their vehicle to keep tabs on me, or risk losing me altogether.

I followed signs to the car park. So did he. I parked, went toward the mall's entrance, hearing his door slamming and the beep of his car lock behind me. The mall was vast inside, maze-like. I found the food court, got a coffee, and browsed on my phone while my man sat on a bench on the other side of the court. I looked at what I could find on Saracen. They were an oil and gas exploration and production company, headquartered in London, interests in Vietnam, Congo, Angola, Mexico. Evidently they found the Middle East too squeaky clean. Robert Carter had bought the company for 12.5 billion pounds and the inflow of fresh capital had funded its Kazakh forays.

London would be waking up around now. I gave Olivia Gresham a call.

"Saracen Oil and Gas. Any feelings about them?"

"Saracen? Jesus, what are you doing with that lot? Is it why you're in Kazakhstan?"

"Possibly. What are they up to?"

"They think there's untapped fields still to be discovered there. The Kazakh government took a lot of money off them for the honor of taking a look."

"Have they had any trouble recently?"

"It's oil and gas — what do you think? Trouble from good people, trouble from bad people."

"Who are the bad people?"

"Rival energy companies, I imagine."

"Who do Saracen employ on the intelligence front?"

"Probably Vectis. Saracen was using them when they drilled in the DCR. Know anything about this? Why are Saracen so hot for Central Asia all of a sudden?"

"I've no idea, but you'll be the first to hear if I find anything."

My watcher was still there, still surreptitiously keeping an eye on me. That afforded me a good look at him. He was ruddy under a peaked cap, graying blond, with a slight curl to the hair, blue-eyed, pink-skinned. There wasn't a team—he didn't have surveillance skills. I was definitely dealing with former military.

I made another call to a friend at Kilgariff & Co., a private intelligence outfit big on energy.

"Do you work with Saracen?"

"No, Vectis have the Saracen contract. Why?"

"Following leads. Thanks."

I knew Vectis Global Insight, as much as anyone did. Boutique, head-quartered in Mayfair, crammed with former spooks of all stripes. The company sold a range of underground services. Their website advertised "strategic advice and analysis for leaders operating in complex environments." There were a lot of complex environments and big corporations paid well. You won't find "espionage" on their books, but you might well come across "security consultancy," a trail that led via a listed Georgian building to some less respectable corners of the earth. As a rule of thumb with PI companies, more wood paneling meant fewer moral scruples.

A lot of them appeared in the 1990s. The intelligence budget was down. The clients that complained loudest were those that had benefit-ted from MI6's commercial and economic espionage department. British businesses said something had to be done—they needed to compete and had money to spend; why couldn't they just give the money to MI6 and keep the reports coming? That didn't look good either. So companies like Vectis appeared, a whole realm of shadow intelligence agencies with com-plex relationships to the state. MI6 officers knew them as potential future employers, staffed by former colleagues, often useful for tips, occasionally making difficult environments even murkier. The ones we called white-hat companies could advertise their services up front; they consisted of retired police and military for the most part, individuals with enough connections willing to check the odd database for them, and armies of poorly paid interns stitching together reports. Black hats went the extra mile. They solved problems in ways the client didn't want to know about, and their front windows were accordingly opaque. They cost more, and were usually worth it.

Vectis was black-hat. Set up by Callum Walker, former SAS, former SovOps desk in Six. I knew this because he'd tried to recruit me a couple of years ago. We'd bumped into each other at one of those posturing, closed-shop conferences that spies get invited to, where CEOs and former foreign secretaries mingle. Walker seemed to know a bit about me. Out of curiosity and habit, I agreed to drinks at the Special Forces Club the following evening. I figured an open channel to Vectis could be as useful to me in various ways as I was to them. At the very least we could avoid treading on each other's toes.

I wasn't interested in going on their payroll, but I liked Walker. He had a blunt, straight-talking style rare in the intelligence services. He seemed more at home in the private sector. He enjoyed showing me the club, hidden behind an unmarked door in Knightsbridge, photographs of fallen comrades across the walls. I wondered if it was one of his current comrades tailing me around Astana.

I called Vectis as Robert Carter's PA from Saracen and got client levels of deference. I said Carter was heading to Astana and wanted a point of contact. I was told the Vectis boss himself, Callum Walker, had just got into town, staying at the Hilton Garden Inn. They wouldn't give more than that but said they'd ensure he got in contact asap. I hung up and began to move.

I paid to go into the spa, reversed my jacket, exited through staff doors. No sign of the tail when I got down to my car.

The Hilton was smart without being ostentatious, stretching the length of a central block just north of Lovers Park. As far as I could tell, the park got its name from a bad statue of a man and woman embracing. Current conditions weren't going to sustain flesh-and-blood romance. The hotel gazed optimistically across it. In a few months the view would thaw.

A young receptionist smiled at me as I stepped inside.

"I'm here to meet one of your guests," I said. "Callum Walker. Has he checked in yet?"

She consulted her computer.

"Yes, he checked in last night."

"Could you call up, tell him David's here?"

She lifted a receiver and her elegant fingers punched 203 on the desk phone. After letting it ring ten times she looked at me regretfully.

"Don't worry," I said. "I'll wait for him in the bar."

The bar was on the first floor. I took the lift to the first floor, then the stairs to the second.

A DO NOT DISTURB sign hung on the handle of room 203. No answer when I knocked. I took a glasses case from inside my jacket and removed a device the size of a phone battery that had made my life a lot easier on several occasions. The beauty of globalization meant that one firm produced sixty percent of hotel card locks. And every single Onity keycard lock has a DC power socket on the base, a small, circular port used to charge up the battery and program the lock with the hotel's own site code. Which means when you plug into the socket, you can read the key from the lock's stored memory, play it back, and turn the handle.

I was about to walk in when a man behind me said, "Stop there or I'll shoot."

17

HIS VOICE WAS CALM, SEMIAUTOMATIC PISTOL HELD STEADY AS HE approached from the end of the corridor. It was my follower from the black Renault.

"Hands out, buddy. Let's see them."

I raised my hands.

When the gun was at my head, he said: "What are you after?"

"Joanna Lake."

"She's not in there."

He tapped me above the ear with the barrel, directed me along the corridor to the emergency stairs. We descended. I had visions of windowless service levels, basements with laundry bins into which a body could be folded. I was prodded into the first-floor bar.

The hotel had gone for a low-lit, burnished-copper theme. Which suited the silver-haired Englishman sitting in one of its armchairs, staring at me. The place was otherwise empty apart from staff and two expensively dressed women in a far corner. My chaperone had made the gun disappear. We were just three men meeting for business.

"Elliot Kane," Walker said.

"Callum."

Walker's suit was crumpled. His eyes suggested an overnight flight. Overall, he had the lingering youthfulness of a sixty-five-year-old with a lot of money coming in, but there was a new wariness to the shine. He looked like a man who had just flown into Central Asia because of an almighty fuckup. I took a seat opposite him and a waiter appeared.

"Have a drink," Walker said. "Warm up."

I ordered a brandy. Walker ordered a Scotch and a bottle of sparkling water. The guard declined refreshment. He had taken the sofa, back straight, hands clasped between his knees. His top button was tight around his throat. The years since military service could be measured in kilograms. Walker surprised me by pulling out a packet of Rothmans, lighting one with a plastic yellow lighter. He set packet and lighter on the coffee table, beside some pink flowers floating in a stone dish, leaned back, exhaled out of the corner of his mouth.

"Where is she?" I said.

"We have no idea."

"I don't believe that."

He spread his hands, face grave.

"Vanished. I thought perhaps you lot might be doing better on this than we are."

"Us lot? I'm not here on behalf of the British government. She contacted me. I came over."

Walker looked skeptical. The drinks arrived with a tray of cashews and a dish of ice cubes. I took a sip.

"You know her?"

"I worked with her. We were close."

"What did she say when she contacted you?" he asked.

"We didn't speak as such. It seemed like she might be in trouble, though. I need to know what's going on before I give you any more."

Walker splashed some water into his whisky. A gold chain rattled on his left wrist. Like his guard, he'd been somewhere a lot sunnier not that long ago; the skin of his ears and nose was still flaked.

"Who have you spoken to?" Walker asked.

"Not very many people. Was she working for you?"

"Yes. Obviously that makes it a sensitive situation."

"I'm sure." Walker hesitated. I pressed. "Right now you're in more trouble than I am. You might appreciate my help." This didn't get an immediate denial. "You're working for Saracen," I said. He tapped his cigarette, studied me again. I knew what threshold we were at—either I was going to be permitted entrance or not. I took a mouthful of brandy. There had been no suggestion they knew about the dead man. That was a card I held.

"Saracen are the client, ultimately. We're hired through a separate PR company."

"I see."

"How much does Vauxhall know about all this?"

"I get the feeling they have an interest—in Joanna, at least. Why would that be? Have you not told them what's going on?"

"Our relationship with your employer is somewhat strained, as you can imagine."

"All sounds very delicate."

"*Delicate* is the word."

I could relate to his impatience with the well-spoken, well-educated men and women at the top of Six and the FCO. There was a no-nonsense edge of grammar school in his intonation, which endeared him to me. When we had last met he had described himself as a fellow scholarship boy, army scholarship to Sandhurst in his case. But he had none of the usual military stiffness, either. You wouldn't have guessed that before Six, Walker had spent four years in the SAS—not if your idea of the SAS was unthinking action men. In reality, the SAS was defined more by mavericks, especially for Walker's generation. They had a restless drive. It meant their thoughts often ended up turning to making money, and they set about it with gung-ho confidence, a lot of contacts, and not always sensitivity to the nuances of a business environment. Walker looked energetic and out of his depth

"Well, I wish she'd tried to contact us."

"How long had she been over here?"

"Eight weeks."

"Spying against anti-Saracen campaigners."

"Along those lines. She went missing six days ago. Last contact was on the evening of the twenty-seventh."

"What was she doing here?"

"Saracen are chasing a big deal. They've got a few active fields, and want to buy a lot more. But their reputation is somewhat checkered, shall we say, which meant activists were on them before they'd even got going. The new owner hired a company called Piper Anderson Communications to try to clean up their profile. Piper Anderson hired us. Obviously we needed to get a feel for the scene out here—the eco community, rival lobbyists, decision makers. So we sent Joanna over."

"How long's she been working for you?"

"Since May."

"Really? She only left the service in April."

He saw what I was thinking: Six had a process for those jumping ship. Intelligence officers were precious and dangerous and sensitive, whether or not you still wanted to employ them.

"We had a few quiet words. They weren't sorry to see her go, it seemed."

"Why not?"

"There had been a falling-out."

There had been a lot more than that, if the closing down of her Shefford project was true.

"Falling-out?" I said.

"Those were her words. I never got details, nor did I ask. My clearance for such matters expired a long time ago. But we softened her landing generously."

"What did she bring for that? Information? Contacts?"

"No."

"But you headhunted her."

"She approached us, actually."

I wondered if I had inadvertently steered her toward Vectis. I had told Joanna about Walker's pursuit of me, mostly to laugh at the oversized salary being touted. I could see how that might have rebounded.

"Why do you think she came to you?" I asked.

"Why shouldn't she come to us? We're a good employer, even if you seemed unconvinced. She wanted out of Six quickly, without losing too many paychecks. And she wanted a change of scene. I told her the biggest danger in Astana would be boredom."

"What did she say to that?"

"She said: 'Good.'" He stubbed his cigarette. A waitress tried to swap his ashtray for a new one and he waved her away. "What did Elena Yussopova tell you?" Walker asked.

"Didn't you hear?"

"Come on, Elliot."

"She thought someone might have approached Vanessa with information. Any idea who that might have been?"

"No."

"Did Joanna have any kind of countersurveillance team over here?"

"None."

"She was here alone?"

"That's right. We agreed minimal contact. She was very much running her own operation. We offered backup, she declined."

That sounded like Joanna. The bigger the team, the more conspicuous you are. Still, I'd never known her to avoid risks. She was someone who liked to step outside the wire, in military parlance. I could see the setup from Walker's point of view: You've got a pro, she says she can run the operation, you save a lot of money. You've won the contract over more established outfits because you promise the client more for less. And it's only a few eco-activists that you're messing with; not exactly Moscow rules. You're looking at the bottom line and someone's abducting your employees.

"Where was Joanna staying?"

"The Park Grand, bang in the center of town."

"Had she packed?"

"Her suitcase was there. It looks like she'd taken some items, though. We've trawled every border crossing, every airline. There's nothing to suggest she left the country. Which just leaves 2.7 million square kilometers to search."

"Did she have access to a vehicle?"

"Not to our knowledge."

"Any hint that she thought she might be in danger?"

"Never. And it shouldn't have been a dangerous job. We gave her a few weeks to get us a picture of Kazakhstan, where it was going. This is about oil in Central Asia, so obviously you're going to be prepared for trouble, but she hadn't reported any concerns. It was mostly picking up gossip."

"Was she armed?"

He looked at me, curiously.

"I've been generous. I think it's time you told us what you know."

It was tempting. Always tempting to confide, with the implication of a burden shared. I wondered what Joanna was doing risking her life for an oil company. Maybe, after all the smoke and mirrors of Shefford, there was something honest about oil. It was real. You could cleanse yourself in it. Maybe she wanted to cash in on her experience. We'd need money, she had said. But I couldn't bring myself to believe she was doing this for us. I imagined that moment of decision, and the thought of Kazakhstan: ice and emptiness. A place in which you'd recognize nothing of yourself. The simplicity of it, compared with the hot and complicated places where we had operated on dubious pretexts. This had been part of the pitch when I met Walker at the Special Forces Club: Get out of the Middle East, out of other people's schemes. And yet, beneath it all, the offhand tone was identical to the conversation that led me over the threshold into Six. "Fancy a bit of adventure? A challenge? Not many rewards, but you'll have a chance to work off your own bat, explore the world." I had the sense that he wanted me there in the way we want friends to share our vices, for both physical and moral companionship. What enticed Joanna to Vectis, of all companies? She wasn't someone who stumbled into things.

"Do Saracen know about any of this?" I asked.

"Our clients aren't interested in operational details. They're looking for oil, not missing researchers."

"And they won't notice the sudden absence of briefings?"

"That's our problem. Obviously this is an embarrassment."

"I hope, wherever Joanna is, she's not too embarrassed."

Walker didn't bother defending the crassness.

"What do you know about her last movements?" I asked.

"She filed a report at nine p.m. on the evening of Saturday, the twenty-seventh of November. Nothing exceptional. Dined alone at her hotel. Staff saw her go up to her room, leave again around ten thirty. That's the last we've got."

"No pickup on CCTV? Card use? Phone signal?"

"None we've got so far."

The amount of resources going unexploited was agonizing. Vectis had money, too. I needed some of that if I was going to sustain my search.

"Reported this to the police?" I asked. "They might know the terrain better."

"Vanessa McDonald was supposedly investigating police corruption. Joanna Lake was a private-sector spy. Which of them do you want the police looking into?"

I thought through the legal situation. *Clear as an oil spill* would be the generous way to put it: a former MI6 agent entering on fake papers, spying on Kazakh citizens, installing surveillance, hacking God knows what, and then Vectis waving guns around when it went wrong. As if sensing this — and keen for an out — Walker said, "You worked together. Could this be something from the past catching up?"

What he meant: Maybe none of this is our fault. Nor need it be anything to endanger an energy deal. I'd considered this, of course. Most of the people from Joanna's past with cause to want her dead were either dead themselves, imprisoned, or doing too well to cause trouble. People don't like stirring history up, certainly not off home ground. But it was true — we had shared environments that didn't forget you. Joanna had also done stints in Serbia and Belarus. That's not a CV to help you sleep at night.

"There's no specific operation for which I think someone would still be seeking revenge. Does Vectis deal with kidnappings and rescues?"

"Not directly. We work with GL5 for that kind of thing. She has full K and R cover, if it comes to it."

Fully insured for kidnap and ransom. Which could help you rustle up a holdall stuffed with used currency, or even some more ex-army types abseiling to your rescue. It rarely happened quite like that. I thought through the various options. If she'd been killed straight off, it meant she was dangerous alive, that her silence was worth the noise generated by a murder. Alternatively, it was a message: Stay away. If she was captive, it was a question of what the captors wanted: money, leverage, or information. Ninety-five percent of hostages, the public never hear about: They're diplomatic tools, assets on the balance sheet. Companies have supposed policies on not paying ransoms and states have policies on not dealing with terrorists, but I'd never known either to be ironclad—it just means the press agree not to cover it. Situations get spun out over years. If the captors wanted money it was straightforward, although you'd expect demands sooner rather than later. If they were pressing her for information, the first you might know about it was a body dump.

"Are you monitoring her family?" I asked.

"We're keeping an ear out. There's been no contact. No whispers internationally, either. All our offices have been chasing this."

"I don't think she's dead."

"Nor do we."

It was time to get a closer look at Vectis. Walker wasn't telling me much, but I liked a challenge and wanted to know more about his setup over here. I didn't believe the search for Joanna was being run out of Walker's hotel room. I was also curious about how they'd react to the video file. So I dangled bait.

"Is the cryptonym *Catalyst* one that you're familiar with?"

"No."

"Have you come across anything over here connected to sophisticated technological deception?"

"What have you got?" Walker watched me carefully. I knew the calculation. You can't trust anyone. But you can't spy alone.

"Shall we adjourn somewhere less comfortable?" I said.

• • •

They knew just the place, it seemed. We took the Renault to an address in the business district, a rectangular block of mirrored glass. Walker swiped us in. The floors housed corporate accountants, software and construction companies. Ours apparently belonged to a law firm called White and Chase, with a desk and logo, a smiling receptionist, and nothing else whatsoever as far as I could see. We walked past empty conference rooms to a heavy door with keypad entry, into a windowless office with three monitors and a Faraday cage to block the transmission of radio waves.

Inside I checked the technology: Dell screens, external hard drives, no phones, ethernet box on the wall. I produced my flash drive and they unlocked a safe in the corner, withdrew a Lenovo laptop with a USB port. It booted up to an empty desktop and factory settings. Walker inserted the drive. The guard stayed by the door at first. When Walker had watched the clip once, he beckoned him over and they watched it together.

"How did you get it?" Walker asked.

"She sent it to me."

"No audio?"

"Unfortunately not."

"Know the other man?"

"No. But I think this may be a room in the Triumph of Astana."

"What do you mean, 'may be'? Don't you remember?"

"It's faked."

"Are you sure?"

"Given that I've never been there, it seems likely. Did Joanna assign cryptonyms?"

"No."

"The video's titled Catalyst."

Walker shook his head, blankly. "You may not be the best person to be visible here."

"Well, here I am. So far I've only had one gun pulled on me today."

"You say someone approached Testimony," Walker said. "That Joanna might have been in receipt of information from that source?"

"Elena Yussopova suggested as much. I couldn't get any more out of her."

"Does she trust you?"

"I wouldn't go that far. But she's not actively campaigning against me yet."

Walker reached into a desk drawer and produced a single cigarette. He used a silver lighter with a small blue flame, then pressed a button, and a fan under the desk sucked the smoke away in a descending stream. Then he continued to watch me, assessing.

"What do you want?"

"Give me access to what you've got so far. I'll find her for you."

Walker massaged his eyes, stared at me again.

"Where does the intelligence service think you are currently?"

"They don't know where I am."

"You'll drag them into this. That will bring attention onto us."

"I'll be back in London before they've got the paperwork signed off. You know Six. But we need to move fast, and for speed I need resources."

"We would have to think how to do this."

"Sure. It's a sensitive situation."

Walker sat silently for some time, eyes open and bloodshot. I tried to imagine what he was thinking.

"I'd like to send the footage for more thorough analysis," he said, finally. "It might tell us where Joanna got it."

"Sure. In return for granting me access to the work she was doing while over here, the details of the setup, and information on the search for her so far."

He nodded slowly, mentally checking through the requests.

"I need to be clear," he said. "We're not in a position to go behind the backs of the British intelligence service."

"You've been managing so far."

He sighed. "We're not entirely renegade."

"Who do you liaise with in Six?" I asked.

"We have a few points of contact. I can't give you names."

"But you haven't told them about this yet?"

"No. Why?"

"She came to me, not them. There was a reason for that."

18

I GAVE HIM MY FOOTAGE TO SEND THROUGH TO ANALYSTS. IN RETURN I got a glimpse of the hunt for Joanna so far. Staff in three Vectis offices, London, Berlin, and Moscow, were trawling intercepts for any whisper regarding her disappearance. Walker gave the impression of big data coming in, which could leave you with a lot of haystack and no needle. He had contacts in intelligence companies that had more experience in the region, and was putting out feelers, but he was reluctant to go begging for help, as they were all competitors for the Saracen contract.

There were a few more complications. MI6—and the UK government generally—were unhappy about Vectis operating in Kazakhstan. A planned £2 billion sale of BAE helicopters to the Kazakh defense forces meant the Department for International Trade was putting a lot of effort into presenting Kazakhstan as a clean place to do business. Neither Saracen nor Vectis was helping. This wasn't the sole reason Vectis had refrained from publicly raising the alarm about Joanna's disappearance, but it provided the backdrop for their reluctance.

I got an hour to look through the reports Joanna had delivered. I had to do it in the Vectis office, at an isolated desk, no phone, watched over by Walker himself, handing over paperwork, clicking files for me.

It wasn't worth the effort.

She had spent most of her time monitoring what Vectis called IMGs —issue-motivated groups. As well as Testimony, these included the usual suspects: Greenpeace, Amnesty International, opposition groups local to Kazakhstan insofar as they were allowed to exist. Additionally, Joanna had mapped power structures: clans, regions, departments, all webbed around the presidential family itself—what in Six we referred to jokingly as bribe maps. The EU and the UN were concerned about Saracen. Laws were being thrown around by rivals and their lobbyists. Shareholders got jumpy. Finally, Joanna provided data for what Vectis presented as "civil unrest analysis": current odds on the whole country melting down.

Data, hacked or otherwise, was processed in the UK, written up and fed through to Piper Anderson Communications. They served as the buffer between an FTSE-listed energy company and people affixing listening devices to coffee tables. I vaguely knew their chief, Lucy Piper: She used to be head of communications at Downing Street. The one time I encountered her in person, she was escorting the PM around Basra, corralling press as they documented a new school for girls. For five hundred grand a month, Piper Anderson offered an all-in-one package: lobbying, damage limitation, agenda-steering, legal muscle, cleaning of the internet, and subversion of any opposition. If you wanted a think tank promoting the concept that human rights thrived on the discovery of oil fields, it would be blogging by breakfast, academics on-message, with politicians having quiet words to journalists over lunch. They had a lot of former ministers on their board. Piper Anderson hired spies so the corporates didn't have to.

I read through Joanna's reports on political groups and systems of decision-making in the Kazakh government, and the tone was flat. A lot of it was clearly gleaned from subscriptions to other business intelligence services, which was common enough practice, but not for Joanna Lake. Some was lifted straight out of the *Oil and Gas Financial Journal*. I could see why Walker wasn't worried about a sudden absence of product.

More useful, to me at least, was a summary of those rival entities with skin in the game, the ones that posed a threat. The US energy company Chevron had big fields in operation in Kazakhstan and had brought over at least three private intelligence firms of their own. Turkey and China both saw Central Asia as their backyard, fielding fierce resources out of vast and well-practiced security departments. Russia's FSB loomed large. Then there was Kazakhstan's own intelligence service, which was made up of KGB remnants. That was worth remembering.

Between Vectis's electronic surveillance and Joanna's inquiries, they had amassed a list of eleven other intelligence operations currently active, state and private, all in relation to Kazakhstan's energy sector. Astana was what the Germans called an *Agentsumpf,* a spy swamp. Things heated up in an *Agentsumpf.* The chaos bred a sense of impunity, of minimal blowback. You ended up giving each other cover. It got messy.

Potential threats to Joanna: first up, rival energy companies who knew she was Saracen-connected and wanted to stop the company's expansion. Against that: Abduction wasn't corporate style. Less likely were activists who'd rumbled her cover and felt aggrieved. No evidence of this happening, and they tended to have sensitive consciences. Then there were always local political thugs who might have bought into the cover and not liked having Vanessa McDonald nosing around. This was plausible, though her nationality should have offered some protection. One long shot, as Walker had suggested, involved individuals whose feathers she'd ruffled in the course of her MI6 career and had chosen this moment to exact revenge. I didn't know where to start with that. All in all, it would have been easier establishing those individuals without a reason to kill her.

I watched some of the documentary footage she'd shot. She stayed off-camera during interviews, so I was denied Jo's face. Still, her voice sent a ripple of electricity down my spine. Interviews with Elena Yussopova, with a writer who'd been imprisoned, with a couple who'd had to move home because of drilling. She'd even managed some interviews with Saracen staff on the ground in Kazakhstan. Most recently she recorded a guy called Craig Bryant, whose company, Auracle, provided tech support for rigs and pipelines. Auracle had been bought up by Carter when he moved into Central Asia. Bryant sat in a bland office with some data pinned to the wall, looking awkward and ingratiating. Joanna was combative and he clearly hadn't expected criticism, opening with a standard pitch:

"*Our technology gives unprecedented sensitivity and range. When you've got a thousand kilometers of pipeline — no human's going to be able to monitor it all . . .*"

Then, when she started throwing around stats on environmental destruction and political corruption, he spent some time trying to convince her it was all more eco now, that he wasn't responsible for the actions of the oil companies themselves and he didn't know about politics.

In the following weeks they went on some dates. Joanna had dutifully logged these events. You could see from phone records that Bryant had been trying to call her since she went missing.

"That's bold," I said. "She interviews him and he asks her out."

"Plucky. But it seems he's that kind of guy. Skirt chaser."

"You've looked into him?" I asked.

"Superficially. Born Sandpoint, Idaho. MIT grad, worked in technology all his life, dropped in by Carter to manage drone operations over here. He's done some consultancy work for the NSA and spoken a couple of times at organizations cozy with the CIA, like the American Enterprise Institute, but that's the extent of it, as far as we can tell."

"Know what exactly these drone ops involve?"

"They have high-end sensors — optical, chemical — which, as far as I understand it, sniff around and help with maintaining pipelines, detecting any leaks or pollution, maybe detecting new reserves."

Walker shrugged as if all this was beyond him. If Bryant struck him as worth pursuing, he didn't show it. I checked the records of their search for Joanna so far. There were her recent ATM withdrawals, card payments, some unenlightening interviews with hotel staff, a copy of her cover itinerary as Vanessa McDonald.

I looked through for the detail that could help me and saw nothing.

Then I found it.

At 11:50 a.m. on November 26, the day before she went missing, there was a purchase on her Vanessa McDonald NatWest debit card. Just under twenty pounds spent at Zara, Mega Astana shopping mall, followed five minutes later by a coffee at the mall's KFC.

You look for things happening on the hour, the half hour. Gratuitous things. Out of character. Joanna was a coffee snob. Given the choice, she'd risk operations before accepting fast-food coffee. Eight hundred tenge, or just under two pounds, to the Colonel, at 11:55 a.m. No other purchases made.

Before going shopping she'd been at her hotel. I brought up a map. There were two other shopping centers closer to the hotel than the Mega Astana Mall. I checked the shops on offer at those alternatives, and they were pretty much the same. It was a significant diversion to buy some accessories and an overpriced Americano.

According to the map, she crossed town, past two larger malls, to be at Mega Astana as the clock struck twelve.

She was meeting someone.

"Any more from this excursion?"

"No. Think it's significant?"

"I doubt it."

If my hunch was right, these were strange protocols: telling nothing to your employer — no pre-contact threat analysis, no post-contact briefing. Maybe this was how they did it in the private sector, but it certainly granted an employee autonomy.

"What are you going to do?" Walker asked.

"Go back to my hotel, shower, think. I reckon I can find her for you but I'm going to need money, at least thirty grand cash in dollars, tenge, and rubles."

This got little more than a cheek-scratch out of Walker. In my experience, people trust you more when you're pushy. They think they know what you want. Walker said he'd have to clear it first.

"Sure. Not with my name attached, though. You're my sole point of contact."

"Of course."

He was nervous about me asking around and suggested that I stay in or close to my hotel. I insisted that he did not mention me by name to the Vectis board in London, and he acknowledged this was wise. I would have to trust him on that. We agreed that unless there were any dramatic developments we would meet the following day for lunch — I'd be picked up at a specified location and brought to the office. Finally I was dropped back at my car.

I waited until the guard and his Renault had disappeared, then drove away from the Hilton toward the Mega Astana Mall.

19

IT WAS AN UNATTRACTIVE LARGE GRAY BOX THAT MADE LITTLE ATTEMPT at enticing Astana's population. But it didn't have to, it seemed: The car park was full. A giant inflatable Father Christmas shook in the Central Asian wind, speakers broadcasting "Jingle Bell Rock."

I walked in, checked the layout, found the shop she'd been in. It gave you a clear view out to the walkway and central plaza: a chance to scan for watchers. A chance to shake them off before doing something. She was here for a reason.

Most of the security cameras throughout were basic domes, with a few distinctive box-style cameras at intervals. A company called MicroDigital made a lot of money around 2014 installing security cameras across Central Asia. These cameras were sold with remote internet access enabled, and default passwords that rarely got changed, which meant it was straightforward tapping into the video feeds. From there, it was a back road into the whole network, including archived footage. MicroDigital's slapdash approach to password security had opened up plenty to me over the years, from branches of AT&T in Ankara to the Golden Times Bath House in Tblisi.

I went to the KFC, conducted my own sampling of its coffee, took a seat at the back of the concession, and opened my laptop. I downloaded a port scanner, then scanned for all the computer connection points in the vicinity. A quick browse gave me cameras and routers being used in the mall. The usual default passwords didn't work, but they were susceptible to what hackers called brute force attack — bombardment with automated guesses. I found the router's IP address and model number, sent a message to Marius at Evotec: I needed Stefan Janikowski. I told him money would be coming from Vectis in the next forty-eight hours. He knew Vectis, and their resources. He confirmed that Stefan was still in Riyadh, and I was authorized to make direct contact. Gave me a new job code.

I called.

"I hear we're back in business," Stefan said. "Your people change their mind?"

"I guess so. I want you to take a look at something."

Within half an hour Stefan had control of the router and was reconfiguring the network rules so that we could take control. Another fifteen minutes, and I was sitting in my hired Hyundai Tuscon with the control board of the mall's security operations center on my laptop. Twenty-one cameras in total. Archived recordings went back two weeks. I checked for KFC. Three cameras covered the area around the fast-food restaurant. It was straightforward enough to search by time and date.

I didn't notice her at first. She wore a short blond wig beneath a knitted hat, with heavy-framed glasses. She carried a shoulder bag and a shopping bag from Zara. She bought her coffee and sat down, opened an HP notebook, glanced toward the entrance.

No one came.

Five minutes later she was still sitting there, scanning the place from behind her laptop. She checked her watch, then closed the device, got up, and left.

I watched it again, disappointed and puzzled. Then I went back to the control board.

Several years ago MI6 realized that physical brush passes — an agent slipping you a delivery hand to hand — could be unnecessary in an age of short-range wireless data transfer. They devised technology akin to Bluetooth, using a particular radio frequency to transmit the data. It gained popularity when encryption became strong enough to neutralize the risk of interception, and receivers became small enough to fit into regular-looking devices. Enabled devices needed to be within a range of twenty meters.

Who was around?

We'd been taught that if a hostile party is watching for an officer to make a brush pass, they'll check the people in your vicinity. But surveillance teams rarely think — or have the convenient means — to look vertically. And in a shopping center, a twenty-meter radius in all directions can give you a hundred people to profile.

There were a lot of candidates, but after half an hour I had a favorite.

Directly above the KFC, on the upper-level food court, was a Dunkin Donuts. At one minute past midday a man walked in. He looked to be in his twenties. He was jumpy, checking in each direction. He wore a quilted blue jacket identical to the one on the corpse I'd seen last night.

The individual bought food and a drink, sat down, set up his laptop. Gray brimmed cap pulled low, scarf up. As close as you could get to obscuring your face without becoming conspicuous.

The timing synced closely with Joanna's. They left within a few minutes of each other. He got to his feet, looked around, moved off fast. The tray remained on his table, food untouched.

I watched three more times, and then I was sure. He typed in a command. Joanna waited. There was the faintest reaction as she saw on her screen that data had been delivered. Then she closed the laptop and stood up.

Her man delivered information. He'd got something. He was a source that required extreme caution, one that she'd decided not to disclose to her employer.

Plenty of potential reasons for that. There certainly had been in Six, where potential agents required a complete risk profile and managerial clearance before you could engage them. It had often been worth sidestepping the bureaucracy at first. And sometimes you wanted to stay like that: Even buried under code names, they were on the system, and systems leaked.

Who was he?

Still nothing about a shooting on local news, nothing about an individual reported missing.

I speculated a timeline. This handover occurs in the Mega Astana. But something goes wrong in spite of the caution. Whatever he's sent causes trouble. The next day they meet at the rented apartment, Joanna's safe house. She's going to get them both out of there. He's packed quickly, ready to leave. She tries to call me off the landline. Perhaps they know their phones are compromised.

But only she got away.

She fled—with an injured arm, according to the staff at the internet café—sent me the video file, then kept running. Where would you run?

I drove out, toward Malakov Street and the dead man. As I was approaching I saw police parked outside. A full forensics team was active. I kept driving in the direction of the internet café. No police at the café. I kept moving in the same direction, north, toward the edge of the city.

Would she try to escape Astana? I checked a map. There was an hour or so of daylight left, and I thought I'd make use of it.

Time spooled backwards as you left the capital, shiny buildings becoming construction sites, bare frames, then gray foundations, then rubble. I passed a police car sitting in the shelter of a billboard with the president's face and the words: PROJECT ASTANA 2050. Then you reached the desert.

It took a while to adjust. With the city still in the rearview, the emptiness stretching to the horizon on either side was less inhuman. You couldn't tell if it was snow or stone or dust, the landscape was just pale gray and lifeless, strewn with loose rocks like a seabed. A sign warned that it was two hundred kilometers to the next town. Tufts of grass and the occasional tamarisk bush stubbled the emptiness; then even these died out. The road divided a lunar landscape and was the only thing in it.

I tried to imagine Joanna fleeing this way. Her injury, if it was true, caused me concern. I had no more leads, though. After ten miles I turned the radio off. The silence was seductive. I stopped the car and felt my soul expand — stretching — searching for other life. The idea that the rest of existence was a fantasy flickered and grew. I zipped my jacket up and stepped out of the car, turned around. An eagle hung in the air, as still as the landscape beneath it, the pupil of an unblinking eye. I crouched and pinched some of the lifeless rock dust, thought of Mongol hordes pouring across it. Lives adapted to the uninhabitable. No wonder, when they reached the civilized glories of thirteenth-century Baghdad, its mosques and libraries and courts, they burned the place to the ground.

When I got back inside the car, there was a message from Tom Marsh. *They're looking for you. They know we met.*

20

No answer when I tried to contact him. I sent a message to Stevenson. He sent back a Threema ID: an app that encrypts voice calls. Plenty do, but Threema's the one that doesn't require a phone number or email address. I downloaded the app and entered his ID, and he answered in seconds.

"Where are you?"

"I took a holiday."

There was a long pause. I could hear a soft exhalation that constituted various entreaties. Eventually he said:

"How does it look?"

"She was working for Vectis Global Insight," I said. "Undercover as an activist. Their client's an energy company, Saracen. Would you ask around? She may have come here because it's a good place to hide. She may have had other reasons. I think she started pursuing her own investigation into something."

"I was about to warn you not to go over there."

"Why?"

"Astana's coming up high on global risk assessments. The Foreign Office has been debating travel advice. I can't establish any details right now. I don't know what, if anything, it has to do with Joanna."

"War? Revolution?"

"Something like that. How does it seem?"

"Okay at the moment."

Tom Marsh's voice came to me: *Maybe the program they were working on predicted something they didn't want getting out. Maybe she saw too much.*

"Any word on the trouble in Shefford?" I asked.

"I'm still trying to find out. I'm in touch with Tom. He's been questioned again."

"Is he okay?"

"Not particularly."

"Have you had any trouble?"

"Not yet. You say you've made contact with Vectis over there?"

"Yes. The boss is here: Callum Walker. Used to be SovOps."

"I remember him."

"Seems to know little more than we do."

"Vectis are huge and dark. Their involvement doesn't give me a good feeling."

"Joanna's involvement doesn't feel right."

"No."

We agreed to speak again in twenty-four hours. I looked a little deeper into Vectis, using a combination of open-source research and calls to acquaintances at some of their rivals. Beyond its oak-paneled façade, Vectis was a global company with a staff of more than three hundred analysts and seventy technology specialists. As well as the Mayfair HQ and some Gloucestershire labs, there was an office on Madison Avenue in NYC, an outpost in Moscow, and one in Berlin on the southeast corner of the Zoological Garden with a dedicated cybermonitoring station. The firm had recently acquired a leading computer forensics and data recovery company, which meant it had its own hackers.

I knew how it worked. Data would be processed and written up by a team of analysts in the UK, some with technical backgrounds, some experts in relevant industries or regions. Finished reports could be seen by up to fifteen people: There were the founders, who were mostly former MI6, then an international advisory board composed of senior figures from industry and government. Far too many former spooks for my liking. Several of the names were familiar; an ex-chief of MI6's counterterrorism branch; another SAS man who became Six's head of commercial liaison. Its management board included two Conservative MPs, both of whom had sat on the Joint Intelligence Committee.

I called the Hilton where Walker was staying and inquired about rooms on the second floor. They had one available which, by my estimation, would be directly above Walker's own. I booked it, then called Stefan.

"I need you in Astana, Kazakhstan. Bring your kit."

"Kazakhstan?"

"It's peaceful here. And everyone uses Windows 95."

I confirmed fees for the job and he said he'd be on a flight that evening.

I was left to think about Joanna's double life as Vanessa McDonald. The interview with Craig Bryant had stuck with me. So had the courtship that followed. Both Joanna and I knew that things happened on operations, through boredom or necessity or both. Neither of us pretended it made anything easy for a partner, or even excusable. Our general philosophy was that sleeping with individuals while undercover was bad form unless really necessary.

In his interview with Joanna, Bryant presented himself as a keen, optimistic technocrat. Her reports for Vectis suggested a womanizer with a drinking problem. In terms of dates, they'd had a meal at Le Dessert near Bayterek, drinks a couple of times at somewhere called Restobar, even gone to the cinema.

Then came Bryant's repeated calls and messages over the last few days:
Drink? I'll be at the usual.
I hope I haven't done something to upset you.
You okay? Let me know you're okay.

I checked his company online. Auracle Geospatial Science was a technology startup that collected and analyzed data from satellite, aircraft, and drone platforms. There were examples of their work on the website: locating and surveying leaks, monitoring gas emissions, detection of oil spillage, the inspection of offshore platforms.

Auracle kept an office in Astana's Special Economic Zone, an industrial park in the heart of the capital: ten acres of tax-free startups occupying low, windowless units, the whole place surrounded by corrugated fencing and razorwire. I drove over. According to the list of businesses at the front gate, Auracle shared it with a lot of warehousing and manufacturing plants for everything from pharmaceuticals to diesel engines. There were guards at the entrance to the zone. I couldn't get in without the kind of high jinks that were liable to see me arrested. But I suspected Auracle kept most of their business out of the office anyway. They'd need it to arrange bribes for launch licenses, somewhere to shoot the vodka, get the tax benefits. Not much more.

From what I could tell, a lot of what their work involved what was in the service we called MASINT, measurement and signature intelligence. I first saw the phrase in training, as we were familiarizing ourselves with the various acronyms. MASINT was where it got weird. MASINT covered the data that human senses weren't able to receive: ultraviolet and infrared radiation, alterations in the electromagnetic spectrum, variations in the gravitational pull of the earth. These were monitored using hyperspectral sensors. All sorts of things revealed themselves.

Most of the interest for the intelligence service was in relation to collecting data on weaponry and bomb tests. It was only when I saw it being used by BP in Azerbaijan that I became fascinated by the imagery produced. I used to stay behind in the offices, scrolling across the data maps of Central Asia. Oil miles underground showed up as hydrocarbon particles in surface soil and water, but the more recent past was down there too. You could see the outline of destroyed cities thousands of years old, and make out mass graves, the Stalinist ones identifiable by their regular shape, then the fainter sites of what must have been Mongol and Scythian massacres.

Bryant's geographical routine had been mapped by Joanna first, then Vectis as they investigated him during their search for her. It didn't deviate much; expats are usually creatures of habit and Astana offered few temptations. Office from nine to five, then an address on Saryarka Avenue, which turned out to be a bar called the Rocks. After eight hours roaming the hyperspectrum, he hit the bottle hard.

I liked the sound of the Rocks. It was the sort of place I would have sought out eventually anyway. A city has currents like any sea, and it was useful for a spy to know the places where loneliness swept a man. Nightcrawling, they called it in Six. Falling in step with the vulnerable. Whenever I arrived on a new posting, I let myself be carried.

It was almost five p.m. Bryant would be getting thirsty.

The Rocks had a four-leaf clover in neon above blacked-out windows. Inside it was dim, cramped, walls painted black between mirrors. The space was divided equally between a square dance floor and a darker, UV-lit bar area with stools around barrels. Clientele were nearly all students, starting to trickle in wearing miniskirts beneath fake fur–lined parkas. You could be pretty much anywhere.

Irish pubs were lucky places for me. The Guinness sign served as a beacon for intelligence agents around the world, looking for venal locals and homesick Westerners. My favorites included McGettigan's in Jumeira, the Blacksmiths in Moscow, Molly Bloom's in Tel Aviv — high times, career-defining recruits. You found CEOs and construction workers democratically leveled by alcoholism; local men and women estranged from their own kind for whatever reason, offered refuge by Celtic tat. And locals drinking with Westerners were halfway recruited already. You found prostitutes and pickpockets, just occasionally an actual pint of Guinness. In short, everything you could want.

The young man behind the bar noticed me as soon as I came in. He was tall, muscled beneath a white T-shirt, with sharp eyes and a quick smile, the bearing of someone running things.

"Hello," he said in English.

"Evening," I replied, happy to play the foreigner.

"American?" he said.

I laughed. "Do I not look Russian?"

"Your clothes don't look Russian."

"English."

"Pint of beer?" His English was good. Good English in a place like this usually signaled frustrated ambitions. Fixer material.

"You read my mind."

My beer came in a frosted glass with a puck of ice in the bottom. The barman welcomed me to Kazakhstan. I imagined him in a country at war, where his combination of charm and street knowledge would come into its own. I tipped well and hoped I did not play a part in his life.

A guy beside me with a ponytail was busy on his phone. I saw Twitter, checked his handle, then looked him up on my own phone. He was Dimash Nurtas, a guitarist. Some of his tweets were in English, mostly about music, some politics: retweets about a pro-democracy demonstration by students in Uzbekistan. He had a few international followers.

"Twitter working?" I said. "I couldn't get it."

"With a VPN."

"Which do you recommend?"

"Cloudflare."

"A lot of people using that?"

"Yes."

"Do people get angry about the restrictions?"

"Everyone."

I leaned back against the bar and watched the room. Too early for the dance floor, but the music was loud. It was Western in style — electronic beats, bassline — with lyrics in Russian and sometimes Kazakh. I tried to hear the lyrics, gauge what the youth of Kazakhstan were dreaming of. Making money, it seemed. Having a good time.

"Been in Astana long?" the barman asked when I got my next drink.

"I've just got here."

"If you want a bar with girls, you know, a nice place, I can recommend one." He lowered his voice: "In London it is like a party town. Yes?"

"Nonstop."

A suited man at the end of the bar got his attention. I watched out of the corner of my eye as the barman slipped him a small package in exchange for several notes. Then I saw who was buying.

Bryant was tall and too smartly dressed for the Rocks, but younger than he seemed in Joanna's interviews. He could have walked straight out of Wall Street or Silicon Valley. Blue shirt, frameless glasses; bright smile with a touch of desperation. Deal done, he got a round in for a lot of the men at the bar, some of whom knew him.

I positioned myself beside him in the queue for the bar and let him hear me order.

"Someone with the Queen's English," he said. "That's music to my ears." He shook my hand. "Craig."

"Toby."

"What brings you here?"

"To the Rocks or to Kazakhstan?"

"Both."

"Kazakhstan for business. Got in yesterday. The Rocks to unwind."

"One day in and you found the Rocks already!" He clapped me on the back. "You chose a fine time of year to visit Kazakhstan. What's the business?"

"I'm looking around for some investors."

"Let me guess: hungry for untapped markets. Exploring this exciting new part of the world."

"Something like that."

He grinned knowingly, drank deeply. His cuff links were sand timers. "How's it working out for you?"

"Seems an interesting time to be here. What about you?"

"I do tech stuff. For the oil industry mostly."

"Good industry to do that for."

"It has its moments."

I bought us more drinks. We grabbed a barrel with stools around it. I wanted to steer him toward revelations, the dark side of this place; his relationship with Vanessa McDonald.

"The oil work ever bring you any issues? I mean, is it still the Wild East—gangsters, oligarchs? You get exposed to that?"

"The company I work for does. It's just a question of—" He rubbed his thumb and finger together. "Bakshish. Whatever."

"Pretty corrupt?"

He shrugged. "In the US they only call a place corrupt when the bribes stop working."

He talked about different nationalities in the city—Saudis, Turkish, Iranians—and about good places to eat and drink, where to find the political class and where to avoid them. He had a story about the president's daughter demanding satellites from an oil company so she could run a TV station. I could see why he was good for background intelligence: atmospherics, as the Americans called it. I could see other reasons Joanna might have taken solace in his company. He was good-looking and over-confident, and a bad choice in terms of her operation, all of which had piqued her interest in the past. There was a wryness to him that I liked, a dark shadow to the optimism. I had come across unadulterated optimism all too often in Iraq and Afghanistan: American men with the same Brooks Brothers suits, fueled by a faith that the world wanted to grow toward the innocence of their childhoods. It soured in the end. Bryant drank with a thirst I suspected had developed since he arrived.

"Is it safe here?" I asked. "Expats had any issues? That's what a lot of my clients ask."

"Mostly safe, yes." He hesitated. Something made him check his phone. He put it away, glanced around at the lasers and the dry ice. "There's ten men for every woman here. Are you up for moving on?"

"Sure."

"Ever been to Chocolate?"

The Chocolate Room was a nightclub by the river, tucked into the base of the Radisson hotel. I drove us there, parked a few meters away from the limos that stretched outside. There was a commotion going on when we got to the place: The side window of a Porsche had been smashed. I caught a glimpse of figures running across the street, bouncers giving chase while on radios. We were inside before I had a chance to see any more.

The place was large and conspicuously expensive, with a stage and a dance floor, booths around the side. On the stage, topless women sat in giant gold picture frames that swung on chains. People on the dance floor paid them little attention—daughters of oligarchs dancing with practiced moves as if they were auditioning for a part. Bryant asked for a table in the corner. For the price of a bottle of champagne and six shots we got a red velvet booth from which you could watch the show and talk undisturbed. He waved away some escorts.

"See the trouble outside?" I said.

"Yeah."

"Get much of that?"

Bryant sipped his Cristal thoughtfully.

"Not yet," he said.

"What do you mean?"

"This country has a problem: It's called forty-dollar barrels. The price of oil has sunk. That means the sweetener's running out, economic brakes slammed on. Which is fine for those strapped in." He gestured at the dance floor. "But the people outside . . . People start to care about democracy when they can't buy what they want."

"Right."

"The government needs a deal from somewhere."

"There must be room for more outside energy investment."

"Yeah, maybe."

"What tech exactly do you do for the oil industry?"

He kept his eyes on the dance floor as if the question was mildly distasteful.

"Collect data and process it. Data from magic technology."

"Satellites?"

"Satellites, drones. Sometimes even guys on the ground."

"For Chevron?"

He smiled. "Not a bad guess. I'm with one of the littler guys, though. Saracen. Know them?"

"They're in Vietnam, right?"

"They've got fields in 'Nam, Mexico. They buy them up, flip them, sell them to the majors for a quick profit. But Kazakhstan's got under their skin."

"Should I invest in Saracen?"

His smile became more enigmatic.

"You could do worse." Then he shook his head ruefully. "Seriously, I'd be killed for talking about this stuff."

"Really?"

"High stakes. And not the gentlest crowd."

"Why? What's happened?"

"Not too much yet. But things have barely started. Why the interest?"

"Just feeling out the landscape."

"Well, let me tell you: You're going to need a stomach for risk doing any business around here."

"It's still on the up, right? There's plenty of oil to come."

"Sure, oil's oil. But times are changing. The president's not going to live forever. He's walked a fine line: tight with Russia, tight with the West; giving us crumbs — oil crumbs, investment crumbs. He's, what, almost eighty? There's no succession plan. He's kept it that way deliberately."

"Where do you think the trouble will come from? Islamists?"

Bryant laughed. "These guys wouldn't know a Koran from a JCPenney catalogue. The trouble will come from the big guys next door." He tilted his glass. "China, Russia."

"A guy I met yesterday was talking about container traffic from China coming through."

"Sure. Doubled last year. Only danger is the Chinese don't know when to stop. They're buying agricultural land, housing, you name it. People aren't happy."

"Better than Russians getting it?"

"They *like* the Russians here. There's an old Kazakh proverb: 'To be the captive of the Chinese is a tight noose — with the Russians, it is a wide-open road.'"

"Sounds like a Russian proverb," I said.

"Every country needs protection. You have the United States. No one wants to be independent without being strong. Anyway, the Kazakhs aren't so worried about infrastructure. They don't like losing land."

"They've got enough of it."

"But it's how they identify. You've got to understand the psychology. There's so much of it, it's everything. That's Kazakhstan."

Another girl came over and he started chatting to her. She looked Indonesian. I went to the toilets, where there was crushed ice in the urinals and a guy in a tuxedo with his head under the taps. The escort had gone when I returned, and Bryant was staring into space.

"Why's there ice in the urinals?" I asked.

"Why is anything?" He shook his head, then tried to drink from an empty glass. I topped him up. He was drunk now. He asked if I wanted to do a line, and I said I was okay. While he was in the toilets powdering himself, I watched the topless women swinging in their picture frames, skin dusted with glitter. I sipped champagne and imagined being Bryant, stuck out here, living the routine as Joanna had figured it. Every expat is an exile of sorts, looking for something to grip on to. You're free to re-make yourself, try things out, which means you end up confronted with who you really are. Then you start drinking. I was drawn to these men and women, all on the run from something, not only because my job depended on exploiting their vulnerability. Bound in with their dreams of self-enrichment—bound in, even, with a hunger to see the world—was always a desire to disappear, and I knew how that felt.

Bryant returned and we leered over the dancers, discussing which we found most attractive.

"Are you dating?" I asked.

He pulled a face. "It's tough. When they hear you work in energy, it's two-hundred-dollar meals for a blowjob. Kazakh women just want to marry you. They want a ring and a visa before you get their number. Funnily enough, the one woman I clicked with was an eco-activist." He looked at me to check my amusement, and maybe something more, sensing he was on uncertain territory.

"Nice. Maybe she was spying on you," I said. He nodded philosophically.

"We'd had a few drinks together. You know, I thought maybe she found it kinky. Then she stops returning my calls. Perhaps that was, like, revenge for me working for the oil industry. Maybe that was a protest."

"Was she Kazakh?"

"English. One of your compatriots."

I feigned surprise. "Working over here?"

"Making a documentary."

"Did she film you?"

"Briefly. But she wanted Kazakhstan. I think she had a romantic idea of the place: dudes riding across the steppe, eagles on their wrists. She asked me about oil companies and human rights. You know, hostile. I was the baddie. I fuck up the planet."

"And then you got a date?" I laughed. "You turned her."

"While it lasted."

"Isn't it risky, if she was doing that kind of political stuff over here?"

"I'm still trying to get my head around this country, in terms of what you can get away with. I certainly wouldn't turn up asking about corruption. Not when it comes to oil and gas. There's a lot of tensions right now: workers' rights, the environment, people getting moved for new drill sites. I chatted to one old Saracen character about communities they were displacing and he said: 'I thought they were nomads.'" Bryant gripped my arm. "Can you believe that? 'I thought they were nomads, why can't they just move?' Jesus Christ. Stick around, Toby. It's about to get interesting."

I helped him finish the Cristal. He had that early-stage alcoholism where inebriation hits sudden and profound. When he leaned in to speak, our stubble rubbed and his hand found my knee. The coke didn't seem to have sharpened him.

"You shouldn't drive," he said. "We can share a cab."

It was an interesting proposition.

We got a cab back to his flat. At a new development, behind the governmental district, Bryant told the driver to stop. He clambered out, sank to his knees in the snow, the driver shaking his head as he waited for his fare. I paid, helped Bryant up, and got him into the right block and to his door. The flat itself was plush, impersonal, with a lot of gray and white. He sat on the sofa and watched me, a slow, seedy smile spreading as if he'd realized something, then fell asleep in his suit. I searched the place, then searched his phone. "Vanessa Campaigner." I scrolled back to their earliest exchanges. She had sent the first message.

It's Vanessa. You were great. I don't know what you were worrying about. I owe you that drink.

To which Bryant replied:

Glad I didn't embarrass myself. Things are crazy at the moment. Next week?

I can wait ;)

I had never known Joanna to use an emoticon. But then, she'd never formally asked me out for a drink. From what I could tell, Bryant wasn't chasing any other women in Astana or anywhere else.

You never know with people. That was what I'd learned in fifteen years manipulating their souls. The closer you look, the more things come apart. One of the big shocks is how readily people will remake themselves for you, shape themselves to your own desires, especially those with shallow roots. No one's depthless, but sometimes you look inside and sense nothing whatsoever beneath the façade. Except, perhaps, a quiet, consistent screaming. People like that will seize any scheme you offer them. The power could go to your head.

I saw his dilated pupils in the light of the Chocolate Room. *You're going to need a stomach for risk.* He'd run a long way from Idaho, that was for sure. I took a photo of his door keys, one of his tranquil face, left him snoring.

21

I GOT A CAB BACK TO THE CLUB TO PICK MY CAR UP. I DIDN'T WANT TO leave it there overnight. And I was still wide awake with champagne and adrenaline.

My Hyundai was where I'd left it, windows intact. I pushed the snow off the windscreen and got in.

A car screeched to a stop in front of me as soon as I pulled out. It gave a flash of police lights. I turned my engine off as a man clambered out, uniformed. No backup vehicles. A second officer remained in the police car.

They must have seen me coming. Which was okay, I told myself: Letting me get to the car suggested a scam rather than a hit. They'd been loitering where the rich might get caught, expats especially. I didn't know the alcohol limit here, but I'd be well over. If that was the worst of my problems, I could handle it. I wound my window down.

"This is your car?" The officer spoke Russian, voice hoarse, eyes heavy-lidded. A functioning alcoholic, forty-something, tall enough that he had to stoop to the window. There was a faded gravity to his jaundiced eyes. A mustache among the stubble seemed like the remnant of a frayed uniform. I spoke Russian back, badly.

"*Ya ne ponimayu.* I don't understand."

"Your car?" he said in English.

"It's a hire car."

"You've been drinking."

"Just one beer."

"You are not in good condition to drive." He wasn't in good condition to police. His breath was flammable. "Papers. And keys."

He took the paperwork and car keys to his vehicle and came back with an old Breathalyzer. He made a show of tutting when I blew. I went along with this. They hadn't radioed in to base. Whatever performance going on was part of a lucrative sideline, not official duties — shaking down unsuspecting foreigners — which suited me.

"Step out of the car. Come with me." His English was proficient. The reasonable English spoken by people who needed to fleece English-speakers.

"We can arrange something," I said.

"Come."

I followed him to his car, got in the back seat with him. There was a younger officer up front. The car was filled with cigarette smoke.

"Where are you from?" the older officer said.

"The UK."

"Here on business."

"Yes."

"Oil." He smiled.

"Something like that."

"You get in trouble here, as a foreigner, it is very bad. Kazakhstan is not England. You would find the prisons very dangerous."

"Prison?" I fumbled with my wallet and made sure he saw money. "Tell you what, we can forget this, can't we? My company would kill me if I got in trouble."

"Four hundred thousand tenge. I give you paper, no more problems."

Four hundred thousand was ridiculous, the better part of a grand, but who could blame him. This con man was growing on me. There was an air of seniority amid the vice, a conflict that told a story. I could envisage a whole portfolio of petty corruption under his control, which opened more doors than those engaged in it usually realized. He'd have connections above and below, colleagues sheltering him, taking their own skim from nicer offices. And I was always drawn to people with ethical voids at their center.

I counted out a few hundred pounds' worth of notes.

"Officer . . . ?"

"Shomko."

"Officer Shomko, I've got a business proposal. You seem a helpful guy. I was just out looking for somewhere I might get a drink, meet some Kazakh ladies. I don't know this city and I don't want any more dealings with police. How about another few tenge, you show me somewhere I can get what I need?"

I showed more notes. The two men consulted one another in Kazakh, assuming I wouldn't understand. Shomko saying I was his, the young man negotiating his cut. Shomko took the money off me and thrust a handful of tenge at his colleague, who got out of the car with a final glance of disdain in my direction.

We drove to a place with a 24 HOUR sign blinking by a small door into the back of what looked like an office block. There was no indication of what was available around the clock, but a vent beside the entrance poured an inverted waterfall of pine-scented steam into the night air.

"You are married?" he said, as we waited for someone to let us in.

"No. You?"

"Divorced. You like Kazakh women?"

"Sure."

"Do not marry a Kazakh woman."

"Okay."

We were buzzed in, hit by the smell of menthol and eucalyptus. A second door led to the front desk of a sauna and massage parlor. A girl lay sleeping on a sofa at the side under a coat. Four men played cards in a side room. A middle-aged woman sat behind the desk watching a Korean drama on TV. Shomko spoke to her about entry fees.

"What does he want?" the woman asked.

"What do you think he wants?"

"What's so special he gets a police escort?"

They haggled over his cut. Shomko quoted me a price.

"You trust this place?" I said.

"It is the best."

"Stick around. How do I know I don't get busted coming out?"

He said he'd wait, folding the money into his pocket. I told him to get a girl himself, paid for both of us. The woman rolled her eyes and told Shomko to shower. She gave us towels and keys for the lockers.

Eyes in the steam watched us pass. There were dead branches in a basket by the door, leaves on the floor. I heard the rustle of birch branches against skin as men swiped themselves.

"Go steam. Your girl will collect you."

"Okay."

Shomko wrapped himself in a towel and disappeared. I went toward the steam, then doubled back to the changing room and broke into Shomko's locker.

His wallet contained some kind of prayer card, Viagra, and ID for the National Security Committee. Lt. Aslan Shomko from the regional department of the NSC, essentially the old KGB with new insignia and less ideology, so it covered a lot of policing, border control, drugs. There were betting slips and numbered tickets: *Bolim Lombard*. Lombard was Russian for pawnshop.

I put his belongings back, feeling hopeful. Midlife crises were where I stepped in. They came at just the right moment, when an employee was well-connected and utterly desperate—you wonder what you have put those years in for, kissing arse . . . you stumble into me. I'm the pleasure you've been denied. I respect you.

In the end I declined my massage and dipped briefly into the hot tub instead, keeping an eye out for Shomko. When I saw him return, I joined him in the changing rooms.

"She give you good service?"

"Excellent."

"Sometimes they are—" He made a hand-chopping gesture. Efficiency? Violence? I wouldn't have drawn out an erotic encounter with Lieutenant Shomko. "Still, I got you a bargain. Usually, Westerners, they make you pay more."

"Money's not a problem." I turned back to my things, letting the statement hang in the steamy air. "So maybe you can help me again sometime."

"Give me your phone." He punched his number in. "You get in trouble, you have my number. Shomko." He patted his chest. We shook hands.

He'd entered his name in my contacts as "Helping man."

In my hotel room I considered how best to use him. Find out if there was a police file on Joanna? On the murder in her safe house? Those were high-risk lines of inquiry. I checked for messages. Nothing from Joanna. Confirmation from Stefan that he was at Dubai International Airport, waiting for a connecting flight. Then the one from Tom Marsh: *They're looking for you.* It wouldn't be long before they found me. I needed to know how my own country's intelligence service fit into this.

I lay down, shut my eyes, and saw the Mega Astana exchange. You get a few bytes of data, traveling through the air like an infection. Shows you something that you can't unsee.

Two people in a room in the Triumph of Astana. What kind of premonition was it? What made it so dangerous for those who'd seen it? Me or him?

22

I TRIED UNSUCCESSFULLY TO SLEEP. I WAS AVERAGING FOUR HOURS A night. In my shallow dreams, when they did come, Joanna and I were in Turkey, setting fire to our fingers. The idea was to erase our identities, in the way we'd seen it achieved by refugees in Reyhanli with blackened finger pads, but our fingers burned like candles and we couldn't put them out.

I was woken by a knock on the door.

"Mr. Bell?"

It was the receptionist. When I opened the door she stepped aside and a team of four men walked in, forcing me back into the room and closing the door again.

"Take a seat," one man said, in English. He wore a suit and holster beneath a gray winter coat. He gestured at the bed. There was another plainclothes officer and two uniforms as backup. One radioed confirmation that I was here and they were in.

No badges or warrants shown. The senior officer was tall, the long coat accentuating his height. He had paperwork in his hand: documents from the car hire company.

"Mr. Toby Bell?"

"That's right. What's going on?"

"When did you arrive in Kazakhstan?"

"Saturday afternoon."

"Passport and visa, please."

I gave him my passport and visa. He checked these while his colleagues checked the cupboards, moved the curtains, peered inside the bathroom.

"What are you looking for?" I asked. They ignored me.

"The nature of your business in this country?" the senior officer said.

"I'm here for work. Why? What am I meant to have done?"

"You have hired a car?"

"Yes."

"Have you been to Apartment 603, Nine Malakhov Street while you've been here?"

"No."

"Would you unlock the safe, please?"

I unlocked the safe and stepped back while he sifted its contents. Then he straightened.

"Get dressed. You come with us, please. It is necessary that we ask you some questions."

"About what? What's going on?"

"Quickly. Then all this will be over."

I dressed smartly, knotting a tie. The younger of the suited men took my passport and the key fob for the Hyundai. They led me downstairs to a black Audi with police lights on the roof. I was squeezed in between the uniformed officers.

"Where are we going?"

No answer. We drove north, the rising sun reflecting off the snow and glass, turning the city into molten lava. After fifteen minutes we arrived at an anonymous, new-looking building, four floors with bars on the lower windows. No state vehicles parked visibly outside, none of the aerials or antennae you'd expect on a police station.

I stepped out of the car. Ten meters of drive led to a narrow, bomb-proof door, with electronic barriers visible inside. Two men in black uniforms stood beside it. It looked like somewhere you went in rather than out. I felt the first stab of real fear. If I was going to run, it was now or never.

Six men against me, at least three carrying small arms, two that looked like they'd be fast on their feet. Most stood to my left, between me and a six-lane road. Best option would be running toward them—past them—which was counterintuitive, therefore surprising; it meant they'd have to turn, with a complicated backdrop for sighting weapons, plus each other getting in the way. We were still in a public space. They were trained, but there would be calculations to make which would slow them down.

There are always worse options than running. I would have the cover of two Land Rovers and then the corner of a building in approximately four seconds. Against a .22 or a .38 from a pistol, a car is going to be an adequate block. But once you start running you can't stop. That was game over. Besides, I felt a step closer to finding what I came for in the first place. And I don't really do running while being shot at.

The bomb-proof door led into a tiny security room lined with thick bulletproof glass. I was searched with cold efficiency. My bag and phone were taken "for security." Then the officer on reception duty produced a device that looked like an iPad. He told me to press my fingers against the screen.

"What's this for?"

"Records."

When they had their records I was directed into a corridor, through two sets of doors with swipe entry, each feeling like another layer of soil above my head, into an office. Not the interrogation cell I'd been braced for. The Kazakh flag was in place behind the desk, beneath a framed photograph of the president, who looked like the Dalai Lama compared with the individual sheltering beneath his gaze. He was small, with dark eyes and a dark suit, handkerchief in the breast pocket, which suggested an ominous amount of pleasure in his role. No visible computer, laptop, or mobile. The phone on the desk was a corded black Siemens.

He was obviously senior. I tried to read the room again, noticed one other framed image on the wall: three men in traditional Kazakh clothing above a line of text: *If there is no owner of the fire, your motherland will be enveloped in flames.*

The man stared at me, tapping the Toby Bell passport against his desk. I prepared myself mentally. Keep a center of calm. But Toby Bell wouldn't keep calm, or quiet, and one technique for interrogation scenarios was noise. The more noise you make, the fewer questions they can ask, the less chance they have of tripping you up. Outrage was a kind of silence of its own.

"What the hell is this? I've been here less than two days. I have no idea what's going on, but you've arrested a British national for no good reason. I believe your government has close relations with the UK, that a lot of potential investment could be jeopardized if Kazakhstan is seen to intimidate visiting businesspeople at random."

"You flew in last week." He spoke calmly, in accented English.

"I flew in two days ago, from Kiev."

His face was a mask, eyes showing neither doubt nor disappointment.

"The flight number?"

"I didn't memorize it," I said. The flight number would start to suggest my circuitous route from the UK, which would start to suggest Bell's circuitous entry into existence. I wanted to delay that revelation. He established my time of arrival and gave instructions to a man beside the door to go and check it. I wondered if they noticed that I didn't ask to speak to my embassy.

"And where were you before?"

"London."

"But you have been in Kazakhstan previously."

"Never."

"Who do you know here?"

I told him about the meeting with Toreali, then asked who exactly I was talking to. He ignored the question, asked for passwords for my phone and laptop. I refused.

"Why do you refuse?"

"Why should I give them to you? I haven't done anything wrong."

"What would we find?"

"Nothing."

He asked which companies I had previously worked for, and then before that, going back years. After a while, as I'd been trained, I just refused, played indignant. I considered making noise about legal representation. Then we started on the proper interrogation.

"You work for Vectis."

"I don't know who that is."

"You know who Saracen are?"

"The oil company?"

"Yes."

"I've got nothing to do with them."

He glowered. I considered. So they'd connected me to the private intelligence outfit. In a way it was a comfort — better than connecting me to MI6, better than making me as a random murderer with no connections out there. After a moment, the man nodded to one of the guards. I was lifted up and pulled out of the room. Then things turned nasty. My hands were forced into metal cuffs, locked behind my back. The guards marched me to the top of steep concrete stairs. Someone pushed me, then caught me before I fell.

"Be careful."

I felt the rising panic of powerlessness. I was slammed face-first into the wall. The front of my skull throbbed.

"Next time you fall down them." One man turned me around and the other punched me hard in the stomach. I dropped to my knees, winded. There was a voice close to my ear.

"You think anyone knows you're here?"

It was a good question. The Lion Hotel's sleepy receptionist had some awareness of my predicament. Callum Walker knew I was in Astana; he didn't strike me as someone who'd make much noise in the event of my disappearance. Hugh Stevenson might raise the alarm after a week or two. Was I about to find out how Joanna had vanished? About twelve people had witnessed me in the hands of the Kazakh State, and not one of them would remember if they were told not to.

A long pause to let the threat linger, and then I was uncuffed and taken back to the office. My interrogator hadn't moved, only the papers on the desk had been rearranged.

"You are sabotaging our country. You come here and bring trouble with you. We are peaceful and you create war."

I shook my head, which was hurting now.

"You think there is no law here?" he asked.

"I've been in this country less than two days."

"We know who you are, what you are doing here."

"Apparently not."

He opened a file and pushed a print out toward me, a poor-quality image of a man walking between a dusty Mercedes and a residential building with steps and an intercom. It took me a few seconds to think where I'd seen him before. It was the man in the faked clip with me. Here, he wore an open-necked shirt and sunglasses. The image looked real enough.

I tried to see the paperwork that came with it, and all I could see was the stamped crest of Kazakh Antiterrorism. I knew that their Antiterrorism was run by a man called Rakim Zhaparov. His name came up in debates over the use of intelligence produced during torture. It seemed he was sitting across the desk from me. Identifying him wasn't entirely comforting.

"What is this meant to mean?" I asked. "Who is he? Why do you think I know him?"

Zhaparov nodded to someone standing behind my right shoulder. A few seconds later something cold and metallic touched my ear. There was a beep and it felt like a nail gun had fired into my brain. I fell off the seat, temporarily blinded, arms wrapped around my head. Before I could recover, I was picked up and sat back down. I felt sick, and registered the beginnings of dread. What was that device? What kind of long-term effects were we looking at? I really didn't want to emerge from this mentally degraded.

"Tell us what you're doing here."

"You've just got yourself in a lot of trouble." My voice came out weakly.

"No, I think you really don't understand who is in trouble."

I could feel the electricity souring my muscles. Everyone has a breaking point, no matter how distant. What did I have to give them, even if I wanted to? What did they want?

The guards lifted me up, one on each arm.

"Have a think," Zhaparov said. "See if you remember."

The doors at basement level were battleship gray with magnetic acoustic seals. The air was freezing. I was pushed into a cell, five meters by five, with a wooden bench along the back wall, uncuffed.

"Your clothes."

"Fuck off."

"Then I'm sure you don't mind if we undress you."

They had restraint equipment—ankle cuffs, fabric restraints, stun belt. Four men, with more behind them. I undressed. They gave me a gray tracksuit, then someone threw a bucket of water over me.

"You have a right to be washed." The door slammed shut on their laughter. I started shivering uncontrollably. I tried to keep moving, heart pumping, brain working. I didn't have long before hypothermia set in. Options: I play along, giving fake information, buy myself time. Or, I wait it out. They didn't want me dead. If they knew who I was, I'd be too valuable. If they didn't, they might be under the impression someone would care. I could try to scare them with suggestions of Toby Bell's own importance. I knew enough about government and the diplomatic service —maybe get the embassy involved after all. Who knew where that would lead? The next flight back to London, most probably. And a lot of questions at the other end.

The door opened three times in the next hour. Once was a cursory check by the guards, once I was given a polystyrene cup of milky coffee. The next visitor was a man with a Russian accent. He had a goatee, black hair swept back so strands fell around his face, an expensive-looking camel overcoat. He saw me, shook his head, and swore at the guards.

"Get him a towel and dry clothes."

The guards looked disgruntled. A rancid towel hit my face, and my clothes were returned. I got dressed.

"Come on," my visitor said, helping me on with my coat. "Let's get you out of here."

23

I WASN'T IN A POSITION TO SAY NO. HE LED ME BACK TO THE RECEPTION, where I signed paperwork that declared my treatment at the hands of the security services had been impeccable. My other possessions were returned. A lot of men watched us leave; I had become quite an attraction.

"Animals," my companion muttered.

He led me to a dark gray Land Rover with a suited driver at the wheel.

"Are you okay?" he asked.

"I've been better. Who are you?"

"Yes, fair question." He smiled. "My name is Sergei Cherenkov. I work on cultural matters with the Russian embassy. Please, get in." His English was good. The vowels suggested time living in an English-speaking country, maybe some education there. Our driver was thick-necked, head shaved. He didn't look cultural.

"Where are we going?"

"Let's get some breakfast," Cherenkov said.

We drove to a side street café that had no lights on, but my companion appeared to know it would open if he knocked. Our driver stayed with the car. The café owner unlocked the door and turned the lights on for us without making eye contact. It was a scruffy place, with scratched wooden tables and blinds down over the windows. Cherenkov ordered teas.

"You drink tea, no?" He took a cigarette from a packet of Kents, shoved the pack toward me, looked around for an ashtray. The health warning on the pack was in Arabic. He wore rings on each hand.

"What the hell is this about?" I said.

"I know your business friend here, Dimash Toreali. I believe he showed you the Palace of Peace and Reconciliation yesterday. I was advising him on an opera he wants to put on there. To sponsor."

"And?"

"I was trying to get in touch with you, at your hotel. You sounded an interesting guy. They said you'd been taken. It took me an hour to find out where you were."

Toreali didn't know where I was staying, but I let this slide. Cherenkov was clearly a Russian intelligence officer — he could have surveillance on me or on the people who'd arrested me.

"What did they want?" he asked. "Those men just now."

"I've no idea."

The teas arrived with a glass ashtray. Cherenkov looked at them with an air of dissatisfaction. He browsed the menu.

"Would you like some eggs? An omelet?"

"No."

He ordered himself some eggs.

"I am not happy at the way they treated you. They are basic, Kazakhs. They think you connect to a murder. I can see you are not a murderer. Could your embassy not help? Where are they?"

"I never got the chance to contact them."

"And what is the business you are on?"

"I'm looking at some investment opportunities."

He nodded, sipped his tea. Eventually he said: "What if I said we knew where she was?" He met my eyes for a second. His were alert, cautious. He looked away again.

I forced myself to say: "Who?"

"We don't. No one does, it seems. But what if we found out?"

"What do you want?"

Cherenkov scratched his goatee.

"I am a lonely man, Mr. Kane." He dropped my real name in without any flourish. "I work with people of simpler minds. They don't care about very much, but I have questions, ideas. Building D," he said. "Shefford. I would like you to give me a glimpse inside. What has been going on there?"

I was transported briefly back to Bedfordshire. He created the link I had been looking for, even if it led through unknown terrain. Joanna's disappearance connected to her earlier work. At the same time, he'd shown me his cards. When you know what your enemy wants, you're halfway to owning them.

"I've no idea what you're talking about," I said.

"You would rather she died than help me a tiny bit."

"If helping you involves providing information that I don't have, we're not going to get very far. If you have something you think it would be useful for me to know, why not tell me? I'm sitting here for another thirty seconds."

"I could learn so much from you."

"You've got me confused with someone."

He nodded.

"I was told you were intelligent. The situation is this, Mr Kane: You are the one in trouble. You need a friend. Not ideal, a Russian friend, but here I am."

"I'm leaving now. Don't try to stop me."

"How could we stop you? At the same time, what are you going to do? I don't want you to be killed. But I think there are people who will kill you, Elliot. If any more unpleasant circumstances arise, we may not be in a position to do much. Then you will want to help us and it will be too late."

Cherenkov reached inside his jacket. He produced a silver case, gave me a business card with the Russian double-headed eagle. *Dr. Sergei Cherenkov, Assistant to the Cultural Attaché, Russian Embassy, Astana.*

"You're expecting me to work for you?" I said.

"In my experience, you're working for whoever keeps you alive. Help us or leave fast, that is my advice. But give me a call anytime. We can find Joanna together." He smiled. "We'll give you a lift back to your hotel."

"I'll walk."

"Wrap up warm." The eggs arrived and he spread a napkin on his lap. I left the café, hailed a cab from the next street, took it to the center of town.

So Russian intelligence wanted to know about Building D. Either Joanna's previous I/Ops work had followed her over here, or she never quit.

Stevenson called a few minutes later. It was good to hear his voice.

"We've got a small lead."

"What is it?"

"A code name, issued June 2014. Perfect Vision." He waited to see my response. "Mean anything to you?"

"No. It sounds like software, a program of some kind."

"That may be the idea. It sounds like software, but it's a hell of a lot more. Tom Marsh extracted it from an internal directory. The budget for Perfect Vision is hidden in Requirements and Production, but it's around seventy million pounds over two years, including the use of Building D in

Shefford Park. Building D had eighty members of staff cleared for entry at the peak of the operation last year."

"That's big."

"Big, maybe compartmentalized. I doubt many of them knew what they were working on. A lot of them were seconded from GCHQ. It was officially designated a research group, but the security setup suggests it was operational. It wasn't just producing papers."

"Who ran it?"

"It bypassed all the usual committees. There was Defense Intelligence involvement, so clearly the MOD was on board, but no one there claims to have heard of it. Like Tom said, six months ago it disappeared as fast as it had arrived, a few days before Joanna ran away. What have you found at your end?"

I said I had some leads, which felt optimistic. Told him some more about Joanna's work for Vectis, then told him I'd run into trouble and had had contact from Russian intelligence.

"They want to know about it, about Shefford and Building D."

"Surely that's a sign we need to pack it in," he said. "Come back. Get yourself killed on home soil, at least."

The levity didn't conceal his fear. I said I'd take one final look around. When he'd rung off I found "Helping man" on my phone, memorized the number before deleting it, then went to a phone booth and dialed.

24

Lieutenant Shomko answered brusquely. When he learned who it was, he told me to wait. He moved somewhere quieter.

"Who are you?" he said.

"We met last night."

"I know we met. I asked: Who *are* you?"

"I've got an offer for you. Meet me and I'll explain."

"I cannot meet."

"Two hundred dollars. Just to hear me out."

There was muttered cursing in Russian.

"Five hundred," he said.

Good man, I thought. "Four."

"Okay. You bring the money. You mess me around, I arrest you on the spot."

"Deal."

He named a bar a long way from the center, said he couldn't get away from work for a couple of hours. That gave me time to prepare.

I took cash, an amount that would be a couple of months' salary for Shomko, split it between two envelopes taken from reception. Then I made a call to a friend who worked for GL5.

There was every chance Shomko would take the money and arrest me anyway, and I'd had enough of that kind of thing for one day. The morning's events had been a wake-up call in more ways than one. I needed backup.

According to Elena Yussopova's research, GL5 private security were plentiful in the area and up for all sorts. I knew GL5 all too well, had people I considered friends working for the company, had had my life both saved and endangered by them. Crucially, I could approach under my own name and count on discretion. And in terms of muscle, they were currently unparalleled. The GL stood for Global Logistics; the 5 was supposedly the five continents on which they operated, which counted Eurasia as one and suggested they weren't on Antarctica, about which I was skeptical. We'd crossed paths regularly since Libya, when they were the first security company to establish a presence post-revolution. They protected the British embassy and so, to an extent, myself. Among intelligence officers, their base in Tripoli, behind Martyrs' Square, was known as a place to get a beer and a game of pool. Open the windows and you could smell the Mediterranean through the security mesh.

I called Jim Baillie, a former captain in the parachute regiment, now running GL5's cash transportation wing.

"Got anyone I can speak to about your Kazakh team? I need a hand."

There was a pause.

"Trouble?" Baillie said.

"Not yet. Could do with a couple of bodies this afternoon, though."

I heard him exhale.

"Geoff Purvis is in Astana. He's a good lad, former Welsh Guards. I can make a call."

"I'd appreciate that. I'm here on the lowdown."

"Got it."

Purvis himself called me twenty minutes later. He listened to my request.

"Reckon I might be able to help. Obviously, there'll be a price attached."

"I understand that."

He asked if I could come to their Astana base. I said I'd be happy to swing by.

Saracen had taken over a sprawling former Gazprom compound on the eastern edge of the city, with a helipad used for flying execs into town and geologists out to the drill sites. Purvis met me at the gates. He was tall, fair hair receded to a reserve line halfway back across his scalp, face flushed with what, up close, you saw were spider veins. His trousers were bloused into desert boots, paratrooper-style. He gripped my hand and shook.

"So you're a mate of Jim's?"

"Good mate. Not seen him in ages, though. Thanks for meeting at such short notice."

"You caught me on a good day."

Purvis signed me in, gave me a pass. We entered the land of GL5, through a guard's block to an expanse of concrete with hangars and barracks-style buildings on its edges.

"You know Jim from Libya?"

"That's right."

"Ever take you to Mama Tawa's?"

"Once. The only brothel I've ever walked straight out of."

Purvis laughed. "Jim's one of the finest soldiers I know, but he's a dog."

We crossed the concrete, passed a helipad with a Sikorsky S-70, then a small heating and power plant. There were long, prefabricated accommodation blocks alongside it. The private security contractors that I could see were heavily kitted out, if not visibly armed.

"They fly in here, get trained, go out to the rigs, drill sites, fields," Purvis explained. "Every few weeks they'll come back for some R-and-R. The kind of places we operate aren't exactly rich with leisure activities."

The canteen at the back of the site was large, with breeze block walls beneath arched corrugated metal. Electric bar heaters glowed. Men in various combinations of uniform and civvies sat at long trestle tables. Liverpool played Arsenal on multiple TV screens. A sign at the bar said dollars accepted, and there were plenty around. Pre-9/11, private security contractors all seemed to be South Africans with rotten teeth. Not anymore. The men here were smart, steroid-pumped, with two-hundred-dollar Oakleys protecting their eyes from the cold neon. It was a multibillion-pound industry now. Of the $21 billion assigned for Iraqi reconstruction, over thirty percent went to commercial security. Contractors came in to defend oil fields, and within a few months they were running aerial surveillance, searching for roadside bombs, and staffing quick reaction forces. Politicians found they preferred their coffins without flags on them. The original teams had been built from the best: men from the SAS and US Marines. But you're not going to get twenty thousand of those. GL5 swallowed smaller companies, picking up thousands of new personnel each time. Then, when they ran out of local recruits, they turned to Peru, Colombia, Eastern Europe—anywhere with a recent history of well-trained violence.

It looked like a lot of them had come off night shifts. Most were watching the game, yawning, smoking, drinking toward daytime sleep. I had never liked these places: the willed ignorance about the surrounding country, the bubble of boredom curdling. But they could be useful. Where there were guns there was a sense of invulnerability, which bred an openness to all sorts of schemes.

The canteen offered a full English breakfast, which Purvis promised me was passable — "No sheep's eyes. No horse sausage." We talked football while we ate, then home generally; he wanted to know what was going on in England and I pretended that I knew. He gave me tips about Kazakhstan, which amounted to not trusting lap dancers. I dropped a few names and places from Helmand, said I'd been in Sangin in 2006. We both knew Brigadier Rob Clarke and had survived raucous nights at the Kabul Serena Hotel. He got us mugs of lukewarm tea — NATOs, as they called them in the army: white tea, two sugars — and we talked some more about former jobs and then GL5. I studied the old regimental tattoos on his arms, and a fresher inscription: *Si vis pacem, para bellum*. I'd seen this tattoo a few times on my travels: *If you want peace, prepare for war.* Curiously, it seemed most popular with the mercenaries. I was never sure in what spirit it was intended. Over time it had gone from seeming like self-justification to an ironic echoing of the flawed logic that had shaped their lives.

"What do you want us to do?" he asked.

"Just be parked where I tell you to park," I said. "And if you see me running, open the door."

"Straightforward enough."

"And lend me a gun."

Purvis sucked in a breath. "What is this?"

"Jealous husband."

"Right. Is this jealous husband armed?"

"Hard to say."

"Does he have his own backup?"

"I doubt it."

"I'd need to speak to Jim."

"Of course."

Purvis came back twenty minutes later with a thumbs-up and an Adidas holdall. Inside it a was Makarov handgun and a box of nine-millimeter ammo.

"Seen one of these before?"

"Once or twice."

"For every second this gun's in your possession it's nothing to do with us. Never was."

I released the magazine, counted seven rounds. Checked the chamber and reloaded it.

"I understand."

"Where are you going to meet this jealous guy?"

I found the address Shomko had given me.

"Casino Zodiak."

Purvis selected two men to accompany us. They shook my hand but didn't remove their shades. One drove; both were heavily armed.

The casino was in the middle of nowhere, which must be why Shomko felt safe here. It had a post-apocalyptic look, plastic-clad with dribbles of rust over the cladding from the bolts that held it in place. It was deserted. Cacti pierced the snow around the front. Industrial scrubland lay flat for miles around.

We were early enough to do a full recon of the place: emergency exit points, potential choke points, sight lines so you could see any vehicles approaching before they saw you. There was a car park at the back, which gave GL5 a place to stay out of sight.

I walked in. There was no one on the front desk, which was shaped like a seashell. Deep red carpets absorbed sound and, by the looks of it, a multitude of burning cigarettes. The gambling must have gone on behind the padded doors. No sound of machines or roulette wheels. The only staff member I saw was pushing a trolley of coffeepots.

I found the bar upstairs, one man in a red waistcoat mopping the floor. When he saw me he put the mop down and went behind the bar, looking at me expectantly. I purchased a bottle of expensive vodka and two glasses, found a back exit, then went to a window that let me watch Shomko arrive and confirm he was alone.

He slammed the door of his car and walked toward the entrance. I was back behind the vodka in time to watch him enter.

He looked uncertain, eyes bloodshot, ice in his mustache. He hadn't shaved since the night before. He felt for his seat before lowering himself down as if it might make a sudden move. He removed his gloves, kept his black wool coat on. I poured the vodka, nudged a shot toward him.

"To the president," I said, in good Russian. The language caught him by surprise. He studied me, then knocked the drink back, wiped his mouth, fumbled in his shirt pocket for a crumpled packet of Marlboros. He removed a flattened cigarette and lit it. I slid one of the envelopes toward him. He looked inside, left it on the table.

"What do you want?"

"That's just for being here, a thank-you. You can take it and walk away now." I put the second envelope down. "This is if you want to help."

He took a deep drag and rested his cigarette in a heavy glass ashtray. I refilled our glasses.

"CIA?"

"No."

"Take my number off your phone."

"It's off."

"Show me."

I showed him. He sat back.

"They have a picture of you," he said.

"The police?"

"Yes. In the airport. Arriving in Kazakhstan."

"Why?"

"They want to know who you are."

"In connection with what?"

"I don't know. Are you mafia?"

"I am someone who does a lot of business here and cares very deeply about Kazakhstan. A man was killed in an apartment on Malakhov Street five nights ago. I'd like to know who he was and why he was shot."

Shomko drew the second envelope toward him and counted the money inside, then he emptied both, cramming half into his wallet, putting the other half inside his jacket. Emboldened by the currency against his heart, he relaxed.

"I know about it."

"Okay."

"There are a lot of resources on this."

"Who is he?"

"I don't have a name. I can try to get one."

"Who do people think did it?"

"They are looking for an Englishwoman."

"Where is the Englishwoman now?"

He spread his hands. "Gone. She bought plane tickets using a stolen credit card. Lufthansa to Frankfurt then on to Caracas, Venezuela."

"Caracas?"

"That's right. They were never used."

"How many tickets?"

"Two; for a man and a woman. Both in fake German names."

This explained the lack of ID on the dead body. He'd stripped himself of identity before coming to meet Joanna. They were about to run.

"What name do they use for this woman?" I asked.

"Vanessa McDonald. It's believed she stole a car just before disappearing."

"What make?"

"Chevy Equinox. Gray. There's no sign of it."

That changed things. Gave me simultaneous hope she got away and a vertiginous awareness that she could be anywhere.

"Checked car parks?"

"I assume so." Astana's underground car parks added up to a city's worth of concealment in themselves. There was no easy way to search those.

"Do cars often just disappear?"

"It's a big country. Could be she headed east."

"What's that meant to mean?"

"I saw men studying a map, talking about the possibility she went east, that she had connections there."

"East like eastern outskirts? East like the border with China?"

"I've no idea," Shomko said. "Did she have connections outside of Astana?"

"Possibly."

"Well, possibly that's something you want to look into."

"Who is in charge of the investigation?" I asked.

"Antiterrorism."

"Rakim Zhaparov."

"Yes."

"Why him?"

"Fuck knows. Maybe she's a terrorist." Shomko refilled his glass and downed it, then wiped the moisture from his mustache.

"It's been kept off the news," I said. "I would have thought this was a big story."

"The news is controlled. This is clearly too sensitive."

I showed him a screen grab of the man in the CGI clip.

"Who is he?"

"I don't know."

"He's on the radar of Antiterrorism. They have a picture of him too: a surveillance photo."

"How do you know who Antiterrorism has pictures of?"

"I know things."

Shomko took a while studying it before shaking his head. I saw him check the newspaper on the table, frown.

"What is this?"

"That's what I'd like to find out."

He ashed his cigarette nervously, flicking until I thought it was going to break.

"So what do you want?" he said.

"I need you to get closer to the investigation into Vanessa McDonald. Find someone on it, recruit someone inside Antiterrorism. They would be rewarded as well. Antiterrorism comes under the National Security Committee, doesn't it?"

"Technically. But they have their own facilities and security clearances, and a separate network for communication."

"You must know people inside it."

"I know people everywhere. Most of them like being alive."

"What's Zhaparov's vice? Does he like guys? Little girls?"

"He likes power. And he's getting more of it."

"He's on the rise?"

"Yes."

I opened the laptop on a map of Astana.

"Which buildings belong to Antiterrorism?"

Shomko dropped his cigarette to the floor and pointed out five locations, three in official state buildings, two black sites.

"Which have cells?"

"All of them."

"Where's the main investigation being run from?"

He showed me the main Antiterrorism headquarters on the map. It was housed within the National Security Committee building.

"And the investigative databases—who gets access to those?"

"Senior personnel only."

"You're senior."

"Not senior enough."

"Password-protected?"

"Yes."

"How often do they change the password?"

"Daily."

He talked me through the building, the security on the doors, the offices, and the integrated IT system.

"Are you searched when you go in?"

"No."

"Searched leaving?"

"No."

"You have access to the report that's been circulated."

"Yes."

"For now, send me everything that's on the open system."

"That is simple."

"Let's start with that, then. And find out where this Englishwoman's gone if she's not in Astana, whereabouts in the east people are looking." I promised him the equivalent of two hundred pounds for every new lead. Five thousand if he established where Vanessa McDonald was. The curiosity was too much for him.

"Who is she?"

"Someone very valuable." I gave him the number for a clean phone. "When you need to contact me, text the number of whatever phone box you're at. I need to know what's going on inside Antiterrorism. In Zhaparov's inner circle."

He shook his head.

"How much do you want?" I asked.

He retrieved another cigarette but didn't light it. His face bore an expression I had seen more times than I wanted: the discomfort of a man calculating what his life was worth.

25

I LET HIM LEAVE FIRST, THEN WENT DOWN TO MY GL5 ESCORT.

"How did it go?"

"Peacefully."

"That's what we like."

I was driven back to their office, where I put a deposit down for any further work. Purvis liked the cash. He didn't ask for the gun back.

"If someone wanted assurance that they could get out of here in a worst-case scenario," I said, "one, maybe two people tops, as quick and quiet as possible out of Kazakhstan—how feasible does that sound?"

"Informal arrangement?"

"Cash in hand."

"It's feasible. I'd have to get some names together. I'm guessing it would be a last-minute kind of business."

"Very. Would you go across the Caspian?"

"The Caspian gets icy, so probably not. We can get to a drill site; there are helis there, a Lynx that will get you to Baku, easy. Five-seater Airbus if the weather allows. We control two helipads in Baku. I'd rather keep wide of Russian airspace."

"Jets?"

"An Embraer Tucano. But it's not for commutes."

"Where do you park that?"

"Away from prying eyes." He winked. Embraer was a Brazilian company. The Tucano was marketed as a light combat aircraft.

"Registered to GL5?"

"Not exactly."

"What sort of price are we talking about?"

"For a civilian?" He considered. "The heli's thirty K. Personnel another ten per day, or two grand each. They'd want a retainer, maybe ten up front. For a mate of Jimmy's, call it seven and a half."

"And how much warning would you need?"

"It depends on the situation. But there's two thousand of us in Kazakhstan. I'm sure I could find some spare hands."

"Two thousand GL5?"

"That's right."

"Working for Saracen?"

"Not just Saracen. We've got contracts with the government: border security, training, cash transportation."

"I'm in the wrong job."

"You could have a good future with us, Elliot. Sector's only going to get bigger."

We agreed to payments and contacts, swapped some final anecdotes, then began back across the concrete.

"What kind of lads have you got over here?" I asked.

"Everything. Thai, Colombian, Ukrainian. Mostly Brits, though."

"Good kit?"

"Take a look at this."

He led me to a hangar. Inside, crouching in the darkness, were forms I didn't recognize: thin struts, metal plates, electronic devices that could have been cameras or lasers.

"It's for a virtual fence. Buried sensors and camera towers all linked to central control centers. UAVs, motion sensors. The lot."

"For protecting drill sites?"

"That's right."

There was something strange at the back: a rusted COSCO container with Chinese markings. I tried to see it as we headed out; it had been half obscured by tarpaulin, but I got a glimpse inside and could make out what looked like a military radio system. Light entered through three bullet-sized holes in the metal. It seemed all sorts of stories sheltered in the hangar.

"You're well-equipped," I said.

"We're doing our job," Purvis said. "We own this market. No one's offering the same level of service right now."

The day outside seemed brighter. Men had stopped on the tarmac. They stood stiffly as gates rolled back and a black convoy with outriders swept in. Purvis put a hand up to stop me.

An armored Bentley swung toward the helipad. It stopped beside the Sikorsky and a guard got out, opening a back passenger door as steps lowered from the helicopter and its rotors began to turn.

"Carter," Purvis said. "The boss."

A lone figure moved between the car and the helicopter, head bowed against the wash. Then he was gone, the stairs folded in, and the heli took off, sending up gritty snow, everyone ducking. Life in the compound continued.

"Ever used the heli for a search-and-rescue mission?"

"There was one the other day, actually. A woman. I was never told what she had to do with Saracen. Hunt her down, we were told. Whereabouts? *Somewhere in Kazakhstan.*" He slapped his forehead and laughed.

"Those were the words used?"

"Something like that. Why? Planning on getting lost? I wouldn't. It's one big, fuck-off country."

"You never found her, I take it."

"Not as far as I'm aware."

"And they said 'hunt'?"

"Hunt, find her, whatever. Something urgent."

I was sitting in my hotel room with the gun in my hand when my phone rang. It was Elena Yussopova.

"Elena."

"John, where are you?"

"I'm at my hotel," I said. "What's happened?"

"I need to speak to you."

"Okay."

"Can you come round? Now?"

"Sure."

"Be careful. Extra careful."

26

YUSSOPOVA'S FLAT WAS CROWDED. IT FELT LIKE A SMALL, TENSE COCK-tail party: cigarette smoke in the air, a pile of coats, dirty coffee cups, and even a bottle of vodka on the table. There were books and files all over the floor. Her wrists were still red from handcuffs.

The crowd shot me hostile glances. I recognized a couple of men and women from the protest photos. One gray-haired man had a case on his lap and was using it as a writing desk, as the group around him talked heatedly about legal options.

Yussopova studied me with a searching intensity. The encounter with Zhaparov hadn't left visible scars, but I didn't look great, either.

"You are okay?" she asked.

"Just. Tell me what's going on."

"I was questioned. About Vanessa. They showed me a photograph of you, John. They know you're here. I was asked if I knew you, if I'd met you."

"What did you say?"

"I said no."

I tried not to think of the risk she was taking for my own lies. I looked across the people and the paperwork in front of them, their plans for a protest; the coffee table with its bug.

"Can we talk in private?" I said.

"It's okay," Yussopova said. "These are good people."

"I don't know them."

We went to the kitchen. I closed the door, turned the taps on.

"Do you know which department they were from?"

"Police, security service. I don't know. It was in the central police station."

"What did they ask about?"

"They thought I might have documents or information — something from Vanessa. I couldn't understand what they wanted. It wasn't just about our work."

"It's to do with whatever Vanessa found out."

"Yes. You should leave here. Go home."

"It may be too late. I was also questioned by police this morning."

A man came in before she could react. He was small, middle-aged, with a pullover under a mismatched brown suit. He looked unhappy to see a stranger. There was an argument in Russian: *Who is he? How do you know? How do you know who Vanessa was? She brings us a lot of trouble.* I gathered this was Andrei, the communications director, back from Armenia. The last one Joanna had contact with. *And who exactly are Reporters for Human Rights? They also appear suddenly . . .*

Yussopova tried to defend me. "John was arrested too," she told him.

This bought me a moment of consideration. I could see the room through the doorway, responding to the news. I mentioned the treatment I received and a young man in the corner said he was a doctor and offered to check my injuries. There was a hushed sense of danger and opportunity: a Westerner, an Englishman, someone who couldn't be ignored. I could draw international attention to their cause. That attention could get them all killed.

"She spoke to you, before she disappeared," I said to Andrei. He stared at me with small, fiery eyes. "What did she want?" Eventually he said:

"She was asking for all those who had helped with previous campaigns. Not just protests but hackers who have helped us. To capture activism in the twenty-first century. She wanted to know who was local, wanted contact details. We gave her access to the connections we have. She wanted help hacking, maybe."

"Hacking who?"

"I don't know."

"Do you have any idea who she approached?"

"No. We showed her a list we have. Now it has gone. Someone wiped it from our system."

"After you showed her?"

"After she disappeared. Who is she? Who does she share information with?"

I was beginning to understand his mistrust, and why it had turned on me.

"She is one of our best campaigners," I said.

"How long has Reporters for Human Rights been established?"

"It is relatively new, but the individuals involved have been campaigning on these issues for decades."

"Tell me about some of these individuals."

"I've been interrogated once today already. I'm not here to defend myself again."

Andrei's phone rang. He stepped back toward the living room, still staring at me, then turned, taking the call.

"I'm sorry," Yussopova said. "Obviously the situation is very tense."

"Of course. I'd be the same. Do you know anything about this list she saw?"

"Just that Andrei believes she approached someone and it created problems."

"You've no idea who?"

"No."

"What did they ask about Vanessa today, when you were questioned?"

"What languages she spoke, how long she'd been working for Reporters for Human Rights, what countries I knew she'd been in . . ." Yussopova trailed off. She was still in shock. She ran a glass of water and in the light from the kitchen window I saw a fresh burn mark on her right arm—a cigar burn. I lifted her coat off the back of the chair and smelled it.

"Who questioned you?"

"A Russian."

"Could you describe him for me?"

"Smart, clean shaven. He had gray hair, parted."

"Glasses?"

"Yes."

"Tall?"

"It was hard to tell. Certainly not small."

"He did this?"

"What do you think?"

There was a knock at the door. The assembled activists fell quiet.

"It's Irina," someone said. A woman came in, indistinct beneath layers of clothing but visibly pale, with bright, scared eyes.

"Timur and Natalya have been arrested. We should not be here. This place may be bugged. They know about our plans."

"Bugged or penetrated," Andrei said.

"You should go," Yussopova said to me. This time she meant *before the crowd turns.* "This is not your problem. It is not safe for you here, John. Leave Kazakhstan as quickly as possible. In England, tell people what is going on. We will try to find out what happened to Vanessa."

"If anyone asks about me again, don't try to protect me, okay? You are in more danger than I am."

"I don't know if that's true."

Cigar burns.

I called Walker when I was back in my car, asked him to compile a list of Russian visitors to Kazakhstan in the week Joanna Lake disappeared.

"There'll be thousands."

I gave specific names to check. After less than ten minutes he came back with a result. It was one I had hoped not to get. From air traffic control: A Russian-registered Gulfstream G280 jet had landed at an airfield a few miles north of Astana two days before Joanna went missing. It had an armed security license for four passengers, including the jet's owner: Vladislav Vishinsky.

27

A HOTEL ROOM IN TURKEY: JOANNA PACING, CRACKING PISTACHIOS AND flicking the shells toward the bin.

"You think I gas kids? For a psyop? You think that's what we do?"

"No. I don't think that's what anyone does. I'm asking if you had seen any intel beforehand that suggested it might happen. Or if this is total bullshit."

"Of course it's bullshit."

Images on the screen: the chemical attack on the village. She kept it on like someone picking at a scab. Russian TV: *UK government seeks inquiry into intelligence blunder.*

Slick, simple, effective.

"They've humiliated me personally."

"If they targeted you it's because they think you're good."

I remembered Joanna, later that night, sitting on the narrow bed, her back against the wall, eyes closed.

"Is that why you were really sent here?" she asked. "You're over here because they don't trust me?"

"They don't trust anyone."

That was the start of her fixation. Fixations were dangerous in intelligence work. Five months later we were in Shefford. It was the first time I'd seen her after Turkey. We were in her Shefford home, before she got paranoid and reluctant to have me over. And I still wasn't sure if that was about security or what was going on inside, which was her own little research project: notes and clippings in carefully locked drawers, which she checked upon entering, refusing to tell me what they concerned.

I picked the locks when she was asleep, reasoning that she would do the same to me. Kept the Anglepoise lamp on her study desk low, moving the sheets silently so as not to wake her.

The top sheets were printed from Russian news sites: female faces — birth and death dates for each face. All were young women who had jumped off buildings in Russia in the past three months, all of whom had self-harm scars. None was older than twenty-three. Joanna had collected pages of interactions on social media, screen shots, photos of wounds.

The main light came on. Joanna stood in the doorway.

"Christ, Elliot. What are you doing?"

"What is this?" I said.

She took a breath, belted her dressing gown.

"A game," she said.

She put on coffee. We talked for the rest of the night. Joanna had connected several suicides to participation in an online game linked to the Russian-based VKontakte social network, Russia's answer to Facebook. The game consisted of a series of tasks assigned to players by an administrator over a fifty-day period; one task per day, innocuous to begin with, ending with them killing themselves.

"The game was an experiment, we believe. The point of the experiment was to see how far you can generate real-world effects through online activity. To test the limits of what can be achieved remotely, through the progressive desensitization of correspondents. It originates with a unit set up by this man, Vladislav Vishinsky." She brought up a photo, a mugshot, early nineties. "It was him, the one we saw in Ukraine. He was the one who fucked things in Turkey."

"You're sure?"

"I'm going to get the bastard."

"How?"

"Smoking him out. Shining a light. We're close, Elliot."

"In what way?"

"We're getting the structure and operations of their Cybercognitive Warfare unit. Vishinsky set it up. We think he was a qualified psychologist before spending time in prison, though it's not clear what his offenses were, as the record's been wiped. His name appears in a document from 1993 called 'How to Win Wars with Children's Tears.' It's a strategy proposal paper, written while he was locked up, drawing heavily on America's experience in Vietnam. He argues that Russia can't compete on defense expenditure and they should fall back on psychology, use targeted psychological campaigns to bring Russia together and to defeat their enemies abroad. In his words, it involves moving from direct annihilation of the opponent to their inner decay."

Joanna spoke calmly enough, stopping to sip coffee. She had the file in her brain, and relayed information as if it was as native to her as childhood memories.

"You have to understand, for Russia, it's central to their view of modern warfare: The main battlespace is the mind. Vishinsky draws on what the Soviet General Staff call reflexive control theory. It means feeding an opponent specially prepared information so that they make a decision of your choosing. Vishinsky says the digital era is a gift in this respect. Using these tactics, they can reclaim Greater Russia. The paper must have reached some influential people. He's released early, sent to Moscow, given resources within the National Defense Control Center. In documents, his work comes up under the designation Unit 19.

"By the early 2000s, Vishinsky's being referred to as Volshebnik, the magician. We had a Russian defector walk into the British embassy in Istanbul, back in 1998. They were able to describe, in very vague terms, something originating in Unit 19 called Alkhimiya — Project Alchemy — which involved the control of populations. That was 1998, for Christ's sake. Nothing was done.

"On the twenty-second of February, 1999, the eve of Russia's annual Defenders of the Fatherland holiday, the defense minister Sergei Shoigu announced the creation of a new information operations force combining cybertroops and cyberpropagandists. It built on existing know-how. They had sophisticated means of tracking the morale of enemy troops. The internet allowed them to extend this to entire nations. Their sensitivity to national psyches allowed them to craft tailor-made psychological campaigns. Vishinsky's GRU textbook even advised different approaches to waging psychological warfare on different NATO members: "abstract-logical" propaganda for the Germans, visuals for the French and Americans etc. Around the turn of the millennium it stopped being simply a tool of Kremlin policy and began to affect the policy itself. Vishinsky was advising Putin directly.

"It was around this time Putin changed his tone. He had started out as a pragmatic realist when it came to world affairs, but now he became Mr. Nationalist. He got an ideology: reclaiming the former Soviet Union. Vishinsky produced speeches and propaganda along these lines and it played well. It was a narrative, a national goal: Make Russia great again. The extra territory would mean access to a lot of oil and gas. And he had persuaded Putin that they could compete, thanks to this new cognitive warfare unit."

Joanna talked through the dawn, but never told me what she intended to do about all this, or who she was working with at Shefford and in what ways this would allow her to claim revenge.

Budget around seventy million pounds over two years; eighty members of staff cleared; officially designated a research group, but the security setup suggests it was operational . . .

Then closed down in the blink of an eye. Six months ago. Sabotaged?

The report from air traffic control gave us Vishinsky landing at a military airfield in Koyandy, north of Astana, at ten a.m. on November 22. I opened my laptop, checked what had been trending on Kazakh social media in the last twenty-four hours. The president's daughter had been chalked up as a judge on *SuperstarKZ*; the regional governor of Mangystau had proposed bird watching as a potential tourist attraction; a Russian woman had been raped in northern Kazakhstan, close to the Russian border.

I clicked.

Several news sites carried high-definition photos of the victim's face, bruised and tear-stained. Her name was Yulia Lysenko; she lived in Schuchinsk. A lot of people with Russian surnames were sharing the story across various platforms, connecting it to an attack a few miles away in Petropavl, a majority-Russian village where a cultural center had been burned down.

The woman was Russian, the rapists were alleged to be ethnic Kazakh. People were posting photos of angry crowds. They held signs that read KAZAKHSTAN IS RUSSIA.

28

"HOW DIRECTLY DOES THE KREMLIN CONTROL THIS UNIT?" WALKER asked.

"Arm's length. But Vishinsky is close to Putin. Nothing's going to happen without approval."

"And it dates back to Ukraine?"

"It predates Ukraine. It's drawn from psychological work their Main Intelligence Directorate was doing in the sixties. But we started getting a concrete picture of how it functions in 2014. I think Joanna was working on it before leaving Six. Vishinsky arriving here now, just as Joanna disappears, feels too much for coincidence."

"What are you suggesting?"

"I've no idea. Are you sure she cut her ties with Six? Sometimes ops evaporate on activation. She might have been using you as cover."

"Lovely. And it's me who has to clear up the mess." Walker looked exasperated. "I'm going to have to report progress soon. Do you still think you can find out more?"

"Yes. But not without some money to spend."

We were in the private room of a canteen inside the White and Chase building, away from other suits, a platter of sushi going to waste between us. Walker had collected me from reception, dropped some unspecified paperwork off in his temporary office, which gave me another view of the keypad and the electronics setup. He'd been hungry so we went up to the canteen, which he'd assured me was secure. I'd decided not to mention my own arrest, or run-in with Sergei Cherenkov, partly to see if Walker knew. Partly because I wanted resources, and the more untouchable I seemed, the more likely he was to give them to me. So far there was no suggestion Walker knew I'd had trouble.

"Vishinsky represents an expansionist, hawkish, ultra-cynical circle at the heart of the Kremlin," I said. "They push the narrative that NATO is seeking to encircle Russia. When they wanted Crimea annexed, Vishinsky had to assure Putin it could work. He masterminded the combining of cyberwarfare, kinetic attacks, propaganda, and what the Russians call Maskirovka: masking, military deception. He was on the ground in the weeks before the invasion, preparing for it. Now he's here."

"Why now?"

"I don't know. I think Joanna knows. She tried to get out. Look."

I showed him the file Shomko had sent through. Walker studied the plane tickets to Caracas, the fake names. If this didn't win his backing, I thought, he either knew where she was or didn't care.

"How did you get this?" he asked.

"I bought it. The investigation concerning Joanna has been moved away from the units you'd expect to be handling it. This is from Antiterrorism. Chief of Kazakh Antiterrorism is Rakim Zhaparov."

Walker nodded as if this made sense. He pincered some sashimi. He didn't push for the source. He understood the rules of the game — an asset is an asset. You don't share.

"It fits the picture we're building. Zhaparov has Kremlin ties."

"What do you know about him?"

"Relatively young, ambitious. Supposedly waging a war against militant Islam. Close to Moscow. Not a pleasant creature if certain reports are anything to go by. And he's caused us problems before. He wants Saracen out of Kazakhstan. Wants all US and European companies out."

"Has he got the muscle to do that?"

"The only muscle in this country is the president, and he thinks kicking out Western oil companies will ruin the place. He's keen for Kazakhstan to seem international, competitive, independent. Zhaparov's a Moscow puppet. Whenever the president gets too cozy with the West, suddenly Zhaparov has resources from Russia, usually in the name of counterterrorism, keeping Kazakhstan a buffer between Russia and Islamists. It was Zhaparov who banned praying in public, and installed pro-government imams. But it's obvious he's also a buffer against the West. Moscow's nervous about Galina, the president's daughter. She's pro-West, loves the UK. When Putin annexed Crimea, she encouraged her father to start diversifying military purchases away from Russia. When Moscow tried to get Kazakhstan to join in with countersanctions against Europe, she pushed her father to decline. And she hates Zhaparov. A few years back, when he was chief prosecutor, he went after one of her boyfriends for money laundering."

"And we're tight with Galina?"

"We shower her with gold."

"How much?"

"Millions. A lot of it is property, mostly for family members. But she's our best chance. Lucy Piper always says that the way to a president's heart is through his daughter."

"Cute, but she's not in charge yet," I said. "What's the president's own relationship with Moscow like?"

Walker considered before responding, dipping a maki roll in soy sauce and then abandoning it there.

"Kazakhstan's always been a staunch Russian ally, but Ukraine made them uneasy. Nazarbayev walks a tightrope. A few years ago, they started limiting Russian broadcasting over here. Russian officials complained, and now it's an offense to even think about preventing them. A lot of Russians came here in Soviet times. Most of those remaining are in the north of the country, close to the Motherland, and the main government policy seems to be not to antagonize them." Walker looked at the police file again. "What did Joanna stumble into?"

"I'm not sure she stumbled. I think she walked purposefully toward an obsession she's been nursing for years. That's what I'm worried about."

Walker groaned. "Robert Carter's going to go mad when he finds out about all this."

"What do you mean?"

"Moscow's scuppered big deals of his before. You know he had plans for a pipeline in Turkmenistan? It was closed down at the last minute as a result of political pressure from China and Russia. Billions written off." Walker shook his head. But even as he expressed his concern for Carter's traumatic experiences with Russia, I could see his eyes glinting. He was one of those men who saw opportunity in traumatized billionaires.

"Your source," he said, "the one who got you the information — you think he can find Joanna?"

"More easily than we can alone. But he costs. I need the money I asked for."

"What about time? How long do you think you need to find out what's happened to her?"

"Five days."

"Wait here."

I watched Walker head in the direction of his office, and then I watched the main restaurant through the doorway: white-shirted men with chopsticks and Breitlings and thick windows between them and the world. Lives lived thirty floors up. As we'd entered the building I'd got another look at the entry procedure, the cameras and stairways; Evotec had produced an original planning application for the block including architectural drawings that gave us the server room in the basement. All this was habit, but so was distrust.

I checked news on my phone, then social media, feeling for traces of Vishinsky and his manipulation of populations. A story had started trending: Two young Kazakh men who'd fought in Ukraine on the pro-Russian side had been sentenced to five years each. *Heroes jailed.* They'd actually been sentenced last year, but the story had gone viral again. Meanwhile someone had painted *This is Kazakhstan* on a hillside in the north of the country in white letters ten feet high. I was wondering how much effort and paint that would take when Walker returned with a laptop case branded ASTANA 2018.

"This is what you asked for," he said. Inside was thirty grand's worth of paper money divided equally into plastic wallets of dollars, tenge, and rubles.

Like most cases of money, it felt dirty, dangerous, and very useful.

When I was in my car I called Stefan.

"Are we playing?" he said.

"Yes. Tell Marius I've got the money in cash."

"Okay."

"I want you in Astana's Hilton Garden Inn. I've booked a room. Target will be directly below. His name is Callum Walker. He may be running countersurveillance, so move gently. I'll tell you more when you get here."

I called Geoff Purvis in the GL5 compound, and we established procedures for a quick escape.

On my way back to the hotel, I stopped at a hunting shop and bought bullets and cold-weather gun lubricant. I drove out to the desert to test-fire the gun but struggled to find anything to aim at, eventually firing once toward the horizon before my fingers went numb.

29

I CHECKED OUT OF THE LION HOTEL AND INTO THE RAMADA PLAZA. IT was more in keeping with the Bell cover, and I had a superstition about sleeping where I'd been arrested. The Ramada put a lot more blue-carpeted corridor between me and the world, even if I knew it was a false sense of security. An eager bellboy, no older than nineteen, helped me with my cases.

"Where'd you learn English?" I asked.

"Here. I like to talk to people."

"Follow football?"

"Of course. My team is Chelsea."

"Abramovich."

"Yes." He grinned.

"Know Astana well?"

"Very well."

"Where did you grow up?"

"Shymkent."

"Deep south. Isn't that what they say? I heard it's like the Wild West down there."

"It is different. The jobs are here."

"Well, you've earned this." I folded some Kazakh currency into his hand. Loyal bellboys were a godsend.

I locked the Makarov in the safe, went to the bar.

The hotel's bar was a cavernous, Hollywood-themed place with a lot of young staff and few customers. It served food through the night: Happy hour was eight p.m. to two a.m. For a city with no evident desire to party the night away, Astana had a lot of places that never closed. I drank a beer and thought of the lines by Thomas Mann: *In an empty, unarticulated space our mind loses its sense of time as well.* He was describing a sea crossing, but it fit Astana. *Our mind loses its sense of time and we enter the twilight of the immeasurable. Dämmerung des unermesslichen.*

I reviewed my knowledge of the situation so far.

Joanna Lake had acquired information and possibly contacts through Testimony. For reasons that remained unclear, she got something from a man who'd now been shot. She got hold of a vehicle, then thoroughly vanished.

But there was a bigger picture that involved her leaving Shefford, the closing down of that operation, her appearance in Kazakhstan and then Vishinsky's arrival.

I wondered if her presence might have alerted Vishinsky to something.

Meanwhile, from everything I could see, it looked like he was preparing the ground for conflict. A psychological war had begun, raising tensions between Russia and Kazakhstan. Did it involve fake videos of myself? Was that the context for Joanna's discovery? She saw what someone had planned, tried to warn me. Here I was.

Stumped.

Cherenkov wanted knowledge of Perfect Vision. So did I. Predicting the future, Marsh had said. I tried to imagine a piece of forecasting software effective enough to inspire the envy of foreign governments. A crystal ball. Or it was something else entirely, some means of defeating Russia's psyops. A truth machine.

Cyber capabilities would give me access to the insides of things — computers, phone calls, locked rooms. I needed Stefan to arrive. There was also a growing ethical issue regarding national interests. If this was a Russian invasion on the horizon I needed to inform the UK. Stevenson's words haunted me: *There's changes in priorities. Russia's got the wind in their sails. Syria's a test bed.* I could inform Six by some back channel. But why hadn't she?

The men who had attacked the Russian woman had now been named on social media.

I typed their names into Google to see if they really existed. It was hard to say without a photo. Meanwhile, two Kazakh brothers had been hospitalized in what sounded like revenge attacks in a village nearby, their family home set alight.

I called the hospital mentioned in reports and eventually got through to a doctor who sounded young, stressed and tired.

"I'm a cousin of the men who were attacked," I said. "Can I speak to them?"

"No."

"But they are there?"

"We can't give you any information."

"I'm family."

"Makes no difference."

"Can I just check — were there any men admitted at all?"

He confirmed that two men had been brought in but wouldn't give any more details. I found the number for a bar in the area owned by a woman called Olga Sergeeva, which was a Russian surname. Sergeeva herself answered.

"This is Dmitry Zubkov from the *Moscow Times*."

"What do you want?" she said.

"How are things there? We in Russia are concerned. How are people feeling?"

"People feel there is a lot of crap around." The woman hung up.

Joanna's voice returned: *He is beyond cynical, Elliot. That is what we haven't understood.*

I know.

You say you met him.

I thought I had. 2003. Baku, Azerbaijan.

I hadn't realized until later that Vishinsky was the individual concerned. At the time he'd been just one strange encounter in a series of them. Baku had been an *Agentsumpf* for sure, a baptism of oil and fire for a young officer. By the time I got to the place there'd been five years of dark-side operations. MI6 had scrambled to help British business mop up what they could of the former-Soviet oil industry. When the wrong man got into power, backed by Russia, MI6 was tasked with sorting out a countercoup. My predecessors set up ratlines: back-door arms channels from dumps in Turkey via Armenia. They got a more amenable dictator in place. Three months later, £5 billion worth of energy deals were signed.

The whole project had been set up by men and women with experience in Bosnia, of drugs for arms networks. Intelligence work doesn't have a rule book, which means people fall back on what they know, which isn't always sophisticated. I arrived to help deal with the fallout. It was one of my first operations for Six, running an agent close to the deposed dictator and trying to anticipate blowback. I was twenty-four, out of my depth, and excited to be there. The experience should have left me feeling disillusioned but I didn't want illusions anyway; I felt only delight at getting the chance to see geopolitics up close. I think Vishinsky sensed that: the vulnerability of appetite.

The old Soviet Intourist Hotel was the only place foreign oil execs were allowed to stay, an ugly concrete slab on Neftchiler Prospekt — Oilmen's Avenue. With the oil came middlemen, warlords, prostitutes, and mercenaries. The US, Turkish, and Russian embassies were all located in the hotel itself. The UK embassy was in the offices of BP down the road, which told you all you needed to know. Azeri security services had comprehensively bugged the place. If you needed to talk to a politician you could say their name in an empty room and they'd turn up an hour or so later. People chained cases to their wrists to move down corridors. No one left the building. Deliveries of paper and whisky came in each morning. If you were curious about what the world looked like you could open your curtains and gaze across the derelict rigs crumbling into the sea.

I thought I was the only one to get out and about. Daily, midafternoon, I'd walk past boomtown Baku, dutifully checking reflections in the windows of Bulgari and Armani to see if I'd been followed, but also spying on the shops themselves — the importation of capitalism as impossible dreams. I'd walk through Bibi-Heybat, a suburb where the first ever oil well had been drilled, to an industrial zone called Black City where refinery chimneys colored the sky gray with smoke. Offshore rig platforms looked like churches floating on air, the spires of the drilling towers hazy in mist. Someone told me they'd sunk seven ships to form the foundation for the offshore platform, one of which was the first oil tanker, *Zoroaster*. Something about that gesture sang to me. I loved the vision, and the name. I put some research into its origins, and learned that Baku used to be a place of Zoroastrian pilgrimage, known as the shrine of fire, with burning gas leaking straight out of the ground. And in this, I felt, was some deep connection through time, a bridge of hunger and worship. In those days I thought like that; I was still writing poems.

When the weather was good, I'd walk to a spot on the coast from which you got a glimpse of *Neft Daslari* — Oil Rocks — a town on stilts in the sea made from two thousand rust-bitten drilling platforms joined by a network of bridges, with floating eight-story apartment blocks for the workers. One particular day was clearer than most and I was trying to make out what remained. I didn't notice the tall, elegant Russian approaching, cigar in hand.

I was sure I hadn't been followed. Yet I could see no reason for someone else to be there. And he made no attempt to disguise the approach — no attempt at cover — he had sought me out, and was happy for me to know it. It was Vladislav Vishinsky, although the name meant nothing to me then.

We fell into polite, mutually curious conversation.

"You are interested in history," he said, which was obvious enough. "I am too."

He told me that when the tsarist regime began to crumble in the early twentieth century, the oil workers of Baku went on strike. One of their leaders was a young Joseph Stalin. Vishinsky gestured to the city behind us and described the whole place in flames, even the waves of the sea, covered in oil from the burning wells.

"And what did Stalin seize first in the uproar? The printing presses." Vishinsky's eyes gleamed. I remember thinking he was intelligent, that he liked the sound of his own voice, that he appeared to have prepared his speech for me personally.

"Stalin gave us a destiny," Vishinsky said. "That was his genius. And then that destiny vanished. The future itself . . ." He waved the future away with his cigar, as if some magic trick had been performed and it still caused him wonder. "You have not felt that. In the West you are children, easily scared and with few memories. You do not know despair. But perhaps you will learn."

We met a couple more times, exchanged numbers. He contacted me after I left Baku. I wondered why he was interested in me. There was a strong possibility these were the first feints of a recruit, I thought, flattering myself. Now I wonder. In retrospect it felt more like a test — the way fighter jets fly into an enemy's airspace to watch the defenses light up. I lit up. Maybe he was attracted to me for less professional reasons.

The following week, back in Vauxhall, I put together a case for playing along. The idea was turned down as too risky. In the chaos of the next few years I almost forgot the whole thing. Then I saw him in Kiev. Or, at least, Joanna saw him.

"He nodded at me," she said. "As if he knew who I was." She showed me the picture she'd got later that night. There was no doubt, it was the man who had approached me in Baku, looking less playful now.

"What do you know about him?" she asked.

I shared the fruits of my initial research, when we were considering engaging him: He was hypernationalistic, believed in regaining lost Soviet glory. Tight with anti-Western circles in both Moscow and Saint Petersburg fighting to restore Russian pride and geopolitical teeth. I thought of him during Ukraine's Orange Revolution, witnessing the people's desire for freedom, for a turn to the West, thinking about how much he must hate it. And I thought of him nine years later when the first *Novorussiya* accounts appeared — "New Russia" — with dedicated websites and domain names. I remembered the phrase from my degree, though no one else in the office seemed to grasp the significance — *Novorussiya* was what Russians called the Crimea in the eighteenth century, when it was annexed by Catherine the Great. Two weeks later, Russian troops took control of the main route to Sevastopol. Men in anonymous uniforms occupied the Crimean parliament building. Across the intelligence service there was disbelief. And the Russians got away with it because the psychological groundwork had been laid.

"They're playing a bigger game than us," Joanna had said then. "They have a vision. We make it up as we go along."

Ten years later, her concerns about Vishinsky were more personal. Over dinner at an Italian restaurant in Milton Keynes she said that she'd been slipped some gossip from a friend on the Russian desk. Vishinsky had a file on us: on the two of us, a supposed team.

"We're on his radar." She got me access to a copy of the GRU report. It included a picture of us in Kiev's Navodnitsky Park, together with attempts at establishing our real identities and, in classic Russian style, the intimate details of our relationship. *Not believed to be sexual partners.* There were question marks over my sexuality. Joanna was labeled *besporyadochny* — chaotic, anarchic, with overtones of promiscuity. The report had been prepared for Vishinsky himself.

"What fueled his interest in us?" I asked.

"He's convinced that we were involved in a US-led coup in Ukraine. Refuses to buy genuine democratic yearnings. I think we've found his own paranoia."

She kept probing me, provoked by Vishinsky's attention on her:

You met him. What did he do? What did he say?

I told her. He said: "People who believe in nothing still believe in oil." And here we were.

I gazed across the windowless bar, its Hollywood-themed memorabilia: old film posters, a gleaming jukebox. TV screens showed news.

The Kazakh rape story had been picked up internationally. But a quick check online showed that it originated from one local news site. The website was called NewAsia: It was big on graphics and pop music, and drew heavily on social media. It had been set up a year ago, and seemed to survive without much advertising. Some rudimentary searches gave me ten VKontakte accounts that appeared to have linked to the story almost as soon as it went up, mostly women, mostly young, with several thousand followers each.

Where had I seen that website? I found the dating app on my phone, checked the first match.

You seem interesting. Check out this site — lots of fun there.

I clicked through to NewAsia, which had put a photo of the victim on its landing page.

30

I SPENT TOO MUCH OF THE NIGHT BROWSING, UNTIL I STARTED TO believe the region's entire internet had been gamed. Stories fueling Russian resentment came up everywhere you looked.

Fired for speaking Russian. Statue removed. Beat up on the way to school.

People in public services were being forced to speak Kazakh rather than Russian; a politician who resisted the new language laws had been assaulted at a rally. Alongside those kinds of stories was a low-level hum of outrage and titillation: mother shamed in Kazakh restaurant, teacher beats pupil; child abducted by Muslims. Meanwhile, on the same sites, the epidemic of homosexuality in the West got good coverage, as did Europe's spiritual bankruptcy in general. NATO was heading for extinction, Russia ready to bring peace to the Middle East.

I logged in as Yuri Cherchesov, my Russian sailor persona, and liked several pictures of "Kazakh militias" targeting Russians in northern Kazakhstan. These supposed militias posed with antique horsebows apparently looted from a museum. They urinated on a portrait of Putin from behind blurred pixels.

Vishinsky's great insight: Propaganda didn't have to be believed to be effective, to make you angry, or act. No more than pornography had to be believed to make you come. It just had to keep you staring, feed your fantasies.

Women's tears, women's shame, everywhere I looked.

There were various ways sophisticated cyber operations could enhance information warfare: Devices and websites can both be infected so you get steered the right way, apparently mainstream news websites look authentic but aren't, selected pages shoot up the rankings. I searched for the same phrases or links appearing simultaneously; big waves of people piling in to comment, then repeating the process at regular intervals. I amassed fifty accounts, ten blogs, and six websites that struck me as suspect or just heavily anti-West and sent them through to Evotec to see if they could get me anything: matches with previous cyber operations, source IPs, syntactic patterns to see how many people were producing this. Every major military power had units running social media now. NATO and US Central Command had poured millions into it in the last couple of years, but they were playing catch-up. The West couldn't compete with the office blocks in Moscow and Shanghai filled with young men and women at this work. You used to be able to analyze the dodgy English: The Chinese skipped plurals; Russian's a phonetic language so spelling tended to be a weak point. But it was getting more sophisticated on all fronts. Bots came fleshed out, with face shots scraped from Picasa and Flickr. The software existed to create hundreds of these a minute, inserting them into comment threads and forums, interacting with people just like a human. But software couldn't do everything.

I called Walker at eight a.m. and talked information warfare. I told him I needed to speak to whoever managed the digital side of Saracen's reputation. He said social media was monitored by Piper Anderson themselves. Piper Anderson's CEO, Lucy Piper, was on the ground in Kazakhstan, currently with a trade delegation. I said it could be useful for me to meet with her, and he said he'd put a call in.

"Does she know about Joanna?" I asked.

"Unfortunately."

I caught up with the delegation in the city center, at the opening of a Saracen-sponsored museum of archaeology. Its creamy imitation marble had been engraved with the message ENERGY AWAKENS ANCIENT HISTORY. A lot of men and a few women circulated in the atrium with branded name badges: BAE, Glaxo, Whitbread; some junior ministers, journalists, a university chancellor. I caught a glimpse of the British ambassador to Kazakhstan, Suzanna Ford, slightly disheveled in a gray skirt suit, laughing and sipping tea. She turned, met my eyes before I could look away, gave the smile of someone having to smile at everyone. I couldn't see Piper.

The new museum displayed fragments of pottery they'd dug up, alongside bad watercolors of a traditional nomad community. At the end of the main hall was a temporary display regarding wildlife protection, signed off by an organization I'd never heard of called Clean Caspian. The ribbon had already been cut and hung limply on either side of the entrance. Four silver minibuses waited to transport the delegation back to the Marriott once a group of schoolchildren had finished burying a time capsule for an unspecified future generation to pore over. The capsule was a Tupperware box, and the hole into which it was being deposited had been created in the icy courtyard with the help of a blowtorch. The ceremony was being filmed, with a lot of effort going into ensuring that the Saracen logo was visible at all times.

When a lull came, I introduced myself to the man with the camera, whose name badge identified him as an employee of Piper Anderson Communications. He said Lucy was at the Marriott dealing with a last-minute emergency, but I could hitch a ride back to the hotel with them.

At the Marriott I was directed to a restaurant, dimly lit, with tables set for the next day. Empty apart from one person.

Lucy Piper stood alone at the windows, phone to her ear. She wore a white suit, her blond hair up in a bun, eyes cool. The screen of a MacBook glowed on the table behind her. She was having a bad day.

"No . . . I don't know . . . It's worse than we thought."

In the low-lit comfort it took me a second to connect her to the figure I'd seen stepping among the former Taliban like some mascara-laden angel of history. I'd been one male face in a large crowd of them, and couldn't imagine she'd recognize me, but it was a risk I was willing to take. Piper looked distracted anyway. There was a lot of paperwork on the table, pinned down with a vape the size of a Colt .45.

She hung up, put on a professional smile.

"Hey there."

"Lucy Piper? I work for Vectis. Toby Bell."

She extended a hand. "Callum mentioned your name. Another former commando?"

"Something like that."

No flicker of recognition. Her phone lit up again and she scrolled through a message.

"One moment."

I scanned the documents lying around as she punched a reply. They had the day's analytics: Google results for "Saracen," "Saracen Kazakhstan," "Kazakhstan corruption." There was an interesting map showing the geographical distribution of anti-Saracen social media accounts in the country. Beside this was a bad photocopy of a petition launched by

Testimony—*The lavish trade mission is a green light to political oppression . . .*—along with a strategy to smother it, which looked like it might involve an organization called the Kazakhstan Business Alliance whose contact number was a London landline.

Piper's company was well-connected, with direct lines to the EU and the UN. But it was their dark arts that kept the clients coming: managing Wikipedia entries, controlling astroturfed NGOs, manipulating Google results so that the first thing you saw when you searched "Saracen Kazakhstan" wasn't a middle-aged woman with blood running into her eyes.

Much brighter were the photos of local kids burying their time capsule. They'd just appeared on her screen as part of a blog post: "British Secretary of State for Industry Leads Largest-Ever Trade Mission Seeking to Cement UK-Kazakhstan Ties."

She put her phone away and sat down, gesturing for me to do the same.

"Any news?" she said. "On the . . . situation?"

"We're working hard to resolve it. Without any great breakthroughs so far. There's an equally pressing matter that's come to light. It looks like we've got something of a Russian influence operation on our hands."

Piper sighed. "Russian influence."

"Have you had issues with any unusual online activity?" I asked.

"Issues? Reality is melting. That's an issue. That's new terrain. How long have you got?"

She clicked on a video, turned the MacBook toward me. Five men in black uniforms surrounded a compact red car, a Daewoo Nexia on a narrow road. They pulled the doors open and dragged three men in T-shirts and jeans out of the car, forcing them to lie facedown on the ground. There was a rocky escarpment on one side of the road, a fence on the other. One of the uniformed men pulled a handgun and fired at the men's legs, making them squirm.

Title: "Saracen Oil's Private Army." Posted today, 7,324 views.

"Genuine?" I said.

"We're checking. There's quite a lot of GL5 in the country. The views have doubled in the last couple of hours, and it's just been posted by Nat Gould, the US activist. All of which shows you why a story about a woman who turns out to have been spying for Saracen and got herself caught up in fuck-knows-what could give us a lot of fires to put out."

The original source of the GL5 video was an account called Miss P, with a picture of a Disney princess as an avatar. Piper tapped a neat nail against the image.

"Eight months tweeting diet tips and inspirational quotes," she said. "*Count your age by friends, not years. Count your life by smiles, not tears.* Fine. There are makeup tips, a guide to Astana, then, on the twenty-third of November, Miss P finds a social conscience and goes in heavy on abuse by private security contractors. Suddenly this is all she cares about. She posts on various platforms and gets big amplification."

A quick glance at the analytics told me it was textbook Vishinsky — or, at least, the textbook his unit had developed. You establish shepherd accounts — active and influential people who kick off a trending topic. For that you need a large number of followers and interaction with high-profile players. Those are difficult to establish, and need to be run by humans, but you only need a few. Sheepdog accounts follow and are also run by humans. They retweet the stories and riff on them, turning up the heat, making the whole thing a real viral moment. Then come the sheep — the zombie army of bots — helping to amplify it and spread the stories across platforms.

Up next on Piper's tour of melting reality was the still image of a young woman sitting in the snow, crying, forked tributaries of blood down her face.

"What happened to her?" I asked.

"Attacked by police during protests in a town called Semey."

"Connected to a rape?"

"I don't know. I don't think so."

The picture came attached to a report on a citizen journalism website called Open Voices. "Tensions Simmer as Protests Continue."

Semey was in the northeast of Kazakhstan, close to the border with Russia. It was famous for hosting Dostoevsky and, a century later, the Soviet Union's primary nuclear test site. Its central square had been occupied, which at minus twenty degrees suggested a serious level of commitment. Origins of the protests were unclear — the report alluded to ongoing refusal by local authorities to allow environmental campaigning or union activities. Last week, three students had been arrested for inciting discord. Rather than quashing things, the situation blew up. Locals were now out in force with photographs of the students and banners demanding justice.

It didn't vibe ethnic conflict, more anti-oppression. People were sing-ing. Some of the elders wore traditional Kazakh clothing.

"The signs say things like 'Put the People First,'" I said. "'Protect Workers' Rights.'"

"Okay," Piper said.

They looked genuine: homemade, not mass-produced—varying handwriting, different paint and ink. Someone lifted up a Styrofoam model resembling the Goddess of Democracy statue erected by protest-ers on Tiananmen Square.

I clicked back to the men being dragged out of the Daewoo.

"Who filmed this?"

"A member of the public."

"Just passing by? It's not filmed through a windscreen."

"That's true."

"Have the British press picked up any of this?"

"I'm managing to keep them at bay for now."

"This is a handheld camera, not a phone."

"You reckon?"

"It's too sharp for a phone, too much detail in the shadows." I listened to the voices in the background, checked the uniforms, then some of the other videos posted which purportedly documented GL5 misconduct: a man in his underwear bleeding on a concrete floor, someone handcuffed to a fence. "At least two of the other videos are from Georgia," I said. "Shot five years ago at least. You can hear the voices in the background, the ac-cents."

Piper nodded slowly, eyes lighting up. "Interesting," she said. "You're sure?"

"That's a Georgian number plate in the background."

She grabbed her phone and stood up.

"Get yourself a drink."

Piper wandered over to the window and made a call, touching her forehead to the glass.

"We may have some ammunition . . . Yes, I'll send that . . . No, we don't want to drive more traffic unnecessarily . . ."

I went through her bag. In a thick Gucci wallet I found a swipe pass identical to the one Walker had used to access the Vectis office block. I pocketed it. I went to the bar and helped myself to a glass of water. She came back thoughtful.

"Do you think your missing colleague connects to all this?"

"Maybe."

Piper took a hit on the vape, disappeared briefly behind an apple-scented cloud.

"Shit," she said. Then she turned to me again, flapping a hand at the steam. "You've been here awhile?"

"Why?"

"You seem to understand this place more than most people."

"I wouldn't say that."

"How do you see it?" She brought up footage of the crowd in Semey. "Is this a revolution? That's what I'm worried about. A Central Asian spring?"

"No. People like the president. They like what he's done."

"These guys?" Piper pointed at a clipping on the table: "Kazakh Police Break Up Strikers."

"They aren't protesting about the president. They want a pay raise. We have strikes in the UK."

She nodded. I felt her warming to me and pressed on, trying to imagine what Toby Bell would say.

"This region's got failed states all around, and here's one that's doubled its GDP, that hasn't been at war. The population's generally happy. It's got religious pluralism."

"That's what we tell people."

"Churches, synagogues. It's a secular Islamic state: modern, open-minded. Isn't that what everyone wants?"

"Where is there a synagogue?"

"Almaty. There's even close ties to Israel. You don't have to draw too much attention to that, but it's true."

"Like Turkey used to be," Piper said.

"Sure, but less complicated. A young, optimistic Turkey without Kurds."

"What are you doing tomorrow morning?"

"Why?"

"Some of the more cautious members of the UK delegation are unconvinced about British involvement here — they still see Kazakhstan as a high-risk environment. Last thing we want is Saracen stakeholders getting cold feet. I could do with them meeting someone articulate, with a few facts at their fingertips. A little brunch to get everyone onside."

"Brunch is good," I said, conscious that I was getting caught up in my own acting ability. We swapped numbers. Piper took another suck of vapor, sizing me up.

"You should meet Galina. She'd like you."

"The president's daughter?"

"She likes English men."

"Why not? I'm a sociable guy." We shook hands. I stood up. "Can I ask a weird question?" I said.

"Sure."

"What was in the time capsule?"

"Time capsule?"

"At the ribbon-cutting ceremony."

"Oh. I don't know. An iPhone, a football shirt, I think. Some poems by local children, their hopes for the future. Why?"

"I just wondered. I'm curious about how they see the future. Any idea what their hopes are?"

"Their hopes? I have no idea. It was all in Kazakh."

31

I drove over to the Hilton, checked that there was no lookout in the hotel's lobby, then walked through to the back stairs and up to the room I'd booked for him.

"I'm going to get some food," I said, knocking, using our usual code.

He opened the door in shorts and a hoody, headphones around his neck. It was good to see him.

"Elliot," he said, gripping my hand once I was inside. "Where the fuck am I?"

"Winter wonderland. I appreciate you stopping by."

Stefan kept his hair cropped military-close, a neat beard with the first touches of gray that made his cheeks look more sunken than they were and brought out the blue, insomniac intensity of his eyes. His room already smelled of energy drinks, a chemical undertone to the pine-scented toiletries. He had the curtains closed, TV on Formula One. There were three computers set up, a MacBook on the bed, two Panasonics on the bureau: rugged, magnesium-alloy-encased laptops of the kind used by the military. One was connected to a Wave Box—a portable device that generously bestowed strong, password-free Wi-Fi to all those within five hundred meters or so. It gave us all of the Internet traffic flowing through it—email, instant messages, and browser sessions.

"What's going on?" Stefan asked.

"Why?"

"I placed a wall-contact mic near the room you're interested in. The occupant makes and takes calls on a dedicated satt phone; deep encryption. Plays white noise from an audio jammer."

Stefan showed me images he'd taken of Walker's hotel room using an under-door camera. The camera was the thickness of a credit card, and one of his favorite toys. Walker's room was neat. You saw the audio jammer on the bureau, a black box barely bigger than a cigarette packet. A suitcase had been lifted to the bed, which was made. There was a suit over the back of a chair and a bottle of whisky beside the bed.

"Is he in there now?"

"He left ten minutes ago. So who am I spying on? What are we doing here?"

"A woman's missing. She was working in Astana for Vectis, the private intelligence company run by the individual downstairs, using the audio jammer. She's vanished. We need to find her."

"Why? Who is she?"

"A former colleague of mine. Her name's Joanna Lake."

"How long's she been missing?"

"Seven days now." I talked him through the mall swap, the email she'd sent from the IT café. Stefan checked the locations on a map, then sat back and sipped his Red Bull. It was a relief to have someone I trusted around. Stefan had been a teenager when I first met him, ten years ago. He came to my attention in a dusty office belonging to New Scotland Yard's cybercrimes division. Seventeen years old, born in north London to Polish parents, he'd been arrested for hacking his school's system, then promptly hacked into the police unit investigating him, before crashing the Home Office website. He already had a criminal conviction for breaking into electronics stores to steal equipment. That placed him in a slightly different, more exciting category for me. After being released on bail he'd tried to escape the country, but was picked up at Dover with his brother's passport. I got him released the next day. A year later he was helping GCHQ develop battlefield capability, and a year after that directing cyber ops in Afghanistan. If he ever wished I'd left him at the mercy of Scotland Yard, he was polite enough not to say so.

A couple of years later I was in Dubai when I heard that someone at the Burj Al Arab was wiping minibar accounts from the hotel system. I found him locked in his room, drinking a cocktail of Mountain Dew, tequila, and zopiclone, war-fatigued and gambling heavily. I paid off his debts and put him in touch with Marius in Romania, who regularly asked for contacts on the ground: people who could infiltrate delivery chains or break into places covertly. We had trained Stefan in that, refining his native criminality. And he had the rare combination of skill and greed that made men return to conflict zones voluntarily. I got him a six-figure salary knowing he was worth twice as much.

"You think she's still in the area?" he asked.

"I think it's a possibility. I think she discovered something that was dangerous for her. Look out for the words 'Perfect Vision,'" I said. "And 'Catalyst.'"

Stefan nodded. He'd heard enough cryptonyms in his time, and knew not to ask for more knowledge than he needed.

"There's a range of places I'd like to know more about: Kazakh security services to start with, then Gazprom offices and the Russian embassy."

I showed him the map I'd marked up with cafés and restaurants near the buildings I was interested in. Often the secret was not to try to directly hack the offices themselves, but find where staff congregated with unprotected smartphones and laptops. Stefan had a Polar Breeze — a remote data-sucking device for tapping wirelessly into nearby computers — and a Stingray, which was able to mimic a cell tower and force all phones in a two-hundred-meter radius to connect to it. From there, it could extract contact information, dialed numbers, text messages, calendar entries. It could also give you a steppingstone into an entire network.

"Most of all, I'd like to know why she's working for Vectis, and anything they might be keeping from me."

I showed him the plan of the Vectis office.

"All their computing's on a closed network, but I reckon we can establish a physical breach." I handed him Piper's swipe pass. He turned it in his fingers. "TensorCo electronic gates at the front," I said. "Dozy security. Two dozen different companies across the building. The swipe will work the lifts as well. Office entrance is PIN code; possibly thirty-five seventy-nine or thirty-five seventy. Facilities maintenance for the building is done by a German company called Apleona, and that includes IT. Server room's in the basement."

"And this is a job for Six?"

"It's a job for me."

"How are your diplomatic relations with the Kazakh government when I end up in trouble?"

"We use the usual contingency plans. There's a big security team here; you don't have to worry about that."

Stefan looked unconvinced. We agreed to rendezvous the following day. I was leaving when he said: "What do you want me to do about the bots?"

I stopped. I'd forgotten my request to Evotec regarding the psychological war being waged online.

"Have you got a lead on it?"

"Got a result for your keyboard warrior."

"Who is he?"

"It's a she."

He typed in a password. The face of a young woman appeared on the screen of the MacBook. She was pale, in her early twenties, Caucasian with a touch of Kazakh; caramel highlights in the hair and a certain force in the dark eyes.

"The enemy," Stefan said. "You wanted to know about online activity; this has just come through from the team. She's the secret author of a particularly effective pro-Russian blog. You'll be pleased to know you're right; there's a massive online information warfare operation going on."

They'd identified over two hundred accounts, a lot simply amplifying a core of ten or twenty with original content — "handwritten," so to speak. The handwriting meant someone with natural aptitude was crafting it. That meant you could compare phrases and grammar to open-source social media and find out who they were.

"She runs this site," Stefan said. "Aliya in Astana. Favorable to Russia. Favorable to the fight against Islamist terrorism. Anti-Western oil companies. She posts heavily on VKontakte."

I studied the face again. There was something haunting about it; someone you'd find yourself watching without meaning to. I wondered if the image was computer-generated.

Stefan showed me a cartoon on the Aliya in Astana site: a drawing of Zhaparov stamping a polished shoe on a bearded mullah. I recognized the style. It looked like those produced by an outfit called Infosurfing, which posted pro-Kremlin graphics on Instagram. Quotes from Zhaparov's speeches had been put into calligraphic fonts, sometimes alongside pictures of eagles or faded-out photographs of balaclava'd special forces.

Aliya also reposted Testimony reports on Saracen malpractice. Only she beefed them up with images: a photograph of Robert Carter and other CEOs in what Aliya claimed was a lap-dancing club. It was set alongside a photo supposedly showing workers at one of the drill sites, malnourished Chinese and Indians squatting around a pan of rice in something resembling a shower block.

"How did she get these?"

"No idea."

I checked her interactions with people online, to see if they matched.

She was good: skilled at counterargument, quick at sourcing memes, often using Western or Asian celebrities. She addressed other commentators by name, often engaging in four or five debates simultaneously across various platforms: about the barbarism of traditional Kazakh customs like "bride kidnapping" — in which a groom abducted his wife-to-be — about increasing use of the veil in rural communities to the south and east of the country. She debated the economic benefits of oil exploration. She originated hashtags: #KZFreedom. #StopSaracen.

I clicked #StopSaracen, got a photograph of a woman burning.

A sixty-year-old woman had set herself on fire outside a Saracen compound in Shymkent. It was the second self-immolation in a week. The only footage that had surfaced showed a Kazakh police officer rushing toward her with a coat in his hands to smother the flames. The woman herself was barely visible, lying on her side next to an electronic gate, hands to her head. Flames consumed her torso, which wasn't as easy to achieve as you'd think, and took a lot of accelerant. Apparently the woman had a longstanding issue with the oil company over compensation for the death of her husband, a rig worker. In the comments section people debated whether it counted as terrorism; whether it was even political or just tragic, some belated *sati*. Others pointed out that there were no corroborating sources.

But there was an interview with her brother, who looked about eighty, weeping tearlessly on a sofa in a low-ceilinged front room. I tried to figure out what felt strange about it. Finally, I zoomed in on the wall behind him. Then I brought up the clip of myself in the Triumph.

"Look," I said to Stefan. "The prints on the wall."

"What about them?"

I showed him the Triumph clip. Both rooms had the same print of a horse and rider traveling through mountains. The rider was bending down asking directions from a peasant with a staff. The path behind him meandered from the woods into a rocky landscape.

"Even the light reflecting on the frames is identical," he said. "What's this clip of you about?"

"I don't know. But someone somewhere is crafting fake videos."

After another moment studying them, Stefan said: "The fire's good." He clicked through the footage of self-immolation, frame by frame.

"You don't think it's real?"

"No. But I think someone's got their effects working nicely."

"Has Aliya posted fake videos before?" I asked.

"I haven't checked. And it's not as if it's easy to tell. The US Defense Department has tried to develop tools for detecting computer-generated material, but there's no silver bullet yet."

"Any more information about her?"

"We located her personal social media," Stefan said. "The name behind the more glamorous persona is Aliya Savinova, a postgrad student at Nazarbayev University. Syntax gets a ninety-seven percent match; so does vocabulary, even typos."

"Address?"

"There's no address online, but we got her IP and Wi-Fi connection history. Every morning her laptop connects to home broadband. Records suggest there are four people living at that address: one is Ms. Savinova."

I took a look at Aliya Savinova's personal social media. It was apolitical. She posted poetry, talked about her short stories as well. The poetry was good, covering urban ennui, romantic longing, thinly disguised erotic musings.

She liked modernism, eye shadow, drinking alone. I wondered if she liked starting wars.

"Think her account's been hijacked?" Stefan asked.

"I don't know. Think she's definitely real?"

"According to her Facebook page, she just checked into a gallery opening two miles away. So I guess you've got one way of finding out."

32

I DROVE TO THE GALLERY, A NEW GLASS BOX BESIDE THE RIVER, sponsored by Credit Bank of Moscow and Emporio Armani. It was already crowded when I got there, with high security for a wealthy turnout. I tried to see the guest list, began to blag my way in, and then the voice of Craig Bryant reached me from the throng.

"He's with me."

Bryant drifted into view accompanied by a woman in heavy makeup and heels that raised her a couple of inches above him. He ushered me in.

"I told you it was a small town at heart."

"Small town with big money."

The smell of paint mingled with expensive perfume and canapés. The crowd was mostly business, the power circuit, a few sharper, younger Kazakhs. The art was contemporary, one room darkened for video installations, one involving bean bags and headphones. The stated theme of "Nostalgic Futures" was offset by models in tight black T-shirts distributing Armani goodie bags. The Russian bank cosponsoring the show kept a lower profile.

If Bryant felt any sheepishness about our last encounter he didn't show it. He introduced me to Dr. Zyabkina. Zyabkina, Bryant explained, was a psychologist working with the Health Ministry to tackle the problem of radicalization.

"How interesting," I said. "The Health Ministry."

"It is a public health issue like any other," she said. "That is how it must be treated, like an epidemic."

I glanced around for Aliya Savinova as I fell into conversation, found myself studying the crowd. The white-painted space was still novel enough to inspire deference. Older attendees circulated obediently; the middle-aged recognized it as a new kind of fun like fast food and rock music. A lot of the young were checking their phones.

Then I saw her. A young woman with black hair, magenta lipstick, glasses. Her reality was a small shock, like seeing a celebrity in the flesh. She had a certain poise that made her seem older than her twenty-three years. She wore black jeans and white blouse. She took photos of the exhibits. Twice, she checked her phone and typed something.

She was accompanied by two female friends. I waited for her to move away from them, saw which way she was circulating, then told Bryant I'd be back. I took a fresh glass of wine and placed myself two works ahead and waited. A semi-abstract painting incorporating symbols from ancient Kazakh rock art. The sign beside it explained that the artist grew up in Mongolia, completed her education in Utah, where she became interested in a new idea of nomadism involving fluidity.

Aliya Savinova browsed a few meters away: a wall hanging woven from fragments of sportswear. She looked unimpressed. I watched her reapply her lipstick, checking her face in her phone. Someone with hidden aspects and desires, I decided, which was what you looked for in a potential recruit. Someone unconvinced by the status quo and her role within it. Espionage, like any vice, is a weapon against mundanity, against being unnoticed or unworthy of notice.

Then she was beside me.

"I'm trying to decide," I said, in Russian. "Is this patronizing?" She looked at me, at the work. "Or culturally disrespectful? Is that an issue?"

"It is ugly," she said. "That is the issue."

"True."

We walked on, past a pastiche of Soviet realism: heroic workers holding games consoles.

"I don't imagine this means much to anyone now," I said.

"It's a concept," she said. "Not much more."

"No."

I introduced myself as Toby. She told me she was Aliya. We continued in step, casually. I saw her friends turn. She glanced at them and gave a wry smile. I struggled to discern the personality she projected online. But then that was the point of an online personality: You could be different. If she was taking instructions with regards to her blog, I wanted to know how the operation was being coordinated. Did she work in a center of some kind? Was Joanna onto this? She reminded me a little of Joanna.

We walked past self-consciously edgy photos of militiamen posing with their guns and uniforms — Kiev, Zagreb, Georgia — into a final room devoted to a triptych of large black-and-white photographs. The central one showed the Cathedral of Christ the Savior in Moscow collapsing in clouds of dust as the Soviets dynamited it. To its right, less dramatically but more hauntingly, was a mosque in Uzbekistan being used as a warehouse for cotton. To the left was a Ukrainian synagogue converted to a center for Communist youth. A banner hung across its back wall, with the old Communist slogan: PEACE TO THE WORLD. This was the title of the artwork.

Aliya studied each image in turn. An older woman with an Armani badge arrived at our side, beaming.

"It is good they are showing this, no?"

"It's certainly a reminder."

"A lot of people still think it was better in those times. Young people, too. They don't know about any of this."

"Do you think that's what it's saying?" I asked.

"I do," she said, less certainly. Someone caught her attention and she wandered off. Aliya leaned closer to the prints, took a photo.

"I was in this country a few years ago," I said. "Further east. I met a man who was ninety-four years old. He used to be a traveling merchant, carrying gold into China, then returning with his camels loaded up with silk. Anyway, he became a butcher in Almaty, settled there, and a friend of mine introduced me to him. I asked what he thought of Kazakhstan now and he said, 'Everything was better in the time of Czar Nikolai II.'"

Aliya smiled.

"Czar Nikolai."

"In the nineteen hundreds. Downhill from there."

"Maybe he was right."

"Are you an artist?"

"A writer. And a student."

"What do you write?"

"Various things."

"I've always wanted to write," I said, ignoring her opacity. "It must take dedication."

"Not so much what I do."

"Do you write fiction?"

"A little. Less so now."

We arrived back at the militias. One thing they had in common, it occurred to me, was that all had been fighting Russia or Russian proxies in the last few years. I wondered about the Credit Bank of Moscow's involvement. Last year, a show of photojournalism in Berlin got taken down when it turned out to be put together by the Kremlin.

"Going to write about all this?" I asked.

"Maybe."

"I've always wanted to read some *young* Kazakh writers, people writing about now. Can you recommend any?"

"Of course." She recommended a writer and said she knew her personally. I repeated the writer's name to memorize it. The canapés had stopped arriving. Aliya's friends were wrapping up for the cold, eyeing the outside in a way that made me think of sniper fire. Craig Bryant drifted into view on the far side of the room. He saw me, lifted a glass. I saw him consider approaching.

"You should get back to your friends," I said.

"I guess so."

"It's been a pleasure to meet you." We shook hands. I began to move away, then stopped. "Aliya?" She turned warily, knowing what was coming. "I'm fairly new to this place. Would you possibly meet me again? Chat some more?"

She looked as if she found this slightly distasteful, or at least awkward.

"Perhaps," she said.

"Of course. I understand, you must be busy. No obligation." She made a final appraisal of me, then gave me her number.

"It's been a pleasure, Aliya," I said. She nodded, and was gone by the time Bryant made it over.

"Get lucky?"

"It's nice to meet some locals."

"I can find you more. What are you up to tonight?" Bryant asked. "There's a bar just opened in Yesil district called Insomnia."

I might have ended up accompanying him to Insomnia if my phone hadn't buzzed with a text: a landline to call.

Lieutenant Shomko answered.

"The woman you are looking for," he said. "I've got something."

33

WE AGREED ON THE SAUNA.

"Room three," the woman said when I got there.

The room was dimly lit, with two scented candles, the bed made up with red sheets, a bowl of condoms next to it, a screen showing music videos on the wall. Shomko was standing beside the window. He'd placed a laptop on the dresser beside him. The scented candles failed to mask his stink of cigarettes.

"I can't do any more for you after this," he said.

"What have you got?"

"I need money."

"I'll give you money."

"Now."

I handed him an envelope I'd filled with cash. He transferred it to his jacket, inserted a flash drive into the laptop, and opened a file. It was CCTV footage. He pressed play.

A back road. It looked like Astana, the backs of office buildings and snow. One car parked up: a broad, black Mercedes S-Class. Then someone approached from the distance. Someone in a parka with the hood up approaching it. Shomko zoomed in. You could just about see a face beneath the hood. It was Joanna.

Shomko went over to the window and checked the street outside.

Joanna appeared to climb into the car. It pulled out while the door was still closing.

Time stamp: 11:31 a.m., 25 November, two days before she went missing.

"Whose car is it?"

He clicked to another shot, seven minutes later. A traffic camera overlooking a busy junction. This time you could definitely see it was Astana. On the opposite side of the junction were gates I recognized as belonging to the Gazprom office next to the Oil Ministry.

The same black Mercedes appeared, stopped before the gates as they slid open, drove through.

"The car's registered to an individual called Aleksandr Kolobkov," he said. "He's a fixer for a man called Vladislav Vishinsky."

I looked again at the images, starting to feel very uneasy.

"A fixer?"

"The driver has been identified as Viktor Trunenkov, former Special Forces soldier now working for Vishinsky."

"You're sure about that?"

"This is why you are hunting her, no?"

The sauna's intercom rang. Shomko peered down from the window.

"Customer," he said.

We both listened to the customer arrive and kept listening until the showers came on. I clicked back to the footage of Joanna getting into the car and watched it again.

"Did you know she was working for the Russians?" Shomko asked.

"That's not what this says."

"I deserve a bonus, no?"

"There's a lot of ways of forcing someone into a car. They don't all involve guns."

"Blackmail."

"What cameras are these from?"

"The footage of the alleyway comes from a camera belonging to the Keruen shopping center. The later footage is from a traffic enforcement camera."

"You took them from the systems yourself?"

"No. Someone else did."

"Have you seen the original footage?"

"I don't need to." He took the envelope out of his jacket and counted the notes. "I must go now. Stay here for at least ten minutes, then return the laptop to the woman on the desk."

"What about the man who was shot on Malakhov Street?" I said.

"I don't know. Maybe he found out what she was really up to."

"What does the investigation say?"

"I have heard nothing about the investigation — except that people want to find the Englishwoman."

"I told you to get information from the investigation."

"I got you information about the woman you want. Five thousand dollars, you said."

"Who gave you these? I need a name — otherwise this means nothing."

"He is trusted."

"Not by me. I don't buy this."

"You don't pay?"

"I don't believe."

"So you were fucking her and she deceived you. Now she's fucking some Russian." He spat. "I am sorry for your heartbreak. Don't fall in love with spies."

34

I LOCKED THE ROOM AGAIN WHEN HE'D LEFT. IF THERE WAS ANY TRUTH in his theory it was too much to contemplate in one go; it would be the universe inverted, and I resisted opening the door on that possibility for now. If this was a highly sophisticated attempt at framing her, then I felt sick at the efficiency, and deeply wary of my involvement. It would explain the suspicion on me and Tom Marsh, on anyone she was close to or came into contact with. True or not, it might explain the closing down of Building D's operation, and her running to Kazakhstan.

I looked again at the shots.

Images are powerful because they suggest you don't have to think. Here's truth. But there's always a story behind them. In the story behind the disappearance of Joanna Lake there was an email to me. *Catalyst*.

One woman getting into a car. I enlarged it on the screen as if an answer would appear, rather than the whole thing fragmenting. It was her; no force, everything to suggest she knew what she was doing and wanted to make it quick.

You recruit someone to the intelligence service because of their confidence and cunning, and then train them to lie for their country. They elect to transfer these skills to a private company working for the energy industry. You ask: Could they ever lose their moral bearings? Go rogue?

But not for Vishinsky. Not in a million years.

In my experience, you're working for whoever keeps you alive. I found Sergei Cherenkov's card, wondered what he knew about all this. Then events took an even more sinister turn, one that momentarily swamped concerns about Joanna.

I noticed the music video on the brothel's TV had stopped and in its place was grainy footage of people running through a shopping mall. Behind them walked a calm, young-looking man, with an automatic rifle.

People dived into shops, pulling doors closed. The man walked past abandoned benches, potted palm trees. The news cut to a presenter reading an autocue: *The attack in Saint Petersburg's Sunlight shopping mall occurred at approximately four p.m. . . . .*

I clicked through channels. Most were showing the same footage. Initial reports said eight people had died, twenty wounded. The attacker had been shot by police. He was Kazakh.

I left the sauna, headed back to my hotel with a bad feeling growing. Where had Kazakhstan's militants suddenly sprung from? What had brought them out of the woodwork now?

Back in my hotel room I went online. A video by a group called the Islamic Movement of Kazakhstan had gone up, claiming responsibility. It showed five Kazakh-looking men in combat fatigues with Korans and AK-47s. The landscape behind them was semi-arid, a low chain of dusty green mountains in the distance. Could have been Iraq, could have been Syria. Could have been southern Spain. It was turning up everywhere, along with their statement: *We demand that Russia ceases all activities in the Middle East and Central Asia. Until Russian troops and their proxies withdraw from all Muslim lands we will wage war against you wherever we find you. You come to our land, we will come to yours.*

The leader spoke calmly, directly to camera, in Kazakh-inflected Russian. A black flag billowed slowly behind him. Shadows lined up. His lips synced with the words.

Kazakhstan was secular, but there were sixteen million inhabitants, and at least some were unemployed young men with access to YouTube. One hundred and fifty or so had headed to Syria over the last couple of years. Wars leak. One or two were going to make it back. I'd come across Central Asian fighters, though not as many as from the UK. I'd come across fighters from most countries: men and women who'd strolled away from their homes, their workplaces, taking in the drab surroundings a final time as the words of a video echoed: *Look around as you sit in comfort and ask yourself if this is how you want to die.* I should know something about walking out of your life into someone else's war.

Once you've gone, you've gone. For most jihadis, returning home meant prison and torture. Life is different when you can't go home. You start dreaming of new things, changing the world so it fits you again. It's an all-or-nothing situation. And when you've been a commander of armed men, saluted and cheered, it's hard to go back to being a mechanic or a hairdresser.

Walker called. "Seen this?"

"I'm watching."

"Know anything about IMK?"

"Never heard of them before."

"Thought it was your side of things."

This gave me pause. What had Walker heard about me, and from whom?

"What gave you that idea?"

"Did you get any more from your contact?"

"I'll let you know when I do." I hung up, deleted the incriminating footage of Joanna from the flash drive, then walked to the TV screen and stared at the grainy shots of the mall shooting. The incident happened around four p.m. in Saint Petersburg, seven p.m. in Astana. Broke eight p.m. Now experts had appeared, nodding over video links: "ISIS has been down on its luck in the Middle East, so it's going to move its attention to those nations that have tried to defeat it. We're going to see increasing amounts of these incidents."

I clicked to Twitter. The attacker had been named as Bakhtiyar Ibraimov, twenty-one years old, born in Aktobe, Kazakhstan. He'd traveled to Syria in July 2015, where he'd fought with a unit attached to Al-Nusra. Arrived in Russia last week on a Saudi passport that might or might not have been fake.

Aktobe was an industrial city—grim prospects. Should have been wealthy with oil, but the lowest incomes tend to be around the oil fields. These were the places to watch. There are always two capitals, the one with the power and the one with the resentment: Benghazis, Aleppos.

From Aktobe to the Al-Nusra Front was far from implausible. Al-Nusra were a tight, effective force in Syria, operating as conventional military or clandestine cells according to need. We'd tried to distance them from Al Qaeda for the sake of some tentative collaboration, but that was a push even for us. Their promotional clips usually came through a media outlet, The White Minaret, which posted to a jihadist web forum called Shamoukh al-Islam. The IMK video wasn't on either.

Aliya Savinova's take on events had just gone out: *Did the Sunlight attacker have contact with British intelligence?*

That gave me a chill across my back. I clicked the link to her blog. Under an old cartoon of imperial powers gathered around a map, she went to town.

Experts have no doubt that the events of 9/11 were the handiwork of the CIA. The so-called "terrorism" in the Middle East is also the handiwork of the CIA and Mossad. Therefore why should Kazakhstan doubt about other possible crimes of the West?

It is known that MI6 sent fighters from terrorist groups to Libya and Syria. One insider has said: "The dangers of 'blowback' were raised but never fully taken seriously."

It is Russia that lies exposed to take the brunt of this "blowback," having led the fight against ISIS while the West wavered. Perhaps certain heads in Western intelligence find this convenient.

The first thing that struck me was the mix of registers. Aside from the quote, which I recognized from an *Observer* article back in 2015, the vocabulary wavered. "Brunt," "Certain heads" — that wasn't the style of English I'd seen her using elsewhere. Second thing was the nature of this material, which felt a little close to home.

There were few people with the knowledge, motivation, and audacity to exploit me to stir tensions, but Vishinsky was a prime contender. It made the idea of Joanna's collaboration improbable. It made me more worried for her well-being. This was personal.

Now I watched the IMK video again. The guns looked like Chinese-made copies of AR-15 assault rifles. Closer inspection suggested the serial numbers had been etched off. China had supplied a lot of knock-off AR-15s to rebel groups in South Sudan. When the Sudanese economy tanked, their government offloaded hundreds to Qatar. Qatar had them airlifted straight to western Turkey for smuggling into Syria. Wars exist in hard-wearing materials, and these circulate. Sometimes that was convenient; Bohren had pointed his Saudi agent toward them. But his weren't the only shady AR-15s around.

Two hundred and forty IMK videos had been uploaded in the last two weeks. That gave me a lot to trawl. But none from more than two weeks back, as far as I could tell.

It looked like they were either trained by the Islamic State's media team or working directly with them. They shared the same slick production techniques: good lighting, careful composition, multiple camera angles. They minimized the color palette, which made the end result sharper. It was typical of the genre. If anything, it was too typical. Then there was the music. I had a guilty fondness for nasheeds, the a cappellas accompanying every ISIS video. There were companies deep in Iraq tasked with nothing but churning these tunes out. Over the last couple of years I'd collected examples in Turkish, Uyghur, English, Bengali, French, and Chinese. I'd never heard one in Kazakh before.

Blowback.

Aliya's blog had been featured on Russian TV: *My blog featured on TV!!* An obscure Christian Orthodox channel had lifted a map from her website, black arrows indicating the flow of Islamists from the Middle East into Kazakhstan. The channel ran it alongside video of right-wing activists chanting in a Moscow suburb.

It wasn't immediately clear what they were protesting against: Kazakhstan, Central Asia, an influx of Central Asian migrants. The protest crowd was ninety percent young men in Adidas and jeans, some sporting black balaclavas or blue medical masks, often football scarves pulled up over their faces. They had some esoteric flags involving swords and eagles, fists and crosses, the yellow of Russian nationalism. It was Moscow, but outskirts. I remembered those places, Yugozapadnaya, Zyablikovo: vast high-rises and little else. I turned the sound up. There was the predictable chant of "Russia for Russians," then "Sport! Health! Nationalism!" which sounded slightly less bizarre in Russian, but only just. For good measure, they threw in the occasional rendition of "Fuck the Jews." One from the repertoire.

I called Alexander Turbayevskiy, reporter on Moscow's *Kommersant* newspaper, but also closely involved with the Sova Center, a Russian NGO that monitored ethnic hatred. He'd been a corduroy-clad oasis of humane intellect during my stays in Moscow.

"Are you watching what I'm watching?" he asked.

"How did they get organized so quickly? How did they get permission to march?"

"It's the tip of the iceberg. The nationalist parties are suddenly loud and everywhere. Nationalist thugs get to march, it seems. All seventy or eighty of them. There were some attacks afterward: three men beat up badly."

"Online activity?"

"Massive. With an increasingly clear narrative: Kazakh terrorism is a threat, shadowy forces are using Central Asian Islamists to attack Russia."

"Shadowy forces like who?"

"Like you, the British."

Aliya's MI6 conspiracy theory appeared on Russian platforms — Live-Journal, VK, the website of the Young Guard of United Russia — alongside stories about the dangers of Islam. One was a rerun of accusations from Ukraine: a Russian boy crucified on the side of a building. The setting had been switched from Odessa to Karaganda, but the details were unchanged. Slightly more grounded in reality was a story from the west of Kazakhstan. A court in Atyrau had just jailed eight followers of a purist Wahhabi sect for destroying a local graveyard. The followers believed that Kazakh traditions of ancestor worship transgressed the rules of Islam. They were shown receiving their sentence in a court of dark green and beige, a line of five men, heads bowed.

I watched more clips on VKontakte. One interviewee, an older man, called the Kazakhs a terrorist threat and said he'd support any Russian intervention: There was a right to self-defense. Russia had a legal obligation to protect ethnic Russians abroad. I watched him five times, convinced that the shape of his head morphed at the edges as he spoke. Authorities in Moscow were looking into how the shooter had got a Saudi passport. Saudi officials denied any form of collusion.

Aliya had tweeted: *They will attack Astana next.*

I looked at the tweet for a long time. Then the comments below: *Don't tempt fate; Keep telling it, Aliya; That would wake these jokers up.*

It looked like any other online prophecy. But I took it slightly more seriously. She'd been blogging about the dangers of an attack in Russia forty-eight hours before Bakhtiyar Ibraimov walked into the Sunlight shopping mall.

I was building a conspiracy theory of my own. Whoever was steering Aliya was steering events.

I picked up the phone, dialed a number I'd hoped not to use again. Mohammad Reza Nikfar answered promptly. Not many people had this number, and if he'd given it to you it was because he valued your acquaintance.

"It's me," I said.

"Don't tell me: You're putting the band back together."

"I'm curious to know what you've heard recently."

"I've been trying to contact you," he said. "Are you back in Turkey?"

"Not right now. What do you know about Saint Petersburg?"

"There's a possibility he connects to our network. Maybe distantly, maybe not so distantly. Can you shed some light?"

I felt vertigo, standing over a pit of my own making, with difficulty discerning the knot of connections at the bottom. The only unsurprising element was the presence of Reza.

Mohammed Nikfar, or Reza to friends, was Iranian born, CIA trained, Peshawar made. He'd been in the dark corners of the CIA long enough to have helped build the Taliban and take it down again. He was the hinge between Langley and Pakistan's Inter-Services Intelligence, the largest intelligence agency in the world. Called Inter-Services because it drew on all branches of Pakistan's armed forces, but I always felt the name described a bigger crossroads, the intelligence equivalent of the arms bazaar in Pakistan's northwestern mountains, where every gang came and no laws applied. Aside from being a reckless visionary, Reza was one of the few intelligence officers who operated at the core of things.

"Do you have the name on the Saudi passport?" I asked.

"Yousef Shaheen."

I had arranged a few Saudi passports in my time: They were gold dust, welcome almost everywhere. I didn't remember a Yousef Shaheen.

"Know when it was issued?"

"No. But something's going on. The shooter was involved in drafting up Central Asians to fight in Libya. On behalf of the UK. He has phone connections with your UK recruitment networks."

I fought against mounting disquiet. "Heard" wasn't a strong verb in intelligence circles; phone connections extended as far as you wanted them to. I stored Reza's conjecture for later reflection.

"Is IMK a thing?" I asked.

"Possibly. Remnants of Al-Nusra and Abu Uzair's men. It's very hazy at the moment. If it exists it's a splinter cell. I'd take the black flag with a pinch of salt, but they did come up in a JIX report yesterday. Where are you? I can send it."

"Kazakhstan."

"You had a heads-up on this?"

"Not as such."

"What have you got?"

"Some leads," I lied. "But I need your help."

"You certainly do. If you're there, you need to see this. Are you on usual channels?"

"Personal ones. They'll do for now."

He sent the information through: a report from Joint Intelligence X, the secretariat at the heart of Pakistan's security services. The time and date put its distribution twelve hours ago. It was one page, light on detail, collating information from sources in Uzbekistan and Afghanistan.

Reza had chased for all information relating to IMK. He got a little more than he bargained for. Intelligence suggested that a group identifying themselves as the Islamic Movement of Kazakhstan was in possession of detonators and four thousand pounds of C-4 explosives. The load originated in Afghanistan: It had been packed in crates on an articulated lorry traveling from Hairatan in Afghanistan to Termez in Uzbekistan. Uzbek intelligence had tracked it by satellite, with the intention of identifying the insurgent cell. Somewhere along the line things went wrong. The transport was stopped, but it was empty; the load had been transferred.

In the twenty-four hours after the failed seizure of explosives, sixteen homes and businesses were raided across Afghanistan. The lorry driver's brother was cooperating. Police had seized a laptop containing research on fuel-air bombs, along with a detailed satellite image of Astana and surveillance photographs of its public squares.

I called Reza back.

"Have any more details surfaced since this report? Like who, where, how?"

"Nothing. It came out of nowhere and vanished into nowhere."

"I'm going to need you to update me if you hear anything more about Astana."

"Of course."

"What put you onto this?"

"A woman from your end, the one you introduced me to."

"Joanna Lake?"

"That's what I was trying to contact you about. Is she legit?"

I felt a stab of adrenaline.

"When was this?"

"About six days ago. Called me in the middle of the night."

"What did she say?"

"She'd seen plans of some kind, relating to those explosives. Wouldn't give me a source."

"I need to know the exact contact time."

He checked, came back. It was two thirty a.m.

"Two thirty in Islamabad?"

"Yes."

Then it was three thirty in Astana, a few minutes before she contacted me. In the very narrow window between fleeing the safe house and vanishing. *She was onto something. Onto whatever is going on here.*

"She's missing," I said. "Went missing in Astana last week."

"Shit. No one's chased me about that."

"What device did Joanna call on?"

"Cell phone. We've run a check: It was clean, it's now dead. Been dead for days."

"I want you to take a look at something."

I sent through a still from the Mega Astana, in case Reza could ID the man in the cap, the probable source for her intelligence. He couldn't. I promised I'd pass any further information his way, took a final look at the anger raging online, then closed my browser.

Where are you, Joanna? What have you led me into?

She'd called Reza. She knew him as one of the only individuals plugged into terrorist networks in all directions. She put him onto an attack in the making. Did that give me some frayed thread of a narrative that contradicted the one in which she sold us out to Gazprom?

Turkey, close to the Syrian border. Looking at the stars.

"When was the last time you kissed someone you weren't trying to recruit?"

"A long time," I said, although it wasn't strictly true.

"Did you know some people do it because they enjoy it?"

"Perverts," I said.

If she was making an accusation of coldness on my part it was neutralized by the beauty of the night. Then she said, as if it followed from her previous thoughts, "Do you ever think about all of that probing they did when they recruited us? All that cross-examination, interviewing friends and family behind our backs, testing us: We thought they were weeding out the corrupt, but what if that was what they wanted? We were chosen because of our flaws."

"I don't think they're that imaginative," I said.

"They chose us because we were already halfway corrupt."

I turned Sergei Cherenkov's business card in my hand and wondered again what light he could throw on Perfect Vision, and what I'd have to do to get it. Be careful, I thought. Exhaustion had begun to fog my judgment. I wasn't going to sleep, so I went for a walk.

The roads had iced. I took my gloves off and touched the hard snow.

It was what Mongolians called a *harin zud,* a black freeze, when snowfall was followed by a sudden drop in temperature. The earth became inaccessible. Out on the steppe it spelled the death of livestock in the thousands. I'd been told of horses eating their own hair out of desperation. People died but it was impossible to dig graves, so they were mummified until summer, organs replaced with pine needles and larch cones. In Astana it meant drivers kept to ten miles per hour, like a citywide funeral procession. Near Bayterek, I saw three crashed cars, one on its side, strands of emergency tape fluttering.

The office blocks changed color, green to blue to red. There was an unearthly metallic ticking sound that I eventually identified as streetlights agitated in the wind. I got the war zone feeling, where everything seems provisional, and when you look at buildings you see their destruction too.

Who else was investigating this imminent attack? I didn't feel in a position to take responsibility for stopping it. Reza was good, but he had more allies in Peshawar than Washington. If no one had chased him about Joanna's contact it was because not many people knew he existed. And it was only because of me that Joanna did.

When she needed access to northern Syria I'd introduced them. We met in the closest thing he had to an office — which was someone else's office behind five walls of concrete and barbed wire. There was a map of Greater Kurdistan on the wall, a photograph of a young-looking Reza with Bill Clinton. Joanna was all charm and only gave me her opinion of him on the flight back: He was well-connected and borderline insane. The CIA, she felt sure, kept him active in the hope that he'd get himself killed.

"You like him because you equate truth with darkness. You think people like him bring you closer to the truth."

"Don't they?"

"They bring you closer to something, that's for sure."

"What do you mean?"

She didn't elaborate. But her observation had become interwoven with my earliest memories of the man. I'd first bumped into him in Tajikistan, the most lawless corner of Asia at that time, controlled by an unlikely combination of Russian soldiers, Islamist guerrillas, bandits, and deserters from all sides. It was ninety percent mountain rock. The only way to make a living was by trading weapons or narcotics. Russia had established outposts along the border, then manned them with drunks and criminals, whiling away long hours as they waited to be decapitated by insurgent Afghans.

I was in the country ostensibly to learn who controlled its mountain passes. Someone in Vauxhall had identified this as important—China was using Tajikistan as a bridge to the Middle East—and I was happy to spend a couple of weeks based in the rapidly developing capital, Dushanbe, heading to the mountains when I could. On the way back to Dushanbe one time, I decided to return through the Yagnob Valley, to see if I could find the isolated village of Yagnob itself. People there were said to be descendants of the ancient kingdom of Samarkand. They spoke a language that hadn't changed significantly in five thousand years. When they prayed, it wasn't toward Mecca but in the direction of the highest mountain peak, the steppingstone to heaven.

I didn't find any Yagnobi. I ended up deeper in the valley than I probably should have gone, especially on a raw February night. When I bumped into a crew of Russian soldiers, I was low on food and water, and almost relieved to see them. I still had vodka and cigarettes, and this, combined with the fact that they were strung out on heroin, saved me from summary execution. They invited me to their camp.

The camp was a dirt-walled hole in the ground. I was led between sandbags into something resembling a First World War trench, where everyone was wasted and they were using fuel barrels to make moonshine. Reza sat among it all, serene, pupils constricted to pinpoints. I thought he was one of the locals, in his filthy kaftan, turban, and beard. Then I heard his American-edged accent. He reminded me of pictures I'd seen of British special forces in Yemen in the 1940s, looking as if the desert wind had whittled them down to a foreign core.

He spent a long time assessing me, trying to establish which intelligence service was on his territory. We ate around a table with a carpet on top and embers burning beneath it. They melted snow for water. Every few minutes someone would raise a toast and we'd knock back another fifty milliliters of vodka. When the Russians sank into oblivion, Reza proposed we borrow their motorbikes and go up the mountain. That was fine by me.

I remembered him howling into the rain at the peak.

"This is it, right? This is what I call getting off base."

Next day we drove along the border with Afghanistan. I'd earned his trust. We skirted the most beautiful and dangerous scenery I'd seen, mountains folded around poppy fields like they were protecting the world's soft organs. We followed a two-lane road toward China. When we were a hundred miles or so from anything, Reza sat me down and we talked about his vision for controlling the region: networks, funding programs, alliances. He wanted to know what I thought, and what support I could get. It seemed a bit crazy, knocking around foreign policy on a mountainside littered with smashed cars, although it doesn't seem so crazy now. On the way back he stopped in at a mud-walled village, "dropping off provisions." While he chatted up locals, I looked inside the remaining parcels on the back seat of his car. They contained encrypted radios and body armor.

By the following week we were solid friends. In 2013 he began making noises about support for rebel militias: Libya initially, then Syria. *Asked for you by name, Kane.* Kurdish-led Syrian defense forces, he said: They're our men. They've got the fighters, Saudis have the money. Boom.

When Joanna needed access to Syria, he linked her up with some Kurdish cigarette smugglers based in Qamishli, a Syrian city near the Turkish border. She had been suspicious before meeting Reza, then disarmed by his charisma and more suspicious. I had mentioned him the last time we met, recalling a conversation the three of us had had about emotional manipulation. I'd used him as an example of what you can't do with computers. "He's mad, but he understands grievances, and that's everything."

"There's software for that," she'd said.

And then I'd given my speech. A machine couldn't give you historical and cultural trauma. How would you program that? Feed in fears, nightmares, poetry?

"Why not?" she said.

GCHQ had a program called XKeyscore, which had already hoovered up data for entire populations. It was stored on more than seven hundred servers at approximately a hundred and fifty sites. The data itself came from satellite intercepts, telecoms access, and what they called overhead: pickup from planes and drones. There was third-party product from twenty-seven countries: content and metadata. Like a lot of industries, the challenge facing the intelligence services wasn't getting all this information; it was figuring out what to do with it. You've got every word used in phone calls, emails, and messaging services in Georgia over a twelve-month period. How do you turn that into knowledge? How can you accept that it doesn't tell you the future?

"So what's next?" I had asked. Part of me was getting sucked in, wondering if maybe Joanna and her secretive Shefford unit really had glimpsed something ahead.

She'd said there would be another incident like the Crimea. Russia wouldn't sit still. We argued about that. I had said the risks were too high.

Now that conversation returned with a more concrete significance. Had something put her onto Vishinsky's next move?

"You don't think they would invade anywhere else?" she asked me.

"I'm not saying they wouldn't *want* to. They want secure borders. Russia's idea of a secure border is one with the Russians on both sides. But there are limits. Think of the potential consequences."

"Nations aren't rational actors. They're bitter old men."

"Yet you can predict what they're going to do."

"You don't need to be rational to be predictable. That's what I'm trying to say."

Sometimes it seemed as if the entire intelligence service had become gripped by the same dream, chasing an infinite meteorology. It had started out simply enough, with a search for algorithms that could warn us of attacks, identifying digital landscapes that had previously led up to terrorist incidents: communications activity, social media, financial transactions, geographical movement. Then it turned to visual patterns: how someone moves around a city, their posture, their silhouette, whether they have a bag, how the bag is carried.

The machines allowed fixation. In the old paper archives you could see the sickness of an obsession, the visible mess of paper, scrawled diagrams and annotations. One click of a mouse could deliver three hundred lifetimes of obsession.

This is mankind's eternal quest, I'd argued. To protect ourselves from chance. To know everything. We'd rather believe we are entirely predictable than that there is a spark of chaos in our heart.

"You think the chaos in your heart gives you independence, but that is the bit you don't control. That's the blind spot. Same with nations."

I returned to the hotel, sat in my room. Chaos driving nations or nations driving chaos. Which was going on around me?

At five past midnight my phone buzzed. A message from Reza.

This her?

I opened the attached file. It was a photo of a group: four men, three women, wrapped up for a hike. They were outside, in snow, a boxy concrete building behind them. One of the women's faces had been circled. She was standing at the back of the group. Almost as if she hadn't wanted to be picked up.

It was her.

Joanna wore a wool hat and hiking boots. Some of the other members of the party had walking poles. Was this Joanna as Vanessa? I didn't recognize any of the other individuals. There was no geographic tag to the image. I was left with the blurred face, some trees that looked like pines breaking the deep snow, the building behind her. A faded sign said Кинотеатр. Kinoteatr. It was a derelict cinema: "Miners' Cinema," according to signage encrusted in icicles.

Reza's analysts had retrieved it from a computer in Berlin they were monitoring, which had received it on Facebook in a posting originating in Kazakhstan. Eco-activists. It had been posted a couple of weeks ago. The activists connected to various campaigns against pollution, but had been careful to remove geotags and any reference to a location. It wasn't Astana. Behind the cinema, a wall of coniferous trees clung to a steep white hillside.

What was Joanna doing there two weeks ago? It matched nothing in the file I'd seen. I asked Reza to get any more details he could, then studied the image again. Well away from Astana, by the looks of it. I thought of what Shomko had told me: *There's a possibility she headed east. She had connections there.*

I tried to call Stevenson, but he didn't pick up. I thought of Aliya Savinova, who felt like the most promising contact I'd made. One way or another she plugged into the online information warfare. In the hotel's business suite, I printed off a story by the writer she had recommended, then returned to my room. I pulled the chair away from the center, so I'd see anyone entering a second before they saw me. Then I removed the handgun from the safe, cleaned it, oiled it, rested it on the arm of the chair.

35

I WOKE UP IN THE CHAIR, LISTENING FOR THE LAYERED SIRENS OF AN attack. The city was silent. It was six a.m. No smoke on the horizon. Just the heat rising out of the top of Khan Shatyr.

I checked jihadi sites, then social media, then global news. Cellophane-wrapped flowers piled high outside the Sunlight Mall. The first victims had been named, photographs of them placed alongside candles and rosary beads.

Still no news of any man found shot in an apartment block in Astana. No news of an Englishwoman missing.

I studied the eco-activists' photo of Joanna again, partly kidding myself I could derive more clues from it, partly because she looked happy in the photo, and I hadn't seen her like that for a while.

Lucy Piper messaged: She'd pick me up for a breakfast meeting at eight, heading to a restaurant on Nurzhol Boulevard.

"Is Callum going to be there?" I asked.

"He's on his way. Why?"

"Just checking."

I messaged Stefan and suggested that it would be a good time to recon the Vectis office. He confirmed.

Aliya Savinova's literary recommendation had fallen to the floor. I picked it up and thought about what I'd read the previous night. A lonely woman fears she is going mad; she contemplates the way in which we believe in unreal things when real things cease to help us, "when a limit is reached and only darkness lies ahead." Lost in fantasy, she succumbs to an ill-judged relationship. It was powerful, well written. The writer's name was given as Salima Qupiya. In Kazakh, *qupiya* meant "secret" or "mystery." There were few traces of her online: a poem in an Almaty magazine, a reference on a literary website from two years ago. No photos. According to a bio, she was the same age as Aliya Savinova. She wrote with Aliya's laconic skepticism. Began studying at Nazarbayev University, it seemed, when Aliya did. Apparently I had found another pseudonym.

I shaved, dressed, browsed a few online literary journals covering literature in translation, putting together a recruitment strategy, feeling for a way into Aliya's heart.

Piper picked me up in a chauffeur-driven Bentley. We drove fast. There were cars sticking close behind us: GL5 protection.

"Whatever's being thrown at us online is part of a concerted operation," she said. "It's at scale, and individuals within UK intelligence have begun to take interest. I don't know if that works in our favor or not."

"Are the intelligence services going to be at the meeting today?"

"Not to my knowledge."

We passed some people grouped outside a police station. They were holding placards. I saw, belatedly, that Elena Yussopova stood to the front.

I turned my face away, swearing under my breath. There was a chance she'd seen me; I had no idea. I didn't have my identities clean — that was the problem. Multiple covers in one city. I was floundering.

We stopped on Nurzhol Boulevard before I had a chance to attempt any more questions. Cafestar was a restaurant on the grand avenue running between ministerial buildings and elite apartment blocks. It was encased in snow. In season, no doubt, the café's terrace would be shared between high-end escorts and ministerial wives showing off Paris fashion and international school English. All that seemed to relate to another world right now.

"Ms. Piper." A big grin from the young waiter on door duty. He beckoned me through. A GL5 guard stood inside like a sullen maître d', jacket fastened over his gun, a nod at Piper, a hard look at me. Callum Walker sat with a man and woman at a circular table in the center of the room. It was a more exclusive gathering than I'd expected. There were no other customers; either the place had been cleared or it wasn't popular with the morning crowd.

I was introduced as an expert on Russia assisting Piper Anderson. No one seemed to want to mention Vectis by name. The man beside Walker was Tim Chambers, former foreign secretary, now lobbying for Saracen. He was freshly shaved, in a tailored navy suit, silk tie, and handmade Italian shoes. With him was Lynn Cook from Saracen in a blue Chanel suit.

We all shook hands. I took a seat next to Chambers. On the table, among white napkins, cafetières, and plates of food, were copies of yesterday's media coverage of the trip and a timetable for today. But everyone's attention was on a phone screen.

Chambers took the iPhone from Walker, glanced at it, passed it to Cook. She raised an eyebrow, passed it to me. The screen showed a dead man on a mortuary slab, face blackened with bruises, mouth a mess of broken teeth. His left ear hung on by a flap of skin.

"He was arrested last night at the protest in Semey," Walker said. "Died in the police station. His brother got the photo."

I handed the phone to Piper.

"Has it gone international?" she asked.

"Not yet."

She shook her head, passed the phone back to me.

"What do these protesters want exactly? No drilling? Human rights?"

"I don't know," Walker said. "I'm more concerned about who's retweeting this image. This one's a troll. Scroll down."

I scrolled down to a clip of Putin giving a speech. It concerned his favorite theme: the breakup of the Soviet Union as the greatest geopolitical catastrophe of the twentieth century, leaving millions of Russians stranded outside the Russian Federation. A minute in, he dismissed Kazakhstan as a recent invention: "The Kazakhs have created a state where there was never one before."

"Is that true?" Chambers asked.

They looked at me. I paused it.

"Technically," I said. "I've not seen this speech before. Where's it from?"

"It's hard to confirm if it's genuine," Walker said. "Our Moscow office isn't aware of it either. It's got over eighty thousand retweets in Kazakhstan alone."

"How many people are even online here?" Chambers asked, looking puzzled. A waiter approached.

"Please," Piper said, handing me a menu. "Everyone, eat. The croissants are amazing. They fly in the pastry."

I ordered coffee and a croissant, double-checked the staff folding napkins in the shadows. The lighting was soft, a lot of it coming from a tall glass box filled with bottles of wine, like a trophy cabinet. Chambers speared the remains of his eggs Benedict.

"You say this is a concerted operation?" he asked Walker. "Kremlin-based?"

"I suspect so."

This provoked a deep breath. Chambers looked to Piper.

"You're keeping Jack in the loop?"

"Daily."

Jack, I thought. Jack Burrows at the Foreign Office?

"We may need to make that hourly."

Piper said: "For now we want to neutralize this as much as possible. It may be that attack is the best form of defense; whack-a-mole isn't working." She looked at me brightly, waiting. "Toby?"

It took me a second to catch up with her thought process. *Attack.*

"Kazakhstan's independent," I began. "Whatever Putin might say, this is a strong, proud, independent country. We've got nationalism on our side."

"Nationalism," someone said, as if testing the word.

"If they're peddling a 'Kazakhstan belongs to Russia' line, you want blogs promoting Kazakh independence, authentic Kazakh identity. A secular one: modern, outward-looking. Nationalism not nationalization."

"Nationalism not nationalization." Piper wrote it down.

"Find some heart-stirring imagery and iconography. There are old Kazakh warriors you could bring into play."

"Any names?"

"One's called Raiymbek, eighteenth century. That could be the pseudonym of someone writing a blog. Say the blog's called Kazakh Independence."

She scribbled furiously.

"And the independence stuff: like anti-Putin?"

"Deeper than that. You've got plenty of history to draw upon: Kazakh servitude to the czars; legends in which they brought together all the clans to fight against Russia." We had a look on her MacBook, found a Romantic oil painting by some Frenchman showing the hordes gathering with incongruous spears. "The Bolshevik invasion saw hundreds of Kazakhs fleeing south. They call it fleeing to the bone."

"I like that."

"Get people talking about historical injustice: the famine introduced by Soviet collective farming; Kazakhs burning their grain and slaughtering their cattle rather than letting them fall into Russian hands. You could have a whole Pinterest board of famine pictures. They're out there."

"I'll get our team on it."

"And, for God's sake, keep the president's daughter onside," Chambers said.

"We've booked the Marriott's thirty-eighth-floor bar for her birthday celebration. There's a catering team coming from Paris. It's under control."

My coffee and croissant arrived. Both were good, as promised.

"Toby," Piper said. "I'm told you read Kazakh."

"A little."

"Can you check this?"

She pushed the draft of an article toward me. It talked about all the good work Saracen was doing. Accompanying the piece was a photograph of the Caspian refinery, its vast metalwork lit against the night. It had a Union Jack flying.

"The piece is great. I wouldn't stick a Union Jack on the Caspian. And I'd get the word 'land' in there," I said. "Land is the main treasure. You're helping them be prosperous so they can keep their land."

"Clearly no one's told them what's under it," the woman from Saracen muttered.

"It's symbolic. Oil will go, not the land."

"But it's oil they're against."

"They're not against it," I said. "They just don't think they're getting dividends. Poverty here's dropped from around fifty percent to four percent in the last fifteen years. That's people not dying. It wasn't because of NGOs, it's because companies got the black stuff out of the ground."

"Hear, hear." Chambers pushed his chair back and rose. "I've got to run. Toby, it's been a pleasure."

Chambers and Cook had to return to the trade delegation. They were late for a tour of a factory manufacturing asthma inhalers. Stefan messaged. He said we had a problem; he'd explain if I could suggest somewhere safe to meet.

36

I FOUND A MOTEL ON THE EDGE OF THE CITY'S INDUSTRIAL AREA. Migrant workers smoked together in the overheated lobby, hi-vis vests steaming on radiators. There was a shop beside reception selling alcohol and microwavable food. I booked a room, checked it, closed the curtains, and returned to the car.

"Meet at the lorry park on the Alash Highway," I told Stefan. "Ten a.m. Pull in; I'll flash my lights, then follow me."

I drove back to the lorry park, then pulled off behind the rusting frame of a disused petrol station beside it, hidden from the road but still able to see the vehicles passing. At five minutes to ten Stefan's rental BMW swung in fast. No other vehicles around. I flashed my lights as I pulled back onto the road and he tailed me to the motel.

Inside the motel room he removed his laptop from its aluminum case, opened it. The screen showed a photo of the Vectis office. Then a second picture, closer to floor level — the junction box for the ethernet.

"Someone's already done it."

"Done what?"

"Hacked them."

Stefan changed windows, logged in to a discussion forum. Halfway down a black screen filled with monospaced text, someone had posted an almost identical picture: same office, same junction box.

"The forum's called Abysm, probably the smallest, most select hacker community on the net. Eighty or ninety members, a lot of them pros. The US Department of Justice has tried to take it down on several occasions. The setup is invite-only: You have to show how you're going to be useful for the other members, so there's a culture of bragging, a lot of sharing tips, trading tools. On Monday, the twentieth of November, a guy calling himself nomad9 says he's been approached for a job, talks about somewhere ultrasecure that he's been asked to get into. "'Been asked to do a thing' were his exact words. It's an isolated systems network, behind multiple firewalls. The target organization's clearly sensitive. All data's encrypted when it's transmitted, so he needs to get access internally. He posts some details; there's a conversation about potential vulnerabilities, a joke about it being banking or military.

"First he thinks about replacing a keyboard with an identical one containing a key logger, thereby getting all the passwords. He says his client would be able to make the swap and then retrieve the memory chip."

"Which suggests his client is someone already inside the organization."

"Right. Talks about rigging a Dell KM7 17."

"That's what they have in the Vectis office."

"Then he says his client reckons the target's too savvy for that. So he sources a replica ethernet box and puts a device in it that can sit on the local area network, between the target and the server, grabbing all the traffic as it passes through. It's a classic man-in-the-middle attack. Gets in, does all the things I did, except then he disappears off the face of the earth."

"What happened?"

"His messages stop. Rumors start a few days later: He's been either killed or arrested. Someone says they think he was in Astana, but there's nothing on the news. Someone knows his family and they say he's disappeared. A few friends drop into the forum to say he's not contactable in the real world either. The last they heard he'd stumbled across something crazy. The whole thing's become news in the community, people circulating the pictures he posted, trying to figure out what he was onto. There are rumors that maybe the British intelligence services were involved; then CIA, Mossad, FSB." Stefan turned to me. "Now I've just tried to hack the same organization."

"Do you know who he is?"

"Nomad9 is a guy called Ruslan Batur. Pretty shit-hot, worked for the Kazakh government on cybersecurity between 2012 and 2014, but fell out over some of the things he was asked to do. He's got a history of using his skills for political ends: hacktivism, connections with human rights groups."

"Got a picture of him?"

"A mugshot, from an arrest in 2015." He brought up Ruslan Batur's mugshot. Batur was twenty-two in the photo, with shoulder-length dark hair, large eyes, and a wispy attempt at a beard. "According to people online, at least ten individuals have been questioned about him over the last few days, in six different countries."

I showed Stefan the CCTV footage of Batur in the Mega Astana Mall on his way to pass what he'd found to Joanna, and then the shots I'd taken of his corpse. Stefan winced.

"Fuck's sake, Elliot."

"You agree that it's him?"

"It's him. You knew it. You knew he was killed and sent me in anyway."

"I didn't know who he was or what he'd done. I've been trying to find out."

"He was doing the hack for your missing woman."

"That's the theory I'm arriving at."

"On her own employer."

"So it seems."

"For a rival?"

"I've no idea."

"I'm trying to figure out who's likely to kill me, Elliot."

"No one's going to kill you."

"This is something big, isn't it?"

"Everything's big."

"I mean really big."

"What makes you say that?"

"There have been attempts to wipe even *talk* of the hack from message boards," Stefan said. "Look." He brought up a page of code. "One hacker site, Black Hat, published a report, nine a.m. US time, connecting the disappearance of Batur to the conversations on Abysm, suggesting he may have stumbled into information to do with an intelligence service. It gets blown offline an hour later. By their own account they were hit by a DDoS attack — they posted a grab of their server log."

DDoS: distributed denial of service — a technique used by criminals, bored teenagers, and intelligence services alike to derail a website by bombarding it with communication requests until it goes into meltdown.

"The style is distinct," Stefan said. "Most attacks piggyback on multiple computers to get scale. This one just fools the host into thinking it's receiving excess communication. It's trying to put together the fragments of data being sent, but getting the wrong information, so it thinks it's overloaded when it isn't. The beauty of this technique is that it leads to buffer overflow. The host starts to wipe the data it already has."

"Seen it before?"

"I helped devise it."

"What do you mean?"

"It looks like what we called Slow Clap. The bosses at GCHQ were queasy about piggybacking civilian PCs to get their mass of attackers, so I helped develop methods using software errors and security gaps that could be run off one PC only. Pretty ingenious, if I say so myself. You can take a target down solo."

"Are GCHQ the only ones with it? What about you guys?"

"We don't have it. But these things catch on fast. Like I say, what's going on?"

"Do you have any idea what Batur got?"

"No."

"Is there any chance of us repeating the hack?"

"There's no way. It's locked down now."

"Do you think there might be a copy of the stolen data anywhere?"

"I'm not sure I'd go looking for it if there was. I'm not sticking around. Sorry, Elliot."

"Wait. I need malware for Aliya Savinova's phone; an exploit for Androids, one that would work on an LG G5."

"Why?"

"I want to get a grip on her. I want to find out who she is so I can persuade her to talk to me."

"I can get them to send something through. But you're not going to crack this alone."

"I don't have a way out."

Stefan sighed. "What's Aliya Savinova going to give you? She won't know who she's working for."

"Everyone knows something. And she interests me."

"She hates the West."

"She likes hating the West. She'll enjoy my company."

37

EVOTEC SENT THROUGH THE MALWARE A FEW HOURS LATER, ALONG WITH a "pattern of life" file for Aliya, including professional and friendship networks, educational history, and financial records for both her and her family. She had some extra money coming in to a personal account with Halyk Savings Bank of Kazakhstan. The account received monthly transfers equivalent to two hundred US dollars from a business account at the Asia Credit Bank in the name of ACT Strategic Communications. No ACT Strategic Communications came up online.

I dialed the number she'd given me. The way someone answers a call is usually informative in itself. Are they in the environment you'd expect? Any suggestion of a delay while devices are initiated? My call was killed after five rings. I sent a text.

It's Toby. Can you call me?

Aliya texted back. *In five minutes.* She called in three and a half. She sounded happy.

"Toby, hello."

"Can you speak?"

"Yes, briefly."

"I read a story by the writer you recommended."

"Already?"

"'The Edge of Things.' I found it online. I began reading it last night and couldn't stop. I think the writer is hugely talented."

"You do?"

"Do you know them well?"

"Quite well."

"I have a friend who edits a literary magazine in London. I think they would be very interested in doing something with her work. He is very interested in literature from under-represented countries."

"Really?"

"Yes. Are they contactable?"

"I think so. I will find out."

I gave it a beat.

"It's very nice to hear your voice. There's not many people here I've met who I have much in common with."

"Me neither."

"Would you meet me for a coffee?"

"When?"

"Today."

"Okay," Aliya said. "A quick one."

"Do you know Café Corso on the corner of Bayanaul Street? I can be there at seven." Corso was far enough away from the governmental district for discretion without it being impractical for her to get to.

"Seven? I think so. I will try."

"I will be there."

"Okay." She hung up.

Too easy, I thought. The doubt was drilled into you over time: No one simply took your hand when you reached out.

I went online, refined my story about contacts at a literary magazine, attached malware to what looked like a link to the publication's website. Then I sent an encrypted email to Hugh Stevenson, informing him that Joanna had hacked into Vectis. I asked him to see whether Vauxhall had any previous concerns about the private intelligence company, but suggested he move carefully.

I bought a new shirt, checked my phone for news. Semey had kicked off in a serious way. News of the young man's death in custody had spread fast. Another protester had been injured and was critical in hospital. The square was filled with chanting, braziers lit, flames promising violence of their own.

Is this a revolution? Piper had asked. A Central Asian Spring? I took a look at inflation rates and average incomes. They gave you something tangible to watch, short of being able to stare directly into the minds of the silent majority, to measure frustration as it approaches that magic point of collective rage when people act. That was what I had prided myself on assessing in reports for Six. A horizon watcher, as Joanna had mocked. There were several online tools for calculating the likelihood of civil unrest, but I didn't feel any of them took enough account of people like Aliya.

I pocketed the Makarov on my way out, wondering what I was trying to protect myself from.

Café Corso was over the top for a first date, but I wanted somewhere with front of house as a line of defense. They did Russian dishes, heavy on cream and pastry. The interior decoration involved doilies and cross-stitch cushions decorated with children sledding. Somewhere a sleazy expat like Toby might think was discreet, but not so high-end that he'd run into government men and their own mistresses. I chose a seat out of earshot of other diners, but with a sight line to the door.

These situations are never my favorite: The fact is that at least one of you might be risking your life by turning up. And yet the appearance of relaxed confidence is all. Nine people inside: five staff, four customers. Two men sat at the counter, speaking Italian; in the center of the room, a man and a woman in dark suits were poring over designs for what looked like a nightclub. Lace curtains on a brass pole divided the front windows in half. Above them, the sky was getting dark. Streetlamps caught fresh flurries of snow in the air.

She entered a few moments after seven. The fur of her hood framed her face, sparkling with tiny diamonds of ice. I got up and hugged her, feeling for wires or weapons. Then I kissed her cheek; it was cold.

"I'm so glad you could come. You must be freezing. Sit down." She placed her bag in her lap, looked around.

"Been here before?" I asked, in Russian.

"Never." She spoke English. That was fine with me. You didn't truly get to know someone unless they were speaking their first language, but if English made her feel safe, or want to show off, English was fine.

"It's okay, a little eccentric. Forgive the cushions."

"I forgive them. You have the word 'kitsch' — is that right?"

"Borrowed off the Germans, yes."

"Kitsch." She tried the word in her mouth. Her makeup was fresh, her drop earrings caught the light.

"How was your day?"

"Fine."

I passed her the menu. "Go wild."

"You take all your women here?"

"Only the ones that write such superb fiction."

She considered this. "Is it obvious?"

"To me."

Aliya ordered hot chocolate with cream. I ordered *sbiten,* a Russian drink with honey and spices. When the waitress left I said, "I thought the story was quite brilliant. The way you used such clarity of language to describe confusion, both lucid and utterly at sea."

"At sea?"

"Lost. You say, in the story, there is clarity in being lost. That is the heart of it, for me. The magazine I have mentioned it to—the *Walbrooke Review*—are very interested. I know the editor there, Sebastian Morley. He's a nice guy. The magazine's small but read by influential people. They've published Anna Starobinets, and Guzel Yakhina—I believe she's of Tajik origin."

"Really?"

"You know their writing?"

"Of course."

"What do you think?"

"It would be amazing."

"What are you working on?" I asked. "At the university."

"My thesis."

"Tell me about it."

"I don't think you'd be interested."

"I'm interested in everything."

"I am looking at the idea of Kazakh literature, and the invention of folk cultures. Many of our heroes were selected by the Communist Party —secular poets and thinkers. Ones that suited them."

"But is it not true that you had 'bards' here?"

"Yes, singers. An oral tradition. But now they are gone. I am not sure people will bring them back, or should try."

"That sounds a provocative angle."

"In a Western university it would not be provocative."

"Do you get funded?"

"Very little."

"But enough to survive on?"

"Just."

Our drinks arrived. She ate the cream off the hot chocolate first. I sipped the *sbiten* and was transported back to a winter in Moscow, when I had decided Russia was the country I loved the most: the hard, magisterial beauty of the place, the cautious friendships, the writers I had met.

"And what exactly do you do?" she asked.

"I advise people investing money. I'm here to do some research. It is very dull."

"I am sure it is not always dull."

It was said genuinely. If I embodied the West, she hadn't attacked me yet. Perhaps her politics were a private matter, to be preserved in fantasy.

"Will you go back to England for Christmas?" she asked.

"I'm not sure yet."

"What about your family?"

I was momentarily thrown. The image that flickered into view was of Croxley Green. It was replaced by Toby's parents, less sharply defined but definitely richer, more glamorous.

"They are dead," I said.

"I'm sorry."

"It's been a long time."

"Are you married?"

"No." She raised an eyebrow quizzically. I changed the subject. "What do you make of recent events here? The ethnic tensions?"

"I think a lot of it is exaggerated."

"Exaggerated?"

"People online causing trouble."

I managed to stifle a laugh at her audacity. "Your family have always lived in Kazakhstan?"

"My father came here in 1970."

The Virgin Lands campaign, I thought. Khrushchev trying to turn the emptiness into agriculture, despatching Russians in their thousands to summon wheat from the steppe.

"What did he think of moving here?"

"He felt he was doing his duty. At that time a lot of Russians came, to farm. It was an adventure. That is what they told them. Building the socialist future. My grandmother was furious when she learned that my mother was marrying a Russian. But I solved everything when I was born. I am harmony."

I laughed. "You are exceptionally harmonious."

"Thank you."

"So your mother is not Russian."

"No. She is from a small village in the south of the country."

"Did your father never want to move the family to Russia?"

"He loves this country."

"Of course."

"And my grandmother is with them. She is not well. Home is not such a good place to be. But I am saving money." She wiped cream from her lips.

"It's interesting times, isn't it? Do you feel free here?"

She shrugged. "You are free until you want to criticize the government. People are not used to thinking for themselves anyway. Do you like it here?"

"Very much so."

"You prefer Almaty to Astana."

"No."

"It is nicer."

"It is pretty. I like places that don't entirely work, though. The less pretty ones."

"Why?"

"I don't know. They are just themselves. People are surprised you are there. I like places that haven't been expecting me."

She drank her chocolate, considering this. "Does England work?"

"That's a good question. Sometimes. Have you been to Europe?"

"No." She hesitated as she said it, which made me curious.

"Really?"

"What do you mean, 'really'?"

"You sounded uncertain."

"I have never been out of Kazakhstan. It is not easy for us. Why don't you have a wife?"

"I'm never anywhere for long enough, I suppose."

She waited for a proper answer.

"I haven't found someone I want to be with. I am a very private person."

"You date Kazakh women?"

"Not yet."

"A rich English businessman in Astana, and you have not found a wife." Her eyes held a wry glint.

"I know," I said. "I can't have been paying attention. Still, I'm not being sent home yet."

"You think you will be sent home?"

"It was a joke. I'm very much my own boss anyway, and I would happily stay here. Perhaps I will."

She looked skeptical. I experienced the lightheadedness that comes as you begin to enter your cover and believe the things you say; when you are most convincing and most vulnerable. Stay sharp, I thought. Maybe it was too hot in here, sudden comfort after the cold. The Italians left, a family of four arrived. It was seven fifteen p.m.

"May I ask," I said. "Is there a special man in your life? A boyfriend?"

She shook her head, stirred the remains of the cream into the chocolate and considered it. "I do not have time. A man will want me to stop working."

"All men?"

"Kazakh men."

"Marry an Englishman." I turned my cup in its saucer. "I mean, I have heard this is still a very traditional society."

"More than ever."

"What do you mean?"

"Traditions are returning. People's idea of tradition."

"Why is that?"

"Now we have some independence, people want Kazakh identity. We have Russia above, China next to us. Both big powers. So we must be Kazakhstan."

"And how do you feel about this?"

"I don't know. You have a lot of questions, but you are the one who has seen the whole world. What do I know?"

"I've seen very little of the world."

"I don't mean to be angry. It has been a stressful week. Do you know where the bathroom is?"

"Downstairs, I believe."

"Excuse me."

She went, taking her bag. I wondered if there was any suspicion bound in with her irritation. I searched her coat pockets: headphones, receipts for lunch, container of pipofezine, an antidepressant. The life report placed Aliya's home twenty minutes' drive away. I'd checked the bus routes, however, and they were slow. And, in this weather, unpredictable. I thought I could find a way to accompany her.

Aliya returned, appearing more composed. I needed to get her out of here.

"You are interested in my politics?" she said, as if the conversation had refused to release her.

"Of course."

"We won't be a serious country until we have democracy."

"But people approve of the president."

"Of course. He is all we know. He has kept us out of war."

"I guess that's all you can ask."

"For now. But soon things must change."

"The people I have met here are good people. I think maybe your country can remain peaceful. Advance, and remain peaceful."

I called for the bill, paid in cash. "I'll drive you home, if you like. I've got a feeling the buses might be difficult."

"Where are you going?"

"Well, I was going to go toward Koyandy. There's a supermarket out there that stocks some European things I can't get anywhere else. It's open late."

"Really? That's quite close to where I live."

"Perfect."

"You have a car?"

"Yes. I'm parked just around the corner."

A home visit was good due diligence. She would invite me in. Hard, if not impossible, to fake a family.

"No. It is not necessary," she said suddenly.

"I am driving you," I said. "No arguing." I was surprised by a burst of adrenaline. I watched her wrestle with something that evidently needed to be said.

"You must understand," she said, finally. "My home is not rich."

38

I'D LEFT THE CAR A STREET AWAY. SHE CLIMBED IN WITHOUT COMMENT. I kept the headlights off for as long as possible, in case someone was looking out for them, only switching them on once we were on the main road. She looked at me curiously.

Night had settled, with a quarter moon sharpened by the cold. Her directions led us into older, eastern suburbs in the process of being brought into line with the new architectural look of the capital. All the surrounding villages were meant to be put in order by 2020. Right now it looked like a construction site: concrete plants, steel frames, tower cranes with aviation warning lights.

"A city changes faster than a human heart," I said.

"What is that?"

"Baudelaire."

"Oh, I know Baudelaire. *Les Fleurs du mal.*"

"He's one of my favorites."

"Do you think it's true, about a city?"

"This city, for sure."

Digital visions of the paradise-to-come decorated the fence panels of building sites. Faceless people moved through an imagined world: hotels, shopping centers, residential compounds with their own golf courses. Build it and they will come. Oil dreams. Baku, Doha, Abu Dhabi. Crude trades at over a hundred dollars and cities appear. You can make any ideology seem successful. But it's not the future — it's just money. It runs out.

I put the radio on: *Semey on a knife edge. Nazarbayev on his way to address protesters' concerns.*

"Have you heard about this?"

"No." Aliya looked as shocked as I did. "Really? He will visit them?" You could hear the crowd on the radio, chanting. When would he appear? The protesters weren't going anywhere. Now even more people would join them. Maybe it was a stroke of genius. If anyone could pull it off it was Nazarbayev.

"The president knows this is it," I said. "This is how things start."

"Yes."

"Think it will work?"

"I hope so."

"He better have something good to say."

"It is Nazarbayev. He just needs to appear."

We crossed the city's ring road. A minute later Aliya directed me left, into a cluster of low, plain houses. Her home was set back from the road, lights on. I stopped the car.

"Have a good night," I said.

"You should come in," Aliya said. "They'll be amused."

"Wonderful."

"In a nice way."

"I won't stay long."

Aliya's mother answered the door. She looked like her daughter: tall, dark-eyed. Her father appeared behind her with a gray mustache and two days' stubble.

"This is Toby," Aliya said in Russian. "He is English. He gave me a lift home."

"A guest!" The father shook my hand, and pulled me in.

I spoke in Russian: "It's an honor to be here."

"You speak Russian?"

"A little."

The living room was low-ceilinged, warm. Filling one end was a dresser with shelves holding Soviet china. The grandmother lay on a couch to the side, face softened toward her toothless mouth and gleaming eyes.

We sat on cushions around a low, lace-covered table. The mother produced a loaf of home-baked *shelpek,* Kazakh flatbread. The father opened a bottle of vodka and found two glasses. I looked around. A rare thing, access to ordinary homes: the people who are not bad or powerful and so rarely worth spying on, but can sometimes change history. Cable TV box, television tuned to Europa Plus, the non–state news station, showing reports from Semey, the crowd outraged in the snow, waiting.

The mother switched it off, as if this were a private concern. I had a quick look at the local Wi-Fi connections on my phone, preparing to email malware to Aliya's mobile. That was the goal I'd set myself, although it was feeling more uncouth by the minute. They had KazakhTelecom broadband, connection speed 5Mpbs. Decent enough.

The father offered me vodka. His right arm was artificial, the hand prosthetic.

"To the friendship of our countries—two great empires, once upon a time." He had the Russian habit of smiling with the eyes alone. I imagined him forty years ago, arriving in this part of the world, in the southern reaches of the Soviet Union, full of wonder about the life ahead of him. Astana was an administrative base for the agricultural project in those days.

Aliya's mother fussed over having company, fetching bowls of pilaf, saucers of sweets. Aliya knelt beside her grandmother. There was a transparent flash of pity, a genuflection. She kissed the old woman's hands, and the grandmother ran a hand through her hair. Then she stared at me.

"Who is he?"

Aliya spoke Russian. "He is English. Visiting."

"A prince?" The grandmother cackled.

"She thinks you might be English royalty," Aliya called over. Her parents laughed.

"I'm the next best thing."

I felt that lightheadedness again. You get moments on a job—especially after a drink—when you're in a life, a home like you imagined a home might feel like. Enclosed in a moment. You're welcome there. But it's always someone else's home, and no one knows who you are.

I watched the grandmother and imagined her surviving the decades, passing through famines and ideologies. Her speech was inflected with something neither Russian nor Kazakh, almost Chinese. Aliya joined us, declined her father's offer of vodka.

"Where's your grandmother from?" I asked.

"Karakol, even further south than Almaty." That made sense. I was hearing traces of Dungan; she was a descendant of refugees from northwestern China, Hui traders who knew the routes west. A rare, linguistic treat. Aliya turned to her parents and spoke quietly: "She is worse."

"Today it is bad," her father said. He asked me about England, how much flights and houses cost, if I was anti-European. He had read on

Russian sites that Britain and America were not friends anymore and was curious about this.

"And what do you think of Kazakhstan?" he asked, when I had given my views on the special relationship.

"It is beautiful," I said. "The landscape."

"Have you been to the national park at Burabay?"

"Yes."

"You are here at an interesting time."

"Really?"

"The honeymoon is over. Many of my fellow Russians returned to the motherland after independence. Others enjoyed the oil boom. But now, without the oil prices, no one knows what will happen. But, please, don't believe this is the next Afghanistan. These are good Muslims. Not like the ones you have wars with. They are people like my wife." He smiled at her. "I am more Muslim than her."

When we had eaten, the parents cleared plates away and remained in the kitchen. Aliya and I were alone with the sleeping grandmother.

"Let me email you the details about the magazine," I said.

"Please."

I emailed them, with the links directing to malware instead.

"Have a look — I've been having difficulty sending documents."

"It opens but the link doesn't work. I get an error message."

"Hang on, I'll try again."

I took her phone, deleted the infected email. I sent her a clean one, clicked to the magazine's site.

"There you go."

No evidence left. But the malware would have been downloaded. Even as we spoke, it was tunneling its way into her device.

"This looks really interesting," she said.

"Great." Her parents returned. "Do you mind if I go and clean myself up? Is there a bathroom I can use?"

The bathroom was upstairs. So were the bedrooms. I took the opportunity to explore. The parents' room had bare plastered walls, a bed and single dresser. A framed wedding photograph stood on the dresser. I listened to the voices downstairs, seated, deep in questioning Aliya: where she met me, what my work was.

I opened the dresser — costume jewelry, bills going back years. Beneath them was a display box with a clasp. I opened it. On one side was a black-and-white photograph of an unsmiling man in the fatigues of a Soviet Tank Division commander. Her father. I recognized the Darul Aman Palace behind him, still intact, and felt a momentary shiver, as if overhearing a stranger discussing my own dream. Kabul, maybe 1979 or 1980. He could have been no more than twenty-one years old. Pinned opposite it was a Soviet Valor Medal with a red, white, and blue ribbon.

Sent to farm, sent to fight. Lives picked up and dropped down. I put the box back, returned to the hallway. The plasterwork here was peeling. All the furniture was old. Military pensions never stretched far. I thought about the medical treatment for her grandmother, and imagined the life of a bright daughter, a lucrative daughter. Responsibility like that could corrupt more effectively than anything else.

Her room was at the end of the corridor. Single bed, clothes draped over a single chair. No PC, but a laptop on the desk. On her shelves: old Russian translations of the English and American writers considered ideologically sound enough to be published under the Soviet Union, a canon about which I'd always been curious — Shaw, Hemingway, Shakespeare, Ford Madox Ford. Then newer, post-Soviet editions: Orwell, Fielding, Proust. A collection of Shevchenko's poems, the revolutionary currently sprayed across Astana's walls. I took that down, leafed through to "My Testament," the poem in question, in case it was marked in any way. It wasn't. On the desk were more current affairs: *The New Imperialism; The Globalization of NATO.* On the wall above the desk was a list of time zones and public holidays in different countries. A key had been left in the top desk drawer. I was approaching when I heard her steps on the stairs. I took a book from the shelf.

"Auezov," Aliya said, when she arrived beside me. She was smiling. "He is a good playwright."

"When I was in Almaty I saw a procession of men and women all dressed in white," I said. "I couldn't imagine what was going on. They didn't look like any particular religion. So I followed them all the way to the central cemetery. Do you know it?"

"Yes."

"They went to Auezov's monument and took turns kissing the statue. Then they sat down nearby and read from his works."

"It is a tradition, on the anniversary of his death."

"I thought it was beautiful. And the cemetery itself was so overgrown.

I loved all the headstones: crescents, orthodox crosses, Stars of David, Red Stars. They all seemed very comfortable together. But only one had worshippers that day." I had never shared the memory with anyone before, and saying it made me realize how much I treasured it. I put the book back. "I should go."

She nodded but didn't move except to tilt her head. I kissed her. She took hold of my wrists and kissed me back with raw, clumsy enthusiasm. When we drew apart she glanced at the stairs. The grandmother could be heard, complaining that I had not eaten. Aliya rolled her eyes. She moved closer so that I was against the wall and kissed me again, her fists against my stomach.

"I'm trapped," I said.

"You are not the one who is trapped," she said.

The family protested when I tried to leave. The father gripped my shoulder with his good hand. The mother gave me some *shelpek* to take home, still warm, wrapped in kitchen towel. At the door, Aliya said, "Thank you for the lift."

"No, thank you. For everything. It was an honor to meet your family. I hope to see you very soon."

"Send me a message."

"I will."

"You are a kind man."

"Not really."

She smiled. "You don't like me saying it?"

"What I've done for you is nothing. Really."

"No, it is something." She glanced behind her, then came out to kiss me once more in the snow. "You are kind, whether you like it or not, Toby."

39

I STOPPED AT A WORKERS' CAFÉ ON THE WAY BACK, HEATED BY AN OVEN in the center of the room, the lighting mostly supplied by headlights coming and going in the car park. More *lagman*, Silk Road comfort food. You could measure where you were in Central Asia by the noodles, which thinned as you approached the Altai Mountains and China. The clientele looked and sounded like rural migrants — *kolkhozn-iki* — on their way to night work at the construction sites.

Lights swept the room as a lorry pulled up outside. The driver came in: a fat man with a swaggering, loudmouth look. He knew most of the people, saw I was out of place. I could feel him watching me, waiting for the opportunity to stir some entertainment out of a turgid night. In the end, I turned and nodded.

"Come far?"

"You are Russian?"

"English."

He said a name. I took me a moment to realize he was saying "Oliver Cromwell" — "Oliver Cromwell, he was a man of the people." The revolutionary Cromwell loomed large in Soviet accounts of British history.

"Some of the people," I said.

"How much does a lorry driver earn in England?" he asked.

"Lots. You're a driver?"

"Thirty years."

"Where have you come from tonight?"

"Balkhash."

"Via Karaganda?"

"Yes."

"How are things in Karaganda?"

"There's people out, you know —" He mimed the waving of placards. "Angry."

"A lot of them?"

"Sure."

"Police checkpoints?"

"North and south, yes."

"What about Balkhash?"

"Quiet. But always too quiet. No women." He laughed, turned to the other men, and they laughed too.

A country in transition. I thought of Aliya's declaration: *Soon things must change.* Kazakhstan had a lot of positive energy in the tank. But states live miracle to miracle—utopias need cash. You have to keep the faith in progress going or the bad dreams start.

I thought of her grandmother's dialect. Not many Dungan speakers remained. My old supervisor at Cambridge would have been fascinated. I saw myself flying Astana to Heathrow; catching the train to Cambridge. It's chilly but bright, Hertfordshire passing by, a winter day that looks like spring. Straight to the college library. The security guard remembers me, nods. I find Victoria Fell's *Literatures of Central Asia* on the shelf. My bookmark is still there from twenty years ago. I sit down.

In fantasies we can be still. Yet that library was a place I had scavenged for means of escape. Linguistically, I had moved outward from the European tongues into the disorientation of Russian and Arabic, then south to the strange ones in between. In my second year I won a prize to be spent on traveling, so I hiked down to Tehran. That was in 2002, two months after Iran got assigned to the "Axis of Evil." It didn't seem particularly evil. A man who ran a pub near where I grew up had told me that in the 1970s they used to drive double-decker buses from London to India via Iran and Afghanistan, searching for pot, opium, mysticism. That was before 1979: before the Iranian revolution, the Soviet invasion of Afghanistan. He had faded photos of himself in tie-dye, the bus painted orange. It felt like learning of an old land route between continents that had become submerged.

But, with the low profile of a solo traveler, I re-created much of the route. The midnineties were tranquil compared to now. With every step away from home I felt lighter. Any anger I had carried from my childhood was becoming counterbalanced by a sense of guilty relief. I could escape.

After Iran, the closest I could imagine to a future was some kind of fieldwork that kept me traveling, so I proposed a thesis on Persianate culture in the time of the Mongols. The violently expanding empires of Genghis Khan and Tamerlane had thrown scholars and poets together, some seeking refuge, others collected by the emperors themselves: trophies and treasuries of knowledge. I was interested in the illiterate Khan, collecting scrolls as he conquered, haunted by the knowledge they might contain. *Hunting truth like the enemy,* my supervisor had said. Here, I thought, was a corner of history obscure enough to hide in.

My supervisor was a brilliant woman. She'd spent time in Sudan and Yemen and written the definitive book on Arabic poetry. Her husband was a "diplomat," as she described it. In retrospect, of course, it was all quite obvious. She was waiting for people like me. The whole place was a honeytrap.

When she first suggested working for the government, I was still recovering from an exercise with the University Officers' Training Corps. My feet were swollen and blistered to the extent that I was forced to wear flip-flops. I remembered sitting in her office like that, my PhD proposal in her hands, wondering why she seemed disinterested in it.

"This is all fine, and I think you would do it well. I wondered if you'd thought about other options." She put the sheets down as if they'd left her unsatisfied and would do the same to me. "You volunteer in the reserves?" she said.

Even while I sat there with bare feet and a bruised cheekbone, it surprised me that she knew this.

"Yes."

"Do you enjoy that?"

I had joined as a gesture against the comfort of the college, the equation of learning with physical ease. And because it seemed an entirely unlikely thing to do. The training felt like the shedding of skin, which reminded me of learning a language. At that time, I was hungry for transformation. I had spent my first months at the university impersonating those around me, fascinated by their ready-formed personas, their postures and ensconced positions in networks that appeared to have arisen spontaneously. I had practiced stretching my vowels, relaxing them as if I too was relaxed, letting my voice sink back in my jaw. I borrowed the grandeur of the college itself like a costume.

But, to my surprise, it was the army reserves where I excelled. The Brecon Beacons, where most of the training took place, was beautiful and desolate. Ten-kilometer runs became twenty with packs, became fifty-kilometer marches with strapless carbines, two hours' sleep in a damp bivouac, then fifty more kilometers. It became clear that they were not interested in your strength so much as your weakness. To know someone well enough to stake your life on them, you needed to know where and when they'd break. But you could only break if you were whole to start with. That was what I learned. The art was to divide yourself in advance; to divide yourself from pain primarily — your own and others' — and then from fear. The training, which had seen two men die in the previous five years, was both a border in your life that you were challenged to cross, and an ineradicable partition within you once you had done so.

I enjoyed map work, and even weapons training, which I approached as you'd approach a class on Japanese woodcarving — an intriguing skill you would never actually need. I remembered the meditative way in which a visiting commander with sunburnt cheekbones and sunbleached hair unrolled a black and white keffiyeh holding an MP5 assault rifle, and arranged the pieces on the scarf, cleaning them, slotting them back together. When he had finished there was the faintest scatter of sand on the Cambridgeshire floor. I looked up. He was watching me looking at the sand. He winked.

"Yes," I said to my supervisor. "I enjoy it."

A delicate first interview overlooking St. James's Park two weeks later, training at Fort Monckton eight weeks after that. All spies have these stories: being chosen, steered. No one wants to believe they sought this profession out.

The car's interior still smelled of Aliya's perfume. I sat in the back seat, opened my laptop, brought up a control board that replicated the home screen of her phone. I opened her contacts and address book, recent messages, check-ins, then closed the laptop and drove back into town.

I was in a shop attached to a petrol station, buying soap and a new toothbrush, when I heard a sound like corn popping. It came from a phone held by a man beside me. He stared at the screen. The crackling sound was gunfire. The man looked around, put the phone away, embarrassed.

Someone moved past, at the end of the aisle, talking on a mobile, an urgency in their voice. I walked back to my car.

Footage had been uploaded to YouTube showing protesters in Semey's floodlit central square, waiting for the president to appear.

It wasn't clear how events turned dark. One moment they were standing, apparently peacefully. The next moment there was chaos.

Two uploads, one from the square itself, one from a window overlooking the square. The footage from the square was jerky, audio distorted with screams. There were voices close to whoever was filming, a man and a woman. *Where are they? Get out of here . . . Where is she? Go up Baiseitov Street.* Then a ripple of tinny gunfire, joined, after a second, by three sharp cracks from a rifle. A woman began screaming some distance from the camera: hoarse, repeated cries of "*Joq.*" No.

I checked the other video. It came from a high window with a clear view of events. You saw the crowd suddenly become ragged, individuals running, turning; some people had fallen. There were voices in the room where it was being filmed. *They're shooting. Oh my god, look. Look. They shot him.*

The camera phone remained steady. Two or three hundred protesters were trapped in the square. They began moving in terror, found themselves blocked. More shots.

Eventually most scattered, leaving dark forms against the snow—the dead and injured. The person filming focused on one man, shot in the leg, dragging himself across the ground. You could see he was young—just the effort suggested he was young—then he shook as if electrocuted as someone unseen fired another round into his body.

I'd witnessed state brutality enough times, but this was breathtaking. I watched it three more times. The shots didn't sound like they came from the standard police rifles I'd seen. Something more heavy-duty, militaristic. There were at least three individuals firing, one from a height. You could see the crowd running right to left of the screen at first, then a louder report, closer to the camera, and they moved in collective panic toward the back.

I felt their shock. You think you're protected because something special is happening. And there are hundreds of you, standing side by side: people who've never fucked with power before and can't imagine that it's as desperate as they are.

Both videos were online for around ten minutes, then disappeared. I had two missed calls from Piper.

"Nine, ten dead," she said, when I eventually got through. "Confirmed. A lot critical."

"Who opened fire? Police? Military?"

"No idea."

"Where was the president?"

"We think he was stuck on the runway. Maybe weather. Maybe sabotaged."

"You're kidding."

"It's localized. It's a local dispute that got out of hand. That's how we're framing it."

"It's going to build."

"What do you suggest?"

"Make it about elements in the Kazakh government close to Russia. Connect it to Zhaparov."

Piper exhaled loudly. I continued: "The president's an experienced dictator; he hates mess. This is an opportunity to move Zhaparov out of power once and for all. That cuts out Moscow."

"We can't afford to inflame things."

"We're on the brink of a Russian takeover. That's not going away, nor is this shooting. So it's a question of how we use it."

"Okay. If you've got ideas of what we might get out there, send them through. I can't promise anything. I need to speak to people."

Khan Shatyr was still open. I pulled into its car park, headed past Tiffany and Hugo Boss up to the Kyoto Bar, where I took a seat at the bar itself. Screens were tuned to a variety of channels, none showing the shooting. It looked like Semey had gone blackout. I found a number for a couple of businesses there, hotels and restaurants, dialed them, and the line didn't connect.

The Kyoto staff were watching their phones. One tore herself away and came over. I ordered an overpriced Japanese whisky and downed it when it arrived.

Joanna had talked me through the principles of psyops: The essential ingredients of a political scandal are that it should be shocking and not immediately refutable. The best lies are simultaneously outrageous and built on truth.

I had a platform. Piper's team had been at work. Raiymbek, the Kazakh warrior, now existed—he even had a picture of himself on horseback with spear and helmet. He worked Twitter hard, posting almost hourly in Kazakh, Russian, and English. The content was eclectic, ranging from footage of Russians abusing a Kazakh prostitute, to repeated links to a blog called Kazakh Independence, which had been up three hours and already boasted eight hundred subscribers. Its first post, on the Bolshevik invasion of Kazakhstan and its accompanying atrocities, had been shared more than one hundred and twenty times.

I lifted an image of some of Zhaparov's elite antiterrorist troops and identified them as the men firing at protesters, emailed it to Lucy Piper, and suggested Raiymbek might circulate the idea that the shooting was on Zhaparov's direct orders.

"Use the phrase 'Putin's puppet.'"

Piper approved. I called a freelance journalist contact, one who was always keen for tips, less keen on fact-checking, and knew how to get pieces fast onto reputable sites that fed into the national press.

"Want an angle on this shooting in Kazakhstan?"

"What shooting?"

"I'm sending something over. Take a look."

She stayed on the line.

"Okay, I'm interested."

"Can you get it up asap? I think there's rivals of yours here trying to break the story."

"I can try. I appreciate this."

A man walked in, stared at me. I paid for the whisky, walked out.

I walked fast, up the escalators. I touched the gun in my pocket, instinctively. The artificial beach was open for another three-quarters of an hour, according to the boy taking my money. I said that was fine. He gave me a towel. It was quiet inside. Snow tickled the glass roof above the artificial waves. Staff were raking the long stretch of sand beside the water. Most of the remaining customers were eating and drinking at tables set up beneath palm trees. No one followed me in.

I got a smoothie, calculated escape through the staff exit, watched the entrance. A message came through ten minutes later from my journalist contact: The story was up.

They'd run it as I'd written it. Headline: "Kazakh Protesters Shot Dead." I used a couple of my social media accounts to broadcast the link, tagged in a selection of anti-Russian figures: Polish, Ukrainian; some Washington-backed organizations, some human rights, some teenagers in bedrooms.

I waited.

Eighty views. Then up to one hundred as I watched.

Sites in the US and Poland were linking to it. Then it got the first pickup from mainstream media in Turkey and India.

Two men came into the beach. I saw a third I hadn't noticed before, beside the water, watching me. All were conspicuous. The two arrivals looked thuggish, with clothing that would conceal arms—one in a cheap brown leather jacket, one, taller, in a black anorak. I finished the smoothie, got up and moved toward the exit. Out of the corner of my eye, I saw one of them speaking into a hands-free mic.

I ran down the back stairs.

A BMW pulled out behind me when I got to the road. I headed to the riverbank, then down the bank to the ice. I heard the car stop and saw its lights above me as I began across the river, slipping and sliding but staying on my feet. Police lights flashed on the left bank. I waited for them to pass, then clambered up snow to dry land, keeping to the darkness, wondering where to lie low. I needed somewhere with the cover of other people, somewhere I could be anonymous, wait, assess. I looked around and saw the neon sign for the Rocks.

The doorman nodded me in. The young barman winked and started pulling a pint when he saw me. I took my drink, moved into the darkness at the back, leaned against the bricks and watched the door. The bar was filling up, the first tentative forays onto the dance floor. Green lasers cut through the artificial smoke like targeting systems.

"Rahmat says you're from England." A girl's voice startled me.

"Rahmat?"

"The barman." She was twenty, maybe twenty-one, heavily made up. She was drunk, eyes narrowed.

"That's right."

"Do you think my English is good?"

"Very." I saw her friends giggling in the background.

"I am a television presenter."

"I bet you're a good one. Where are you from?" I asked.

"Astana."

"Really? I didn't think anyone was born here."

"Yes. I wish I could go to England."

She bumped a hip drunkenly against me. I watched the room reflected in the mirrored walls.

"Let me ask you a question," I said: "Who would you choose as president?"

She frowned at me. "Nazarbayev."

"I mean after Nazarbayev."

"Someone modern."

"Is it important to you to vote?"

This was funny to her. "Loosen up. It's, like, a party here." She disappeared into the smoke. I looked around. The man with the brown leather jacket sat at one of the barrels, staring at me.

There was only one exit, and he'd positioned himself between me and the door. I was potentially outnumbered, but we were in a crowded bar and people would pile in sooner rather than later if a fight broke out. I moved the Makarov from my pocket to my waistband just in case. Then I saw Sergei Cherenkov, assistant to the cultural attaché, Russian embassy, walking out of the dry ice toward me.

He wore a waistcoat over a white T-shirt, hair gelled back. He held two bottles of lager, gave me one.

"We're not the threat, Elliot. For fuck's sake."

"Are those your men?"

"Yes."

"What do you want?"

"I suggested that you keep in touch with me or get out of Kazakhstan. Can you see the problems you're causing?"

"I'm not sure I introduced the problems here."

"Let's sit down."

"Have you found Joanna?" I asked.

"Please, let's sit."

We took a booth. It was dark, and Cherenkov sprawled on the leather seat opposite me. "I haven't found her," Cherenkov said. "No one's found her. People found the body of her hacker, of course. Tomorrow the story's going to come out. The line they seem to have decided to use is that Ruslan Batur was working for a gang: organized crime. That's what they'll say. Shot by a Makarov pistol, like the one you're carrying."

It was possible. Equally possible was the idea that Cherenkov was trying to disorient me, force me into a position of desperation.

"Your prints are there, Elliot. Either you killed him or Joanna Lake killed him."

"Or someone else with a Makarov."

He gave a disappointed sigh.

"I haven't found Joanna, but I found this." Cherenkov took his phone out, swiped down videos, and played one. It was Joanna and myself in Café Corso.

I was wearing what I'd been wearing when I met Aliya. I could even see our drinks on the table. Only, the woman who sat across from me was Joanna.

The sensation was bizarre — poignant and chilling. Cherenkov gave me the phone and I watched it again. She looked younger than I remembered her the last time I'd seen her, as if this was part of the fantasy. She held herself in a way that was accurate, but the facial expressions weren't right. She smiled too much.

I thought back to the café, tried to figure out how I'd been filmed: what this meant for my security and for Aliya Savinova's.

"Is it real?" Cherenkov said.

"No."

"Is this?" He leaned over and tapped the next video. It was a couple having sex. They were in a hotel room, bedsheets tangled. None of the flamboyance of porn, just two bodies, naked and entwined. The shot was static, low-quality, from a camera that must have been on a dresser or behind a mirror. It looked like surveillance. Cherenkov gave me the phone. It could have been my back. The hair was right. I had to wait another minute before my face was visible. Joanna's was clear enough.

"Why do I have this?" he asked.

"You tell me."

"I have it because some guy in Moscow got it from a friend in the German Federal Intelligence Service who got it from a contact in Six. One way or another they wanted it to land in Moscow. Why is that? You and Joanna Lake?" He sipped his beer. I gave him the phone back.

"Are you working with Vladislav Vishinsky?"

"No." He laughed. "Vishinsky? I would love to catch his eye. I am nothing."

"He's here in Kazakhstan. What does that mean?"

"You're here. What does that mean? That's what we're asking ourselves. You have quite a reputation in our circles."

"Do I?"

"Why did you leave Saudi Arabia? You went back to London, then came here. What were your instructions?"

"My instructions were not to."

He considered this, then glanced at his phone again. "This is a question I've heard people ask: Can you blackmail someone over something they didn't actually do? Perhaps the question is: Can someone feel shame over something they didn't do? What do you think?"

"I don't feel ashamed because someone is trying to play games with me."

"Are you ashamed of the things you do while you are someone else?"

He tore his gaze from the phone and met my eyes. I didn't answer. Cherenkov let the question hang for a moment, then took a deep breath.

"You like Russia. You wrote on Russian poetry. You have friends there: Denis Tretyakov, Daria Nikitina."

"Are you threatening them?"

"I'm showing you your new life. Because I don't think you can go back to the UK now. Not as a free man."

"No?"

He waved the phone again. "Why are they exposing you? A great officer like yourself. I understand ingratitude, Elliot. Look at me. They used to send us to Kazakhstan as a punishment. You think that has changed? Here I am, and all I can tell you is that something is not right."

"You can tell me this: Is Joanna Lake working for you?"

"Not for me personally. Whether she's working for anyone else, I'd like to know."

"If she's in Russia now, just say and I'll clear off."

"Not as far as we're aware. Explain to me what exactly she was working on in Shefford."

"I don't know what she was working on."

"Well, you've got a day to find out, by my reckoning. You know where the Russian embassy is: Aleksandr Barayev Street. You'll be safe there. We can get you out of here, start making sense of things."

"The cold war ended a while ago."

"So we're told. But you don't need an ideology to defect, Elliot, just a life. I was sorry to hear about Hugh Stevenson."

I grabbed his arm as he got up. A bottle fell from the table and smashed. People turned.

"What's happened?" I said.

"The question I'd be asking is: What hasn't happened? Why are *you* still alive?"

I pulled him back into the booth, got my fingers around his larynx. His protection detail moved in.

"What's happened to Hugh Stevenson?"

"I'm trying to save you," he gasped. I released him before his heavies arrived. Cherenkov gathered himself together, then walked out, followed by his team.

40

I SEARCHED ONLINE FOR NEWS OF STEVENSON ONCE I WAS OUT OF THE club. A BBC report had been published two hours ago: "Body Found on Hampstead Heath Identified as Senior Government Official."

The body of senior Foreign Office official Hugh Stevenson was spotted by a jogger on Hampstead Heath in the early hours of Tuesday morning. It is believed his wallet and phone were missing. The area, a notorious cruising spot, has seen two violent robberies in the last week. A police spokesperson has said that there are no immediate suggestions of any connection, but individuals are being warned to stay away from the area after dark. A government spokesperson has said that a full investigation is under way and it would be inappropriate to comment at this time.

Cold-blooded bastards. The wind was knocked out of me. Ruthlessness like that spelled desperation. But whose? That kind of strike on one of its own was unprecedented for Six, as far as I was aware. But the subsequent misdirection was slick in a way I found hard to imagine being directed from abroad. I looked around, and the absence of any visible company was threatening in itself. *The question I'd be asking is: Why are you still alive?* Then the absence filled with guilt. I saw Stevenson in the library, where I'd first met him, flapping the pages of a newspaper as if in endless irritation. Over a long career, there were only two other individuals for whose death I felt directly responsible, but they happened in the course of authorized operations. I could offload some of the guilt. Not here.

Marsh had tried calling twice in the last hour. I went to a public phone box, exhaling with relief when he answered.

"You're okay?" I said.

"Just."

"When did you last speak to him?"

"The afternoon before he was killed."

"What did he say?"

"Hugh was trying to establish what was going on. I'm sensing divisions, schisms, right up at the top level of Six."

"Like what?"

"I don't have any details. Hugh just said a crisis was going on. He wouldn't give me more than that."

I wondered what that reflected, and how I fit in. Genuine penetration by Russian intelligence? Clashing agendas, or governmental interference?

"Any suggestion of who killed him?"

"No. But the story's wrong. Hugh was killed less than a couple of hours after speaking to me, not at night like the papers are saying. I spoke to his partner, Sunil. He said Hugh had a taxi booked to go somewhere. He was killed before he could get there."

"Where?"

"Cording House, St. James's Street."

I could picture St. James's Street: gray-stoned Georgian blocks between Piccadilly and Pall Mall. According to Marsh, Cording House was currently the headquarters of a company called Talon.

"It does defense technology — research and development. Used to be part of the government's Defense Evaluation and Research Agency. Still comes up as List X."

I'd heard of Talon. It was one of several companies created in the early 2000s, when the government privatized its defense research. List X contractors were those approved to handle classified governmental material, with sufficient in-house security of their own. Which made sense if they used to be a governmental department and were still supplying tech to the UK military.

"Any idea who he was going to visit?"

"No. Apparently he knew someone with information. Someone he trusted. Maybe someone who knew what was going on."

When I was back in my hotel room, I brought up a number listed for Talon Inc. But I had no idea what I'd say to whoever answered. A company like that would be stuffed with individuals close to government and intelligence. Hugh could have known any number of them.

What did I have? A lot more from the last few hours, but a lot more mystery with it.

Semey. Sergei Cherenkov. Reza. *Called me in the middle of the night. She'd seen plans of some kind, relating to those explosives. Wouldn't give me a source.*

All came down to those final minutes. Contacted me, contacted Reza. She spent some time in the internet café. Injured, life at risk. What was she doing? Who else was she contacting? What else was she searching?

I took one of the unused phones and called Stefan. He had checked in to the St. Regis Hotel, next to the Astana airport. The political situation had rendered flights scarce, but he was well positioned to grab one at any sign of trouble.

"We need more on the internet café Joanna Lake used," I said. "It's the last known location we have for her. She was in there for a while. I want to know what she did on that computer aside from contacting me. The search history was wiped, but I reckon the PCs might be monitored by the owners, in which case there will be records on the central system."

"I can take a look."

I searched for more information on Stevenson's death. There was nothing online. A few stories speculating on his intelligence service connections had vanished.

Meanwhile, overnight, a lot of accounts had appeared making anti-Chinese comments. About two hundred of them, mostly in Russia, some in Kazakhstan. Aliya was on a Sinophobic jag of her own: Chinese companies buying up Kazakh land, Chinese men stealing Kazakh women, Chinese dams diverting water from Kazakh lakes.

Who was steering her? Vishinsky? Was this Russia using residual Kazakh prejudice against the Chinese to ensure that their own grip on the region wasn't supplanted?

Aliya linked to aerial shots of prison camps in Xinjiang, supposedly housing thousands of ethnic Kazakhs. There was an interview with a man in Almaty.

My wife went to China in 2016 and hasn't returned. A year and eight months have passed since then and we have had no word from her. We've just recently found out that she's in a re-education camp. I'm begging our government, our Ministry of Foreign Affairs, to return the mother of my children. We're living in a kind of hell at the moment.

I switched the laptop off, lay back on the bed, and saw Stevenson walking toward the lamplight and the pond. I felt the darkness returning. The only way of staying sane in this job was to remain detached. Other people's tragedies defeated that or rendered it psychopathic. Joanna called intelligence work the stupid game. You involve people, telling yourself it's under control, draw them in. You risk their life.

I could still feel Aliya's kiss. I sat up again, opened the laptop, and went back into her phone, planning to wipe all traces of myself. I would take a look first, though, considering all the effort of gaining access. *Lord, let me be pure, but not yet.* I checked text messages and WhatsApp first. Friends, social occasions, advice to one girlfriend about a breakup, plans for a holiday. Eighty-one entries in the address book, fifteen landlines, sixteen addresses outside Astana, none overseas. I activated the camera. It was dark, the phone facedown on a surface. I reversed directions, selfie-mode, got a blade of ceiling fan. I kept the visuals open in the corner of the screen, put headphones on and activated the microphone. Listened to what sounded like crockery being set down, then her parents' voices.

Seventeen anodyne videos stored. I watched through them all: someone's baby, a friend's birthday party, a 360-degree view of mountains. Her photos were similar. It was all so generic, I started to wonder again if she was real.

I checked the sent file. A lot of people didn't realize it stored sent images even when the original had been deleted. I looked through until I got to a view that made me stop.

The Houses of Parliament.

Aliya stood in Parliament Square, Big Ben behind her, smiling and saluting.

April 23 of last year.

Similar photos beside the Thames, in a London park, Chinatown. A view from a hotel window across the London skyline. Then one inside the hotel.

It showed a large hall, with tables lined up. There were oil paintings on the wall, large vases of dried flowers. The tables were laid out with what looked like conference packs, lanyards. No name or sign was legible to suggest the nature of this event.

I went into her messages and scrolled back to April; there were several to a girl called Sabina.

I've arrived.

Still don't really know what this is about!

They've asked us not to use our phones while here. No more pictures! See you when back!

The cutlery of her home clinked. The family conversation involved Semey: how many dead, what the protest meant. The image from her phone camera moved as Aliya picked it up. I killed the connection. A minute later my own message light blinked.

Good night, Toby. Thank you for this evening. See you soon. x

I sent her a good night, put the phone down and stared at it. Then I picked it up again.

So she had been to London.

Smartphones embed GPS coordinates in each photo they take. The information is stored as metadata embedded in the photo files themselves. All you had to do was view the file's properties and look for it.

I opened the hotel jpeg, went to Info, clicked on the GPS tab. Latitude and longitude coordinates appeared in the header. Lat — N 33.00, 56.00, 17.82, Long — E 19.00, 9.00, 39.85. I entered the coordinates into our mapping software and arrived at the Millennium Hotel, Earls Court.

I gave them a call.

"Hi. I don't know if you'll be able to help me. I attended an event at your hotel in April last year, April twenty-third. I need to speak to the organizers but have lost their contact details."

"What event was it?"

"I can't remember the exact name."

"Hang on . . . We had several events that day."

"Could you read them out?"

"Asperian Retirement, The Association of Vice Chancellors, Worldwide Media."

"Worldwide Media, I think."

She gave me a phone number, but it didn't connect. There were a lot of "Worldwide Medias" online, but none that seemed more dubious than any other marketing company.

Why London, I wondered? It seemed to point toward whoever was behind this, but there was a range of options: UK government, a UK company, an outsider trying to make it look like that. Plenty of Russians in London. Plenty of international companies.

Hacking a hotel was easy enough. You could just email as a current supplier, a guest, or a wedding planner, with malware-infected specs attached. A conference would leave plenty of traces.

I sat on the edge of the bed, wondering what my next move involved. I was going to have to keep the connection to Aliya's phone. Once again, someone else's duplicity justified my own. I looked at Aliya's photograph of London again, then videos of the shooting in Semey going up and getting taken down.

41

PEOPLE IN THE CROWD HAD GUNS. THAT WAS THE FIRST DEFLECTION used by officials in Semey trying to control the news agenda the following morning: Salafi jihadists running amok. By nine a.m. it had traversed the news, entered social media, and attracted angry, widespread derision, cracking the surface of Kazakhstan's usually respectful forums. The president, as ever, played a smarter game, announcing an immediate investigation and calling for unity. He identified a spiritual crisis in Kazakh society. WhatsApp and YouTube were down. Tumblr had vanished amid accusations that the platform hosted pornography.

In photos on surviving message boards you could see volunteers tending to the wounded in what looked like a mosque, padding around in socks, oxygen cylinders and plasma bags set up between stone arches. People had formed human chains in front of Semey's police station, while solidarity protests erupted in three other cities. This was it: the point of no turning back. I felt that dizzying, glorious fascination of being there; seeing what happens when the limits of what is possible are breached. Spring again. I used to hear the chants in my dreams: *The people demand the fall of the regime.* It was slicker in Arabic but still had something wistful about it, even when there was hope — something measured and legalistic. Chanted by people who had never chanted before, spreading across Tunisia, Egypt, Libya, carried by a shared language, the language of the Koran, suddenly a vehicle for this democratic virus.

On British sites, news of Stevenson's death had gained a note of caution: "Question Marks over Intelligence Officer's Murder." That would turn the heat up. Spies dead on home soil. Whatever Vauxhall's involvement, they'd be working overtime to defuse that scandal.

Sirens outside.

For the sake of not keeping still, I went for a drive.

I drove past Kiber Sports. There were police vehicles parked outside. It looked like it had been broken into. So we'd been beaten to it, I thought. I wondered who had the data. That was a precious lead gone.

I continued past the places you might expect protests in Astana: the main square, government buildings, Bayterek. In the long, landscaped park that stretched from Bayterek to Khan Shatyr, the committed had turned up, in clusters of eight or nine, wrapped against the cold. But it only made the surrounding silence more conspicuous. A city without a past does not really have a population — everyone is dependent on keeping the fantasy alive. It felt like being swaddled in one man's dream, which was a generous way to describe dictatorship but had some truth here.

When I logged in to Aliya's phone, I could see her also searching for protests. She'd caught the bug. *Where and when are people meeting?* I logged out, sent a text message:

Awful news about Semey.

Really awful. Did you get back ok last night?

Yes. Thank you again.

Will be in touch v soon. Stay safe. I added: *Keep clear of crowds,* then deleted it. A message came in from Stefan. He was still stuck in the St. Regis waiting for a flight. He had something I might be interested in.

I wound my way around the city center a few times. When I was convinced there was no one following I headed over to the airport hotel.

Stefan answered his door looking unslept. There was a hard drive on the carpet, connected to his laptop: the beige case of the PC it had belonged to beside it.

"Is that what I think it is?"

"That's right."

"You took it from Kiber?"

"I couldn't sleep so I went out. The door was practically open. They have everything on here. This must be her, right?"

On the screen of his laptop was Google browsing history from the time she'd been in the café. She'd been browsing for me: It included the search strings: *Elliot Kane; Elliot Kane Kazakhstan; Elliot Kane MI6.* There were also four different cover names I'd used on operations.

"She's trying to see if you're out there, what you're up to. Less than a minute later she starts searching for up-to-the-minute satellite imagery."

He showed me. Joanna checked through a series of sites that let you search recent satellite data: Digital Globe, the European Space Agency, finally Earth Explorer, which gave you access to NASA's land data feeds. In each, she typed in the same coordinates.

"She's trying to get up-to-date imagery of a particular region," Stefan said.

I punched in the GPS coordinates she'd been searching. They took me to white spaces in the east of Kazakhstan. I heard Shomko's voice — *I saw men studying a map, talking about the possibility she went east.* I thought of the photo of activists Reza had found. Then I thought of the chain of events he had reported: Before disappearing she stole a Chevy Equinox. Had she headed there? Semey was close by. It was near the Russian border.

I looked at the imagery again. What I had initially taken for blankness had a faint pattern visible: roads that appeared to have faded. I crosschecked with Google Maps, then official Kazakh maps. Neither recorded anything for the area. But zooming in on satellite view, I could make out right angles suggesting manmade structures.

"You think she's there?" Stefan asked.

"Something is. Can you check to see if anything with a nearby geotag has been uploaded? Photos, video, anything."

My phone screen lit up. It was Callum Walker. I didn't answer. I brought up the photograph of Joanna that Reza had sent through the previous day — the one of Joanna in a group of people — feeling increasingly sure this connected to the location in the east. Ten minutes later, Stefan had the satellite images up again. He said: "It's wrong."

"What's wrong?"

"The weather doesn't fit current reports." He showed me two current weather reports. "I think someone's hacked the satellite feed."

"What about local uploads?"

"Nothing at all. I think internet's blocked."

"Someone's trying to hide something."

"They've succeeded."

I clicked "directions" on Google Maps: 240 miles.

"Six hours to find out."

"Google doesn't allow for people trying to kill you on the way," Stefan said.

I nodded. It wasn't entirely a joke.

"I'm going to give it a try," I said.

"I won't be here when you get back."

"Well, next time somewhere sunnier."

"On me."

This was the manner in which we always parted. But I realized something was new. We were genuinely worried, even if we weren't going to show it.

42

I FILLED THE CAR'S TANK AT A PETROL STATION WITH A SUPERMARKET attached, then filled two spare jerry cans. I reckoned I could cover the distance in less than the estimated six hours if I put my foot down. But I bought eight liters of water, three days' worth of food, and spare batteries just in case. I put the gun under the seat.

The only plausible destinations in this direction were Pavlodar and Karaganda, although it was still insane to be driving across the desert. What was my cover? Karaganda had a football stadium and power plant. Pavlodar had Sary-Arka Airport twenty-four kilometers to its south. I went online and bought a plane ticket from Pavlodar to Istanbul — my excuse for this travel, should I need one — then got in the car to drive east. On Joanna's trail again.

A Toyota Yaris passed in the opposite direction, seemed to slow. I watched the mirror as it continued away from me. No other vehicles appeared. Eventually I left the last construction sites behind and plunged into a landscape like a white sea. The city receded behind me — civilization, other humans — the elastic stretching until the view in the mirrors was as empty as the one through the windscreen, and I was alone.

Desert rules: Beware men flagging you down. Give lorry drivers a wide berth — most are wrecked on crystal meth. Don't lose the road: It was level with the desert either side, no barriers, no lights. An old Soviet road, potholed, bleeding into the landscape. I focused on its line. There was something comforting about being able to see endlessly in each direction. I had escaped, for now. I had no idea what I was heading toward.

A few miles farther and the road became white gravel. That dragged my speed down. A rusted line of containers stretched along the horizon. I passed one dust-coated lorry marked Dong Feng, driver expressionless behind shades. Around two p.m. I saw a settlement a couple of miles to the east. They cropped up at intervals along the railway; track gangs, who might try to rob you but would possibly sell you some stale food and black market fuel. The railway itself was invisible but would be a single track carrying cargos of oil and gas from the Caspian to Druzhba on the border of China. I could smell the diesel fumes when I opened my window a crack. After another five miles I could see the oil tanks themselves, stained black and smeared with rail grease.

The railway veered away, replaced by mountains alongside me, and then the mountains retreated. No landmarks apart from the road itself. Sometimes that vanished beneath snow and I had to check coordinates and pray. I'd read of intrepid Roman travelers who had reached these parts trying to navigate by the stars like sailors. I'd been trained in astral navigation, but it was a long time ago and I hadn't had to call upon it recently.

Any variation meant a lot: small shifts in gradient, the appearance of a ruined fort on the horizon, occasional nomad tombs — domes a few meters high, made of well-preserved mud brick. Then the gradual appearance of low, blunt mountains to the east, striped in bands of pink and gray. The snow thinned, and then I realized it wasn't snow anymore. The dirty white landscape beside me was salt flats. I'd read stories by people in this area who claimed to have witnessed centuries-old corpses brought up perfectly preserved. It stayed like that for the next hour, and then I became aware of company.

I made out the horsemen a few minutes before I reached them. Two figures alongside the road, rugged as the land around them, leading horses visibly starving beneath blankets. A few hours from the glass and chrome of the capital. They seemed inexplicable, and you had to remind yourself that this was the scale of their world.

They came over when I stopped. The horses were gaunt, ribs vivid, their owners wrapped in layers of weathered rags. I greeted them in Kazakh and explained where I was going, asked if there'd been any trouble. They shook their heads.

"Where have you come from?" I asked.

They had come from a village thirty miles to the east, looking for pasture. That was the only trouble they were aware of: starvation. I asked if they needed money and they said no, just food for the horses. I wished them luck.

I drove on, wondering how much they knew of the nation around them. If there was a war, would they realize? There would be signs and portents; people like me passing through their emptiness, loaded with a meaning we carried away with us. Perhaps that would be all. Fifteen years ago, traveling through the south of the country, I'd encountered a group of hunters and fallen into conversation with them. My concern that they would connect me to contemporary geopolitical affairs soon evaporated. They had spoken as if the Soviet Union still existed. With regards to England, a couple of them knew that England had once invaded India, that the English were bloodthirsty but weren't convinced that the country still existed. Events reached them like the light from dead stars.

I didn't pass any other vehicles. The road surface was reasonable, and I had five hours of daylight left. The nearest town was over one hundred miles away. Around four p.m. I passed a twelve-ton China Transport shipping lorry crashed on its side, a day's snow on it. The windscreen was cracked but not by a bullet. It had Jiangxi plates, straps for the canvas sides hanging loose. Beyond it, pylons thickened across the landscape toward a town as if catching it in a web.

I checked the GPS. I was heading in the right direction. Heading into gulag territory. Kok-Terek, where Solzhenitsyn had been imprisoned, lay thirty miles to the east. Dostoevsky ended up nearby after his release from Omsk. There were a lot of towns around here where men freed from the gulags had settled, too exhausted to go farther. Or unwilling, for reasons that never quite clarified for me, but made me think of Solzhenitsyn's advice for survival in the camps: Let go of the idea that your life ahead will be anything like the one behind. A new mountain range occupied the horizon, all gray shards. Then I hit a problem.

Two vehicles appeared in the distance, parked across the road. A block of some kind. I couldn't see any men.

I touched the brakes. There was still half a mile before I reached them. One was a black Subaru Outback, the other a UAZ minibus of the kind you see being used as dirt-cheap public transport in former Soviet countries. There was nothing else around for miles.

No point turning. I would have been seen. And my destination lay beyond them. I'd driven for over five hours now and wasn't inclined to turn around.

I advanced slowly, stopping twenty meters short of the block. The closer you were the fewer options you had. I left the engine running. The signals on my phone indicated they were using radios, but not police band.

Three men climbed out of the UAZ. One of them, the oldest, was in a heavy ankle-length winter coat. The other two wore desert fatigues under fur-trimmed bomber jackets and carried Kalashnikovs. They moved with the stiff caution of men who are bored, cold, but prepared to kill you if it comes to it. The older man was craggy, thick-featured, with an ugly stare. A black-handled pistol nestled in his holster.

He approached my window shaking his head and wagging a finger. Then he saw my face and peered closer. "No farther," he said in Russian.

"Why?" I asked. His men stepped either side of my vehicle.

"Papers, please."

I handed over my papers, gave my story about the flight, and showed the e-ticket on my phone.

"I need to get to Pavlodar," I said.

"The road's closed."

I offered money. The captain rejected it sullenly, like someone taunted. Which meant there was a big old chain of command beyond them. It had them scared.

I turned the car around, making a show of irritation, and wondered what I'd encountered. The mixed uniforms and weaponry suggested a militia. The younger men had the determined eyes of insurgents. I drove a kilometer back until they were out of my rearview then turned off-road. According to the map I could loop them. If I went a mile east I could re-join the road beyond the men, unseen. I could also lose my bearings and never find another road again.

I marked my GPS position and set off. After twenty minutes of rough driving I found myself back at something approximating a path, but it was not the same road. I'd gone wrong somewhere. That was when GPS chose to go screwy. And even if I was still heading in the right direction, I wasn't going to get there over raw desert. I had half a tank of petrol left, plus the jerry cans. I swigged some water, got out, and checked the tires. Then I saw a faint pall of smoke a mile or so away.

More humans. Whoever they were, there would be a track of some kind connecting them to the world, surely. But it was a random place to settle. An outlaw kind of place. Still, there was a good chance it was the last contact for several hundred miles and I needed to get my bearings. So I headed toward the smoke.

After ten minutes I saw a cluster of makeshift buildings. There was a chance I was about to be robbed, but I didn't have much choice. I contin-ued, past a starved-looking dog chasing a plastic bag, into what seemed to be a herdsmen's village. The houses were low and misshapen: rough walls of mud bricks, occasionally plastered over and painted white; small windows, roofs of corrugated iron weighed down by bricks. A grotesque parody of a nomadic camp: Winter cattle sheds had been built from whatever lay to hand: fragments from dismembered trucks, old tires, rusted bedposts.

The smoke puttered out of an unlocked shack. Two men lay among empty vodka bottles beside a stove filled with white ash. That was the only furniture. They looked up at me as if I was a hallucination, and made no attempt to communicate. I walked past to a fence made of flattened drums that, according to their markings, had once held sodium chlorate. Behind it was an adobe house. At the back I found an ice-encrusted water tank and a pile of scrap metal.

I was leaving, despondent, when I felt eyes on me. A girl, nine or ten years old, appeared among the scrap.

"*Privyet*," I said. "Hello." An identical girl appeared. They were twins, clothes grayed and patched beneath their coats. One whispered something to the other and they giggled. I searched my pockets and gave them a protein bar. Then the mother appeared, saw me, and began scolding them.

I showed her the map on my phone and asked where we were. It was too cold to be outside, she said, and invited me in.

The home had a warm, damp, close smell. Hanging carpets hid the dirt walls. Furniture was a double mattress and cushions. An antique sewing machine took center stage. A stove poked its chimney through the roof. A man's boots hung off a nail along with a rusted horse bridle.

The woman heated a samovar. I recognized that code of hospitality, lost in the developed world, where you rarely found yourself truly at the mercy of strangers. I would never forget the individuals who had invited me into their homes without question: Aleppo, Afrin, Shatoi in Chechnya. It was the code of the sea, an obligation to help vessels in distress, and an Islamic tradition, a religion of the desert; the knowledge that the absence of hospitality was death.

"The weather is changing," she warned as the tea heated. "Where are you going?"

"Pavlodar," I said.

"Not tonight," she said.

She asked where I was from, what on earth I was doing here, and I embellished my tale of trying to get to the airport, describing a bad hour of getting lost without mentioning the roadblock. The girls poured the tea, watching me openly. Both had an extra finger on each hand. It jutted out, slender and perfectly formed, like a second stalk beside the little finger.

"Hello," one said in English. "How are you?"

"I'm very well. How are you?" They laughed. They saw me notice their hands and giggled and I concentrated on their faces.

"What is your name?" the other said.

"Toby. What is yours?"

I didn't get an answer.

"They are learning English," the mother explained. She brought out what I thought might be an exercise book but was a leaflet from Testimony.

Know Your Rights.

Beneath the charity's logo, and an oil tower with a line crossed through it, the leaflet quoted local residents who had been harassed in connection with energy company work. It outlined steps individuals needed to take if they encountered problems such as compulsory purchase orders, limits on organizing and protesting, an enhanced security presence. It even gave legal contacts, and listed medical issues to watch out for connected to nearby drilling.

There were pictures of heavy machinery, security guards, children in hospital beds. The text was in English, Russian, and Kazakh.

The girls read some words out loud — *health, oil, protect* — then looked up at me, smiling.

"Who gave you this?" I asked.

"The people who came." The woman passed a hand through one of her daughter's hair, mimed cutting it.

"People who cut their hair?"

"Just a little."

"A sample?"

"Yes."

"Have you had oil companies around here?"

"I don't know. I don't know about any of this."

"Protests? People angry?"

She shrugged.

What were Testimony doing passing through here, taking hair samples? This definitely seemed to connect to Joanna's presence in the area, and made me to keen to keep moving. Light was fading. I finished my tea, checked the map again. The woman studied it with me and advised on passable roads.

I tried to give some money as I left. The woman refused, then shyly took it.

"You are crazy. You should not go farther."

The girls cleared the cups away without taking their eyes off me. I said goodbye and they waved. I smiled. I walked past the rusting scrap and the old sodium chlorate barrels.

Half a mile outside the village, signs appeared on either side: AGRICULTURE BANNED.

Sodium chlorate was used in the mining of uranium. Northeastern Kazakhstan was used for an atomic bomb program for forty years. They were still testing bombs as the Berlin Wall came down. Moscow men would make a trip to watch the mushroom clouds. Locals had been exposed deliberately as guinea pigs. The steppe was a laboratory, riddled with unfissioned plutonium.

Trees appeared ahead: a dark canopy of Scotch pine on emaciated-looking trunks. But just inside the woodland, the road had been blocked. Square slabs of wood lay across it, painted white with signs nailed into them: DANGER. NO ENTRY.

The signs looked new. I got out of the car, listened, checked for fresh footprints. Then I checked for sensors, cameras, land mines. Nothing that I could see.

The wooden slabs were heavy, but I managed to work a solid branch beneath them and use it as a lever to roll each one a couple of times. That was enough to squeeze the car through. I stopped on the other side, got out, and rolled them back. Then I flattened the snow where they'd been moved.

Trees closed in as I continued, the spectral white trunks of aspen and birch among the pine. Then they thinned out and I glimpsed a dried-out lake, a decrepit jetty reaching into mud. I checked the map: nothing for one hundred and twenty miles. Which made it unnerving when I cleared the trees and saw the outskirts of a small town.

43

THERE WAS ONLY ONE ROAD IN AND IT WENT PAST THE CONCRETE RUINS of a guards' post: a booth with broken windows, struts in the ground beside it where a barrier would have rested. Any metal that could be lifted had been stripped from the place. There had been a fence once. The roof of the booth itself had been pried off.

Two red-and-white-striped factory chimneys rose up a mile out. Closer than them were three apartment blocks, hinged into shallow V shapes, pocked with hundreds of dark windows.

It had been a closed town, one of those the Soviets considered too sensitive to have people moving in and out freely. Abandoned for a couple of decades by the looks of it. Which made the fresh tracks of a vehicle — with deep tread and ten-inch-thick wheels — a worrying sign.

The apartment blocks came into focus as I drove in, windows smashed, faded murals flaked from the end walls: a woman with arms aloft before a globe; two miners, one with Slavic features, one Kazakh. Silver water pipes snaked above the ground. The ice that ran down from them formed a low, opalescent curtain, waist high. It was minus eighteen outside, but the wind straight off the steppe took another ten degrees off.

I drove further in, slowly. Perturbed by the fresh tire tracks. By the Testimony leaflet I'd seen. Getting closer to a zone that had been hidden from satellite view. Two redbrick buildings the size of churches had collapsed into themselves, filled with piles of their own bricks. Trees grew above and through the buildings. The water pipes wound between them, scattering lagging across the ground.

In the center was a town square. I saw the *Kinoteatr* in front of which Joanna had been photographed. The car was struggling on the snow now. I stopped, got out, pulling my scarf tight, sealing myself into my jacket. It seemed a good moment to explore, to literally retrace Joanna's footsteps. Past the cinema was a town hall, then a school with cracked plasterwork the same color as the snow. I continued into a park with a playground and a sculpture: a sphere of blue and white oxidized copper beside a bearded man in a suit. I cleaned the plaque at his feet. IGOR VASILYE-VICH KURCHATOV. NUCLEAR PHYSICIST.

I laid a gloved hand on a roundabout in the playground and it turned, smoother than I'd expected. Every blank window seemed to watch me. I wondered how far I was from another living human.

I kept moving, as if obeying the logic of the place itself, toward the derelict factories.

The factories arrived a mile or so before the mine itself: two roofless chemical plants, stripped like carcasses. One brown bricked construction was more intact. Squares of late sun decorated the floor inside. Fixings remained where the machines had been. Nests filled the corners, and black pelletlike droppings scattered across the floor from bats. Turbines and gangways had been left to rot. There was an office in the corner with a rotten jacket hanging on a peg, rusted circuit boards from a computer on the floor.

Beyond the factories, indentations preserved the direction of a narrow-gauge railway running toward the old mine. Alongside these, I made out the tire tracks again, more this time — leading back into wilderness, on the opposite side of town from my entry point.

I returned to my car. I wanted to find out where they led.

I followed the tracks until the town disappeared behind me. Then a warning sign appeared, this one bright and startling, placed on a gate in the road in the past few weeks: DANGER. PRIVATE PROPERTY. GUARDED BY GL5.

The chain had been cut. I opened the gate, drove through.

It was getting dark, the white disk of sun sinking. Clouds moved fast, as if getting out of the way of the approaching night. I was entering woods again when my petrol light came on. I got out and refilled from the canister, grateful that the trees blocked the rising wind at least. That left me with twenty liters of backup. By the time I started off again, I needed headlights but was reluctant to use them. Then my phone lit up: There were radio frequencies ahead. Military radios.

I stopped, wound the window down and listened, then reversed slowly into the trees, positioning the car so that passing headlights wouldn't illuminate its reflectors. It was bitterly cold once I was outside. I could make out faint light ahead: pervasive, artificial, illuminating the sky above the trees. I tucked the gun into the back of my waistband, put gloves on.

Whatever lay ahead, it connected to Joanna's visit here, and her subsequent disappearance. What was she pretending to protest against? Why hadn't it been included in the reports I'd seen?

The road felt conspicuous, so I stepped off the tarmac into the trees and continued deeper into the woods until I was out of sight but close enough to the road that I didn't lose my orientation. I could hear activity half a mile ahead: the low hum of what sounded like a construction site, scraping of tools and wheels and engines. I was forty miles from the Russian border, I estimated. The signals pattern on my phone showed layers of radios. Then the trees were interrupted by a chain-link fence, and I heard Russian voices.

I reluctantly flattened myself on the forest ground. Torch beams came closer, snow crunching between boots. I risked a glance to assess what I was up against. There were five of them, bulky with black combat gear — the pouched tactical vests of Special Forces, assault rifles with mounted night sights. No insignia that I could make out. Vehicles had Kazakh plates. Kit was carefully generic. But these weren't local farmers.

The steps stopped. My body was already starting to shake. I needed to move but the noise would reach them. I needed the cover of some other sounds. None came. Two of them spoke a language that wasn't Russian. It took me a second to place it as Serbian. That was unexpected. It suggested mercenaries. I was considering a run for it when they adjusted kit and walked on.

I waited a moment, then eased into a low crouch, trying to still my shaking and stop my hands from going numb. They were a distance away now, themselves keeping low. It looked like a surveillance unit. They'd wandered away from the source of the noise. I moved fast, following the fence to a gate that had been forced open. Another GL5 warning sign, no guards, a clear passage through. I went in.

It was another fifteen minutes stumbling through trees before the gradient afforded a clear view. Floodlights lit a flattened square of compacted mud half a mile across, cleared for a drill pad. Bright yellow diggers looked small beside it. Security guards patrolled with sniffer dogs. To the east was a pit large enough to bury a five-story building. Pipes and cables waited to be laid, stacked beside two holding tanks bearing the Saracen logo. Around the edges, unlit, you could see the ruins of the old mine: a mountain of gray waste, the rusting towers of the extraction plant. A new road ran from the site to a complex of temporary buildings, porta-cabins with gleaming black GL5 patrol vehicles beside them. So I'd found a few more of the two thousand currently in Kazakhstan.

The level of security suggested there was something special about this site. I didn't have time or warmth to search for it now. I headed back toward my car, but hit a problem.

Five men stood around it, the Russians and Serbs, quiet now, scanning the surroundings with their weapons up as one of them radioed details. The boot was open, more men approaching through the trees. I stepped back.

Their own patrol vehicle was parked a few meters away, closer to me than it was to them: a light cargo truck, mud-colored canvas over its flat bed. No one had stayed with it. I took a few steps closer to the truck, saw keys in the ignition. Then I slid into the vehicle, praying that it moved quickly. They all turned in my direction. I turned the key.

"Hey!"

I dropped low in my seat as the truck began to move. I drove straight at them at first, which caused some temporary disruption and blinded them with the headlights, then I dragged down the oversized steering wheel and circled away. A bullet pinged off the front engine. A second smashed the back window. Shifting gears was a fight, but the horsepower felt good.

Once on the road, I floored the accelerator, glad to put several miles between myself and whatever crew was nosing about. Twenty minutes later I was still so focused on threats behind that I didn't see the Toyota Cruiser speeding toward me, less than a second from a head-on collision.

44

THEY REACTED SLOWER, WHICH MEANT I WAS THE ONE WHO STEERED off-road. The truck bounced over ditches, throwing me up against the roof, tearing the wheel out of my hand, but slowing the vehicle so that when I crashed into trees I didn't go straight through the windscreen. I slammed into the steering wheel and came to a stop.

Three balaclava-clad men appeared in the headlights, Kalashnikovs pointed at my windscreen. I raised my hands. One of the men tore the door open and I was dragged out, forced to the ground, searched. My face rested in the snow as I tried to imagine various ways this could unfold and kept arriving at my death. It felt too soon, rushed, and with this came rising panic, and then a faint accompanying awareness that I needed to keep control of myself if I was going to have any chance of surviving.

One turned and called: *Hna*. Another man appeared from the trees, unmasked. *Hna*. Here.

Arabic.

I was lifted to my feet. Four men now, two in camo fatigues, two in a mixture of nondescript khaki and civilian clothes. I could see narrower Kazakh eyes behind the balaclavas of the khaki men. The lead camo fatigues wore gray gloves and looked Middle Eastern. He was the jumpiest, the one I was most cautious about, scarf pulled up to his eyes, shoulders hunched, combat-jittery. The arrival from the woods had broad, blunt Slavic features, a fair beard beneath his chin encrusted with ice, but mustache shaved. All of which said Chechnya. The sharp, unmistakable scent of unwashed fighters cut through the cold. No alcohol on their breath, though. Weapons held professionally, kept angled down when they spoke to one another, movements controlled, pupils undilated. No visible radios: an underground crew, guerrilla-smart.

The jumpy one barked orders in Arabic without taking his eyes off me: "Check the vehicle, check the boot, check the road." The choppy, guttural language sounded startling among the snow. When he spoke to me he used Russian, which was understandable, as I'd been hauled out of a Russian military vehicle.

"On your knees."

I was forced to my knees, the barrel of his Kalashnikov grinding against my temple, told to put my hands on my head. The flash eliminator at the end of the barrel dug into my forehead. Was this the Islamic Movement of Kazakhstan? Did they regard themselves as such? It wasn't unusual to come across men who didn't know who they were fighting for that week. Deals were made several ranks higher, sometimes countries away. My phone was torn out of my pocket, then thrust at me. I entered the password, watched out of the corner of my eye as he tried to scroll through with gloves on. I tried to decide which cover story was least likely to get me shot immediately. One of the Kazakhs was going through the truck. There was a debate along the lines of *Should we kill him or take him?* It turned out to be my lucky day. My hands were bound behind my back with duct tape and I was marched to their vehicle, a blue Toyota Cruiser with roof rack, where I was offered the boot.

The only other time I'd ridden in a boot it had been voluntary and got me out of Kashmir. That one had been more spacious and more recently hoovered. I rested my head on a coil of old rope and wondered if I was going to freeze to death before we got anywhere. When the car started I jammed my feet against the metalwork to stop myself being bounced too hard. I kept thinking through a cover, feeling out any remote possibility of surviving the night.

After thirty minutes we pulled over ruts. I was hauled out and a bag came down over my head. We entered somewhere heated, which felt like a reprieve in itself. The bag came off.

We were in a brick-walled farmhouse. I was put in a side room with a concrete floor and a small barred window. Twenty minutes later another vehicle stopped outside and I heard more men arrive. My cell door opened. I looked up to see a man in his fifties or sixties, a hard-looking Afghan or Iraqi. He had a nickel-plated Kalashnikov slung over his shoulder, his hands gnarled.

While the rest of the men explained finding me, I pondered this multinational get-together. Chechens got around; in Syria, at least one vicious rebel crew was Chechen-led. You found Chechen Islamists wherever there was the opportunity to fight Russians — especially since Russia had gained the upper hand at home. And Russia had pushed plenty of its own Moscow-loyal Chechens into Syria to fight for Assad. Same war, different country. Many of the Islamists joined ISIS.

It made some sense that they'd head north again.

I could see how Russians encroaching on Kazakhstan would be a provocation to them. I could see how jihadists encroaching on Kazakhstan would be a provocation to the Russians. Could see, with sickening clarity, why either side would cut my throat with nonchalance.

A rifle butt slammed into my face. I thought it might have broken a cheekbone and experimentally moved my jaw and checked my sight. I was intact. I was forced to squat with my back against the wall, thighs parallel with the ground, while the boss questioned me: *Name, commanders. Which unit? Which battalion? Why no uniform?*

"You are Russian."

"English."

"The jeep—"

"I stole it."

"What are you doing here?"

In training you're told to ride out the first few hours, when the situation's new and everything's terrifying. But then things become known and it's not always uplifting.

"Where is the man you took?"

They thought I was involved in the abduction of one of their men. I wondered who was. I had nothing for them. I'd stumbled into a warzone, it seemed, but was playing catch-up. We kept going around in circles. *Why are you here? What are your plans?*

After a while the questions stopped. A new length of rope was looped around my hands and tied to a bolt in the wall. He left one of his own guards to watch over me, one of the youngest of the men. I hadn't been fed or watered, which meant they intended to kill me. They wouldn't spend a second night here, and I was a travel liability.

An hour passed. I stretched and relaxed as far as my restrictions allowed; recited poems in my head to keep alert and conscious. I listened to the voices of my captors and let them carry me to various points of the globe. I was back in the Caucasus Mountains, two years into my career. It was a dream job, among the tribes, up in the clouds and jagged white peaks, tasked with establishing a picture of gang operations. I befriended the locals. I was shown how to chew certain flowers against altitude sickness. In the mornings I watched my shadow cast up into the mist half a mile in height. My official brief involved ascertaining hierarchies, but these people didn't do hierarchy, they did blood feuds. That was their life. And the only way to step beyond the endless, innumerable tangle of feuds was to establish yourself as *abrek*. My predecessors had translated the word as "bandit," which missed the sense utterly. The *abrek* were outcasts, gathered high in the hills, forbidden to work the fields or engage in business. They survived alone, feared but respected. These were the men I was trying to reach. I outlined the anthropological phenomenon of the *abrek* in a detailed report sent to the Central Asia desk in London, for which I was informed that I was not at Trinity anymore. It elicited a smile, even now.

A spade hit the frozen soil outside. I listened to the clink and shuck of its blade. As the darkness began to soften, my guard stepped out of the room and I watched his shadow on the bare concrete floor as he knelt and prayed. *Fajr*, dawn prayer. A time worth marking. I tried to remember all the men I'd watched praying: complacent ones, desperate ones, ones who did not know they were about to die. His shadow pointed to the front of the house, which meant Mecca was in the opposite direction to my barred window. That was southwest, then; at least I had my bearings. There was something unusual about his muttered prayers, and after a while I realized he was praying in Dari. A Dari of West Afghanistan, cut off from Kabul by five hundred miles of mountains. I thought of the deep blue lakes of Band-e Amir, and the pristine Panjshir Valley, and the people there, as serene and welcoming as the landscape, as if environments worked so transparently. I watched his face when he returned.

"From Herat?" I asked, trying to rustle up what remained of my own Dari.

He looked suspicious.

"It's a beautiful place," I said.

No answer. From West Afghanistan to Kazakhstan: that sounded like a heroin route. I thought through the various warlords who controlled the trade.

"Can I stretch for a few seconds?" I asked, sticking to Dari. "I can't feel my legs."

He kept the gun on me as I got to my feet, bent my body left and right to stretch the spine. A vehicle pulled up outside and there were two new voices: talk of firefights, low ammo, faulty radios.

Around six a.m. I was untied and marched out. They'd dug a shallow grave. Given the frozen soil, it was more trouble than I was worth. Eight men stood around and I scanned for the weapon intended to kill me. No one had a knife out; no camera ready to film. One of the new arrivals, arm in a bloody sling, came and looked at me. He wore the uniform of a Kazakh border guard.

Borders, I thought. Heroin. Northern Kazakhstan . . .

I was led to the edge of the grave, hands still bound. The sky was a washed-out blue. In its half light you saw the spindly fence around the farm buildings, dividing a hazy, infinite pallor. Every mission you go on, you prepare mentally for death. Which is a different thing from preparing for life-threatening scenarios. In those you have years of training to fall back on — focusing, keeping calm, maintaining connection. Then there is the moment when death becomes inevitable. You prepare a final, hidden handful of thoughts and images that might bring you peace in your final moments. I didn't want to miss that. I thought of Joanna, but it didn't bring me peace. I didn't like dying with a mystery unsolved. I watched the fence appear in the gray light and thought of borders. One man controlled the roads all the way from Balkh in Afghanistan to Kazakhstan's border with Russia. I had sat on a carpeted floor with him, toasting our friendship with fermented camel's milk. And with that, a plan solidified.

"Kneel." My knees touched the cold ground. The Chechen raised his gun. I said:

"Akan Satayev."

"What?"

"I know Akan Satayev," I said in Arabic. "I've worked with him."

The boss came over.

"What are you saying?"

"I was at his wedding two years ago in Aktobe. Akan's. I imagine you came here via Mingdon, on the Uzbek border, under Akan's protection." I didn't expect anyone to believe me — I just needed to make killing me potentially too risky.

"Who are you? What are you doing here?"

"Tell Akan it's Christopher Bohren. The British want to help."

The safety catch eased down. Someone lifted me to my feet and I found myself eyeball to eyeball with the boss.

"You lie."

"You've got half the Russian army coming in," I said. "How long are you going to last without help? Let me speak to Akan."

The senior men consulted. I was made to go through my story once more before someone produced a satellite phone and gave it to the chief.

He disappeared to talk inside. I didn't hear what was said. After five minutes he reappeared. I was begrudgingly given a blanket, driven again.

45

I WAS SPARED THE BOOT THIS TIME. WE DROVE IN A STRAIGHT LINE EAST, by my estimation. After twenty miles or so there was a change of vehicles. I was blindfolded, passed over to someone with a different grip, led over broken branches for a couple of hundred meters to a car with good heating and leather seats. We drove for what felt like an hour. Then I was pulled out.

Ten meters of tarmac underfoot, into the warmth of a building with a smell of bleach. I was led down a long flight of stairs through two doorways with beaded curtains. Someone unknotted my blindfold.

I stood in the basement dining room of a restaurant with plastic vine leaves over the ceiling. Akan Satayev sat at the farthest table, watching me. I was shoved into the seat facing him.

His hair had grayed, eyes dark. He wore a creased suit jacket, and a white shirt that wasn't fresh today. A rich man who hadn't slept in his own home for a while. We'd both aged less than we deserved. His career had clearly done better than mine, although, until last week, he was more likely to be the target of an assassination. Hence the missile-proof basement, I imagined.

One guard stood to the side of Satayev. Another took the doorway, gun on me. Satayev studied my face.

"Christopher," Satayev said. At the hint of personal warmth the barrel pointing at me relaxed a touch. But it didn't drop.

"It's good to see you, Akan."

"Are you sure?"

He studied my damaged face. The wars and deaths since our last meeting had carved a depth behind his eyes. He retained some of that aura of the rich, of moving through the world in a slightly slicker substance, but there was a gravity there, a melancholy that I associated with military figures more than with criminals or businessmen, both of whom could go a long way without knowing the names of those killed on their behalf.

Satayev had started out as a regular midlevel thug. His family had clan control of the region — the transportation of heroin and lapis lazuli in particular. He became boss, gained some notoriety for extortion and kidnappings, then the Kazakh president had some trouble with local Cossack gangs. Satayev was given carte blanche to get rid of them, which he did, ruthlessly. That handed the Satayev family not only regional power, but control of the smuggling route across the border.

Afghanistan is the world's biggest producer of heroin. Russia's the world's biggest consumer. In between the two lie Uzbekistan, Turkmenistan, and Kazakhstan, depending on your route. One hundred kilograms of raw opium cost a thousand dollars in Osh. In Moscow you could sell it for fifteen times that, more again in Western Europe. Labs around Moscow processed it into heroin. Smuggled into Sweden by boat, then all over the world — the addiction epidemics raging meant big money. I'd spent a lot of time beside the US-built Nizhny Pyanj Bridge that connected Afghanistan and Tajikistan, getting blind drunk with border guards, but not so blind I couldn't see the bulky sacks coming through on the backs of Satayev's trucks. From Tajikistan, the heroin and opium should logically pass through Uzbekistan, only the Uzbeks are paranoid, hate their neighbors and so actually pay border guards to do their job. Which meant Kazakhstan was good traffic.

Satayev got filthy rich. And like any businessperson who finds themselves sitting on several million dollars, he expanded. Guns, oil — but most of all, he controlled men. His money funded the armed wings of various criminal enterprises in Iraq, Afghanistan, Kyrgyzstan, and Kazakhstan. He was a blissfully unidealistic fulcrum of several shitstorms, which made him as appealing to MI6 as he was to anyone else. His routes were precisely those along which NATO liked to move armies. So I set up shop beside the historic Jayma bazaar in Osh — buying cheap cotton for a fictitious textiles company — and in less than a month I was sharing boiled sheep's head and negotiating payoffs.

Like a lot of barely literate, power-hungry criminals, he had an instinctive grasp of international diplomacy. But it had been a while since his name did me any favors. I hadn't seen or spoken to him directly for over a year. It was possible he'd kill me anyway, but there was a shred of comfort in being killed by someone who knew at least one of my lives.

My phone and gun lay on the table. The table's polished black surface reflected the plastic vine leaves above us so that they seemed to reach up like pond weed. A decent restaurant suggested some habitations nearby. I considered the scale of the place, the distance driven—I guessed a town between Semey and Pavlodar.

"It looks like you have trouble," I said. "Maybe I can help."

"*I* have trouble?"

"We have trouble."

"You were sent to find me?"

"I was sent to assess the situation."

"And you found me. I think this is too much for coincidence."

He ordered my cuffs removed and sent one guard away with orders to bring water and tea.

"Is this a good place to talk?" I said.

"That is why we're here."

"There are Russian mercs up near the border. What do they want?" I said.

"What do you think?" I let this ride, curious. The drinks arrived. Satayev stirred a sugar cube into his tea. He continued: "There have been drone strikes on my men, my vehicles."

"From across the border?"

"We think so. Russians closed the border, set up checkpoints. Their men came into the country, no official uniforms. Said they were a 'local militia' defending ethnic Russians against fanatics. Bullshit. They are trained forces."

"So you got some jihadis."

He dismissed the word with a flick of his hand. "I don't believe you've become that naïve, Elliot."

"Are your men connected to the Islamic Movement of Kazakhstan?"

"I've never come across any such group."

"But you're using Chechens and Afghans, Akan. That's a controversial look. It's not going to win you friends."

"Who would you like me to use? Or shall I tell the Russians that Block Nine is all theirs?"

"Block Nine?"

"What do your bosses say to that? Is the UK government willing to hand oil to Russia?"

"I don't know about Block Nine," I said. Satayev looked puzzled.

"Why do you think Saracen are here? Why are they so desperate to get extraction rights for the field?"

"Tell me."

"Because it's big. Their big new discovery."

"How big?"

"Thirty trillion cubic feet of gas, over five billion barrels of oil."

I stared at him in astonishment as my brain did the calculations. If what he was saying was true, it was the biggest energy discovery of the last twenty years. Satayev, at least, seemed sure of the numbers.

"You've seen data?" I asked.

"I've seen data."

"Where did you get it?"

"Friends in Russia."

"Where did they get it?"

"Stolen from Saracen. Hacked, leaked, I don't know."

"I need to see that data."

"Of course — if you're in a position to help. Saracen have been buying up every square kilometer of land around. They use front companies, but we're not stupid. Nor are the Russians. You could have saved yourself a lot of trouble by speaking to me in the first place."

He reached into his pocket and tossed over a dog tag: four digits, no name. The numbers given to soldiers by the Russian defense ministry usually have a single letter of the Russian alphabet followed by a six-digit number. Russia's PMCs — private military contractors — in Syria only had four.

"Sigma Group," I said.

"You know them?"

They'd turned up in Ukraine aiding the separatist forces of the self-declared Donetsk and Luhansk people's republics. Then we picked up the exact same men in Syria, fighting on behalf of the Syrian government. Their chief mission was capturing ISIS-held oil fields.

A former special forces brigade commander was in charge, and the company was named after his old call sign; he headhunted elite troops, some from the Russian army's Nefte Polk, the oil protection regiment created to protect Chechnya's oil infrastructure, some Spetsgruppa A, a counterterrorist subunit of special forces. The company was registered in Argentina, offices in Saint Petersburg. By our estimations Sigma Group controlled over six thousand men. They got good pay. In return, they signed ten-year confidentiality clauses, handed over their phones, received a nameless dog tag with a four-digit number. I handed it back.

"Private military," I said. "Possibly used as cover for Moscow, possibly more renegade."

Sigma had a Serbian unit that had cropped up briefly in Palmyra. That startled the GCHQ listeners initially, especially those who'd been around in the nineties. Like the West, the Kremlin had become keen on private military contractors as a way of lowering official casualty numbers—but the situation wasn't without friction. When US air strikes ended up killing a lot of Sigma men involved in attempting to capture a Kurdish base last year, there were accusations that information hadn't been shared by Russia's Main Intelligence Directorate, and suspicions that the defense ministry might have been hostile toward private entities conducting a major operation without its approval.

The scale of things made sense now. The concerted Russian information warfare, Moscow's cultivation of Zhaparov, Sigma turning up. It looked like Akan needed help, which was fortunate for me.

"Who else are you speaking to from the UK?" I asked.

"No one."

"You have contact with GL5?"

"Informal."

"They pay you so they can operate here."

"Yes."

"And when did the Russians arrive?"

"Six days ago."

Just after Joanna had gone missing. "Have you come across an Englishwoman?"

"No."

"Possibly with eco-activists."

"Those aren't my problem."

Satayev may not have been able to help directly with finding Joanna, but he was certainly a potential ally against the people I suspected of targeting her: the encroaching Russians.

"Still in contact with Jan Jágr?"

He nodded. Jágr was a former military translator turned arms dealer. He ran an air freight company based in Namibia, with two Ukrainian-registered Ilyushin-76 cargo aircrafts originally designed for delivering machinery to remote areas of the USSR. Now they mostly delivered light weaponry. The hulls were sheathed in lead to deflect bullets, and he could land them almost anywhere. More important, he was a master of paperwork, with a web of thirty or forty front companies under his command, frequently reregistering aircraft and keeping his money moving between territories. He'd survived three decades as a priority for Interpol. Still, I had to get him out of German custody last year, so he owed me a favor.

"You can contact him?" Satayev asked.

"I can try."

"We need communications equipment, ammunition, satellite pictures, and radio interception. But until I have the roads back, I cannot throw money around. I cannot fight the Russian army out of my own funds. They are already raping, cutting throats, stealing homes."

"I can get you what I can."

"That is all you'll say? After I saved your life?"

"I need to speak to people."

"How do I know you have people to speak to?"

"You know me, Akan."

"You disappear from the scene, cut all ties, then turn up again driving a Russian truck. Explain to me why I have saved your life."

I explained that a private intelligence company was working for Saracen, and staff there could guarantee my role and any potential payments.

"Speak to Saracen, tell them you've got a Vectis employee here." I gave him a number to call. He walked off. I was left watching the vines in the tabletop and feeling the tickle of the gun on me. So I'd been picked up by a new militia. More men with nowhere left to go except back into conflict. I had a vision of the future: swarms of mercs and militias chasing each other around the globe as we lock ourselves into shopping malls.

Satayev came back ten minutes later. I don't know exactly who he spoke to, or what was exchanged, but he seemed keener.

"They say you should go back to Astana."

"Who does?"

"Saracen."

"I see."

"I told them I'd help," Satayev clarified. "I have experienced men. We can hold the road from the border. There is only one clear route from Russia to the field. I propose a five-kilometer exclusion zone. There is a river to the west. It provides some natural defense. Officials will be on your side as well: the regional administrator, the police chief. You will find that useful."

He told me about jets I could use for returning to the capital, and then we talked supply routes for equipment.

"What about your American friend Reza?" Satayev said. "Are the Americans with you on this? You have the Saudi money?"

"This is a different situation to last time, Akan. I need you to understand that. I may not be in such a strong position."

The illusion of my continuing significance, my connection to the British intelligence service, had kept me alive so far, but it wasn't a roleplay I could back out of easily. Satayev's faith in this was based on desperation. He needed to believe I could help, and I needed that too.

"Saracen have given me their guarantee," he said. "They will help us; you will help us."

"Okay. But then we need to be clear on styles: no suicide bombs, no beheadings. No bearded men on YouTube waving rifles."

"I understand."

Did he? We exchanged secure means of communication. I asked where I was.

"Glukhovka."

"Where's that?"

"Northeast. I can arrange a flight to Astana. I have contacts in Astana who can collect the money from you."

I was a hostage, essentially. But playing along was the only way I was going to get out of here. And I'd been in Satayev's jets before. They had coffee machines. Things like that can help you feel immortal.

"Checks at the other end?"

"Not for an in-country flight. Not with my setup. I have jets in Semey or Pavlodar. Pavlodar is probably safer right now."

"What's the news from Semey?"

"Twenty dead. More protests."

"Twenty dead?"

"So it seems. Fifteen shot in the square, five died in custody."

"I'd like to take a look."

"It is on the edge of going very bad."

"Give me an hour in the town. I heard it has a Dostoevsky Museum."

"A Dostoevsky Museum?"

"I thought I'd check it out while I'm in the area."

46

MY BELONGINGS WERE RETURNED, ALTHOUGH THE GUN HAD NO bullets. I was led back upstairs. Glukhovka, it turned out, was a crossroads with a petrol station, a restaurant, and not much else apart from six blacked-out armor-plated SUVs scattered across the frozen mud.

One of them took me to Semey. Two men sat up front with an AK-47 propped between them. The driver chain-smoked, glancing in his mirror at me then looking away instantly when our eyes met. The dashboard clock said eight a.m. We drove back into barrenness: snow and rock.

So I had one missing piece of the puzzle: an oil field. In my experience, that was usually the central piece. The question was how it had made Joanna vanish.

Block Nine was a supergiant — the largest class of field, with a billion or more barrels of ultimately recoverable oil. Fewer than forty had ever been found, and two-thirds of those were in the Persian Gulf. People hunted hard, but for years the word was that there were no more out there. Until now. I did the maths. Even if the estimates were optimistic, it was vast. Thirty trillion cubic feet of gas, over five billion barrels of oil: That would meet Europe's energy needs for years to come. All buried fifty miles from the Russian border.

I had a message from Aliya, sent while I'd been in the care of Satayev's men: *How long are you in Astana? Let me know if you want another coffee. Got something for you.*

I texted back that I was briefly out of town and would get in touch asap.

I messaged Walker with confirmation of my encounter with Satayev, confirmation I was now returning to Astana. He rang back.

"We got a call from this Akan character."

"What did you say?"

"We asked him politely not to kill you. But it seems he may be a useful contact. What the hell are you doing out there?"

"Trying to find Joanna. I found Block Nine. You didn't mention it."

"It's incredibly sensitive. Are you able to get back here safely? We need your experience. Satayev said he would only work with you. That needs to start immediately."

I told him I was on my way, and hung up.

The more oil around, the less I trusted people, and my trust levels had been minimal to start with. But the hardest question was always whether you could trust yourself. I thought through the exchange with Satayev and felt the ice of Christopher Bohren hardening around me again.

I fell asleep in the car, and when I woke Semey was visible on the other side of the Irtish River. Ten a.m. on the dashboard. The town looked innocent enough, in the way of medium-sized towns: snow-crested, a scatter of older buildings among the concrete, arranged between the river and the mountains behind. A suspension bridge crossed the river toward it. Population 300,000. No sign that twenty of them had been killed in the last forty-eight hours. I wanted to assess which way the wind was blowing among the locals, whether they were ready to join Russia, who was in charge of them, how far they were prepared to go. Call it occupational habit.

We crossed the bridge, above lumps of ice floating downstream. The town was called Semipalatinsk until 2007: seven-templed city, named after the ruins of a Buddhist monastery. By the time they decided it was time for a rebrand, the name meant nothing but nuclear tests. I'd met a nurse in Moscow who used to work in Semey's central hospital and remembered terminally ill children running around the wards pretending to be radiation.

Now Semey was metamorphosing again.

I told the driver to stop once we'd crossed the bridge. I could already see police vehicles parked on the main road. It would be wiser to approach on foot. The men refused money, and as soon as I was out, the driver pulled a fast U-turn that left me wondering what I was heading into.

I ditched the gun in the river; it wasn't much use without ammunition, and would only get me in trouble. Once across, I kept to back streets. The few people out and about were moving quickly, nervously. Patrols of men, military, and police appeared every other block. Most shops were closed, phone signal intermittent.

The main public square was taped off, with teams of armed police at each corner. The ground had been hosed, but broken glass glinted in the cracks between paving slabs. A block away I found a café open beside a small frozen park. A stone Lenin rose up above the cold shrubbery of the park, right arm thrust out as if seeking to shake hands. Most of these monuments had vanished over the last two decades, usually removed in the dead of night. I wondered what kept this one here. Proximity to the Motherland? Distance from brave new Astana? I ordered coffee and a hot pastry, then took a seat in the center so I could see the windows but would be mostly obscured from those looking in.

I warmed my hands on the coffee, then sipped, my insides contracting in surprise. I ate the pastry slowly before ordering more food and another coffee. Events of the previous twenty-four hours repeated in my mind with stabs of dread, yet interwoven with a sense that I was still walking in Joanna's footsteps. When I had sufficient caffeine and carbohydrates inside me, I focused on the view.

The patrols were a mix: local police, Ministry of State security, Kazakh army. I wasn't inclined to get involved with any of them; enough escaping death for one day. I brought up a map of the town on my phone, checked the routes out, the location of the police station, the university. According to conversations around me, only four bodies had been released to the relevant families. There were ongoing disputes over the rest: Relatives were being told to sign waivers before they could see the remains of their loved ones. The Kazakh authorities were trying to keep a tight, anxious grip on the situation, stop it from exploding. A funeral scheduled for tomorrow morning had been canceled.

There was low talk of more protests, simmering anger, nightfall. I kept my gaze on the street outside and assessed how easily the paving stones would come up. What other ammunition was there? No loose bricks, hardly any street furniture. I finished my coffee, walked up Lenin Street, past a T-34 tank on a plinth, which turned out to be a monument to Kazakh independence. Small memorial stones lined the pavement, inscribed with the names of local military heroes. At the end of the road was a shabby department store. I bought two rainproof jackets, a black hoodie, a small backpack, then shaving kit and concealer cream from the pharmacy. At the shop next door I bought a disposable phone and prepaid card.

I spent a moment circling back alleys to make sure I was alone, then headed up Dostoevsky Street to the rundown edge of the city, past the apartment blocks rising from the snow. Set back, as if removed from the present, was a log cabin, its shutters and window frames painted pale green. A small sign at the front announced the museum, with a picture of Dostoevsky and a list of prices. It looked closed, but the door opened when I pushed and an old woman stirred in the half light. She tapped a price list taped to the desk in front of her. I paid three hundred tenge, took a ticket, and walked in.

It was empty of other visitors, which made the ghost of the novelist more present. They'd reconstructed the place as it might have been when he lived here. I listened for the drop of coins behind me, the printing of a ticket. No one else entered.

I made my way through the writer's sitting room, its solid furniture, chintz prints, matching armchairs. In the study was a walnut writing desk with photographic reproductions of Dostoevsky's notes amid stationery. My movements were now followed by a second woman who'd appeared, solid and suspicious, a remnant of the Soviet Union's weaponization of nosy grandmothers. I considered the study dutifully, just reverentially enough, and recalled various other unlikely museums I had used as refuge and countersurveillance.

In the final room was an exhibition about the author's time in the gulag: portraits of prison laborers, quotations from *The House of the Dead*. Murals traced his journey through suffering to religion. What had Dostoevsky written? *If they drive God from the earth, we shall shelter Him underground.* I wiped dust from the window and gazed out across an empty square to the mint-green Tatar mosque.

No one waiting, no one watching. I changed into my new clothes in the first-floor toilet, binned the old ones, and used the concealer to cover my bruising as much as possible. The gift shop contained an odd assortment of memorabilia: Dostoevsky's works in multiple languages, postcards of the building itself, then general Kazakh souvenirs—boxes of chocolates, etched glass ornaments all bearing the yellow and blue of the Kazakh flag. You could buy pictures of Nazarbayev, of Astana's skyline, and flags themselves, cheap nylon on plastic poles.

"How many flags do you have in stock?" I asked. I had to repeat the question a couple of times. The woman on duty showed me the wholesale box. I checked the supplier.

"Do you have more?"

"One more box."

"Okay, thank you. The exhibition was fascinating."

I cut south again, in the direction of chanting. There were buses parked on back streets, blocking them. The passengers stood around the streets beside them, smoking cagily. They were men, all between the ages of eighteen and thirty-five or so, with military-style haircuts. Governmental muscle, content to hold back for now. A few minutes further on, I found a crowd of thirty or forty locals across the road from the main police station, young and old, many of the elderly in conservative dress, white headscarves, fur hats. Flames licked from a brazier. Twenty police stood across the street from them, warily observing. Older women led the chanting, fists in the air. Placards had photographs of young men and women pasted on.

I walked on past the university. A thin crowd of students braved the cold in front of the gates, handing out flyers. I took one, checked the names of the arrested individuals listed on the flyer, then looked around for someone to speak to.

A plump, bespectacled student appeared to be in charge, wearing a thick tweed jacket as if dressed for premature responsibility.

"I am an English journalist," I said. "John Sands. I work with Reporters for Human Rights." I waved the flyer. "I know Natalya Atakhanova and Timur Bekmambetov. What happened to them?"

He led me to one side.

"Thank you for coming. We feel very isolated at the moment. Natalya and Timur are in Dolinka Prison."

"Both arrested?" I said.

"Two days ago."

I shook my head, tried to read the crowd around me. The anti-Russian signs outnumbered pro-democracy ones. FUCK PUTIN. HANDS OFF KAZAKHSTAN. It wasn't how I wanted it to go, even if I bore some responsibility. On one placard, I glimpsed a portrait of Raiymbek Batyr, my Kazakh warrior. The faces in the throng were all Kazakh. No suggestion that they were anything more than students, though; not armed, not ready to fight.

"What are people saying in England?" he asked.

"They're concerned, but not as engaged as they should be. We need to get images to them, stories. Who fired? Do you know?"

"We don't know anything for sure."

"What's your plan?"

"We are arranging more protests. We will resist the curfew. There is no going back now."

"How are you communicating?"

He showed me some of the apps they used, and basic encryption.

"For tonight," I said. "If you're organizing protests, download Gate-waySMS. They'll cut the internet again, but you'll still be able to communicate with anyone in the group. And it's secure."

I made sure he understood what I was talking about. He grasped the concept enthusiastically.

"Thank you."

"What do you want?" I asked. "At the end of this?"

"Justice. That is all."

"Have you thought about using the flag? Maybe the colors in it. Doesn't the blue symbolize peace and unity? You're proud of Kazakhstan. You want to defend it, defend Nazarbayev's legacy for everyone. All ethnicities. The Western press understands that."

"Maybe."

"Any famous people supporting you? Celebrities?"

"Not openly."

"Okay. Keep in touch." I didn't feel optimistic for them and wondered if they knew they were on a front line.

"Please, tell the world."

I went to shake his hand and he hugged me.

Satayev's armed guard were waiting for me a mile west of the city center, as promised. It was a ten-minute drive to the airport. As we drove, I experienced the faint flickering of what I eventually identified as hope, a sense that this could be the good revolution I was owed, the one that was going to go right.

All of which should have been a warning sign.

The Semey airport was small and low tech. A side gate opened for us, well-rehearsed men averting their eyes as we drove straight onto the smooth tarmac of the runway. We passed helicopters and one cargo plane, rolled right up to a crisp, white forty-seat Tupolev jet, just as the cockpit lights came on.

Once on board I was given a drink and the code for the Wi-Fi. There were others traveling—three well-dressed men, none of whom spoke to one another, one of whom might have been a low-profile chaperone for me. They all glanced at me but seemed unfazed by my bruised face. A pilot with gold teeth shook our hands. A free newspaper told me the president was making efforts to address concerns around the country: Long-serving men had resigned, though not Zhaparov. Independence Day was coming up on December 16 and would be an opportunity to show the world that Kazakhstan stood united.

When we were in the air, one of the men gave me a folder: "From Mr. Satayev."

Inside was a copy of a document from the Russian military intelligence service's Asian Directorate, carrying the *CEKPETHO* stamp for highest level classified: Lt. General Grigory Tanayev, to Anton Kirkorov, head of the Russian Federation Ministry of Energy. Timeline: 19:07, 25 November. Topic: Block Nine estimates.

The source for this intelligence was an agent named Serenade. It consisted largely of stolen hyperspectral data, translated into 3D sections of the Earth, veined with Day-Glo pinks and blues.

This was the dream: that with equipment sensitive enough — with the ability to read the near infrared spectral band — you might get a sniff of something to which your rivals were oblivious. Down beneath the abandoned Soviet tools, the skeletons of loyal comrades, in among the Miocene fossils: five billion barrels of light, sweet crude. It was calling out to change history.

At the bottom of the computer imagery it said *Property of Auracle Inc.* Someone had stolen it off Craig Bryant's company, given it to Russia ten days ago.

47

THE FLIGHT GAVE ME TIME TO THINK. I SPENT A LOT OF TIME STUDYING the Russian intelligence report, piecing together a variety of potential chronologies. The one I was trying to counter: She chases Bryant; she sells the data. I kept seeing that CCTV, Joanna getting into the car, which I tried to analyze with a cool objectivity I didn't feel.

Would Vishinsky trust her? Only if she'd been working with him for a while. A long game, then. Had I been lied to for years? I dissected our relationship from the beginning, feeling my way along it for an alteration in Joanna's behavior. There were enough unexplained events. The recent closing down of my Saudi op, for one; her disaster in Turkey. Everything invited new focus. Under harsh courtroom lights I saw details I hadn't seen the first time around—the insincerity of a smile, a canceled meeting, the appearance of a new phone. I considered an interpretation of my life in which Joanna was working for Moscow: our relationship, its feints and circumlocution. Vishinsky had a file on us, I knew that much. He had been interested in me. Say he got Joanna instead. Joanna was tasked with getting as close to me as possible. She resisted this at first, no doubt; relinquished under God knows what pressure. Finally, the order would come: Invite Elliot over. Get him to help. What a victory for them. And I would have been good. Would I have been tempted?

Perhaps she had reasons of her own. Revenge on the intelligence service. This speculation led me onto a parallel track of thoughts regarding her disappearance. I remembered a conversation with Joanna, around the time Russia poisoned Sergei Skripal. While the media and politicians railed in outrage, we saw it pragmatically. He was a former GRU colonel. We had some sense of what he potentially knew. Of course they were going to try to kill him. What we debated was whether Six would do the same. Hunt down a traitorous officer? Terminate them?

That conversation felt more pointed now. I tried to remember Joanna's face as we spoke. If a senior member of the intelligence service defected to Russia, risking the exposure of dozens of operations, should Six try to stop them by any means? The ethical concerns were moderated by the number of lives they could endanger. Potentially thousands. That put the morality of it in an entirely new light. Every day for years we had shared a workplace with people arranging deaths for the sake of preventing other deaths. Those were the men and women queuing beside you in the canteen. The only question, once you moved beyond drone strikes on insurgents, concerned limits. You heard rumors about the outer edges of Security Branch, about former agents who disappeared after turning bad. But you didn't hear more than rumors.

That was one explanation for Cherenkov's ignorance of Joanna's whereabouts. It would explain the ignorance of everyone in Six at a less-than-senior level.

Or it was all very carefully constructed bullshit. Oldest psyops in the book: Get departments to tear themselves apart over moles that don't exist. That way, you don't even need to penetrate — just sow doubt. And the Russians were old hands at it.

My gut instinct: One way or another, this was Vishinsky's idea of victory. Joanna had been working against him in some way since Turkey. Perfect Vision, whatever it was, represented that attempt. Vishinsky had ensured that both Six and Vectis turned against her, got the Shefford operation closed down, undermined her reputation. He was destroying not only Joanna but her identity. I knew he would make sure Joanna was aware of this: her disgrace in the eyes of those who loved and respected her. Perhaps she was being made to watch it from her cell.

My immediate mission was clear: Stop the Russian incursion he was masterminding.

As we dipped toward Astana, the intercom came to life, the pilot clearing his throat and informing us that it was minus twenty-five degrees on the ground. The time was three fifteen p.m. Beneath us, two C-130 military transport planes sat fatly on the airport runway, a line of fifty-ton army trucks parked along the perimeter fence.

Touchdown was smooth. We exited via a lounge with car magazines and a white leatherette sofa. No passport control, no camera in the face. I was met by a GL5 Mercedes with Walker in the back. I got in. We started heading into the city.

"What took you east?" Walker asked.

"I was following a lead."

"And you found Akan Satayev."

"He found me. So did Russian special forces on Kazakh soil."

"Definitely Russian?"

"Russian, Serb. Probably Sigma Group."

"We're going to the Saracen HQ. They need to hear what you saw."

That was okay with me. I was being invited into the heart of a company whose actions could determine what happened in this region. I needed to know what they were planning.

"The president is terrified of upsetting Moscow," Walker said, after another moment. "That's our problem right now."

"Does the president know how big the discovery is? Over five billion barrels?"

"As of yesterday, it seems. The Kazakhs are asking Saracen for eight point nine billion dollars just to start pumping. Saracen have secured credit up to eight. They're trying to get it within that. Money's not the biggest problem. Gazprom have crashed in out of nowhere. They don't have that kind of money, but they've got a hell of a lot of influence. If Saracen gets the Conqueror field for eight, they've got a bargain."

"Conqueror?"

"That's what they've named it."

"Jesus Christ."

We passed striped office complexes, emerald towers, clouds held in glass, moving around corners.

"Gazprom crashed in out of nowhere?"

"There was a leak," Walker said. "Carter knows there was a leak. He knows the Russians have our data."

I nodded. A stiff silence fell. After another moment we pulled up at the Saracen HQ. Four armored black Lexus limousines sat in front with motorbike outriders waiting.

"I want you to meet Robert Carter," Walker said. "I told him you know what's going on."

Armed guards searched my pockets, ran a scanner around my body, then waved us through. Everything was calm until we got to the sixth floor, where more than sixty Saracen personnel were working phones and computers. I was brought up to speed as we marched through, past geological surveys and dense spreadsheets. Experts across Saracen's divisions had been ordered to abandon everything else and number-crunch the bid. The European Investment Bank had their own people coming over to conduct a feasibility study. On the plans I saw, wells stretched out in all directions once they got underground, thousands of feet long, running to multiple reservoirs. Tight oil: light crude held in shale, which meant digging deep and fracking.

A meeting with the president and the head of KMG was lined up for eight a.m. tomorrow. Two hundred more GL5 contractors were set to roll into Kazakhstan by nightfall.

I was shown into a glass-walled side office with framed pictures of flare stacks and six tense individuals standing around a table of contracts. Lucy Piper was there, typing away, one phone between ear and shoulder, one flashing on the table beside her. She raised an eyebrow by way of greeting. I was introduced to Jill Friedman from Credit Suisse, then Ahmad Suleiman representing Qatar's sovereign wealth fund. Carter stood at the back, arms crossed, bristling. He had a rugby player's build and a drinker's flush to his face. He had taken a big gamble and was a presidential signature away from breaking the casino. I recognized him, seeing him up close, and knew I'd been in his company before but couldn't think where. His chief negotiator stood beside him, sixty-something, thinning white hair, tight-jawed. Ronald Steiner. I'd heard about him in Iraq: former Exxon, former Shell, fierce reputation, go-to man for oil contracts.

Walker was playing an audio file off his laptop. It involved two men talking Russian in what sounded like a moving car. Walker's translator — a young, pale woman no older than twenty-three — was struggling.

"A *pon-yatino* is like an understanding, rather than a written agreement."

"Not a legal term," Steiner said.

"No. More than that."

"More than legal," he said, witheringly.

The men on the recording, I gathered, were the head of Kazakhstan's state energy company and the Russian Minister for Oil and Gas. It sounded like the Russian wasn't keen on Saracen, and the Kazakh energy chief was trying very hard to be as noncommittal as possible. Saracen had extraction rights on any new discovery, but it seemed the Kazakhs weren't compelled to grant those rights unless certain criteria had been fulfilled. The criteria were spread across the table in front of me alongside speculation about Gazprom's proposed offer, as well as satellite images of the field with potential Sigma activity circled.

The voices on the recording continued. A Western company operating the field was diplomatically unacceptable. The Kazakh president had spoken to Putin. The translator tried to keep up, cautiously aware that she was a messenger in the line of fire.

"The field or the line is unacceptable?" Carter said.

"Both, I think."

I was trying to figure out what *the line* referred to, then I saw it. Among the paperwork on the table was a map showing a proposed route for a pipeline. It ran west from the field to Aktau, then under the Caspian to the terminal south of Baku in Azerbaijan. From Baku to Erzurum in Turkey, up through Bulgaria and Romania to the hub at Baumgarten in Austria. Plans came courtesy of Bechtel Engineering. Either a team of hundreds had worked overnight or there were long-standing ambitions in play.

"My colleague has just been assessing the situation on the ground," Walker said.

Steiner shot a glance at me. "You've been to the drill site?" he asked.

"Just returned."

"How does it look?"

I talked them through the situation, indicating that there were highly trained Russian fighters coming in. I mentioned the local support they might need to draw upon, alluding to Akan Satayev without actually using the phrase "heroin-trafficking warlord." When I'd finished, Steiner clicked a mouse and a map appeared on a wall-mounted screen. It was Kazakhstan, only divided horizontally by a meandering dotted line. It took me a second to understand what I was looking at — then I felt sick.

"These are the regions we think the Russians would go for: Akmola, Pavlodar, East Kazakhstan." I followed the dashed line that signified the Russian border sinking south.

"Those regions mostly have forty to fifty percent ethnic Russian populations. Then there's West Kazakhstan and Kostanay, which are less clear."

Piper waved her phone, cleared her throat. "Foreign Office on the line. Jack Burrows."

"Get him a copy of this," Steiner said, gesturing at the map as he gathered his papers. "I want him to see this."

The Saracen crew moved as one toward the secure communications area, leaving Walker, Piper, and myself. We all stared at the map.

"The Crimea rerun narrative is strong," Piper said, eventually, managing to sound level-headed. "We let Russia get away with that. Not again. This is a challenge to the world. Red lines."

"Where did you get the map?" I asked.

"Analysts. Does it fit what you've seen?"

"It fits a nightmare. Why exactly is Robert Carter on the phone to the Foreign Office?"

"Saracen want guarantees, backed up by military commitment if Russia oversteps the line. They're in conversation with the EU as well, with regards to the pipeline. People are up for this," Piper said. "The field's a game-changer."

"I really wouldn't push the pipeline-to-Europe angle," I said.

"Not up front, no," Piper agreed. "In-house perhaps, for Westminster. Energy security."

"The whole thing's a step too far. It cuts Russia off from Central Asia."

"Should we shed tears?"

"They won't let it happen. They never do. I can tell you at least three similar schemes in the last ten years, all of which led to a protracted conflict and no line." I stepped closer to the map and traced the new border with my finger, then down into the empty spaces. There were few population centers or strategic points. An army could gain a hundred miles with a single battle.

"Apparently the military base in Omsk has become lively," Walker said. "A couple of hundred ground forces from Russia's Central Military District arrived in the last few hours." He seemed phlegmatic, the SAS man in his comfort zone. "Russia's Armenian bases have also lit up. Same with the airfield near Bishkek. And we're getting repeated reports of Russian civilians arming in Kazakhstan. GL5 are holding fifteen of them who came near the site: possibly Sigma, possibly amateur local protection units."

I didn't want to dwell on the legal sensitivies of a private security contractor holding fifteen Kazakh citizens. I concentrated on the big blank map.

"If Russia makes a move, it will be fast and on the ground," I said. "Government buildings, roadways, telecom cables—they'll have them within hours."

"We're preparing for that, lines open with the Kazakh military. GL5 have some advanced capability: the means of blocking radar and electronic jamming."

"What about China?"

"What about them?"

"They've invested too much to let Russia march in. Any annexation would destroy their new Silk Road. That's our biggest asset: China won't tolerate interference."

"For sure."

"And the other Stans?" I asked. "Who would they side with? Could they turn against Russia?"

"We're hearing positive noises. Certainly Uzbekistan and Kyrgystan would be reluctant to fall in line with Moscow, if it came down to it."

"Find out what kind of loans Russia has given Kazakhstan, and how much China's put in. Most war is debt collection. See who's left out of pocket."

Walker agreed. He began to collect up his devices.

"I'm going to speak to our analysts in London. Keep thinking," he said. "This is where we earn our money."

I was briefly alone with Piper and her press releases.

"Whose idea was it to call the field Conqueror?" I said.

"Not us."

"You should try to find something local, something Kazakh."

"We can try." Piper thought. "This is about independence, right? Local strength. What could be more independent than selling your oil to Europe?"

"When you've got five thousand miles of border with Russia, that's not a joke. Eight billion pounds: a flagship for the Kazakh economy, the largest-ever foreign investment in Kazakhstan. Money from this deal will keep the peace, keep Kazakhstan at the heart of international values and progress. And Gazprom don't have the technology. They won't get it out of the ground."

"Are you sure?"

"I've no idea. But it sounds right, doesn't it? This is fracking, horizontal drilling, new advances. Show diagrams, flag up old Russian kit. Get photos of dead herons from Gazprom fields. Russia will be ready to exploit environmental issues. Spin Conqueror as a cleanup operation. This isn't wilderness, it's a brown site. We're going to leave it in a better state than we find it. We'll clean up the groundwater, dispose of the radioactive tailings. Then get the British prime minister over here, on Independence Day. Now or never. Gold fountain pens."

She stared at me, unblinking, tongue pressed against her teeth.

"That's a big ask."

"What you get the man who has everything is moral approval. The president doesn't need more money—he needs to look good in the eyes of the world. Calm his citizens down, regain the magic. It can be twenty-four hours in and out."

"I'll put out feelers."

The door opened. Walker returned with fresh paperwork.

"Kazakhstan owes Russia five billion for arms sales alone. Then there's about three billion in cash-for-oil financing: prepay deals."

"China will have more," I said.

"China's loaned this place fifteen billion in the last two years. Mostly through joint ventures."

"Fifteen billion," Piper said, wide-eyed.

I'd been expecting a lot, but not that much. You look in the accounts book and the whole thing's floating on thin air. It's a shell game, and then something threatens to bring it down and the tanks appear.

"It makes it pretty obvious," I said. "There's no way Beijing would let Russia invade."

Walker handed me the report. The China Investment Corporation had issued billions of dollars in bonds to underwrite construction in Kazakhstan. They needed to make a profit of twenty million yuan every day just to pay the interest and operation costs. What the report didn't note was that Chinese workers on big infrastructure projects were often trained in military skills and could provide a ready-made militia if need be.

"You know, the Chinese refer to Russia as the Warring Nation," I said.

"I hear you." Piper wrote this down.

"Do they try to hack us?" I asked.

"The Chinese? Only about ten times a day."

"Put the annexation map on the system, take the security off."

"I'm not in a position to do that," she said, more like a disclaimer than a fact. "But I'll pass the suggestion on." Her phone rang. She checked the screen and got to her feet. "You can still make the party?" she asked me, heading for the door.

"The party?"

"Galina's birthday. Tonight."

"Of course." It felt unreal. But I could see that the event wasn't entirely a distraction.

"Will you get a chance to shave?" She was serious. I thought briefly about how I must look.

"I'll try." She smiled, then she was gone.

Walker said, "People are asking about the local support on the ground you mentioned, as a temporary measure for keeping the field secure. How much of a politically acceptable option is Akan Satayev?"

"He's the only option."

"He's militant."

"No, but I imagine some of the men he employs will be."

"How many does he control?"

"He's probably got two or three hundred in the area now. And it's a clan system, with alliances: Each of those men can bring in thirty or forty more. There are gangs in Tajikistan and Uzbekistan that ultimately answer to Satayev. They can be protecting Conqueror in days."

"What would he need in order to work with us?"

"A fair amount of cash, I reckon. Get his trucks moving, crossing borders, his men equipped, confident that they've got backing. In the longer term, with the field, it may come down to giving him a cut of final profits."

"There's no way he's getting final profits," Walker said. "But keep that channel open."

"He'll need reassurances. Concrete ones."

"You know more about that side of things than I do. There are options. Keep him onside, if you can."

"Sure."

He glanced outside the office, then shut the door, locked it, turned to me. The mood changed.

"Did you ever have suspicions about her?"

"About who?"

"You know what I'm talking about, Elliot."

"This wasn't Joanna."

"The Russians had data from Auracle."

"There's a lot of ways they could have got that."

"Are you in on this with her?"

"This is bullshit."

"We know she pursued Craig Bryant. All Carter knows for now is that there was a leak of some kind, somewhere along the line. They want to sue Auracle."

"That's going to get messy."

"We're going to make sure it doesn't. We're going to bury the whole Joanna thing. Understand?"

"No, I don't understand."

"Yes, you do. Your police officer friend gave you footage of Joanna getting into a car with members of the Russian security service. Are there any other copies floating around that we should know about?"

This threw me off-balance. My muscles tensed, and I glanced across the room for objects I could use as a weapon if it came to blows, wondered how much of his training Walker remembered. Where did he get that information? Shomko? From taps on me?

"Your pisshead police officer needs to forget he ever saw it," Walker said.

"And the computer-generated clip I showed you? What has that got to do with spying for Vishinsky?"

"What's it got to do with anything? What are you really doing here, Elliot?" He was too cool, too experienced for all-out anger. And he held cards. "Both you and Joanna have been on a caution list since 2010, with some heavy question marks by your names. Security Branch are very, very keen to speak to you right now, as you can imagine. So be thankful you're sitting here and not in Belmarsh."

"Do you know where she is?" I asked.

"Moscow, I expect."

"I was hunting her for you."

"I don't remember asking you to come over here. Joanna Lake's seen getting into a car connected to Vladislav Vishinsky on Saturday the twenty-fifth. Over the next forty-eight hours there's huge Russian activity: flights booked, meetings arranged, money transferred. The first troops move down to the Kazakh border. We've checked imagery from the last week down to minutes and hours. On the evening of the twenty-fifth, Vishinsky arranged an emergency meeting at which he presented data to Gazprom. The next morning there's a payment of half a million dollars into a Cayman Islands account Joanna set up the previous month."

He produced the last fact with a flourish and enjoyed watching me hesitate.

"How do you know?" I asked.

"We know."

"That's my point. She's a trained officer. You think she sets up a visible account in the Cayman Islands?"

"Elliot, do you really think it's impossible she'd do this?"

"She'd do it better. This is being handed to us."

"So why didn't you tell us about the footage from Lieutenant Shomko?"

"Why would I trust you?"

Walker sighed. "The phone line here's secure," he said. "Sigma troops are massing on the border. Call Akan Satayev, tell him to name his price. Unless it turns out you do favor Russia. If so, I'd find a way of moving there."

He walked out. I didn't call Satayev straight away. I called Craig Bryant. I was surprised when he answered. He sounded like he'd been drunk but sobered by my call.

"Toby, what's happened?" he said.

"Why? You okay?"

"Not really. The company's had some problems."

"What problems?"

"Big problems. You struck me as a guy who might hear things. Have you?"

"Nothing. I don't understand."

"Shit, Toby. You work somewhere like this and you know it's not going to be Houston, but I'm not equipped to operate in a jungle."

"A jungle?"

"We spoke about that woman, Vanessa. Ever hear anything else?"

"The documentary maker? You think she caused you problems?"

"This town, Toby . . ." It sounded like he dropped the phone. I heard him shuffling around, then his voice returned. "Are you going to the party later?"

"I reckon so. Are you?"

"If I don't show my face, people will talk."

"What will they say?"

"They'll say I'm not there. See you later, Toby."

I studied the annexation map, then social media: houses burning, cars laden with mattresses and furniture and mirrors. It looked like Bosnia to me, but the license plates were Kazakh. I went to the window. Astana remained calm. The dome of the Presidential Palace shone blue through the snow. The Triumph of Astana muscled into the horizon beyond it.

I called Madrid, where my contact for Jan Jágr, the arms dealer, was based, and once the contact had called back I spoke to Akan Satayev.

"Jágr's on. If you can find somewhere for a plane to land, he can get you the equipment you need. What about your own expenses?"

Satayev gave his quote: 1.5 million US dollars in cash, hand-delivered to his connection in Astana. I had to stop myself from laughing. The naked greed was nothing if not audacious. I reminded myself, once again, that he was a gangster, a man who knew when he had you by the balls.

"I'll ask," I said. "If they do agree, that's going to take some time."

"The Russians are not taking their time. More men are coming in every hour." He lowered his voice. "I had a call from Moscow. They understand that I am a businessman. You know that means I have to have a hard heart."

"I understand, Akan. I'll see what I can do."

I left a message for Walker: *1.5 mill.*

When I tried to leave the HQ, it turned out I needed an escort: The lifts were PIN code entry. And, before anyone would summon me a lift, I was searched and my phone checked for photos. All this was happening when I saw Carter march back from his call with the foreign secretary, poker-faced.

I could see the strain, and sense a deepening pessimism in the office. I heard someone mutter: "The President's blocking."

I thought of the *Herald Tribune* clipping I'd seen at Elena's: *Both rivals and shareholders claim he has paid well over the odds on a quixotic and personal mission.* It was so close to paying off. To being the luckiest of gambles—buying up Saracen, choosing Kazakhstan as the place to drill, billions of his own money thrown in. The chips were stacked high, the ball spinning. I tried to imagine how it felt having the whim of one human being standing between you and victory.

The guard returned my phone and the lift doors opened. I took a last look at Carter's face and tried to think where I'd met him before.

48

SIX HOURS TO PARTY TIME. I LOOKED A MESS. AT THE RAMADA PLAZA
they seemed surprised to see me.

"Mr. Bell!"

"How have things been?"

"All very fine here. We have an Oriental buffet in the restaurant tonight, if you are interested."

I went up to my room, stood there in the light of the TV holding a
crumpled shirt. Semey on the screen. I glanced across the faces in the angry crowd, looking out for the students, thinking of my experiences there.
Thinking of Akan Satayev and his men, who weren't on TV. Not yet.

Message in from Piper: *Conqueror situation not looking good. President set to say no.* Galina was trying to persuade him otherwise, but she
wasn't a match for the Kremlin.

No answer from Stefan when I called him. Marius in the Evotec office
answered, told me Stefan had messaged to say he was booked on a flight
that morning. Presumably he'd got on it. I hoped he was enjoying the
complimentary G&Ts.

"One other thing," Marius said. "You asked for him to look out for ref-
erences to 'Catalyst'?"

"Yes."

"Stefan sent us an email saying he'd intercepted someone or something about an issue regarding Catalyst attending a party tonight. Does
that mean anything? He wanted you to know."

"He said Catalyst was going to be at a party?"

"Someone said that. Stefan picked it up."

"Galina's birthday party?"

"I've no idea. Stefan couldn't get hold of you, but wanted us to pass the
message on."

"I need the exact message."

Marius read it out: "If you speak to EK, tell him that Catalyst will be at party tomorrow. People are concerned re issues arising. More details to follow. He'll understand."

I wished that was more than half true. Marius believed the information had come from a phone or computer Stefan had gained access to, but Stefan had refused to give details over an open line.

"Any idea when he lands?"

"No."

"Any suggestion what the 'issues' are?"

"That's all we've got."

"Okay. Would you tell him to contact me as soon as he's on his phone?"

"Will do."

The party had gained a new edge of significance. I watched the clip of myself and the Central Asian man again, to ensure I had his features memorized, as if I hadn't been thinking about them for a week.

I shaved. I went to the Kerulen Mall and bought a new shirt and tie. On my way back I told the taxi to stop early and walked to the river. It was getting dark but there were lights on the ice, music playing. People sledded down the banks, others skated in the center. I wondered how they knew when the ice began getting too thin, who told them it was time to stop.

The front drive was full of cars when I got to the Marriott, the hotel lobby thick with bodyguards. I went through three security checks to get to the lifts, then had to share them with half of Gazprom's board, stinking of expensive cologne.

The thirty-eighth floor was packed. Suits and gowns, pyramids of Champagne coupes, everything — everyone's consciousness — inconspicuously centered on the president, who stood at the back of the room talking to the Chinese ambassador. Banners declared that Saracen Oil and Gas Exploration wished Galina Nazarbayev a happy birthday. There was a Kazakh flag and, beneath it, the Saracen logo. I squeezed through diplomats and spies, looking for my Triumph video companion; equally alert for Cherenkov, and for representatives of the British embassy. I found Lucy Piper looking tense. She needed help with Carter's speech.

"Something Kazakh, a quote or something."

"Abai's their national poet," I said. "He's quotable." I pointed her toward some lines. She walked off, already searching on her phone. I took a drink as it floated past.

The optimism on display was impressive, as if a deal could be willed into existence through sheer decadence. The banners, the waterfall of champagne down the stacked glasses, the *moelleux au chocolat* birthday cake. Saracen was putting a determined face on things. Every situation changes.

All the intelligence services had gathered, surreptitiously checking the president for IV drip scars, for slurs in his speech; noting who he spoke to, who he avoided. They studied the demeanor of CEOs, engineers, financiers, and go-betweens, every player among these men and women whose lives had become devoted to the carbon molecules of buried plankton, the energy from three-hundred-million-year-old sunlight.

Galina sang two songs by Céline Dion with a world-class Czech pianist who had apparently insisted on ten grand for every hour spent on Kazakh soil; Piper introduced me to European journalists and I told them Kazakhstan was a peaceful country at heart — "We have homegrown terrorists in the UK, you know, and nowhere's going to become a liberal democracy overnight." I met rich people and heard myself saying: "It's a family-run Swiss school, but it follows the British national curriculum so it's probably your most *British* international school." Guests swayed with bonhomie. A lot of the newcomers had been drinking hard since the flight over. Fireworks exploded outside, unannounced. A Tajik warlord flinched — so did a security officer from the British embassy. Then everyone loosened their ties and began to do shots.

I met Anastasia two drinks into the evening. Bryant introduced me. She was one of two women with him when he lunged sweatily out of the crowd.

"Toby!"

"Craig."

"Toby, can I introduce you to Olga and . . ." He looked to the other woman for help. She wore a dress of gold sequins.

"Anastasia."

I noticed her Moscow accent and her eyes. *There you are*, they seemed to say. Her blond hair was cut into a bob that framed clear features. She had the assured good looks of escorts and honeytraps. After a few minutes, Bryant vanished with Olga. Anastasia and I ended up on a sofa. It was all suspiciously slick.

"So, an Englishman in Astana. You are either rich or here to get rich."

"I am here to see history being made," I said. "To broaden my mind."

My companion looked skeptical. She touched a hand to her necklace as if it might protect her. Her cocktail was down to slush. She smelled of Miss Dior and was being watched by a man at the bar wearing a concealed handgun.

"People from England come here for business."

"This is a young place," I said. "There are not many of those. Once or twice in a lifetime, if you're lucky, you get to see somewhere being born rather than dying." I gestured at the room. "This is the future."

"The future's drunk," she said.

As if on cue, the UK's secretary of state for Business, Energy, and Industrial Strategy roared with laughter, followed a few seconds later by some unsteady Chinese pipeline engineers, and a man with a greasy smile who did PR for the Kazakh government.

"And you?" I said to my companion. "What brings you here?"

"I am a designer. I design interiors: shops, hotels. I am working with the Sheraton group."

"That sounds a dynamic career. One that lets you see the world." If there were Russians trying to seduce me, I wanted to know. If she was innocently attached to Russians, with potential access, I was equally curious. And in the back of my mind, there was Stefan's message: Catalyst at the party. I leaned closer. "I'm glad I met you," I said. "I was slightly dreading this whole thing. I have a suspicion that you're one of the more interesting people in the room."

She studied my face, then leaned back into the sofa. I considered my next move. The party was going to seed. Sushi congealed on platters, and condensation from the ice buckets had made a soggy carpet out of brochures about renewables. A raucous foursome from the state energy company were raising toasts by the bar. They knocked into the gunman, oblivious, but he didn't react. The holster was strapped crossways under the man's jacket; he was overweight and kept his jacket buttoned, which meant it was tight on his back when he turned. He wore the gun on his right hip, making him sit twisted on his stool. The holster suggested a license, someone official or well connected, as did getting past the scanners downstairs. He used the mirror behind the bar to watch the crowd. The local offices of Chevron and Merrill Lynch had turned out in force, as had representatives from the French and German embassies.

Robert Carter made his speech, sweating hard, colored lights reflecting off his face.

"In the words of Abai, your excellent national poet, Kazakhstan should be a convivial meeting place of Russia, the West, and Islam. Ambitious perhaps but, as I believe he also said, 'A clever man can set fire to the snow.'"

Polite laughter rippled. The president said something to the British minister. Galina beamed and would have clapped if she hadn't been holding a glass of champagne. Carter smiled gratefully at the crowd.

There was more applause when he finished, then a toast to Galina, the birthday girl. I watched the Russians to see if they toasted and they did so unreservedly, downing the Veuve Clicquot. The president himself moved away from the stage, and everyone went back to their previous conversations.

Bryant was talking to the Chinese. The head of Extraction for an Italian oil firm was nearby, sharing something on his phone with the man who ran the central bank, but no one was conspicuously hustling. The mood was carefree. Outside, the snow was thickening in the air, to the extent that I wondered if we were all going to become trapped, and how that would pan out. But for now all were drunk, and we could stop pretending that power was anything other than ridiculous good fortune. Almost eleven p.m. and there was the hilarity of getting away with it.

Anastasia checked a silver iPhone then dropped it in her bag. She transferred her gaze to the room. Bryant caught my eye and winked. The man at the bar saw this, checked Bryant, turned back to the mirror. He had tan lines from wraparound sunglasses.

None of this was how I'd manage an assassination.

"Did you always want to be an interior designer?"

Anastasia glanced across the crowd. "No. When I was young I wanted to be an artist. But there is no security in that. My family needs me to earn money."

"A country only truly develops when people stop caring about their family," I said. "That is what developed means." She raised an eyebrow, considering this.

"Come with me," I said. I took her hand and helped her up, leading her to the windows. "Did you know, the Germans call this *Lichtarchitektur*: the architecture of light."

Glass towers shimmered. The smiling woman in the Samsung advert lifted her phone in eternal expectation. Her pale face lit the canvas roofs of three troop carriers parked beside the building. I lifted my own phone and took a photo of the skyline.

"And let's take one of us," I said.

She stiffened. "I hate photos."

"Come on, something to make my friends in London jealous."

Anastasia rolled her eyes, but flicked her hair away from her face compliantly and leaned in.

"So many photographs," she muttered.

In the bathroom, I locked a stall and put the image through facial recognition. Four separate names came up: same face, three nationalities. That was enough for me. I was being targeted. It was time to get out of here.

I passed Galina in the corridor on my way back, Lucy Piper adjusting the zip on the back of her blue Versace cocktail dress.

"Toby, have you met Galina?" Piper said. "Galina, this is one of my stars: Toby Bell. A true English gentleman."

"I've heard about you," Galina said. She reached toward me. I moved forward so we could shake hands without the dress being torn from Piper's hands.

"This is an honor," I said. "I thought your singing was amazing."

"Thank you. It's been a wonderful event. Am I right that you were involved in arranging it?"

"Hardly. But I'm glad you're enjoying it. Your father is looking well."

She smiled, as confident in her father's immortality as the rest of the nation. "He is well. He is well, thank God."

"And next year, perhaps, we will have the honor of seeing you on television again. SuperstarKZ."

"Maybe."

"You must do it. You're such a natural. It would bring a lot of joy to the people of this country."

She beamed. Bryant appeared from the main room. Galina sashayed passed him. Piper gave a cursory nod at the American and leaned toward me, speaking low.

"Some of us are going back to the palace. Moving now. Come with us — she'd like that."

It was an electrifying invitation. Piper disappeared back toward Galina's entourage and Bryant was left grinning at me.

"Hear about the jet?" he said. "What are they going to get her for Christmas, for Christ's sake?"

"I'm not sure they celebrate Christmas." I began moving past Bryant toward the main room, trying to calculate how to get my coat from the cloakroom while avoiding my honeytrap.

"I'm getting us some shots. You'll have one. Or are you busy?"

"I'm busy," I said, but Bryant kept grinning. On the far side of the main bar I could see Anastasia waiting, toe tapping the air; a woman conscious of sitting alone in a room of drunken men. A woman with a job to do. She exchanged a glance with the gunman, who got to his feet, adjusting his jacket. Bryant headed to the bar. I cut back through the crowd, saw Anastasia moving in my direction.

"Toby."

"Anastasia, I'm so sorry. I've got to run." I slipped her a business card. "Dinner? Can you forgive me? Have you been to Le Dessert?"

I could see Galina's entourage moving. They were going down to the convoy. It looked like the president was already downstairs. Piper came up to me. "Ride with us. Galina says it's all good."

Anastasia had a hand on my arm.

"You are going with them?"

"I've made a promise. I really am sorry." I kept moving. At some point, presidential security would kick in, I thought. Or she could come to the palace, kill me there. That would be chic. The entourage had gone by the time I made it to the corridor. The lifts were blocked by a crowd of oil execs. I went for the stairs.

Someone followed. I heard the door slam, footsteps behind me. Then a man's voice.

"You forgot this." It was the gunman. He held up a wallet that wasn't mine. He sounded English. I thought through the various options for incapacitating him: eyes, throat, knees. Then it became irrelevant.

An explosion shook the building. I found myself on the floor beside the wall, in the dark, thinking: that sound, the one that gets you in the stomach. A car bomb. Thinking: I'm alive. The president . . .

I got to my feet. There was plaster over my skin. I continued down the stairs, checking myself for injury. I was okay. I'd been lucky.

I'd been saved.

Screaming began on the seventh floor. Windows had blown in from the fifth floor down. Then I was stepping over debris, over a car door. A woman's bare arm lay on the third-floor carpet, severed at the shoulder, bracelet gleaming.

Dust filled the reception. The heat of the explosion lingered. There was no front wall. The central spine of the revolving doors had become implanted in the reception desk. A car lay on its roof beside a stump of the lobby's fountain. One security guard sat in a spreading pool of blood, gun out, no right leg beneath the knee.

A few dazed, dust-caked figures wandered in the snow outside. Thick smoke plumed from two burning cars, turning the snow black. I made out a twenty-foot crater in the driveway's tarmac, halfway between the hotel's entrance and the gates to the street.

The security who had survived were coming to their senses, trying to clear the area. More often than not there was a second bomb. Sometimes the second bomber waited for the emergency services to arrive. I couldn't see any unattended vehicles. The first sirens were approaching.

Saved. I turned back, thinking I might see my guardian angels emerging from the dust. There was a woman in shredded evening wear, blood down her chin, mouth working silently. I gave her my coat and continued into the storm.

49

I STUMBLED AWAY FROM THE SCENE THROUGH A CLOUD OF BLACK flakes, gripped by a sense that I should have known. The first emergency vehicles tore into the hotel grounds, almost hitting me.

A minute later I was still walking, starting to shiver with early-stage hypothermia. I flagged a car beside Lovers Park. The driver let me in. He had his family with him. He was agitated, seeking information rather than a fare. The sirens were endless now; a troop carrier tore past us. I could still smell synthetic materials burning and see the smoke plume in the light of adverts.

"What happened?"

"A bomb."

"I must go home. I can't drive you."

"I just need to get to somewhere indoors."

He took me to a Ramstor all-night supermarket. I found a coat on the rails, put it on, and crouched in a corner, warming my hands. My phone rang. I couldn't move my fingers. Eventually I managed to answer the phone by putting it on the ground and using my knuckles. It was Piper in a state of high anxiety.

"You're alive. Oh my God. Where are you?"

"A supermarket. A Ramstor, at the end of Respublika Avenue. What do you know?"

"Nothing. I'm in a car somewhere around the Northern Lights complex. We've been stopped at a roadblock. We're trying to get to the Saracen offices. It's just . . ." Her voice wavered with shock. "It's going to be a holding situation. Until we know how this is going to play out."

"Nothing's going to hold."

"No."

"They'll try to pin this on us," I said.

"I know."

"Who's alive?"

"The president's critical. He's at City Hospital Number One. Galina's also at the hospital. She might be okay."

"This is fucked. How did they drive up to the hotel?"

The line went. I checked social media for IMK, then Twitter feeds for Al-Nusra, ISIS in Central Asia, Hizb ut-Tahrir. No one was claiming credit for the attack.

The art of an assassination is controlling what happens next. That's not the sole prerogative of those responsible—they've just got a head start. On Russian news they were cutting between footage from Astana and a story about a GL5 maritime patrol vessel caught illegally patrolling in the Caspian: *In the last five or six hours a Russian coast guard patrol rammed and water-cannoned a boat belonging to a UK-registered private security company—a 183-foot vessel with a crew of fourteen and a helicopter pad.* The contractors had been arrested. There was footage of men in GL5 uniform sitting on the ground, hands on their heads like drug runners.

All domestic flights were grounded. The first posts suggesting how convenient this was for Saracen had appeared less than twenty minutes after the attack. Oil was up five points, FTSE closing just as Saracen started to lift.

I saw a store security guard watching me from the end of the aisle, speaking to two men in GL5 uniforms, then realized they were talking about me. The contractors walked over.

"We've been instructed to get you somewhere safe," one of them said.

"Where would that be?"

"Everyone's convening at the Saracen headquarters. We may have to get out of the country." I said I'd make my own way. They were having none of it. The guard watched me escorted out, and if he was aware of the stolen coat, it wasn't his major concern.

The contractors were silent as we drove, eerily calm, the man in the passenger seat cradling a submachine gun. He looked Southeast Asian. Inside the vehicle were steel lockboxes for weapons, medibags, an ax affixed to the back of the driver's seat.

"Know anything about the patrol boat in the Caspian?" I asked, to get a reading of them, at least: their tension, their accents. "Is this true?"

"We can't comment on that," the driver said.

"Are you guys in the Caspian?"

"No comment."

The business district was crawling with police and military; sniffer dogs, red and blue flashing lights. At least two helicopters crawled the night sky, unseen but loud. Only speed, visible weaponry, and a uniformed gravitas kept us moving. Piper called again. "Galina's conscious. She was still in the hotel when it happened. The bomb went off beside the president."

"There was a battalion of security at the hotel. How did the bomber get that close?"

"I don't know."

We sped up. I was on the verge of asking Piper about the security setup at the hotel when it occurred to me that GL5 must have been involved somewhere along the line. I said I'd speak to her at the office and hung up. My chauffeurs faced frontward, unmoving. The doors were centrally locked. I reached down and clicked the release for the hand ax, then checked we were on the correct route. We arrived at the Saracen offices a few minutes later. I was hustled past security barriers to the lift, where, to my surprise, we went down.

Doors opened directly onto a bunker office, one half of which was crowded with staff, the other half, through a glass partition, was a conference room with a large oval table. Both ends had multiple TVs showing CNN, BBC, Al Jazeera, Russia's Channel One — plus screens carrying maps and satellite feeds of the various fields. The lift kept chiming, Saracen executives arriving from the party in their eveningwear, faded by ash. Medics had set up a small first-aid station in the corner. Piper was there, on the phone, running on disbelief. It looked like she had a list of names, checking off all employees and members of the trade delegation who were in the area. Some of the Kazakh staff were crying.

I went over to a live satellite feed of the Conqueror field and tried to see activity. Nothing, which was ominous in itself. The Sigma battalions were surely preparing. Piper hung up and came over. Tiny specks of glass glittered in her hair.

"We've got a plane on standby to evacuate the delegation, as soon as we know it's safe to get there. Trying to get clearance to fly."

"Where's Callum?"

"On his way. I just spoke to Galina. Obviously she's not in a good way psychologically, but her injuries are superficial. She wasn't at the front when it happened."

Through the panic and confusion, the trained officer in me still felt the need to brief those in a position to act.

"There's no succession plan as far as I'm aware. There's nothing to guarantee she ends up in charge."

"That's what we're worried about. This went live a few hours before the bomb." Piper showed me a website on her phone: An organization called Corruption Watch, based in Helsinki, had come into possession of data hacked from Galina's financial advisor: emails concerning a BVI-registered shell company used to buy a twenty-three-meter yacht and three properties in London. Someone had got footage flying over one of them: tennis courts, some sports cars, and a pool. The cover was off the pool. It had been filmed months ago.

"We can get it onto the second page, at least. That may be all. Same accounts pushing photos of Galina with Carter at the party last night, and a story about Galina wanting to take Kazakhstan into NATO."

It was on at least three reputable sites. Her photo was placed beside one of the NATO secretary-general. *It is unlikely the invitation to begin accession talks will appear anytime soon, but the meeting indicates Galina's willingness to reorient the country her father has steered for so long . . .*

"That one appeared about an hour after the bomb," Piper said. "It's total lies."

A lot of anti-Galina accounts had begun demanding free elections: bots, calling out for representation: *The Kazakh people deserve to choose!* They had memes: ballot boxes with the Kazakh flag on the side, a cartoon of Galina stealing a map of the country behind the backs of grieving citizens.

"Get pictures of Galina injured," I said. "She's a hero now. She survived an attempt on her life. Remind people that democracy's divisive and what we need now is unity. Make it clear that any free elections would be won by Islamists. Point toward Egypt."

"Okay."

"So we're going to let Galina unite Kazakhstan and steer us through this difficult time. Emphasize that she's a victim of last night's attack. Get pictures of her injured face. Everything needs to be about her now. Continuity."

"We can't get access to the hospital."

"They didn't get access to the party, but they've got pictures of it. Photoshop something."

Politics has two speeds: glacial and crisis. Crisis is a storm in which all the little laws are up in the air, the dice of history are tumbling. You have a window in which the impossible is possible, before reality congeals again. Hours, sometimes minutes.

By three a.m. Saracen had managed to assemble all their big names. Those in Kazakhstan stood around the conference table in the corner office. Their London colleagues streamed in on a video screen. I recognized Charlene Hayes, who used to chair the Joint Intelligence Committee. I also recognized John Weston, former British ambassador to NATO. Walker turned up to brief them all just as it was kicking off. He was pumped, carrying two phones, almost looking like he was enjoying this.

"The president's dead. That's confirmed. The bomber's believed to be Samat Baysufinov: Kazakh, from Shymkent. Twenty-eight years old, no known affiliations."

Baysufinov hadn't previously been flagged by the services. From what they could glean off surviving CCTV, he'd hired a black Mercedes 220, then attached fake diplomatic plates. He drove up to the front of the hotel at 11:03, past six hotel security and almost twice as many members of the presidential guard. That was insane, and suggested inside support, which was currently a high-priority line of investigation. The president had gone downstairs at 11:10.

Forty-two injured, seventeen dead. If I'd made it downstairs thirty seconds earlier it would have been eighteen.

"Do we have a group responsible?" Weston asked.

"Not yet."

People kept one eye on the TV screens as it hit. Normal broadcasting ceased. Kazakh channels cut to visibly distressed presenters. *The president is reported to have been injured . . .*

Someone had to say it. In the end it was Hayes.

"Who's going to be giving the green light now, when it comes to Conqueror?"

"There's a number of options ahead of us," Walker said.

"We're going to have to move carefully," Piper said. "We know Galina's been supportive so far. Obviously we don't want to seem to be taking advantage." Her voice was tight. She turned to me.

"Thoughts, Toby?"

"This is going to plunge their economy into crisis," I said. "That's our opportunity. Objectively speaking, they need this deal now more than ever. Show them UK investors standing firm. We won't be cowed, Kazakhstan won't be cowed."

There were nods. I felt like I was watching myself from a distance. Everyone agreed to speak again in an hour and dispersed. I took Piper aside, removed some of the glass from her hair. She looked at me with a strange smile.

"Toby, are there any aspects of Vectis that I need to know about? What you do, what's going on?"

"What do you mean?"

"I mean aspects of Vectis that I *shouldn't* know about."

Walker joined us before I could think of an answer.

"Zhaparov is directing pretty much everything, as far as we can tell." He had reports from Vectis's Moscow and Berlin offices, focused on Kazakhstan's chief of Antiterrorism and Kremlin favorite. "The head of the Kazakh Defense Force is on his way to the Antiterrorism HQ to meet him. We tracked calls from Zhaparov's advisors to senior figures in the Kyrgyz, Uzbek, and Russian governments, all made less than an hour after the bomb. The calls lasted five to ten minutes, enough to get guarantees, establish details, chains of command."

"And China?"

"Expressing concern."

"That's screaming 'Fire,'" Piper said, as if we hadn't just had our inconclusive exchange. "For Beijing."

"We have fairly strong indication that there's going to be another attack in Astana," Walker said.

"What kind of attack?"

"Another bomb. That's all I know. We need to get delegates out sooner rather than later."

"Who's supplying you with this?"

"Reliable sources." He wouldn't say more.

The attack hit international news at five a.m. *Word of an alleged terror attack at an event attended by Kazakhstan's president.* Statements from world leaders scrolled across the screens. *Grave concern . . . The scourge of terror must be defeated . . .* Nothing yet from Kyrgyzstan, with its Russian bases. Nothing yet from Tehran. Mass arrests had started under Zhaparov's instructions. They included his rivals and opponents. The official Russian statement arrived a few minutes later: *Nazarbayev was a pillar of stability in the region and Russia will do everything it can to preserve peace and security for the people of Kazakhstan.* Which meant it was ready to invade.

I logged in to the VKontakte social media account of Aslan Cherchesov, my fake Russian seaman, and checked his military friends. Leave had been canceled. I posted: *Can't believe leave's canceled. Going to miss my girlfriend's twenty-first birthday. Where are you being sent?*

Then a hush fell across the headquarters. I looked up and saw Zhaparov on the screens. He stood in the lobby of Kazakhstan's Parliament House, surrounded by senior military.

"The president is in a very critical condition," he said convincingly. "I want the people of Kazakhstan to know, we will stop at nothing to catch those responsible. Nowhere on earth will be safe. They will see what happens when the Kazakh people stand together."

Zhaparov declared a state of emergency. I made out Vladislav Vishinsky in the crowd behind him. I was still watching when Walker touched my arm.

"Come with me."

Was this it, I wondered? Was he leading me to some form of incarceration or worse? I considered running. In the end, I pocketed a pen on the way as a very last-ditch form of defense.

We walked the length of the ground floor to a door that opened into a gym. No cameras. One shaved-headed individual guarding a scratched brown briefcase. The man departed with a nod at Walker. The case sat there beside a rowing machine.

"It's what he asked for," Walker said. "There'll be another million in Satayev's designated account if the deal goes through."

I lifted the case by the handle. It was heavy. I sat on a bench, pulled it onto my lap, and slid the locks. The money was portioned into clear bags of several thousand dollars, a mixture of bank-fresh and used notes, both with plain seals.

"I've arranged guards," Walker said.

"We need to keep it light."

"I get that. You can appreciate our concern."

I messaged Satayev. He called me back within a few minutes.

"We're in a position to help," I said.

"We are ready to fight. But people need to hear your government say they are with us."

"I've got what you asked for. I'm not doing this on behalf of any government."

"I understand."

"It's the truth this time. I need you to know that."

I told him how much money I was about to deliver, and he relaxed.

"Take it to my colleague."

"This is a big delivery. You're sure you can trust them?"

"He is my right hand. I will give you the address."

"Go for it."

He gave me an address in the Triumph of Astana.

50

APARTMENT 601. NO NAME. I WAS TOLD TO BUZZ, SAY I HAD A DELIVERY, get the lift straight up.

Satayev ended the call, and I was left staring across the gym equipment.

I was being swept along by something. This was my last chance to escape, I thought, but I knew I was kidding myself. That moment had long passed. I wanted to know what story I was in.

Walker had arranged a driver. He put a tracker on the case, the size of a memory card.

Morbid curiosity kept me moving.

The dawn felt fragile. A few people out on the street acted as if life continued, ignoring the helicopter that circled above them. Some huddled at bus stops in the gray sunrise, looking at phones. There was heavy activity around the government district, convoys of tactical vehicles containing Special Forces driving into town. A city in shock. Viewing it through tinted glass didn't help shake the feeling of traveling through a dream. Toward a dream.

I kept the case on my lap as my GL5 chauffeur drove me there, but that made me self-conscious so I put it on the seat beside me as if it was just another load of paperwork. I had an earpiece that connected to GL5 high command, a discreet microphone on my jacket. The vehicle would be tracked on satellite. None of this made me feel secure.

We turned north. The Triumph appeared. There was a heavy, sleep-deprived wave of dread growing in me. Something was making sense in a way I could only associate with impending death.

"I want to walk in on foot," I said, trying to gain some kind of control on the situation.

He shook his head. "That is not possible."

We entered the building's shadow. Barriers for the underground car park sank into the ground and we sped down the ramp toward a lot of high-end vehicles under neon.

There was a lift in the underground car park, with its own armed guard.

"I think I'll be okay from here."

"We'll stay by the car. Ten minutes. Then we come to get you."

The car park lift took me to the ground-floor reception, where I had to cross the lobby to another set of lifts. These lift doors opened to reveal a gleaming interior of polished brass and mirrored walls. I stepped inside, reflected to infinity—me and one and a half million dollars rising through the building—asking myself why I was still alive.

The doors opened on a long, carpeted corridor, five doors in each direction. Number 601 was the farthest to the left.

I knocked. The door opened. He wasn't in the dark suit, but it was him, the man in the clip. He wore a white shirt, open at the neck, sleeves rolled up, beltless black suit trousers, leather slip-ons. He glanced at the case.

"Come in."

The place was overheated. I followed him down the corridor to the room where I had been filmed.

It was the same room: same view, same cupboard with mirrored panels. The rug had gone and there was a new sofa: brown where the one in the clip was pale. A TV showed troops marching. *The assassination opens up a Pandora's box as Russia, China, and Turkey contest for control of the region.* An emergency summit had been called in Brussels including EU leaders, the UK prime minister, the French president. The first crowds had appeared across Kazakhstan holding images of Nazarbayev. *Nation in shock.*

"We must be quick," he said.

I glanced up to where a camera might be. I couldn't see anything, or anywhere you'd hide one. I walked over to the mirror, ran a thumb nail over the crack, then stood back and looked at myself in it. I still gripped the case.

"Who are you?" I said.

"A friend of Akan Satayev." He watched me curiously.

"I don't work with people I don't know."

"You don't need to work with me," he said.

"Do you know who I am?" I asked.

"Akan says you can be trusted." The man wanted this over, but was cautious. There was no decanter, as in the video. No traces of comfort or gestures of camaraderie. I checked the view from the window. "We don't have long," he said. "Show me what you have."

Strange anticlimax. You meet your destiny and it just wants to take the cash and run. I had a hunger to talk. I realized I was staring at my companion, and this was making him uncomfortable. Part of me couldn't help investing him with knowledge, as if he might bear a trace of the oracle that had created him. I had finally got here, and there was nothing for me.

I lifted the case to the coffee table, unlocked it, and nudged the money toward him. He checked a couple of the blocks, then went to the next room and made a call.

I looked for papers, post, anything with a name, pressed the pedal to open a trash bin in the corner, but it was empty. I picked up a jacket slung over the arm of the sofa and retrieved a receipt for a Visa card in the name of B. Golovkin. Golovkin, if it was him, seemed deep in discussion in the kitchen — I heard the words "two hours" and "cleaning up." I messaged the name to Reza Nikfar, picked up an open laptop beside the table. No folders or documents saved, just news streaming: Turkey had stopped a Russian ship from passing through the Bosphorus Strait. NATO vessels from Spain and Italy were moving toward Georgia. Saudi Arabia had described Kazakhstan as a friend, and any threat to the country's independence as unacceptable. There were Chinese troops at Khorgos, on the Kazakh border. The ruble had sunk to fifty-nine per dollar.

West united in warning to Russia. Territorial integrity is the foundation of international law.

The man returned and nodded.

"Okay. Now we move forward. Akan will be in touch." He took a packet of cigarettes from his pocket and tapped one against the box. That was when I saw his fingernails. They were blackened and stunted — where they'd grown back at all. It meant someone had seen fit to remove them at some point. Time spent in the hands of those people explained the care with which he moved, the unblinking eyes. I imagined seeing him through bars, without the suit, in Kabul's Policharki Prison, in Baghdad's Karrada District hellhole. What else did it explain?

"How long have you lived here?" I asked.

"I don't live here."

I returned to the mirror. The bruising, the traces of ash, the new coat I'd stolen — you start operations in control, you end up looking like you're on the run. Reza messaged back: *Golovkin = high alert. What do you know? Call me asap.*

I returned to the case, picked it up, and walked out.

"What are you doing?" he said.

51

I GOT INTO AN OPEN LIFT AND HIT THE BUTTON FOR GROUND FLOOR, hearing Golovkin's steps approach. The doors closed and I began to drop. The feeling I had was that I was ready to wake up now, and that was going to take a fight. I had a message from GL5: *Confirm delivery.* I crossed the ground floor to a doorman who held the doors open for me and my case as we walked out.

Then I ran.

I took the tracker out of the case, threw it into the back of a pickup waiting at traffic lights, and kept going. Half a mile south I stole a boxy old Honda Civic from beside the university. I threw the case on the back seat and used the car to put another mile between myself and the Triumph.

An unmarked car screamed past, sixty miles per hour with a siren on and someone sitting in the back, head bowed. Police were everywhere now, stiff with live rounds. After another moment I realized they'd turned the adverts off on the sides of buildings. My instinct was to get out of the city. Main roads were being used by military. I kept to the back roads and sank low in my seat, cutting toward the airport.

I called Reza as I drove.

"Who is Golovkin?"

"Elliot, you're on an Interpol red notice."

"Issued by who?"

"The States."

"Under what name?"

"Your own. Links to terrorism."

A red notice was an instruction to locate and provisionally arrest an individual pending extradition. It was issued by Interpol when a member country had produced a valid national arrest warrant.

"I've been set up."

My phone vibrated. I had an alert from Cognizance, the facial-recognition app, which meant a face resembling my own had shown up online. I groaned inwardly.

"Are you back working with Akan Satayev? Is that what this is to do with?" Reza asked.

The phone buzzed again. I took vibrate off.

"I'm not working with anyone. Who's Golovkin?"

"One of the twenty or so cover names used by Serik Ten. He's the money man for ISIS in Central Asia. His name just came up in connection with the truck that took the explosives to Astana."

So the CGI clip showed me consorting with a terrorist linchpin: MI6 stirring Central Asia against Russia.

I was the catalyst.

"We have an individual in custody talking to us," Reza said. "He claims there will be a vehicle-borne attack in Astana today, targeting civilians. Can you confirm that?"

"I don't have that intelligence personally."

"People believe you do. We identified seven Kazakh terror cells allied with the bomber. They've gone dark as of two hours ago — a surge in electronic chatter, then total silence. Something's about to happen."

I said I'd call back, then braced myself and checked what the facial alert was bringing up. Online I'd gone viral. *Police release footage of British citizen accused of conspiracy to provide resources to a designated foreign terrorist organization.*

Bohren crossing the lobby of Jeddah's Waldorf Astoria; Bohren on security cameras leaving his gallery in Lausanne.

Russian sites: *Who is Christopher Bohren?* Me in Queen Alia Airport, crossing the departures hall, a red circle around my head like a halo. Then a more blurred shot as I entered the GL5 compound. *Questions must be answered regarding Bohren's connections with GL5, the private security contractor now suspended from all security work at UK military and governmental facilities . . .*

I stopped the car, took a wad of cash from the briefcase, and ripped it open. I checked for watermarks, metallic thread, ran my finger over the print. It looked real enough. Hard to tell. Another call came in: Marius from the Evotec office, sounding uncharacteristically tense.

"Where's Stefan?" he said.

"I thought he was on his way back to you."

"He never got the flight."

"Why not?"

"We got word via contacts: He was abducted, flown to Moscow. Russia thinks we were involved in hacking them on behalf of China."

"You're joking."

"Critical infrastructure in Russia went down a few hours ago—Sberbank, Lukoil, Rosneft: all hacked. China's Cyberspace Administration was taken down in return."

"By the Russians?"

"Not by us, that's for sure."

"I'll get you Stefan. I'll sort this out."

"We can't work with you anymore."

"Leave it with me."

I put thoughts of Stefan's probable interrogation out of my mind and checked Aliya's VKontakte account. It was still broadcasting messages.

She had moved on from conspiracy theories about the president's death to conspiracy theories regarding Christopher Bohren and terrorist funding, and was now encouraging Astana's citizens to come together in memory and defiance. She was urging people to meet at Independence Square.

I logged in to her phone, looked at her London photos again, then checked the phone's current location. It came up as the Eagilik bookshop, Kenesary Street. According to social media, people were gathering there in preparation for a march or memorial or protest of some kind: No one seemed entirely sure which.

By the time I got to the bookshop, individuals were spilling out, some with candles, others with placards. I saw Aliya among them, pulled up alongside her, opened the passenger door.

"Get in."

"Toby?" She looked terrified. Her companions stared.

"I need to speak to you."

"I know who you are."

"I doubt it. Please, get in."

"You are Christopher Bohren. You work for MI6."

"Close. You're in trouble, Aliya. I need to know why you went to London."

Now it was her turn to feel the heat of her friends' attention. It was a tense morning, and my presence wasn't making it any more comfortable for anyone.

"Please," I said. She said something to one of her friends then got in the car.

"Aliya?" a young woman with a candle said. Then, to me: "Where are you taking her?"

"It's okay," Aliya said.

I began to drive.

"Who are you?" she said.

"I'm the one who's going to stop you from being arrested. I can get you out of here. But I need you to trust me. I need you to tell me about Worldwide Media," I said.

"I can't."

"Yes, you can."

"Let me out."

"In a minute."

She sat frozen, silent while I drove. I didn't want a scene in the car. I wanted her somewhere isolated.

When we got to the motel she panicked, tried to grab the wheel. I stopped the car, persuaded her again that I wasn't the threat, which was sounding less convincing by the minute. She stayed in the car while I paid for a room. I bought a bottle of vodka from the shop. We went into the room and I set the vodka down, fetched tumblers from the bathroom and gave her one.

"Have a drink."

"You kissed me." Aliya shook her head. "Drive me back. Please."

"I will drive you back. Now, or anytime you want. But I am concerned about what you're involved in, and I think it might place you in danger. You know about attacks before they happen. Have you noticed that? Recently you've been tweeting about another bomb attack on Astana. Is that going to happen?"

"It's nothing to do with me."

"But it is. I think it is, other people will think it is. That brings danger to you and your family."

Her glass whistled past my head, smashed against the wall. She went for the door, then changed her mind and came at me, slashing my face with her nails. I got her wrists.

"Don't you dare threaten my family."

"I'm not the threat. Talk to me. You said you had something for me," I said. Her face went blank, then she gave a pained laugh.

"Something for you?"

I released her and she backed off, reached into her rucksack, searched beneath her MacBook and found a brown paper bag. She threw it onto the bed. A book fell out.

It was a secondhand paperback. Baudelaire. *Les Fleurs du mal* in Russian translation.

For a moment we both stood still, looking at the book, as if neither of us understood what it was doing there, how it had appeared from out of a lie and survived. I felt my heart twinge. I opened the case of money, turned it toward her.

"Help yourself."

She stared at the bundles.

"Just give me ten minutes," I said. "Explain why this is nothing to do with you. Tell me who it's to do with. Then I drive you back with as much cash as you want."

"I don't understand who you are."

"I'm the person who's going to stop you from being arrested. I can get you out of here. But I need you to trust me."

I poured her a drink in the remaining glass, then took a swig from the bottle. She sat down on the bed, holding the glass, staring through it at her knees, then knocked it back.

"I did what they told me."

"Who?

"Worldwide Media."

"What do Worldwide Media do?"

"They create online content. Marketing, advertising, connecting companies with Kazakhstan."

"What happened in London?"

"It was like a job interview. They paid for me to go."

"To do what job exactly?"

"Write for them. They wanted young people in Kazakhstan. They'd read my blog. They said they were looking for young people who knew the local perspective: music, celebrities, customs."

"Who else did you meet while over there?"

"Lots of people. Other organizers, other people being recruited."

"How many being recruited?"

"Around twenty of us."

"Were the recruiters English?"

"I think so."

"Did you ever visit any kind of office?"

"No."

"Receive any correspondence with a company address?"

"No."

I put on a bedside lamp and turned off the neon tubes. We were talking now, and I needed her to continue. I needed to arrive at a point where I understood who was behind this, and what they wanted. I topped up her glass, then asked Aliya to lead me through the whole experience from first contact. She took a breath and began to speak.

After a few emails, and Aliya's confirmation of interest, they'd arranged a travel visa for her. She flew British Airways, via Helsinki. Picked up at Heathrow by a woman called Natasha, who was accompanied by two men, neither of whom was introduced to Aliya. She'd spent five days total in London. Most of the recruitment and training was handled by Natasha and a man who called himself Mark. Aliya described him as slick and energetic: He spoke about social media tactics, building profiles, persuasive writing. No conspicuous security was visible during her stay, though she was accompanied on outings, which they did as a group, and she was asked not to bring her phone to the training sessions.

"What else did these sessions involve?"

"They wanted to know about me: what languages I spoke, what I cared about, what my passions were. Also how I felt politically. Did I think representations of Russia were fair? What are hot topics in Kazakhstan? I did some written exercises: short pieces about news stories they showed us."

"Then what happened?"

"I got the job."

She had signed a nondisclosure agreement but no official contract. That was the last time she met anyone involved in person.

I asked her to talk me through the protocols they'd arranged. The first thing she did each day was to switch on an internet proxy service, which hid her IP address; then she accessed an encrypted cloud-storage service. It contained instructions from Worldwide Media: files uploaded with material, wiped after seven days. She followed the instructions; money appeared in her account.

"Some of it's just translating news articles from English to Russian. Or they ask me to leave comments on news sites."

"They tell you what to say?"

"I'm allowed to say what I want. They sometimes send me graphics and videos to use; sometimes ideas and articles they want me to think about, suggestions about which websites to post on."

"All under your name?"

"No. I have other names; other personas."

She told me about Maria Zagitova, who was very anti-Chinese, and Sabina, a housewife in Shymkent who concentrated more on traditional Kazakh values. Sabina wrote in Kazakh. The third identity Aliya controlled was a fortuneteller named Cantadora. She passed on advice from the spirit world, often regarding sex or relationships, occasionally geopolitics. She believed the future lay with Russia.

I handed Aliya the MacBook from her bag.

"Show me the dropbox."

She hesitated, then logged in to a Boxcryptor online storage account.

"This is just the last few days."

It was enough—more than forty files. I read a few.

Then I stopped.

Russia's idea of a secure border is one with Russians on both sides.

My words to Joanna.

I scanned through the bullet points. There were other ideas I remembered from our conversation.

Kazakhstan is an attractive prospect to Russians nostalgic for the territorial reach of the Soviet Union.

Invasion itself would not present a problem for Russia's military. Kazakhstan's limited forces of some 70,000 could not offer significant resistance.

Seizing their "rightful" portion of Kazakhstan would bring Russia substantial resources and enormous geopolitical advantages. It would also gain control of China's border to the west, thereby getting a monopoly of control over China's energy imports and any manufactured exports that pass west through Kazakhstan.

I took my phone out, accessed my encrypted files, and found the image of Joanna taken from the mall CCTV.

"This woman," I said.

Aliya stared at the image, puzzled. "That's Natasha."

"This is definitely Natasha?"

"Yes."

She sounded certain, and calmer now; it was my turn to deal with bewilderment.

"What was Natasha's role, exactly?"

"She runs the company. She was in charge."

In charge, I thought. Joanna's part in all this lurched from victim to presiding genius. Then back to missing.

"What did you think it was all for?"

"To generate clicks, drive traffic. Why else?"

I checked the latest file, dated Monday. Aliya was being prompted to tweet about people protesting, encouraging them, announcing the gathering in Independence Square.

"Why this gathering? What do you know?" I asked.

"Nothing." I caught a look that teetered between uncertainty and mounting terror. She topped up her glass shakily, drank again. Then she asked if I had cigarettes. I went to buy some from the front desk. When I returned she had vanished.

So had the case with the money.

No sign of her in the car park. I checked the road. She was nowhere to be seen. There was nothing to suggest she'd been abducted. Her laptop remained on the bed, next to the Baudelaire. She must have hitched a lift. Good luck to her, I thought. I hoped she was going to use that money to get herself and her family as far away from here as possible.

I picked up the Baudelaire, smelled the paper, returned it to its bag.

The dropbox was still open on the laptop. The zip file within it contained twenty or so links, suggestions, and articles. The latest set of instructions included a map showing areas of Kazakhstan that Russia might annex in an invasion, identical to the one I'd seen in Saracen's offices. *If you can include this map, that would be great. Thanks.*

So who had created it?

I ran a reverse image search online. There was one result. The map had appeared previously, in an academic paper by a professor at Southampton's School of International Relations, entitled "Russia's Southern Front."

The author was a Professor Romas Kleiza. Lithuanian-born, expert in Cold War history. A quick browse gave me a sense of Kleiza and his career. Not the most successful scholar — he had one book to his name, *World Without the West,* regarding a plot by Russia, China, and Iran to dominate the next millennium — but popular with right-wing think tanks and anti-Russian lobby groups.

He'd created another, more popular map: *The world in June 2030. Political structures after NATO.*

It took a moment for my eyes to decipher. Poland was misshapen, its eastern regions absorbed into the Russian Federation. Same with Estonia. Ukraine had disintegrated entirely. Turkey was pocked with Russian bases. So were Syria, Libya, and Egypt.

A lot of Western countries lay in fragments; broken rocks on the shoreline of a great sea: Central Asia and the Middle East, including the Gulf states, divided between Russia, China, and Iran. Symbols indicated their ports, airfields, shipping routes, oil and gas pipelines. As a bloc, they controlled ninety percent of energy and trade to Europe.

According to his website, the map had been used at a conference, Approaches to the New Russia-China Threat, put on by the Eurasian Futures Foundation.

That name rang a bell.

A lot of Kleiza's work, apparently, had been made possible by the generosity of this foundation. EFF, as it styled itself, had been active between 2013 and 2017, supplying quotes, statistics, and opinion pieces to the media; generously funding conferences, journals, and research projects.

I had a closer look at their website, to see if I could discern who had supplied the Eurasian Futures Foundation with their money. The name that came up was Robert Carter.

Robert Carter, I found after a few minutes' browsing, had put millions into EFF. The launch of the foundation was recorded in the press as another front in Carter's lobbying war. To celebrate the occasion, the *Spectator* ran a think piece under his name.

We're told NATO is coming apart, EU defence pacts are in tatters, and the West, defeated in the Middle East, will now bow out gracefully from affairs on our doorstep. For new powers are on the rise. Well, some of us will not stand by as the two most autocratic, undemocratic, and merciless regimes gang up to make liberal democracy a mere memory. The cynical alliance between Russia and China is the greatest threat we face. Their machinations, combined with America's increasing absence from the global stage, is bad news for the free world. It is up to all politicians and diplomats to ensure the twenty-first century won't turn into the Sino-Russian century.

Then I knew where I'd first seen him. He'd been at the event where I met Callum Walker.

I took the bottle of vodka to the doorway and stared across the car park's deep snow, awed by an approaching tide of realization.

I thought back to that night, two and a half years ago, which had been a memorable one. The conference had taken place in Wilton House, an eighteenth-century mansion in Buckinghamshire used by the Foreign and Commonwealth Office for strategic forums. Undercroft had instructed me to attend. He wanted me to ascertain whether there was anyone there who shouldn't be; the sensitivity of the discussions and exclusivity or not of the guest list. I agreed, partly curious to see the place, which had originally been commandeered as a site to interrogate German prisoners after the Second World War. I was thinking about this as I arrived.

Helicopters on the lawn, sculptured topiary around the edges; inside the house, a sweeping staircase, iridescent chandeliers, then an ornate room with Greek gods painted across the ceiling. Beneath the gods, international political figures mingled with heads of banks, energy companies, retired military, stooped to hear one another's small talk, eyes scanning the crowd, taking their seats for the night's performance.

There were three talks, each more swivel-eyed than the last. They involved fantasies of Russian schemes and capabilities, of our incapacity to respond, and visions of various futures in which it was too late. Most guests nodded along, minds already made up or indifferent. With the décor and candlelight, the whole thing felt like a strange court masque, an attempt at decorating power with ideas. There was no way it would be of use to an intelligence officer, I thought—ours or anyone else's. It was a waste of my time, and I wondered why Alastair Undercroft had suggested I attend. For it had been his idea, I was certain now. I could see the invitation squared on his desk before he slid it over. Even as I scanned the crowd I had felt that someone was keeping an eye on me. After the final speech I moved to the bar, feeling superstitious and wanting to clear the crude, apocalyptic visions away with whisky. I was looking forward to getting back on a plane to Kurdistan. I met Callum Walker. I tried to see that moment: Walker stepping over the threshold of my life. Had he approached from the crowd or been at the bar before me? What was his opening line? *So, what do you make of all that?* He wore a leery smile, eyes bright with what I had assumed was drink but may have been reflected gold. His business card was in my hand when I sat down.

I returned to the laptop. The Eurasian Futures Foundation website listed events, sponsors, speakers. I was scanning down names when one caught my eye in the list of sponsors: Talon.

Hugh Stevenson had been on his way to their offices when he was killed.

I called the number for Talon. It had just gone seven a.m. in the UK and I wasn't optimistic, but a receptionist answered.

"I believe someone at your company may want to speak to me quite urgently," I said. "I'm not sure who. My name is Elliot Kane, and I believe they want to speak to me about Hugh Stevenson. Possibly about the Eurasian Futures Foundation. I'd appreciate if you could identify the relevant employee and give them this number."

I thought I sounded insane. The man on the other end remained polite. He said he'd see what he could do. I didn't believe him.

My phone rang in less than two minutes.

"You know I can't tell you much." It was a woman's voice, soaked in decades of power and finished with money. I could hear birds chirping in the background, an English dawn chorus. I had a sense of her moving out into a well-tended garden.

"Who is this?" I said.

"You don't need my name. Hugh suggested you might call. He said if anything happened I should speak to you. You have to understand, I am not part of the privileged circle. But I was at the initial meeting."

"Go on."

"The first of March, 2014. I won't say where. I was told it was going to be a closed conference on Central Asian policy, put together by the Eurasian Futures Foundation. We'd donated some money, mostly to keep Robert Carter friendly. I'm not even sure we knew the full parameters of its work. There was an astonishing array of figures present: the Foreign Secretary and Chief of Six, the army chief of General Staff. There were representatives of the NATO Psychological Operations Working Group, CEOs of the top British energy and defense companies.

"Carter himself led the presentation. We were shown forecasting on Central Asia, a set of scenarios that could unfold. All incorporated loss of

Western influence, financial losses of billions, a complete shift of global power. A lot focused on the potential implications of a Russia-China alliance. Carter had intelligence regarding a meeting in August of that year between China, Russia, and Iran. He claimed that Russia persuaded its allies that the West had become politically incapable of coordinated military response. More specifically, we lacked the means of responding to their psychological operations.

"Carter presented data that showed Russian dominance of online media in more countries than not. He said the effects of this would only be fully understood in the coming decades. By way of conclusion there was a report recommending we step up our own offensive psyop strategy before it was too late. The British government needed to take these warnings seriously. Attack was the best form of defense. It was now or never."

"Any specific psyop strategy?"

"Not that I was ever aware of. They began talking about invading Syria and Iran, and how we would need Russia distracted et cetera. That was the point at which I detached myself, so to speak. I decided they were fantasists. Now I believe they had very real alliances within the MOD and beyond, in the States: individuals who backed a more aggressive foreign policy."

"What happened after the meeting?"

"I don't know. As a naysayer, I was closed out. I can't say with certainty how things proceeded, but I know Robert Carter bought Saracen Oil and Gas Exploration a few months later. Saracen hired the intelligence company Vectis. Their founder, Callum Walker, had been one of the more encouraging voices at the meeting."

"Callum Walker was there?"

"He was there in 2014. I've no doubt his connections within the intelligence service helped win initial support for whatever unfolded."

"Alastair Undercroft?"

"Also there. Another big name lending their voice to the project. Now suspended from his post, I'm told. The government *did* spend millions on this. My own acquaintances in government were able to share that much. No other information came my way until six months ago when those acquaintances suggested that my initial instincts had been right. The PM got cold feet, balked at the scale to which things had grown. You can imagine the government's response: We can't risk starting World War Three. Thoughts along those lines."

"And then people left Six," I said, as the pieces came together.

"The big names associated with the project seemed to feel their time in state intelligence had come to an end. There was quite an exodus. Carter ensured that most of them had a soft landing."

"Joanna Lake?"

"Lake, yes. She moved to Vectis."

I went to the motel window, stared at the car park as my mind reeled.

"Do you think the operation *was* closed down?" I asked.

"What do you mean?"

"The individuals involved — did they jump ship or just change ship?"

"I see." There was a long pause. "I wouldn't want to speculate. I've probably said all I can for now."

"Wait. There are elements in the service now aware that something continued, yes? The project didn't stop as intended. That's why Alastair Undercroft's been suspended."

"Certainly. Senior elements."

"Are you in a position to contact them?"

"I'm not sure . . ."

"A lot of lives are at stake. I need you to tell them I'm willing to help. I'm in Kazakhstan. They need to work with me."

"I can try getting some word through."

"Tell them to contact the ambassador here, Suzanna Ford. You can give her this number. She'll find me."

"I'll try."

"I appreciate it."

"Hugh was a good friend."

"Mine also."

She rang off. Olivia Gresham had messaged with a link to an article about me: *Is this real?* Reza Nikfar: *Call asap.* I returned to the car and began to drive through the outskirts, blank with regards to my next move. Lie low? Escape? Hand myself in? I called Reza first.

"Got a possible ID for the attacker," he said. "We're looking for Yeldos Tanatarov, another Kazakh, from Karagandy Province. Seventeen years old. Spent time in a correctional colony of some kind, near Almaty. Next seen in Raqqa, blind in one eye, learning how to take apart an AK-47. His brother was arrested last year, but young Yeldos must have had some decent training as he's been off radar since returning to Kazakhstan."

"Where's he going to bomb?"

"That's the question. Would be nice to answer it before he does."

I saw the aftermath of an explosion: detached body parts, decapitated children, bones jutting through skin.

"Listen, Reza, you said Joanna Lake put you onto this attack in the first place when she called. I think she'd just seen the plans — I think she'd accessed something that told her what was going to happen. She was going somewhere to try to stop it."

"You think she got there? She tried to stop terrorists singlehandedly?"

"I don't know. You've got the cell number she rang you from; you may have her last location."

"Give me fifteen."

"Five."

"Alright. Five."

Gresham was still trying to get through. I answered.

"Where are you?" she said.

"Astana."

"You're on the news."

"Ignore the news."

"Are you okay?"

"No. What have you heard about the situation here?"

"The president might be dead."

"The president is dead. What are people saying about Saracen? About the deal?"

"It's up in the air. If there is any oil at all."

"What do you mean?"

"Something's wrong on the estimates. I'm hearing five billion barrels, I'm hearing three billion, then zero billion; I'm hearing a line into Turkey, then people saying that's a no-go. Others telling me the field's sixty million years out, and all the oil is gone."

"Who's saying that?"

"Smart people. Apparently there's been drilling around Block Nine for years. The fossils coming up are Cretaceous rather than Miocene — so say people who know about these things and what they mean. It's clay all the way down."

"Saracen use new sensing technology," I said.

"Auracle."

"Right."

"Sources tell me the Auracle data might be cooked. It's fake. No one had heard of Auracle or their drones until two years ago. Now they're not answering calls."

"I know they've had issues," I said uncertainly.

"Can you find out if these issues involve inventing several billion barrels of oil? Because that — that's going to have consequences."

"I'll try."

"Are you really on a Wanted list, Elliot?"

"So it seems."

"Connected to terrorism?"

"More than you'd believe."

"I gave you cover."

"I know. You'll be okay. I promise."

She groaned softly. I could sense Gresham struggling to balance her clandestine past and financially exposed present.

"I don't think I can help, Elliot, but if there's anything I can do . . ."

I promised I'd message with an update asap and hung up. I was a few blocks east of the Special Economic Zone, where Auracle kept its office. I could do better than calling them. I turned the car around and headed in their direction.

Astana's citizens were out in force. Many carried flowers or wreaths. I passed two satellite broadcasting vans, then heard the first chants. At the corner of Independence Square I saw the crowd. Two thousand or so men and women drawn together by shock. Most stood without any banners or placards, but a contingent had brought the abstract nouns: "*Freedom,*" "*Justice.*" Police lines protected the governmental palace. Military groups waited beside armored vehicles at the corners.

Three security police waved me away. I turned east, kept going, into narrower, poorer back streets, turned another corner and saw two black Land Cruisers, ten black uniforms. A kid was down on the snow, clutching his face, eight more individuals with their hands on their heads, noses pressed to the wall. An open doorway led into a prayer hall with overlapping rugs on the floor, a speaker on the wall, prayer books in a case by the door. I checked the uniformed men, most in full-face balaclavas. They looked tough, well-equipped, with Glocks and MP3s. Looked like Zhaparov's personal unit.

I reversed fast, then circled back to the gates of the economic zone. Two guards kept uneasy watch. They asked for my pass.

"I'm visiting Auracle."

"No visitors today."

I talked my way in by virtue of being a white European and passing them my last handful of cash. Besides, it wasn't a day for excess propriety.

The businesses were housed in identical warehouse-style buildings and it took me ten minutes to find Auracle's unit. The door to the office was locked, but no alarm went off when I smashed a back window. Inside, it was pristine. Abandoned. With little sense of having ever been particularly inhabited.

Computers, desks, a coffee machine, a shredder. A whiteboard had been smeared. A small kitchen contained a kettle and plastic cups.

I sat down in a swivel chair at an empty desk. The wall beside it carried a relief map and a graph above a diagram of drone components. But the technology I thought about was the software Joanna had described.

"They have software that can tell you how long a relationship will last," she said.

What does that allow you to do? What are we, marriage guidance?

"It means, if you wanted a relationship to end, you could run the program backwards and see what steps would engineer that outcome."

BBC News website. Moscow was demanding the release of ten Russian tourists arrested by the Chinese in Manchuria, accused of spying for the GRU. Two Russian Su-27 fighter jets had intercepted a Chinese reconnaissance aircraft above Khabarovsk.

I brought up real-time satellite imagery of the Kazakh border with Russia. This was what Joanna had been doing in the internet café, I realized now: watching the creep of war. The hacked data showed her a project that had burst its banks. A psychological operation that was out of control. I couldn't discern any change at the border.

There were no more updates from Aliya in Astana, or her other personas. No reply when I messaged her, which was understandable. I logged in to her phone, switched the mic on, heard a crowd chanting. She had joined the protest. She could have chosen safety and she chose history.

I tried Walker, then the Vectis office. Both lines were dead. I left a voice message for Suzanna Ford at the British embassy, with my phone number and a suggestion we work together. Either that would mean something to her or not. There was no way I had time to explain what was going on. I stood at the window and stared out at the corrugated walls of the industrial estate, then back to my phone. According to local news, Zhaparov was due to address the Independence Square crowd in an hour, flanked by senior officials from Russia. He was branding it a mass vigil, in an attempt at keeping the square occupied by grief rather than anger: *Kazakhstan united against terrorism.*

In 2014, Islamic State published instructions for building and deploying vehicle-borne explosives. They encouraged targeting mass gatherings. They advised on components that weren't going to trigger security trip wires, and suggested waiting to construct the device until just before the operation for maximum discretion.

According to Reza, police had seized a laptop containing research on fuel-air bombs along with a detailed satellite image of Astana and surveillance photographs of public squares.

Fuel-air meant thermobaric. Thermobaric explosions were unlike anything else. Mix in enough petrol with your military-grade explosives and you got a second-blast wave as the air itself caught light, sucking up all the oxygen. Most forms of defense were useless, since the fuel cloud flowed around objects and into structures. What tended to kill people wasn't just the pressure wave but the subsequent vacuum, which tore lungs apart.

In a crowd like Independence Square, there would be more than five or six hundred in the kill zone.

But how would you get the bomb through? No parked cars, area checked by sniffer dogs, airspace closed. Blocks on every approach road. I sat on a swivel chair in the abandoned office, hearing the last moments of peace outside, finite, tangible, precious. I made a fist of my left hand, then opened it and stared at the scar.

Reza called.

"We have the last location of Joanna's cell phone."

52

THE LOCATION WAS TWO MILES OUT OF THE CITY. I COAXED THE HONDA
Civic to seventy miles per hour, prayed that its wheels would hold on the
icy road.

The coordinates led me into nothingness; level snow as far as the eye
could see. I considered the possibility that Reza's readings were off, or
even that GPS signals were being scrambled, which wasn't unheard of
during states of emergency. A mile later, as I was about to turn back, I
saw something.

It looked like a village in the distance, with low brown buildings. As
I got closer I saw that the buildings were tombs — the village was a cemetery, mud-built graves surrounded by a low fence. Not a soul in sight.

I left the car by the fence and walked in. Graves were snow-capped,
some domed, others square mausoleums of stone or clay. They were
carved with images of camels and swords and inscriptions in Arabic.
Poles jutted out of the snow, tied with bundles of horse hair. A low tree
in the center shrieked with colored rags that had been wound around its
dead branches.

Families had cleared snow from some of the tombs. A path had been
dug to a small brick mosque with barred windows and a crude water
pump beside its door. A few hundred meters behind the mosque were the
low concrete ruins of a collective farm.

I knocked at the door of the mosque, then turned back toward the
cemetery and considered my next move. I searched the landscape, as if I
might see Joanna out there. What I saw was odder. A hundred meters beyond where I'd parked, something glinted on the ground. It looked like
water, which was impossible, so I walked over. As I got closer I saw it was
a hard material, reflective: a panel of gray metal. I kicked it, knelt and
touched the surface. I thought it was a car door, and wondered how it had
become detached, then realized it was the car's roof and it hadn't.

I needed a shovel. Heart thumping, I ran back to the mosque, knocking hard on the door. When no one answered, I pulled on the handle and it opened. I walked in, searching, and a figure moved. It was an old man, head shrouded, face sunken. A caretaker of some kind, scared.

I tried various languages before realizing he was deaf. I mimed digging, then pointed out, toward my car. That did the trick. He disappeared into the shadows and came back with an ancient-looking spade. He followed me, and seemed curious when I started digging around the buried car.

The Chevy Equinox sat in what must once have been a hollow. There was a ridge of earth on at least two sides. These would have obscured the car from the road, but also left it exposed to the east—the direction that the snow had blown in—and had served as a trap.

After ten minutes digging, I had the top of a window. I crouched to try and see through, but it was too dark inside. The caretaker watched as I dug furiously. I shined my phone light through the glass, couldn't see anything. When I had another few inches of window exposed, I took the shovel and smashed the glass in.

The car was empty but for a laptop, a blond wig, and the contents of a first-aid kit spilled across the front seats. Down by the pedals was a nylon pouch used for carrying a spare box magazine for a handgun. The gray fabric of the driver's seat was bloodstained. There was blood smeared on the window and the door handle.

The caretaker called out. He stood closer to the cemetery, waving for me to come over.

A few meters away from him, I saw the fabric showing through the snow.

I dug with my hands, not minding that they went numb in seconds. I uncovered strands of hair, then skin, clearing the snow gently around her closed eyes. Joanna lay on her side. The snow remained pink around her right arm where she'd bled from beneath a shoelace tourniquet. Her lips were parted, frozen.

I crouched with my face to the exposed skin and felt the illusion of warmth. The caretaker muttered a prayer in Arabic: *O God, forgive our living and our dead . . .* Yes, I thought. I'd heard those words many times but they'd never felt so necessary. The stupid game. She knew that and she'd kept playing. I saw the girl at the recruitment interview, climbing through the window and out of her life. I had loved her then. I couldn't remember why we waited, why we had let them rob us of our lives.

Some pins remained in Joanna's hair. I took one and pocketed it. I touched my lips to her frozen cheek because that was what I wanted to remember doing. A unique intelligence had gone from the world, a dangerous, discontented one that involved some understanding of me, and that was gone too. I didn't want to leave her here. I thought of people I had encountered in Abkhazia, exiles from a flurry of war who had dug up the corpses of their relatives to bring with them, all shrouded in tarpaulin on the back of a pickup truck. Who was going to collect Joanna Lake? Not Vectis. The embassy, perhaps. I imagined her loaded onto a plane, unloaded tactfully on British soil. A spy's repatriation: indistinct and unmourned.

I returned to the half-excavated Chevy, managed to retrieve the laptop. It was the one I'd seen her use on the mall CCTV. The battery was dead. I looked around, thought of her last minutes here. Terrified? Surprised by an incongruous euphoria? Still fighting, I thought. Where was she trying to get to? Why was she here?

I pointed toward the abandoned farm buildings at the back.

"Anyone there?"

The caretaker shook his head. Then a thought occurred to him. I saw his sunken eyes come to life. He said something in Russian — *skoraya pomosh* . . . ambulance? "An ambulance came?" I tried both Russian and Kazakh. He lifted a hand as if to say "Wait," went into the mosque, and returned a moment later with a torch. He guided me toward the farm.

Blades of abandoned threshing machines lay around — dismembered combines, tractors. An air of desolation hung over the place. We went through to a long, breeze-block shelter, with rusted doors sealing it shut. The chain that had sealed them lay on the floor. The caretaker gestured for me to help him pull the doors open, and they scraped over the concrete.

The darkness inside was almost total. He clicked a torch and pointed it. Hessian bags, more rusted metal, a stained floor. Then, in the farthest corner, a pile of new medical kit: stretchers, a wheelchair, a drip stand, dressing pads, boxes of latex gloves.

There had been an ambulance here. It had been stripped; even the seats had been ripped out. There were also approximately forty empty petrol canisters lying in a pile. The petrol would have been transferred to breakable containers, probably mixed with nails or other shrapnel. I estimated the volume of an ambulance as around 400 cubic feet, which would hold a horrific amount of explosive power.

My phone rang as I ran back to the stolen Honda. Number withheld. I answered.

"Elliot, this is Suzanna Ford, the British ambassador in Kazakhstan. I've been in contact with various individuals in the UK, and we appreciate the complexity of your situation. Right now, we're focused on preventing this attack. I'm sure that's your priority too."

I got in the car, started the engine.

"He's using an ambulance," I said. "That's all I know. What resources do you have to stop it?"

"I've got a six-man team here. We're equipped."

"That's not going to do it."

"Elliot—"

"I'm going to enable GPS on my phone. Track me."

I called the number on Sergei Cherenkov's business card. It was time to engage the Russian intelligence service. He answered promptly.

"I have what you want," I said. "We need to be quick."

53

HE TOLD ME TO HEAD STRAIGHT TO THE RUSSIAN EMBASSY. I WAS stopped ten meters before the gates by three men in Russian military uniform, one with a pistol drawn. They searched me. Joanna's laptop was taken, along with my phone. I was patted down, steered through the gates, pushed into the building.

Embassy stucco, pastel walls, a framed picture of Putin.

I was made to wait in a corridor beside a double set of doors into what must have been Cherenkov's office. I felt the clock ticking. They'd weaponized the ambulance. They weren't going to sit around. After a couple of minutes I pushed the doors open, walked in.

Cherenkov sat behind a table of dark wood in a room with silk wallpaper, oil paintings, and a suite of antique furniture. He looked up from Joanna's laptop, saw me, and told the guards it was okay. He looked unslept but smarter than usual, the sleeves of his white shirt rolled up.

"Take a seat."

"We don't have long. There's going to be another attack. I think we can stop it."

He gazed at me, processing this. I saw the laptop screen. It contained multiple images: more CGI versions of the room in the Triumph of Astana; me and Serik Ten. I sat down opposite Cherenkov and he nudged the laptop toward me. I clicked through low-quality images from other locations: my body on the ground with a spread of blood across my shirt; Joanna hanging from a belt in a toilet cubicle. Me and Joanna unconscious in the front seats of an SUV.

"Different ways of wrapping it up," he said.

"Looks like it. My part, anyway. There's going to be a vehicle-borne attack in the next hour, using a stolen ambulance. I think the target's Independence Square, where a lot of your senior officials are gathered."

"You arranged this?"

"No. You have to stop it and then stop a war — convince Russian high command that this is an unauthorized, nongovernmental psyop strategy. But we've got minutes, not hours."

Something was coming together. Cherenkov relayed instructions to the uniformed men: communication channels to open, combat preparations to initiate.

"First tell me about Perfect Vision," he said. The door closed. Just the two of us. A well-upholstered interrogation room. "We're not going anywhere until you tell me what you know."

"Where's Stefan Janikowski?"

"He's fine, and we can arrange his release. But he doesn't know as much as you do. Talk to me."

"Perfect Vision's a large-scale psychological operation, set up to hit back at Russia, developed by MI6 after you invaded Ukraine. The idea's to inflame issues between you and your allies, China in particular. Kazakhstan's being used for that."

Cherenkov absorbed this information expressionlessly.

"And the oil field?" he asked. "How long have you known the scale?"

"There is no oil field. No oil. Just an attempt to get Russia muscling into Kazakhstan, which would set China on the defensive, introducing a crack in their special relationship. It gets Russia mired in Central Asia again, distracted from the Middle East, discredited amongst the Stans. You can see the logic. I think it started as Joanna Lake's idea, but she wouldn't have taken it this far. Some people tried to close it down, but there's no monopoly on starting wars anymore. When the British government pulled its support, the whole thing moved into the hands of individuals under less scrutiny and with more resources. Robert Carter and his billions kept the operation afloat. It allowed him to pour a private army up to the Russian border. You need to get word of all this to your bosses before things kick off in a big way."

"And you?"

"I'm proof that it's real. They wanted me here because Vishinsky knows what I represent. I create trouble, as you implied."

Cherenkov nodded thoughtfully. "Vishinsky's not going to be very popular if this is true—if he got fooled."

"That would be one positive outcome."

"And what about Joanna?"

"Joanna knew she wasn't being given full access to the scheme, so she hired Ruslan Batur to hack in. She saw the faked clips of me, tried to save my life, and paid the price. Saw plans for the bombing as well. Batur was shot by GL5. She was injured, escaped, almost made it to the explosives stash."

"You don't think she knew that you were going to be used?"

"I've no idea. It doesn't make much difference now."

He leaned over and clicked the mouse. The screen filled with an email. It came from the Vectis private network, from Undercroft to Callum Walker.

> *This is broadly how it would work if we choose to drop in CATALYST. I agree with your comment that he'd be more effective as an unconscious operator. He would trigger the right alarms in Moscow. And, impressive as they are, these fake images are no substitute for the real thing.*
>
> *Bringing him in from his current operation is not a problem. The issue remains re Joanna Lake and their history. Would she object? If so, how compartmentalised can this be?*

Cherenkov looked to me, as if to say: *I can give you this, at least.*

"I have to say, you played your part well," he said.

The email was a validation of sorts. My grief could retain some purity. But this relief would be inconsequential if we didn't move fast.

"Those files also contain information about the upcoming attack," I said. "The final straw that forces Russia's hand."

"And the attacker's using an ambulance?"

"An ambulance loaded with two tons of plastic explosives. He's probably on the move now."

Cherenkov called a guard, instructed him to bring up a connection with Moscow, then got to his feet.

"Stay here." He ordered one man to watch over me. I was sitting there, feeling the seconds counting down, when I heard raised voices at the front, some speaking English. My guard hesitated, drew his weapon, then went to look.

I followed.

About twenty GL5 blocked the road in front of the embassy. The men wore helmets and full combat uniform and were armed. Cherenkov was in heated discussion with their team leader, voices raised. The British-accented GL5 boss seemed to be saying that it wasn't safe, the Russians should stay inside. That wasn't going down well. No one stopped me from getting close enough to hear.

"You have no jurisdiction," Cherenkov said. But neither did he. It was quite a standoff. Then I saw Callum Walker arrive.

He climbed out of an armored SUV, moved through the GL5 officers, pistol in his right hand. He approached me cautiously, as if I was the one who was armed. "Come on, Elliot. Let's go." When he was a couple of feet away he lowered his voice. "Let this play out. This is what she spent years building." And, when he was even closer: "I tried to keep you out of it."

I leaned in and whispered, "Thank you."

Then I drove the base of my right palm into his face. The cartilage of his nose crumpled. I gripped Walker's wrist as he began to fall and unhooked the gun from his fingers, pulling him up by his thin hair and ramming the barrel of the Browning into the side of his skull. Blood streamed into his mouth. His hired backup froze. I turned to Cherenkov.

"Go," I said. "Find the ambulance."

But it was too late. More trouble pulled up with a screech: a crew of six British SAS in two Land Rovers. They jumped out, taking up combat stance. Suzanna Ford appeared from among them. She glanced at me and Walker.

"Elliot. We can take him off your hands."

"Please do," I said.

Ford gestured to her men. They approached, one eye on the Russians, one on the GL5 contractors, and grabbed hold of Walker. Then, before I knew what was happening, I had Russian hands on my arms, moving me away from the embassy, my feet getting no purchase on the snow, vaguely aware of Cherenkov's gun close to my head as we approached a vehicle with the doors open.

It was moving, with me inside, before I could do anything. I saw Suzanna Ford in the mirrors, giving chase—an arm flung out to stop her men firing—yelling for my captors to stop before heading back to her own team.

54

I WAS HURTLING THROUGH ASTANA IN AN ARMORED MITSUBISHI Outlander filled with military communications systems, a compact signals intelligence suite, Sergei Cherenkov, and four Russian Special Forces officers dressed in civilian clothes but operation-ready. I saw a couple of AK-12 assault rifles, stun grenades, respirator kits, and a sniper rifle. There were headsets and a blocky laptop monitor. They had the Special Forces habit of looking as unlike soldiers as possible. The driver was unshaven, gloved hands on the wheel, earpiece in. Beside him sat a malign-looking figure with a ponytail and webbed body armor over a denim jacket. A sniper sat behind mirror shades in the back beside a signals operator with a tactical data link system, involving a headset, mic, and two screens on a portable box. It looked like they had a quad drone up.

Cherenkov turned to me.

"You speak Russian," he said.

"Yes."

"Tell them what they need to know."

I detailed the vehicle we were searching for as we continued into the center: the explosives, the likely target, the time pressure. Cherenkov brought up security camera footage of the square on a laptop.

"Know if the bomb involves chemicals?" he asked me. "Gases? Radioactive materials?"

"I don't know. Try not to cause panic over the radio — we need to keep the streets clear. Have you got access to this city's Emergency Command?"

"Not directly."

Cherenkov's live feed showed the square packed edge to edge with people. They were still pouring in, holding candles and posters. The man who was working the data link touched his earpiece, checked the laptop screen, said:

"Look at that."

He prodded the screen. The roof markings made it conspicuous from the air: one ambulance, heading north. They were less than half a mile from the square.

"Got its lights on, moving fast."

"We've got about four minutes," I said. The Mitsubishi accelerated. I checked the map again.

"He's going to circle and come from the east," I said. "That gives him the longest run-up. Either Akhmet Street or Jumeken. There's no obstacles on either. He'll get up to serious speed. We need to reach him before that."

The driver muttered curses in Russian. Radios crackled. Cherenkov was struggling with his Kazakh counterparts.

"Yes, I am FSB. Russia. The situation is live . . ."

"It's already inside most security checks," the signals operator said. "I don't see any further blocks between it and the square, until you get to the guards around the square itself."

"What defenses do they have?" I asked.

"Crowd-control barriers. They wouldn't stop a push bike."

We tore through the city, Cherenkov desperately trying to radio various Kazakh commanders.

"Evacuate the square," the driver said.

"You'd need to evacuate more than half a kilometer," I said. "People will go straight toward the ambulance. They'll block the road."

"He's just crossing the M-36 into the center," the man with the satellite feed said. "It's at Sarayshyq Street."

"Get them to close the roads down," the driver said. "It's only going to get more crowded as he approaches the square."

"I can't establish the chain of command," Cherenkov said. "We're on our own."

"Target now on Respublika," the signals operator said.

"He's parallel with us," I said. "Take the next right. We can cut him off."

It was a high-risk suggestion. The driver checked his map, swung the car to the right.

Aside from the gathering, the city center had emptied entirely. The PA system from the memorial service echoed across deserted streets. We were conspicuous. As we reached Respublika Avenue, four heavily armed Kazakh troops tried to wave us down.

"Fuck them," the driver said.

We sped up. The troops caught a glimpse inside our vehicle as we drew close, became uneasy, hesitating just long enough for us to pass. When we were clear and no shots had been fired, everyone breathed again.

Then the ambulance appeared ahead of us.

"There it is."

Lights flashing, low on its wheels. There was a silence inside the Mitsubishi, save for the clicking of three safety catches.

"Go easy," Cherenkov said.

We narrowed the gap between us. Either of the next two turns could take him to the square. I could see the crowd through gaps in the buildings. The street tightened ahead. I thought we could block him at least, but we'd have to move fast.

"Don't panic him."

"He's stopped."

"Shit."

"They've stopped him."

I tried to see what was going on. There were barriers in front of the ambulance, blue uniforms; a checkpoint of some kind. The ambulance's sirens blared. If he detonated now we were deep within the blast zone. Cherenkov got on the radio and tried to ascertain if the Kazakh soldiers ahead knew who they'd stopped. Our driver twisted in his seat, staring through the back window.

"We're blocked," he said.

The Kazakh troops we'd passed had tailed us and now parked two armored personnel carriers a meter or so behind our vehicle. They got out, shouting, pointing their guns in our direction. The ambulance was also boxed in, vehicles on three sides, concrete barriers on the fourth. Speeches continued from the stage. This was it, I thought.

Then people appeared, running. I don't know what sparked the panic. Word must have got through to someone.

"An attack!" a woman shouted. It was followed a second later by an order over the PA system: "Please evacuate the square in an orderly fashion."

"Not now. Shit." Cherenkov was frozen with his hand on the door handle. His men awaited instructions. The road began to flood with people. Distracted by the crowd, the guards on the roadblock were no longer paying the ambulance attention.

"They're going to let him through," Cherenkov said, as the first barrier was pulled aside.

"They've got no idea."

"We've got to go, try to stop him."

We climbed out of the vehicle. The Kazakhs behind us had their weapons ready, still pointing in our direction. They stepped closer, six paramilitaries, then ran toward us. The Russians took up position behind the doors of the Mitsubishi. I stepped aside. Then the Kazakhs were past us, approaching the ambulance.

"Maybe they do," Cherenkov said. The crowd parted as the Kazakhs swarmed the ambulance. They took up positions around it, then, at a hand signal, three men smashed the windows of the driver's cab. I heard two shots, then two more. Then a second's silence before the crowd began to scream.

Everyone moved at once. We were pushed back a hundred meters by terrified individuals and roaring Kazakh soldiers. On a corner across from the National Museum I managed to stop, get a vantage point. Cherenkov and the Russians were still alongside me. They were ready to dissolve into the city, mission over. In their current getup, they were more liable to be shot as terrorists, which made them edgy when other troops arrived. They saw them a second before I did: British faces in the chaos. It was Suzanna Ford and her SAS detail. She locked eyes with Cherenkov. The man beside her had a gun, low but intent, focused on the Russian intelligence officer.

Ford was reading the situation, reading me. She beckoned me closer. I took a step toward her and nodded.

"Good work." She glanced in the direction of the ambulance. When I failed to react, she said, "We collected her body. I'm sorry, Elliot. If it's any consolation, we're holding Callum Walker. Going to need a full debrief from you, but you'll be protected."

Cherenkov caught my look of skepticism.

"The invitation's still open, Elliot. Moscow for Christmas. You'd be treated well."

"Maybe next time," I said. "*Prosti.*"

He stepped back, eyeing Ford and her gunman.

"I mean it," he said. "Keep my card." Then he disappeared into the crowd. His men were already gone. Ford winked.

"Welcome back, Elliot," she said. "We'll get a brew on the plane." She turned to the SAS team and began coordinating our own evacuation. They studied a handheld device with a map on it. I walked back toward the ambulance, against the flow of the crowd, initially curious to see the seventeen-year-old martyr, then changed my mind and walked into the square instead. The ground was littered with placards, trampled into the snow. I continued over them, keeping an eye out for Aliya, and then I was on the other side and still walking.

55

NO ONE TAILED ME THROUGH ASTANA'S FREEZING BACK STREETS. I CUT
north, flagged down a car, ended up at the train station. I bought a third-
class ticket to Beyneu, near the border with Uzbekistan, picked up a loaf
of bread, some biscuits, two bottles of local vodka. I called Evotec from a
public phone by the ticket office and they confirmed Stefan had been released and was on his way to Moscow's Sheremetyevo Airport before anyone changed their mind.

The train was modern, but the cheap carriage felt Soviet-era as it filled
with farmers and traders, women who sat down amid bags of produce.
Those who made the journey regularly settled themselves with blankets,
the first-timers stiff and staring out of the small windows. I studied hands
and nails to see if they matched the clothes. I passed my vodka around.
They shared lamb and flatbreads doled out of newspaper, the president's
assassination smudged to whorls of black and gray. I told them I was from
Belarus, which was as exotic and distant as England to them, but less wor-
thy of attention. I said I sold electronic equipment and was visiting my
wife, who was in Tashkent with her family, and was ill.

I checked news over a neighbor's shoulder as they swiped an iPhone.
China's troop movements were on hold. CNN showed Russian tanks rolling back from the Kazakh border. I thought of Joanna's serene face in
death and felt, in some small way, I had completed the journey she had
been trying to make.

Bukhara, in southern Uzbekistan, had a tenth-century mosque ru-
mored to be built on the remains of a Zoroastrian fire temple. I'd always
wanted to visit. I'd been told that a Sufi sect survived in the area, still
worshipping God by staring into flames. The city had once been a great
center of world civilization. I knew of a remote border crossing on the
Zhanaozen–Turkmenbashi road where you could cross into Uzbekistan
on foot.

Around midnight the train stopped and troops boarded it and

marched through, searching for something or someone. I felt torchlight in my face, and when it continued onward I imagined the moment as a kind of benediction. We moved off again and five minutes later passed a lit platform with one guard holding a flag. A sign said KOSHOBA. You could see the scattered lights of oil derricks a few miles away. My companions fell asleep on each other's shoulders, and I relaxed into the violence of the train, the relentless shudder of metal as if it had to drill through the space ahead of us.

I wanted to see the fire temple and Bukhara's fortress that had once contained a vast library of ancient manuscripts. From there onward was straightforward: two nights in Dushanbe in Tajikistan, where forged paperwork would be available. Then keep moving south and east, through the world's deep places: Kashmir, maybe Nepal. I would fix myself. Regain equilibrium. Until the day came when I looked up, met someone's gaze and they looked away. It would turn out that they'd been asking after me. That night I'd unlock my room and the man would be sitting there, neatly suited and well spoken. "Elliot, excuse the intrusion, rather hoped you'd be able to lend a hand." No introduction is necessary. "Not much money in it," he explains, "but you might find it diverting. Needs someone like you: a field officer." And I'll perform some reluctance before agreeing, mainly out of curiosity. Just to see, I'll tell myself. What else is there to do?

Acknowledgments

Thanks to:

Matthew Plowright, Tom Nuttall, Gulliver Cragg, Olga Nikonchuk, Yulia Erlykina, Calum Murray, Kuralay Kabdeshova, Rahat Tuyakbaev and his friend behind the bar, Clare Smith, Veronique Baxter, Judith Murray, Jaime Levine, Gráinne Fox, Alison Kerr Miller, Rana Feghali, Stephanie Cross, Joanna Lillis, Ranjan Balakumaran, Neil Arun, Robin Forrestier-Walker, N. B. Ray, the Young Roots team, and one individual who has asked to remain anonymous.

Very special thanks to Suzie Kim Jihyon.

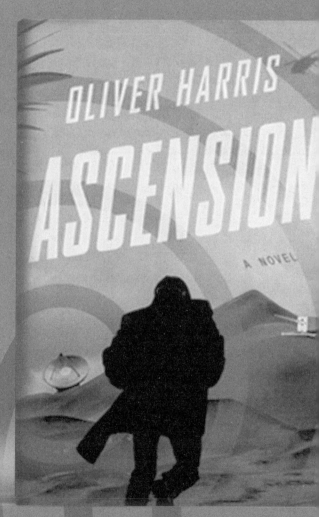